RAIDERS of the LOST Heart

Jo Segura

BERKLEY ROMANCE
NEW YORK

BERKLEY ROMANCE
Published by Berkley
An imprint of Penguin Random House LLC
penguinrandomhouse.com

Library of Congress Cataloging-in-Publication Data

Names: Segura, Jo, author.
Title: Raiders of the lost heart / Jo Segura.
Description: First edition. | New York : Berkley Romance, 2023.
Identifiers: LCCN 2023013971 (print) | LCCN 2023013972 (ebook) |
ISBN 9780593547465 (trade paperback) | ISBN 9780593547472 (ebook)
Subjects: LCGFT: Romance fiction. | Novels.
Classification: LCC PS3619.E4158 R35 2023 (print) |
LCC PS3619.E4158 (ebook) | DDC 813/.6—dc23/eng/20230505
LC record available at https://lccn.loc.gov/2023013971
LC ebook record available at https://lccn.loc.gov/2023013972

First Edition: December 2023

Printed in the United States of America
2nd Printing

Book design by Daniel Brount

For Mommo and Daddo,
I hope it's not too spicy for you.

CHAPTER

One

YES. A THOUSAND AND ONE PERCENT, YES.

Corrie Mejía's thighs tensed under the antique wooden desk in her office as she gripped the arms of the matching chair. The old Mexican pine creaked under the tension as she forced her body to remain calm and commanded her face to appear as if she were still considering the offer presented by the balding, middle-aged man sitting across from her.

This was the moment she'd been waiting for since the day she'd decided to become an archaeologist. Now that it was finally happening, it took all her strength not to launch out of her seat and accept the job without knowing any details—not that it would be the first time. But who cared about details after hearing those glorious words, words she'd longed to hear for decades:

Because you, Dr. Socorro Mejía, are the world's most brilliant archaeologist and the leading expert on the subject, we want you—and only you, because no one else could possibly measure up—for an all-expenses-paid and no-expense-spared expedition to

*Mexico to search for the remains of the Aztec warrior Chimalli
and the tecpatl sacrificial knife he stole from Moctezuma II when
he fled Tenochtitlán right before the downfall of the Aztec Empire.*

Well, okay. He didn't say it *quite* like that. It was more like
*I've been sent here by an anonymous investor to offer you a posi-
tion on a Chimalli expedition.*

But the implication was still there—no one knew more about
Chimalli than Corrie. And she *was* fucking brilliant.

The dusty old clock she'd inherited from her grandmother
ticked in the corner of her tiny office at Berkeley. Her office was
only half the size of those of the other faculty members. *Once
you make tenure, you'll get a bigger one*, she'd been told. Funny
how that had never happened. It wouldn't have even crossed her
mind if this stranger wasn't practically right on top of her in the
cramped space, able to observe every flinch. Every forced effort
at maintaining composure.

The ticking grew louder with each passing second. And with
each hammering beat, Corrie's abuela's words echoed through
her ears.

If it's too good to be true, there's a catch.

Corrie had learned the truth behind those words the hard
way. Now, at thirty-five years old, she'd trained herself to tem-
per her gut reactions. Suss out the motives. Put in some evalua-
tion before the adventure. Or, you know, maybe at least get a
detail or two in advance of saying yes.

Because why—especially after rallying hard for the last eight
years to find someone to finance this exact dig—would this
güey she'd never seen or heard of in her entire life be coming to
her now, offering her the job of all jobs. Her dream dig on an
all-expenses-paid platter.

There had to be a catch. There was *always* a catch.

A knock on her door cut through the tension in the room, allowing her to release her hold on the chair.

"Come in," she called out, giving the stranger a quick glance before swiveling her chair toward the door.

Her mentee, Dr. Miriam Jacobs, entered, clasping an assortment of books and papers under her arm.

"Hi, Dr. Mejía," she said, noticing that Corrie had company, "I'm here for our one o'clock to discuss next semester's course outline."

Corrie glanced at the clock, and sure enough, their meeting should have started more than ten minutes ago. Right. Those were the details she should have been focusing on, given that the fall semester would be starting in a few short weeks. It wasn't like her to be late or to blow people off. She wasn't an "absentminded professor" or one of those *my time is more important than your time* types like some of her colleagues. In fact, Corrie prided herself on being down to earth. Someone her students admired rather than feared. A professor who was as entertaining over a pint of beer as she was in the classroom. A mentor for other young female archaeologists like Miriam to help navigate the patriarchal holdovers of the formerly male-dominated field.

But this unfamiliar person had showed up fifteen minutes ago and immediately started with, "I have a proposition that you'll find very enticing," before she could tell him she had an upcoming appointment. How was she supposed to refuse without at least hearing him out?

"Oh, I'm sorry, Miri. The time got away from me. Just give me—"

"Dr. Mejía won't be handling any courses this fall."

The stranger's words about knocked the wind out of her.

Enticing or not, Corrie Mejía did *not* take kindly to men speaking for her.

"Ex*cuse* me?" Corrie said, slowly cocking her head in the man's direction.

"Dr. Mejía is leaving for Mexico in a few days," the man clarified, speaking to Miriam as if Corrie weren't in the room, "and she'll be there at least through the semester." He took off his glasses and pulled a handkerchief from his pocket, proceeding to polish the lenses as if it were no big deal.

As if leaving for an unplanned trip to *Mexico* in a few days were no big deal.

"I'm not sure if you realize this, but I haven't agreed yet," Corrie snapped back.

"No, but you will."

"Oh, I will, will I? Says who?" She folded her arms and leaned back in her chair.

"Says the person who sent me here." The man returned his glasses to his face. "I wouldn't be here if there was even an inkling of a chance that you'd say no."

Corrie's mouth slackened, but nothing came out. Person? What person? Various names swirled through her head, but none made any sense. It couldn't be any of the people she'd previously approached for funding, because why the need to remain anonymous? And she didn't really know anyone else who had the financial means to pull off something like this, and certainly not someone who knew her well enough to be so sure that there wasn't even *an inkling of a chance* that she'd say no. Few people knew Corrie at all—at least, not the *real* Corrie.

"Corrie?" Miriam asked, her voice strained with worry and confusion, pulling Corrie's attention to the matter at hand.

"Um, uh, yes," she said, standing and walking toward the door. "How about I e-mail you this afternoon and we can reschedule?"

Corrie held the door open for Miri, who took two tentative steps back while nodding and taking one last glance at the stranger before she closed the door. With her back to the man, she took a deep breath, then turned and leaned flush against the wood-paneled slab.

"Who sent you?" she asked.

"I'm sorry, Dr. Mejía, but that's confidential."

"All right . . . Then where would I be going?"

"Also confidential."

Her eyebrow quirked up. "Okay . . . How am I supposed to direct this dig if I don't know who I'm working for or where I'm going?"

"You'll be assisting, not directing. The specifics will be left to the lead archaeologist."

A tiny laugh escaped her lips as she tossed back her head and looked at the ceiling. He couldn't be serious. No way was Corrie agreeing to play second fiddle on a Chimalli dig. Not even if succeeding on this dig could finally launch her into archaeology's gated inner circle where she might be taken more seriously.

"Hold on. Let me get this straight. Not only will I not be the lead, but you want me to agree to go on a job not knowing who sent you, who I'll be working for, or where I'll be going, and I'll be leaving in a few days? And, let me guess, your name is confidential, too?"

The man didn't flinch.

Oh, there was a catch, all right. She laughed again, but this time it was a full-throated laugh filled with disbelief and annoyance. Without further hesitation, she whipped the door behind her wide open.

"Well, you can tell whoever it is that sent you that they clearly don't know me at all. I'm going to have to pass."

She signaled toward the door with a nod of her head, then crossed her arms. And the man smiled. Corrie wanted nothing more than to wipe that smile off his face with a full-handed smack as he finally rose from his seat and walked to the door to leave. But before he did, he stopped in front of Corrie, his face two feet from hers.

"Sorry to hear that you don't want to partake in the discovery of your ancestor's remains. When you change your mind, there will be a ticket waiting for you on Sunday morning at the United Airlines counter. Flight leaves at five a.m."

Corrie stood at the door, eyes wide, as the man walked down the hall without turning back. In one word, the man had convinced her. *Ancestor.*

Whoever sent this man knew her better than she could have ever imagined.

· · · · · · · · ·

MEXICO IN AUGUST WAS EVEN HOTTER THAN CORRIE HAD ANTICI-pated. She'd been many times to visit family, go on vacation, and participate in other digs, but never in August.

She'd also never gotten on an airplane after being propositioned by a man with no name, but the time to question her decisions had already passed. There had been a brief moment at SFO when she'd debated her own sanity—sometime after realizing that the man with no name had somehow gotten her passport information, but before boarding the plane. A quick call to the Anthropology Department's administration office confirmed that Mr. No-Name had verified the details of the expedition and her travel arrangements in advance. That at least gave her a sliver of confidence that she wasn't en route to her demise.

"Last call for passengers on flight 5468 to Houston," the loudspeaker bellowed out.

She glanced at the note accompanying her ticket to board flight 5468 to Houston, along with its companion ticket to her final destination in Oaxaca, Mexico, once more.

We knew you'd agree. We'll find you outside the airport once you land.

Oaxaca. There'd been many theories on the final resting place of Chimalli, Oaxaca not being one of them. Based on her research, that wasn't the final destination. No, this was merely the jumping-off point.

Most people thought he'd fled south of Tenochtitlán into the pine-oak forests of the Sierra Madre del Sur. Others thought west, near Lake Chapala. Corrie had other ideas.

The Lacandon Jungle. The outskirts of the Aztec domain, not far from the abandoned settlements of the Olmecs, Zapotecs, and Mayans. The Lacandon provided thick cover from enemies and had an abundance of flora and fauna to consume in the absence of farmed foods. Its terrain and conditions matched perfectly with what Corrie believed were the most credible accounts of Chimalli's disappearance.

And it was located not far from Oaxaca.

Part terrified and part eager, Corrie had boarded that damn plane, determined to at least find out who the hell had the nerve to think they knew her better than she knew herself. Besides, she could always back out if things looked shady once she arrived. Unless this was all a ruse to kidnap her. Or worse.

She walked out of the Oaxaca airport to a blast of hot, humid air and meandered under the shaded walkway, rethinking her decision to wear long pants and sleeves. The sticky heat invaded every nook and cranny of her outfit. She tossed her bags atop an empty concrete bench, then stripped down to a formfitting black V-neck undershirt while she searched her things for a clip to keep her hair off her sweaty neck. Not exactly the professional archaeologist image she'd been going for, with her boobs practically on full display, but red-faced and reeking of sweat wasn't any better.

Who was she waiting for, anyway? The man with no name? Someone else? She glanced at the note one more time: *We'll find you.*

Suddenly those words felt much more ominous than they had a few hours earlier. Everything about this seemed like a bad idea. Or, hell . . . maybe this was a super elaborate practical joke from the UC Berkeley Department of Anthropology as a congratulations for making tenure.

Though that would be quite an expensive practical joke. Her colleagues had barely wanted to shell out ten bucks apiece to upgrade their coffeemaker a year ago. But with the passing of each excruciatingly long minute, the chances that this was a practical joke were more and more likely.

Forty-eight minutes. At what point would she call it and inquire about catching a return flight home?

You've been played, Dr. Mejía. Remember . . . there's always a catch.

She closed her eyes and winced at her gullibility. *God, this is embarrassing.* It wasn't like her to cry. No, tough chicas didn't cry. So when the prick of tears formed behind her eyelids, she squeezed them tighter.

Always confirm the motives in advance. She chastised herself for failing to follow her grandmother's advice and for falling back into her impulsive adventure-seeking habits. Had she asked a few more questions or demanded answers, maybe she wouldn't be sitting alone on a bench in Oaxaca trying to figure out how she was going to explain this to the head of the department. Taking the semester off on such short notice had put a real wrench in the department's curriculum. *"This isn't another one of your wild Lara Croft adventures, is it?"* the department director had asked. After her last dig had resulted in an emergency evacuation, all on the university's tab, they had a right to be concerned. This time, she'd practically had to beg.

But admitting she'd been duped and having to grovel to resume her original course plans? The idea made Corrie want to vomit.

One hour. One hour and then she'd call it. And she'd figure out how to grovel on the flight home.

Once the threat of crying subsided, Corrie slowly opened her eyes and noticed a blurry figure approaching. A man in sunglasses and a Panama hat came into focus as she blinked a few times to dissipate the tears. Not the man with no name. No, someone else.

Someone . . . familiar.

"Well, well, well, if it isn't Dr. Corrie Mejía," the man called out with a distinctive, friendly voice. A warm voice that had shared hundreds of laughs with Corrie over pints and cheese fries at the Village Pub during grad school.

A voice Corrie would recognize anywhere.

"Ethan!" she said, leaping from the bench and running toward her old friend. Her spirits lifted as *he* lifted her from the ground into a hearty embrace, sending his hat toppling to the ground.

"What are you doing here?" she asked as he set her on the pavement, though she refused to let go of him for fear that he'd vanish into thin air.

Her old compadre smiled at her with laugh lines that hadn't been there the last time she'd seen him and a few grays streaking through his otherwise jet-black hair. She'd always thought he was good-looking—not her type necessarily, but still pretty cute—but time agreed with his features. God, it was good to see him.

"I'm here for the same reason you're here, obviously," he said with a wink. Like it was a secret mission.

Which, come to think of it, wasn't an incorrect assessment.

"You mean, you're here for"—she brought her voice to a whisper and checked her surroundings—"*the dig?*"

He laughed. "It's not MI6, Corrie. Yes, I'm here for"—he shifted his eyes back and forth and crouched a solid foot to reach her level—"*the dig.*"

It was just like Ethan to tease her and her suspicions. Blame Abuela Mejía and all her warnings about motives and catches for that. But after thinking she was going to be kidnapped less than fifteen minutes ago, she'd take Ethan's teasing any day. That still didn't stop Corrie from punching him in the arm.

"Glad to see you've still got spunk. You're gonna need it for this one," he said.

"Why all the secrecy?" she asked.

"They're worried about dig robbers. If anyone knew what we were doing here, we'd be screwed."

Grave robbers were nothing new. Every high-profile dig had to contend with them. "No, I mean with bringing me down here?"

Ethan's eyebrow quirked. "Er . . . we wanted it to be a surprise."

A surprise? She'd been on top-secret jobs before, but she'd never been in the dark like this. And they certainly didn't keep things from the archaeologists as a fun "surprise." But, then again, Ethan had always had an interesting sense of humor.

"So where are we going? Aren't the locals curious?"

"It's about two hours east of here. Heavily jungled, no locals to keep an eye on us. We all stay in tents, with a shipment of food and supplies every week."

"Wait, wait, wait," Corrie said, bringing up her hand and shaking her head. "I thought the dig was just starting. How long have you been here?"

"Since May."

"May?" Not that Corrie had any information to go on, but something wasn't adding up. Why was she being brought on now if they'd already been digging for more than three months?

"I thought you knew that. Didn't Calvin explain everything when he asked you to come?"

Calvin? Who the hell was Calvin? Oh . . .

"You mean that bald dude with the glasses?"

Ethan raised his eyebrows and laughed. "Oh boy. Yes, I suppose I do."

"Well, *Calvin* didn't tell me shit. He only said it was a Chimalli expedition with an anonymous investor and that there would be a plane ticket to an unknown destination waiting for me at the airport."

His eyebrows lifted even higher. "And you actually *came*

based on that description? I'd heard about that whole makeshift-paragliding incident on that expedition in Thailand, but you're more adventurous than I thought."

Corrie jostled her head and opened her palms face up. "Well, what the heck, Ethan? You're the one who wanted me to come here."

"Um . . . no," he said, rubbing the back of his neck with his hand and scrunching his face. "That wasn't me."

Never mind. Maybe this *was* a practical joke. Corrie's brow furrowed and she opened her mouth to ask yet another clarifying question when another voice came from behind her.

"*I* asked Calvin to send for you."

Her entire body clenched as she sucked in a breath. That low, sweet, delicious timbre sent an unwanted fiery blaze across her skin. She knew that voice, too. Even better than she'd known Ethan's.

No, no, no, no, no, she silently repeated as she slowly turned to confirm the speaker, her stomach swirling with a strong brew of contempt mixed with lust.

"*You*," she growled, and narrowed her eyes at the disgustingly handsome man standing tall before her in his army-green cargos, hiking boots, and an untucked white button-down with the sleeves rolled up to his elbows. Time had been fucking *unfair* when it came to him. After having spent countless hours staring across the lecture hall at him during class, Ford Matthews's attractiveness never ceased to amaze her.

He also never ceased to irritate the *crap* out of her, which had nothing to do with his emerald eyes, always perfectly tousled sandy-blond tresses, and obviously chiseled six-feet-something physique.

She'd never wanted to hate-fuck someone so badly in her life.

But she could never give him the satisfaction or allow herself to be another notch on his certainly already full bedpost. Especially not after everything he'd done to her.

And to think, at one point she might have actually considered it.

A warm tingle fluttered through her core at the memory before she quickly tamped it down and took a step back, bumping into Ethan's chest. Great. Trapped. Her body was far too close to Ford's for comfort.

"It's lovely to see you too, Corrie," he retorted with a sly, enigmatic smile. A smile that was the complete opposite of the scowl lodged on Corrie's face.

"It's Dr. Mejía," she demanded through her sneer.

A slight chuckle escaped from the corner of his mouth. Goddamn did she want to smack that smirk off his perfect face. "Well, you don't need to call me Dr. Matthews. I'm fine with Ford. Or *boss* is okay with me, too."

Boss?

Her mouth started to fall before she pulled it into a snarl as her eyebrows snapped together. *Smug motherfu—*

She should have suspected Dr. Ford Matthews would be the lead archaeologist on this dig. Leave it to Ford to take yet another thing from her. It wasn't enough for him to steal the fellowship that had been all but offered to her eight years ago after graduation. Now he wanted to stake claim to her passion project? To have *his* name written in all the history books about the discovery of Chimalli's grave. Chimalli, *her* ancestor, not his.

She rolled her eyes and looked away as she folded her arms. "I'm sure it is. Un-fucking-believable," she grumbled under her breath.

"I see you've missed me," he said with his charming sarcasm.

He took a step closer, and she eyed the gap closing between them. What was he doing?

"The only thing I miss about you is your absence. What is this? Some sort of joke?" she snapped at him as she stepped to the side to back away.

"Far from it." Another step. *What the—?*

"Then what am I doing here?"

He tilted his head and squinted those brilliant eyes at her from behind his thick, black-framed glasses. *Oh please.* He couldn't *possibly* be surprised that she was confused. "Isn't it obvious? We're searching for Chimalli. Thought you might want in on this, you know, given that he was the subject of your dissertation. And rumor has it you've been searching for funding for the past few years . . ." His know-it-all voice trailed off.

She wasn't buying the ole good-guy act. No, Dr. Ford Matthews hadn't invited her out of the goodness of his heart because he thought she *might want in on this*. Ford didn't do anything for anyone but himself.

As he'd more than sufficiently demonstrated throughout their four years together in grad school. But it would be a cold day in hell—or, rather, the Mexican jungle—before Corrie got burned by him again. Chimalli or not, she couldn't work with Ford.

And she *especially* couldn't work *for* Ford.

The realization brought her back to reality. "You know, I'm going to have to pass. I got what I needed—confirmation that this was too good to be true. I just wish you'd saved both of us the trouble by letting Calvin know it was *you* who wanted me here so I could have declined in Berkeley." She then turned to Ethan, placing her hand on his forearm. "Ethan, it was great seeing you. Let's catch up when you get back to the States."

With that, Corrie spun on her heel toward her things, calculating in her head whether she could afford a first-class seat, because, well, she deserved it after all this. She'd make up for the expense in free cocktails.

"Corrie—" Ford started, followed by an audible punch and a grunt. "I mean, Dr. Mejía, wait!"

She stopped in her tracks, never having heard such a tremor in Ford's voice. What was that? Fear? Worry?

Was Ford Matthews *pleading*? The corner of her lip curled up.

"Calvin didn't tell you it was me because I knew you wouldn't come and . . . and . . ."

The words hung on the tip of his tongue, and the curl of her lip fell. Of course Ford wouldn't ever admit to doing anything wrong. She took another step—

"I need you!" he blurted out.

A small, devilish smile formed on Corrie's lips like the Grinch who stole Christmas. Those words were utterly delectable coming from him. "I'm sorry, what did you say?" she asked as she slowly turned, fighting to keep her smug smile to herself.

"You heard me," he said, grinding his jaw and digging his fingers into his hips as he stood in front of her.

This time *she* took a few steps to close the gap. "No, I don't think I did. Because the Ford Matthews *I* know would never ask for my help. Or at least he'd know not to," she said, matching his stance with her hip cocked to the side and her hands placed on either side of her waist.

Ford's nostrils flared and his broad chest filled as he took a deep breath. Corrie pictured tiptoeing her fingers up his tight torso with extreme delight. Oh, how it pained him to be the one needing help. Ethan grumbled something in his ear, but Corrie only caught the latter half. "Tell her, will you?" he said.

Ten seconds into their stare down, Ford finally gave in.

"Fine," he growled, tossing his hands in the air. "I need you. Things started out great, and I thought I had it figured out, but we're three months in and something isn't right. I'm sure you know I wouldn't have sent for you if I had any other options."

He had a point. Ford despised Corrie as much as she despised him.

"So you're desperate?"

He rolled his eyes. "Obviously. But you're the only person in the world who has even a remote chance of being able to help, so here we are. Now, are you going to help me or not, because if we don't hit the road soon, it's going to be dark by the time we make it back."

"What's in it for me?" she asked.

"Fortune and glory not enough for you?" Ford said, crossing his arms.

Corrie started to open her mouth, ready to hurl another argument, but Ethan jumped in to stop her. "Why don't you come for the night? In the morning we'll show you the site, and then you can decide whether you want to stay."

"We can't show her where we're going if she doesn't agree to stay," Ford protested under his breath.

"It will be fine," Ethan reassured him. "She's the only person I trust more than you, and she's not going to steal anything. I promise. Right, Corrie?" he asked her.

"Of course not. I don't take what's not mine. Not like *some* people," she said, leaning into her words.

Ford glared as the words flowed from her pursed lips. Good. She hoped they stung.

"So are you in?" Ethan asked.

Corrie gave Ford a once-over, searching his face. Despite the scowl, she noted the panic in his eyes. Worry that she might actually say no.

Clearly, they were onto something big, and he was afraid he might lose it if he didn't have her help. Finding out more was worth the pain of having to spend a car ride and an evening in Ford's company.

At least the scenery was decent.

"All right, I'm in. But I reserve the right to change my mind in the morning."

Both Ford and Ethan breathed sighs of relief as their shoulders relaxed, and Ford walked toward Corrie. A rush of heat washed over her at his proximity.

"Trust me . . . You won't be changing your mind," he whispered in her ear as he reached down to grab her bags.

His warm breath, laced with spearmint, tickled behind her ear, sending another sizzling inferno soaring through her body. Though, unlike the last time, this one was centered around her nether regions.

But if there was one person in the world she didn't trust with anything—*especially* her nether regions—it was Dr. Ford Matthews.

CHAPTER
Two

THIS WAS A BAD IDEA. A VERY BAD IDEA.

The wind whipped through Corrie's hair as they traveled down the dirt road. Even though she had it pinned to the back of her head, a few unruly deep brown waves dipped with dark honey danced through the air, brushing across the smooth golden skin of her face.

Dr. Corrie Mejía was even more beautiful than he'd remembered.

Too bad she hated his guts. Not that he could blame her. Hell, sometimes he hated himself, too, or at least the times when he put on that smarmy act like he'd done at the airport. But he couldn't help it. Whenever he was around her—her and only her—Ford the Douchebag always made an appearance.

He couldn't believe he'd actually told her she could call him *boss.*

Douche. Bag.

He shook his head thinking about it, catching Corrie's curious glance in the rearview mirror. A glance that quickly turned intense as those rich brown eyes bore through him like lasers. Perhaps this was her attempt at being menacing. Little did she know, however, that the only thing on his mind was wondering what those eyes would look like staring up at him from his bed. Staring at him like that one night they'd spent alone in the library.

Did she ever think about that night, too?

This dig was *way* too long to be on a forced sexual sabbatical while in the Mexican jungle with Corrie around, *especially* if she kept wearing outfits that hugged every single one of her soft curves the way this one did.

"How much longer?" she called out.

"About fifteen minutes," he called over the wind and the roaring engine as they careened down the bumpiest dirt road in all of Mexico, lined with Mexican elms.

"Good. My back's killing me," she said as she arched her torso, pushing out her breasts even farther.

Why? Why couldn't the only person with any possibility of helping him look like a troll? Or at least not be a goddess like Corrie? Ford wouldn't mind her tearing off his clothes given the opportunity.

A small part of him hoped that she'd change her mind. That they'd get in one of their infamous arguments once he showed her the site—or, preferably, even before—and that she'd leave. In many ways, it would be better to simply let the investor know that they'd failed rather than have to put up with Dr. Corrie Mejía for who knows how long. He already knew from experience that they worked terribly together, if you could call it *working together* at all. He didn't need to add sexual frustration on top of it.

Because if there was one thing Ford knew, it was that he and

Corrie could *never* sleep together. Ever. No matter how many times he'd thought about it. Because if there was *another* thing he knew, it was that sleeping with Corrie would end disastrously, giving her yet another reason to hate him more than she already did.

But Ford was desperate. So desperate he'd willingly risk all the wrath and fury of Corrie Mejía if it meant he might be able to save his mother.

A tear pricked his eye, and he quickly blinked it away, though not before earning another curious look from Corrie. He wasn't sure how he felt about that, Corrie always watching him. He couldn't tell if it was suspicion or something else, but every time he caught her eye, his X-rated imagination strayed and kicked up the temperature another couple of degrees. The conditions were bad enough as it was. More heat was the last thing Ford needed.

Well, that and another failure to add to his growing list.

Dusk settled over the heavily canopied jungle, casting darkness over the area. He'd hoped they would arrive earlier so they could give Corrie a tour this evening, but now it would have to wait until morning. With this new arrangement, though, and the potential that she might pull the plug in the morning, he didn't really want to get into all the specifics of the dig. Maybe Ethan trusted her, but Ford hardly trusted anyone in this business, at least not until they'd had time to build a solid foundation. What he was doing on a dig funded by a complete stranger was beyond him. But, so far, the investor, Pierre Vautour, had come through on every promise. No expense spared. And despite his rocky relationship with his boss at Yale, he trusted that Dr. Crawley wouldn't have sent him astray by introducing him to Mr. Vautour in the first place.

One thing was certain, though—Corrie didn't trust him, which didn't exactly instill the confidence in Ford that would make him want to divulge any specific details until she agreed to stay. After all, what if she hired someone to sneak into their camp and snag the artifacts? Assuming they ever found them, that was. He didn't *think* Corrie was the type, but then again, she had an axe to grind. People did strange things when they wanted to exact revenge.

"We're here," Ethan called out to Corrie as Ford slowed down and eased the Jeep into the camp.

Several large tents outlined the perimeter of the small clearing in the forest—a few bunk tents for the crew and interns and two singles that Ethan termed "glamping" tents for Ford and Ethan—all built on platforms to protect them from the frequent unrelenting downpours. A larger mess tent with picnic tables and a makeshift kitchen sat in the center of camp, and a couple of padlocked equipment sheds sat outside the main camp area near the bathrooms, although calling them *bathrooms* was generous. They consisted of little more than pit toilets and flimsy stand-up showers. But the fire pit was the best part of camp. Out there, the team could unwind after a long day, drinking, telling stories, singing songs. Out there, surrounded by the towering mahogany and ceiba trees, abundant feathery palms and ferns, fluttering bats, and raucous spider monkeys, they were a family.

The lights strung high in the trees' vines were already turned on as the rest of the team sat around waiting for dinner. Just in time. Even with all its creatures and mysteries, the middle of the jungle wasn't so bad with home-cooked meals every night. If anything, Agnes's cooking might help tip Corrie in favor of staying.

"All right, this is it. Home sweet home," Ford said, putting the Jeep in park and shutting off the engine.

"Where's the site?" Corrie asked, taking in their surroundings.

"We've gotta hike in. It's about a mile from here," Ethan responded.

Her eyes flickered for a moment, as if realizing the additional demands placed on the participants in this expedition. Not wanting to wait until morning to clarify that it got even worse, Ford added, "The terrain is treacherous. Uneven and hilly. Virtually impossible to get a vehicle through. And when it rains, which happens almost daily this time of year . . . well, it's a mess."

Ford didn't particularly enjoy tramping through the mud and muck on a daily basis. Was it really so bad that he missed hot showers and dirt-free living quarters?

"I've been on digs, you know," she sassed. "Besides, isn't getting dirty part of the fun?"

Her rhetorical question ended with a flourish and a hint of suggestion, piquing his interest and sending a healthy surge of blood to his core. *Well, when you put it that way . . .*

"Let's introduce you to the gang and then have some dinner," Ethan said, snapping Ford out of his *dirty* thoughts.

"What about my things?"

"They'll be fine in the Jeep for now. We'll grab them later," Ford said, climbing out and offering Corrie a hand.

But one sneer at his hand and she jumped out without assistance. Sigh. Yep, it was going to be like that.

"And here I thought you two went into town to go drinking without me." Lance, Mr. Vautour's personal associate, emerged from the outskirts of camp, turning Ford's attention away from Corrie.

Ford smiled. "And ditch the third amigo?" They slapped their hands together in a solid handshake. Lance might have been there to make sure everything was going according to plan, but they'd formed a sort of friendship over the last few months, despite the fact that he preferred scotch over rye.

"Who do we have here? A new recruit?" Lance asked, looking past Ford and eyeing Corrie curiously.

Shit. Ford hadn't really thought this through. The last thing he needed was for Lance to report back to the investor that they were stuck and that they'd sent for reinforcements. Especially when those reinforcements happened to have been the investor's first choice for this expedition.

"Uh, Lance, I want to introduce you to Dr. Socorro Mejía, our old college buddy."

Corrie's brow quirked up as both she and Ethan shot suspicious looks over at Ford.

"She's here, uh, for research," Ford said, ignoring their glances. "Dr. Mejía, this is Lance. He works for the investor."

Her head raised an inch, as if understanding the awkwardness behind the introduction. "It's nice to meet you," she said, shaking his hand.

"Likewise. How nice that the three of you have maintained your friendship after college."

"Oh yes. Ford, Ethan, and I were the *best* of friends in grad school. We had *so* much fun together, didn't we, Ford?" she asked, playfully punching him in the arm with a little too much oomph.

"Mm-hmm," he murmured, fighting the urge to massage the sting in his bicep.

"Will you be staying long?" Lance asked.

"Not sure. We haven't really talked about it. This was somewhat of a surprise trip," Corrie responded.

What was she up to?

"A surprise trip to Mexico? You archaeologists sure do live fascinating lives."

"Totally. I mean, it was *super* easy for me to drop everything to come down here, and I just had to see what Ford and Ethan were up to. Plus, I missed them so much," she said, laying it on thick. *Too* thick.

Fortunately, not being familiar with Corrie's sense of . . . humor, Lance didn't seem to catch on.

"Well, I'm taking a few pictures before dinner," he said, holding up the camera that always accompanied him, "but hopefully we'll get a chance to talk more later."

They waited a few moments, ensuring Lance was far enough away, before Corrie turned to Ford. "'Old college buddies,' eh?"

"Look, it's complicated."

Corrie burst out with a laugh. "Are you talking about the dig or is that our relationship status?"

Ford tensed. That was one way to put it. But hearing her refer to anything they had as a *relationship*—whether good or bad—sent a funny feeling roaring through his stomach.

"Come on," he said, choosing to ignore the bait.

They walked over to the camp, stopping to say hello to various people along the way as they meandered through the trees. Sundays were off days, so most of the crew were relatively clean and showered. At least Corrie wouldn't be bombarded with the typical aromas of dirt, sweat, and BO that usually lingered in camp. Most of the crew were men, and with only two other women in camp—Sunny, Ford's sweet but annoyingly perky intern, and Agnes, the sixty-two-year-old chef—the camp often felt more like a fraternity than a top-secret archaeological dig. Agnes chastised the men on a daily basis for their disgusting habits. Sunny, on the other hand, didn't complain about anything. Not the smells, or the muddy treks to the dig site, or having to share a tent with Agnes—purely their choice, not that he could blame them. Heck, Ford thanked his lucky stars that he had his own tent every single night.

And, as if right on cue, Sunny came bounding out of her tent like an excited ocelot and rushed straight over to meet the new arrival. Corrie froze alongside Ford at the sight of her and recoiled seconds before being assailed by the ball of pure energy that was Sunshine O'Donnell.

"Oh my God, you must be Dr. Mejía! I've heard so much about you and I've read all your papers," Sunny said, fervently shaking Corrie's hand.

Ford snickered to himself at how uncomfortable Corrie looked. He'd never taken Corrie as a "girl's girl," or the type to be a fan of bubbly personalities like Sunny's. Corrie Mejía was far too serious for that sort of poppycock. No, she was driven and focused, and while Corrie had moments of friendliness—hell, she and Ethan had acted like they were practically besties back at the airport—she didn't seem like the type who had hordes of friends.

She also wasn't a woman who could successfully hide her true emotions, something Ford knew from firsthand experience.

As Sunny rambled on about one of Corrie's most recent papers published in *Archaeology* magazine without taking a single breath—or allowing Corrie to even learn her name—the crease on Corrie's forehead grew, and she tilted her head. *Er . . . this might not end well.* A pit started to form in Ford's stomach. Perhaps he and Ethan should have given her—or, frankly, both of them—a warning. Corrie, about Sunny's, well, *sunny* disposition. And Sunny, about Corrie's . . . lack thereof.

He probably should have held off on their introduction until *after* Corrie agreed to stay.

Ford waited for it. Waited for Corrie's inevitable explosion when she had enough nonsense for the day. She opened her mouth, and he readied himself so he could jump in to save Sunny from Corrie. And . . .

"I'm sorry, but I didn't catch your name," Corrie said, politely cutting Sunny off and smiling.

What the . . . ? Ford glanced at Corrie out of the corner of his eye, scanning her profile. *Who is this person and what did she do with Corrie Mejía?*

Sunny let go of Corrie's hand, then pushed her auburn hair behind her ears as she bowed her head with embarrassment. "Oh God, I'm sorry. I'm Dr. Matthews's research assistant, Sunshine O'Donnell, but everybody calls me Sunny. Sorry, I get excited sometimes, and when I get excited, I ramble. And when I heard that you were coming, I couldn't believe it because you're my idol—no offense, Dr. Matthews," she said, turning to Ford. "And it's like my brain thinks I need to tell you everything, because what if I don't get another chance like this, and oh my God, I'm doing it again, aren't I?"

Corrie laughed. Laughed as if she was charmed by Sunny. The *old* Corrie would have had little tolerance for someone babbling on like Sunny during a lecture. But this person? Ford barely recognized her. He had to admit, Corrie had a great laugh. The sound of it relieved the tension in his body. And it was nice to see an actual smile on that gorgeous face of hers.

"Well, I've never had a fan. I'm surprised you even know who I am," Corrie said with a playfulness to her voice.

"OMG, you're joking, right? You're only, like, the most badass archaeologist of modern times. No offense, Dr. Matthews."

Never mind about that tension. Ford changed his stance as

he felt a twang in his neck. No offense? Hearing it for the second time, he started to think maybe he *should* be offended.

"I mean, you chased that group of thieves in Belize. Stole
back that jade necklace from those crooks in Panama City. And
then there was that time you outran the jaguar in the Amazon—"

"It was injured," Ford clarified, and Corrie tossed her head
in his direction, the heat from her gaze palpable. Whatever.
He'd heard that story, too.

"Whatever. Bad. Ass," Sunny continued. "You're like a real-
life Lara Croft. And just as hot as she is, too," she said with a
sultry upturn of her lip and waggle of her brow.

Ford snapped his gaze at Sunny. Wait . . . was she . . . *flirting*
with Corrie?

"Wasn't Lara Croft a tomb *raider*—aka, *not* one of us, the
good guys?" Ford said, yet again offering his unsolicited opinion. For Pete's sake, Sunny was acting like Corrie was swinging
from vines and jumping out of helicopters.

Though he supposed she was right about that whole *hot* thing.

"Now, now, Dr. Matthews. We all know you're impressive,
too," Ethan joked, patting Ford on the head.

Really? Then why didn't *he* make the list of Most Badass
Archaeologists despite going on well over fifty digs, uncovering
that whole set of pictographs in Arizona, and discovering a previously unknown Mayan temple in Guatemala? He deserved *a
little* credit, didn't he?

"I'm just saying," Ford said, shrugging Ethan off, "I'm not
sure being like Lara Croft should necessarily be taken as a compliment."

Was he . . . *jealous*? God, he sounded like an entitled brat.
Yet again, his inner douchebag was coming out.

"Well, thank you," Corrie finally spoke up. "I truly am flattered, *despite* the comparison. And you'll have to forgive Ford. He and his namesake aren't too keen on raiders."

Ford's nostrils flared and his jaw clenched as he glared at Corrie.

"Ford? Oh my God, were you named after Harrison Ford, Dr. Matthews?" Sunny asked, shifting her attention to him.

It wasn't something he liked to advertise—the fact that his parents had, in fact, named him after Harrison Ford. And that their obsession with Harrison and the Indiana Jones movies was what had gotten him into archaeology. But ask any archaeologist born after 1981 whether Indiana Jones was their hero, and not one would say otherwise.

Okay . . . fine. Lara Croft was pretty freaking awesome, too.

"Sort of," he said, trying to quickly brush it off. "Hey, Sunny, would you mind checking with Agnes to make sure she updated the head count for dinner?"

"Oh, I talked to her about an hour—"

"Why don't you double-check?"

Sunny scanned all their faces one at a time—Ethan and Corrie eyeing Ford, and Ford looking nowhere in particular—before she finally took the hint. "Well, I guess we can chat more later," she said to Corrie.

"Sounds great. Looking forward to it," Corrie responded, tenderly placing her hand on Sunny's forearm before Sunny finally did as Ford had asked.

Once Sunny was out of earshot, Corrie spun around toward him. "Jealous much?"

"Oh, please," he said with a *tsk* and a roll of his eyes. "Jealous of your reckless adventures and the fact that you've almost gotten yourself killed half a dozen times? I don't think so."

So, in other words, jealous and very much so.

"Oh, I don't mean all that. I know you're much too delicate for running through jungles or chasing after criminals. But I'm talking about you not being the center of attention. Something tells me up until a few moments ago, Sunny probably looked at you in much the same way. And now . . ." Her voice trailed off as she smiled and shrugged her shoulders.

Smug much?

"Wow. Two smiles in one day. Since when did you become Miss Congeniality?"

"Aw, hon. You noticed," she said, batting her eyelashes and curving her body toward his. Ford pressed his lips together as he glared at her, wanting nothing more than to wipe that cocky smirk off her face.

"All right, you two. Seriously, you're like a couple of bratty teenagers. Doesn't it ever get old?" Ethan asked, stepping in to break up the bickering.

"Nope," Corrie and Ford both responded at the same time without taking their narrowed eyes off each other.

"Well, I'm starving, and I can't take another one of your spats unless I have some food during the entertainment, so can we give it a break for, oh, I don't know, fifteen minutes?"

Leave it to Ethan to be the rational one. One of the many reasons Ford had asked him to join this expedition. And now that Corrie had been invited, having Ethan as referee was an added perk.

"Fine," Corrie responded, releasing his gaze. "I have to use the bathroom, anyway. Where might I find it?"

"Over there." Ethan pointed toward the toilet tents, or the TTs as they'd been calling them. Saying *I've gotta hit the TT* sounded a heck of a lot better than *I'm heading to the shitter.*

Corrie nodded, though not without one more sharp look, then took off toward the TTs, her fabulous hips swaying with each step, mesmerizing Ford. Drawing him in and practically erasing the annoyance he'd felt moments earlier.

"What is your problem?" Ethan asked, smacking Ford across the stomach and snapping him out of his *hip*-notic daydream. "We need her, remember?"

"I know, I know," Ford said, bowing his head, frustrated with himself. "She's just so . . . so . . ."

Dozens of words circled his brain, but none that he wanted to say out loud.

"Sexy?" Ethan finally answered for him.

Great. Was it really that obvious?

"What? No. Jeez, Ethan." Ford rolled his eyes and sneered.

"Okay, sure, Ford. Whatever you say," Ethan said with one raised eyebrow. "Look, you can admit that you're attracted to her. Claiming you're not only makes me more certain that you are."

Annoyance rolled through Ford's body. "That's not what this is about," he said, trying to turn the topic back to the matter at hand.

"Then you admit it?"

"Admit what?"

"Admit that you're attracted to her. I'm not going to tell her."

His mouth twitched and his nostrils flared as he fought to keep the words in. What the hell did this have to do with anything? Best friend or not, it wasn't any of Ethan's damn business who he found attractive. But even in her absence, Corrie's intoxicating hips, pretty mouth, and heavenly eyes taunted him.

"Fine! Yes!" he blurted, tossing his hands in the air. "Yes, she's hot. There, are you happy?"

A wide smile formed on Ethan's face. "I am, actually. Thanks.

You two always had some weird sexual energy going on back in school. Until you started dating Addison, that is."

"Okay, can we not talk about this, please?" Ford said, rubbing his forehead and growing impatient with the conversation. "Like I said, that's not what this is about. I can work with Corrie—if she even agrees to do it, which right now I put at about a fifty-fifty chance—despite the fact that, yes, I find her attractive. She's a beautiful woman, and I'm sure everyone in this camp would agree, yourself included. Sunny, too. So don't stand there acting like you've cracked the Da Vinci code, because it's really not all that surprising, is it?"

"Nope, not to me it isn't," Ethan said with his chin up, clearly proud of himself. "Nice to finally hear you say it after, what, twelve years?"

"You really are a dick sometimes, you know that, right?"

"Absolutely. But so are you, you know. Maybe cool it with the animosity. She's really not bad, once you get to know her. And neither are you."

Oh, he knew her, all right. That night in the library had revealed a different side of Corrie—and he'd liked it quite a bit. She'd managed to break down his walls. And, in turn, Ford had softened Corrie's hardened edges. It was quite synergistic when he really thought about it. Too bad he didn't know how to get them back to that place.

And too bad that side of Corrie was locked away.

"I know. She's just so . . . so . . ."

"Impressive?"

That was one word for her.

"I was going to say cocky."

Ethan laughed. "Don't you think that's a little too *pot calling the kettle black*?"

"Hey, I'm not *nearly* as cocky as she is."

Ethan patted Ford on the shoulder. "Sure, you're not. You two, I swear. It's hilarious that you both think it's the other one who's got the problem. You're unable to acknowledge how similar you actually are."

Similar? Please.

"Corrie and I are nothing alike. I stick with the facts and the rules. She's one of those goes-on-instincts kind of people. A plays-by-no-rules archaeologist. And, frankly, she's a bit reckless."

"Yet you still sent for her."

"Yeah, because she's also fucking brilliant. She might have her weird methods and all, but clearly whatever I'm doing here isn't working."

Not that he'd ever been on a job with Corrie, but he'd heard the stories about the spiritual connection she seemed to have with the land. An instinct for where to dig. An understanding of the earth. No one could explain it, but when Corrie Mejía was on an expedition, things always magically worked out, even if there were some mishaps and wild escapades along the way.

After three months into this dig and finding little more than a couple of jagged bits of obsidian, he could use a little dose of that Mejía magic. He'd never flat out told Ethan why he wanted to bring Corrie of all people onto the dig, though he assumed it was obvious. Still, Ethan's brows raised and his jaw lowered, as if shocked by Ford's confession.

"Wow. I have to say, I'm surprised to hear you admit that."

"Believe it or not, Ethan, I do have a little humility. See? Me? Not the cockiest." Ford smiled, knowing his friend appreciated his humor—and knowing that deep down, Ethan was only looking out for him.

They'd traveled the world together. Been on dozens of digs.

He was the best friend Ford had, though lately Ford had been closed off. Ever since his whole life had gotten turned upside down. Sure, he could acknowledge his humility, but not this. Not his fears that he deserved all the crap that had been thrown his way these last few years.

"Well, maybe if you admitted that to Corrie, *maybe* she'd be a little nicer to you," Ethan said, pulling him out of his thoughts.

"What? Me not being the cockiest?" Ford joked.

"No, you jackass," Ethan said, smiling and rolling his eyes. "That you think she's brilliant. I'm sure she'd appreciate your approval."

Ford brought back his head. "My approval?" He laughed. "I doubt Corrie would be all that impressed with my approval."

"You'd be surprised," Ethan said, with suggestion in his voice. Like he knew something he wasn't telling Ford. "Because maybe you're not aware, but you're pretty fucking brilliant, too."

Ford smiled.

"Aw, you think I'm brilliant," he joshed while batting his lashes. He'd never dare to admit it, but it was actually quite sweet and probably the nicest thing anyone had ever said to him.

"Yeah, yeah. Don't forget we started this conversation by calling each other dicks. Now, come on. I'm starving."

CHAPTER

Three

EVEN IF SHE WASN'T GOING TO STAY, CORRIE DIDN'T MIND HAVING a little fun getting under Ford's skin in the meantime. It was easy. All she had to do was open her mouth and *bam!* Let the battle commence. Though he really was being a baby about the whole Sunny thing. Leave it to Ford to not want anyone else to be in the spotlight. In his world there could only be one shining star.

But even the brightest of stars eventually burned out. Hence why Corrie didn't care much for pretty shiny things or anything else that inevitably faded. Things like diamond rings. Fresh flowers. Or love. Life was much easier on her own, anyway. No one to answer to. No one to stop her from jetting off to Mexico on three days' notice. No one to chastise her about her dangerous antics. If she died while trying to outrun a boulder careening through a booby-trapped temple, then at least she'd go doing something she loved. At least she'd go while having an adventure. Prima donnas like Ford who never bent the rules or took a risk for fear of getting hurt . . . well, they'd never understand.

Corrie wandered around the small clearing that held the camp, the rumble of the crew talking while waiting in line for dinner adding to the hoots and chirps of the jungle. Even well after dark, the air temperature had barely dropped. It was definitely gonna be one of those never-feel-fresh digs, always coated in mud, sweat, and a muggy sheen. So how did Ford manage to still look so . . . appetizing?

She shook her head. Why? Why did her mind keep going there? Must have been her stomach talking. She circled back around toward the mess tent. Smelled good. Having a cook flown in was better than most digs, where they shared cooking duties or had nothing but individual camp stoves and dehydrated food pouches. If she never had to eat another packet of rehydrated scrambled eggs with "bacon" in her life, she'd call that a victory.

She walked up to the tent, grabbed a tray, and cycled through the line, loading up with a biscuit, a pat of butter, a small green salad, and a hearty bowl of beef stew.

"You made this all out here?" Corrie asked the cook as she handed her the bowl.

"Sure did. Real food only. None of that freeze-dried or pre-packaged crap here," the cook said, holding her head high. "You must be Dr. Mejía."

"Corrie." She reached out her hand for a shake.

"Agnes. Guess we'll be bunkmates, eh?"

"Oh. Well, I, uh . . . I don't know." Corrie glanced around the camp, just now realizing the person-to-tent ratio. *Well, damn.*

"Well, if you'd rather bunk with those burping, farting, loudmouth boobs, then by all means," Agnes said, motioning toward the rest of the group—all men aside from Agnes, Sunny, and Corrie. Not that she minded coed sleeping situations, but she was a thirty-five-year-old woman who liked her privacy. She didn't even want to live with a cat, let alone other people.

"No, I mean, we haven't discussed sleeping arrangements. And frankly, I'm not really even sure I'm going to stay."

"Not going to stay? Then why did Dr. Matthews have me bust my budget getting these gosh dang Jamaican coffee beans?" Agnes reached over to grab a clipboard and looked at what appeared to be an order form. "Said we *had* to have them," she mumbled as she turned her back and reviewed the form.

Warmth spread over Corrie's skin. He'd remembered. He remembered her love for Jamaican coffee.

She had to admit, he didn't really seem the thoughtful type. No, Ford Matthews was always in it for himself. Perhaps that was all this was—his way of buttering her up so she'd sign on for this dig. *See? We even special ordered your favorite coffee, just for you, because your being here means soooooo much to us.*

Then *wham!* Ford's name gets slapped on one of the greatest discoveries of their time and all Corrie gets is a smooth, rich cup of delicious Jamaican coffee.

Then again, that long evening they'd spent in the library drinking coffee together out of Corrie's thermos was ingrained in her brain even after all these years. Maybe it was ingrained in his as well. She could still picture his lips pressed against the tiny red plastic cup of her thermos. Or at least it had looked tiny in *his* hands. His lips, touching the same spot where her lips had been, savoring that coffee as she'd savored his emerald eyes staring back at her from behind his glasses, never taking away his gaze. She remembered how the low moan in his throat had fanned the fire building in her core as the creamy yet bold and zesty coffee hit his taste buds. And how he'd licked away those few droplets that clung to his lower lip before wiping his mouth with the back of his hand and returning the cup to her while brushing his fingers ever so lightly across her own.

Yep, she'd analyzed what that night meant many times, especially in light of the fact that a few days later she'd found him sucking face with Addison Crawley, daughter of the famed Yale professor Dr. Richard Crawley—Ford's eventual boss. Who should have been *her* boss.

Corrie turned toward the tables, searching for Ford.

There.

He quickly looked away when she spotted him, but he'd clearly been watching her, which sent another tingle, though this one was focused in her midsection.

All right . . . maybe she wouldn't try *quite* so hard to get under his skin. After all, perhaps this was *his* attempt at trying, too.

"Dr. Mejía! Over here!" Sunny called out from their table, waving her arms frantically in the air.

Oh boy. Deep breaths.

Ford had been right—Corrie would never have been a contender in a Miss Congeniality contest back in the day. But unlike Ford, who got things handed to him simply by being charming (and, apparently, by sleeping up the food chain), Corrie had had to *learn* to be likeable. And once she'd started teaching, well, she'd realized that excited students meant *engaged* students. After getting to know her students and mentoring her younger colleagues and seeing that they shared her passion, well, it made the whole experience even better. Sometimes those students and colleagues even became her friends. People like Miri.

Besides, what was the saying? You kill more bees with honey?

Oh, wait . . . or was it *catch*?

Eight years ago, Sunny would have annoyed the hell out of

Corrie. But today, she found Sunny to be the much-needed bright spot—no pun intended—in an otherwise cloudy, craptastic day.

"Dr. Mejía, here, I saved you a seat," Sunny said, shooing a younger guy out of the way as Corrie approached.

"You can call me Corrie."

"I thought you said, 'It's Dr. Mejía' earlier today," Ford grouched from across the table. Though his snipe was quickly met with a jab in the ribs and a whispered grumble from Ethan.

"Well, my *friends* call me Corrie. Is someone going to introduce me to everyone?" she asked, looking around the table at the other four faces.

Ethan took the reins, going around and introducing Ford's other interns and Ethan's research assistant.

"Dr. Mejía—" one of the interns started.

"I told you, please call me Corrie."

"Oh, okay . . ." he said, looking at Ford as if asking for permission, clearly unsure if doing so would be rude and insulting. Ford merely shrugged his shoulders before stabbing his spoon into his bowl of stew. "Well, Doctor, I mean Corrie, can you tell us about that time you got flooded out and had to build a raft to float to that Native village in the Amazon?"

Even though the world's most prominent archaeologists didn't find her escapades very . . . refined, Corrie enjoyed that she'd gained something of a following among the younger generation for her outrageous adventures. Ford let out a quick huff as he stared at his tray, making it obvious which camp he belonged to. Appeasing Ford wasn't exactly high on Corrie's list, but she also didn't need to fan the flames or get into yet another spat with him, especially not in front of an audience. They were his students, after all.

Though she didn't understand what he was so salty about. They were good stories. Even *he* should have been able to admit that. And if they *really* thought she was so great, they would have chosen to go to Berkeley rather than Yale so they could have studied under her instead.

But best not to poke the beast.

"You know," she deflected, "it seems like you all already know about me. I'd like to learn more about all of you," Corrie said.

Ford's eyes looked up and locked on hers, as if acknowledging that she'd done that for him. *Yeah, remember that the next time you start being an ass again.*

They went around the table, telling Corrie about their studies. How they'd gotten into archaeology—a lot of Indiana Jones and *The Mummy* franchise fans as per usual. What they wanted to do once they were done with school. A few funny stories about Ford's classes that garnered an endearing smile and a few playful ribbings from him. It seemed his students enjoyed his teaching style, and based on their banter, it seemed he enjoyed them as well.

Ethan's assistant, Gabriel, talked about his position at the Field Museum in Chicago. Unlike the others, he'd opted not to get a formal degree in archaeology, studying history instead, but that didn't stop him from volunteering to go on digs whenever he built up enough vacation time. Luckily, this dig was a paid gig, courtesy of Ford convincing their investor that he needed Ethan, and Ethan convincing Ford that he needed his assistant. Ethan and Gabriel were both skilled in archaeological techniques, which made up for the fact that Sunny and the other interns were not.

The interns all had their various reasons for wanting to go on the dig. Experience. Credits. One, Mateo, was originally from Mexico and wanted to participate in a dig in his native land. Though she'd been born and raised in the US, Corrie understood the desire to study one's culture. For the most part, they all said they were enjoying their time on the dig, though at three months in with little to no contact with the outside world and no real end in sight, their excitement seemed to be waning. Digs were hard no matter how you sliced it, especially remote ones like this. Being away from home. Being sweaty and dirty all day. Sleeping in tents with no access to running water. But the secrecy surrounding this particular excursion added an extra layer of frustration. They couldn't tell their friends and family where they were or for how long. They couldn't discuss what they had or hadn't found. No, the only people they could *really* talk to were those crowded inside this tent.

And seeing as one of those people was the person Corrie despised most in the world, she wasn't sure she was ready to limit her interactions to her present company.

"How did you become so knowledgeable about Chimalli?" Mateo asked.

"Yeah. What got you interested in Chimalli in the first place?" Gabriel followed up.

Corrie opened her mouth to speak, but Ford beat her to it. "Well, Dr. Mejía over here thinks she's Chimalli's descendant." His voice carried an air of skepticism—and a healthy dose of arrogance. He didn't believe her. Few people did, in fact, so she typically kept that information to herself.

Now she was regretting ever mentioning it to Ford, especially seeing as he'd used that information to get her here in the first place.

"Seriously?" Sunny asked, her eyes wide and full of wonderment.

"Well, uh, yes. My grandfather traced my family history, and it appears that, yes, I could be one of Chimalli's descendants."

"Except for the fact, however, that it was widely assumed that Chimalli was infertile, having been castrated with the very knife he took when he fled Tenochtitlán," Ford felt the need to clarify.

Corrie glared at him. "Yes, that's *one* version. But Diego Mendoza's account presents a different version of the events."

"Oh, right! You mentioned that in your dissertation, didn't you?" one of the interns asked.

Her dissertation? She perked up in her seat.

"You . . . you've read my dissertation?"

"We all have. Required reading assigned by Dr. Matthews," Sunny clarified.

She shot a glance over to Ford, sitting with his elbows on the table and taking a swig of water. "What? It's a good paper. I mean, it's practically the textbook on Chimalli," he explained.

Was that . . . was that a compliment? Well, fuck. She pressed her knees together. His now calm, casual demeanor oozed with sex appeal, but a compliment? If *that* wasn't the biggest turn-on Corrie had ever experienced . . .

Sure, there wasn't much concrete documentation on Chimalli, and she *had* gathered almost everything there was to know about him within that one document, but surely Ford didn't admit—to his own students, no less—that she knew more about Chimalli than he did. Did he?

Nearly speechless at the revelation, Corrie finally turned back to the students. "Well, I . . . uh, yes. I mentioned it. But, as evidenced by your professor, it's not a widely believed account."

"Can you tell us a little more?" Mateo asked.

Corrie glanced at Ford again, as if checking to make sure he was okay with her telling the tale. It was his dig, after all. Not that Corrie really felt she needed his permission, but it was a professional courtesy that even Ford was worthy of receiving. It was still surprising, though, when he motioned with his hands as if to say, *By all means.*

"Okay. Well . . . there are two main theories about what happened to Chimalli. The first and most widely believed is that Chimalli was a high-ranking official in Moctezuma the second's army and that to pledge his allegiance, he allowed himself to be castrated, signifying that his commitment would be to no one other than the gods. Not a woman. Not a family. Only the gods. But once the Spaniards arrived, Chimalli got scared and fled the city alone, stealing the knife, thinking he could trade it once he was far enough away from the empire.

"The problem with that theory, in my opinion, is that it doesn't make sense that he would be so dedicated to the gods as to be castrated, but then flee at the first sign of the Spaniards, especially when their initial arrival didn't appear hostile. It doesn't add up."

"Yeah, except that people do strange things when their lives are on the line," Ford chimed in.

True. But Corrie knew many men, and any who would be brave enough to get their balls cut off—i.e., none of them—wouldn't then be afraid of a foreign invasion. *Especially* not if they thought they had the backing of literal gods on their side.

"Then what was Mendoza's version?" Mateo asked.

Her favorite part.

"In Mendoza's account, Chimalli had actually fallen in love with a macehualtin, a commoner named Yaretzi from a village near Tenochtitlán, but their relationship was frowned upon because Chimalli was a member of the pipiltin, the noble class of warriors. Some of the high priests found out and set to have her used as a sacrificial offering during the festival of Panquetzaliztli. But on the eve of her scheduled death, Chimalli rescued her and stole the tecpatl—the sacrificial knife. After they fled the city, they then had a child and lived a relatively peaceful life away from the demise of the Aztecs."

"How did they have a child if he'd been castrated, though?" Sunny asked.

"He wasn't castrated. According to Mendoza, that was a lie Moctezuma the second's most loyal disciples had started as a way to discredit Chimalli, or lessen his worth as a man," Corrie explained.

"Do you know what the tecpa . . . tepa—"

"Tecpatl," she clarified.

"Right, the tecpatl," one of the interns said. "Do you know what it looks like?"

She shook her head. "No, though a few tecpatl have been discovered, so we have some general idea. The double-edged blade is likely made of flint, possibly white flint. And the handle is likely elaborate, possibly a carved figure such as an animal made out of wood. Maybe adorned with a mosaic of shell pieces or gemstones like turquoise, malachite, or mother-of-pearl. They're quite beautiful, considering what they were used for. But it was all part of their culture."

"If there are these two versions, then why don't most people know about Mendoza's? Or, better yet, why don't they believe it?"

"Because Mendoza was a Spanish Army deserter who couldn't be trusted, that's why," Ford responded. "And the only written account of this *version* is Mendoza's own, unlike the other version, which is supported by paintings in Tenochtitlán and multiple written accounts by other Spaniards."

Yet again, chiming in with his unsolicited opinions. His sexiness was starting to wear off. Corrie rolled her eyes. Sure, there was more support for version A, and in many people's eyes castration made for a sexier story. You know, sexy without the sex. But despite the lack of it in her own life, Corrie believed in love. She *wanted* Mendoza's version to be true. She *wanted* Chimalli to break the barriers of the archaic rule and risk it all for love.

And to steal the knife as a fuck-you while he was at it.

But the fact of the matter was, they didn't know. No one did. So unless and until she had definitive proof, Corrie was going to acknowledge there were multiple possibilities, but hope that Mendoza's version proved true.

"Don't you think there's a possibility that, like Moctezuma the second's supporters might have done to Chimalli, the Spanish Army could have planted lies about Mendoza to discredit him?" Corrie asked Ford. "Because according to Mendoza, he wasn't a deserter. Rather, he fell down a ravine and was left for dead until Chimalli came upon him and saved his life. Why else would the Spaniards write about an otherwise low-level nobody like Mendoza?"

"Slow news day?" he joked, garnering a few laughs from the others.

Corrie's blood started to boil. Typical. Just like when they were in school and he'd try to undermine her arguments with a silly remark that would steal everyone's attention from the real issue. It had worked back then, and it worked for him now. And why wouldn't it? Ford had a charm that few possessed. Despite his arrogance, he was the kind of person who could command anyone's attention simply by walking in the room.

Addison Crawley, case in point.

"Real cute, Ford," Corrie said to him, unable to keep from scowling.

"Oh relax, Corrie. I know many people might prefer the Prince Charming version where a warrior like Chimalli put it all on the line for love, but the facts are facts, and in this instance, they point to castration."

Another snicker from the group stoked the fire burning beneath the surface of her skin. Fuck Prince Charming.

"As a practicing archaeologist, you should know that at this stage, there are no facts. Only theories."

"Hey, I'm only pointing out the more obvious scenario."

The inferno was ready to release its wrath when Ethan the Pacifier jumped in yet again.

"Well, that was fascinating, you two. Let's see if you can put those critical thinking skills to work tomorrow morning."

Corrie was starting to think Ford didn't deserve her help. For all she knew, Ford was out here looking for Chimalli's balls rather than trying to determine what *really* happened to him.

"You're right," Ford said, clapping his hands together. "We've got a big day tomorrow, gang, so let's make sure everyone is rested and ready to hit the trail by eight a.m., okay?"

The students all nodded and got up, saying their goodbyes and good nights, leaving Corrie, Ford, and Ethan alone at the table. It was still relatively early, but if this was anything like the other digs Corrie had been on, the last evening after a break was always the toughest. You needed the evening to get back in the mind-set and rest.

All she needed was a good night's rest.

Hmm.

"So . . . uh, what are the sleeping arrangements here?" she asked.

"Didn't Ford tell you? You're sleeping in his bed," Ethan teased, and was immediately met by a shove from Ford.

What the . . . ?

"Will you knock it off?" Ford spat at Ethan. "You're about to get fired if you don't cut it out."

Corrie eyed them curiously. She'd missed something, clearly.

"We ordered a tent for you so you'd have your own space, assuming you stay and all," Ford continued once he got his annoyance with Ethan out of the way. "But our deliveries only come on Mondays so it isn't here yet. But you can stay in my tent tonight—*alone*," he then clarified, glaring at Ethan. "I'll bunk with some of the other guys."

"Oh. Well, I don't want to put you out or anything. I can share with Agnes . . . and Sunny I presume?"

"You don't want to bunk with Agnes. She snores," Ethan offered.

"How do you know?"

"Sunny told us, in the politest, most *I really don't want to throw anyone under the bus* sort of way," Ford said, unable to hold back an endearing smile.

He looked good when he smiled. Not that smarmy, douchey smile he sometimes tossed her way. Like when he *really* wanted to irk her. But in genuine moments—the moments where Ford acted like a real person who actually had feelings and cared for people other than himself—well, in those moments, Ford went from being a hot jerk to a handsome man.

He also seemed to genuinely like his students, a sentiment Corrie shared. She could tell he had a soft spot for Sunny in particular.

But Corrie didn't know what to make of all this—Jamaican coffee, charming smiles, and the offer to relinquish his tent for the night? Either he was *really* working to get her to stay or maybe Ford Matthews had matured over the last few years. Corrie wanted to think he could change. After all, she wanted to think that *she* had changed since they'd last seen each other.

Maybe she needed to cool it on the jabs. At least for the night.

Ethan stood and grabbed his tray. "I'm going to let you two sort this out and retire to my solo tent. It's nice seeing you talking civilly, at least. Now, good night. I bid you adieu," he said, bowing and taking his leave.

And allowing an awkward silence to settle over the table.

"I feel bad taking your space," Corrie finally said, breaking up the stillness. "Really, I don't mind rooming with Agnes and Sunny. Besides, it's just for the night."

They were the only two left under the mess tent, everyone else either sitting over by the fire and passing a bottle of booze or going in and out of their tents, readying themselves for the evening. Even Agnes had packed up, leaving Corrie and Ford to have to clean their own dishes.

"It's fine, Corrie. Besides, unless you want to bunk with some of the guys, we'd have to move an empty bed from one of the other tents, so it's easier this way. Come on, we should clean up."

He stood and took both their trays over to the makeshift kitchen area where a tub of water sat waiting for them. "I'll wash. You dry," he said, handing Corrie a towel then rolling up his sleeves slightly higher. Aside from the hoots from the howler monkeys and the throaty squawks from the scarlet macaws, they washed and dried in silence, a rare occurrence for the two of them. Corrie's mind blanked as her gaze wandered over him under the low camp lights. From his height to his hands. And then to his forearms. The muscles flexing beneath his skin with each movement.

A flash of ink peeked out from under the cuff of his rolled-up sleeves, on the inside of his elbow. Letters in cursive. *CM.*

Corrie's heart skipped a beat. *CM?* As in Corrie Mejía?

"What's that stand for?" Corrie asked as nonchalantly as possible as she took one of the bowls from his hands.

He looked at what she was referring to, and tugged at his sleeve, covering the tattoo so she could no longer see. "It's nothing."

Well, that was bullshit. Seriously, though. Was it possible that he had her initials tattooed on his arm? No . . . there was no way.

Right?

"It's my mom's initials," he said a few moments later as he kept his focus on the suds in the dirty water. Corrie scrunched her face in embarrassment, thankful he didn't notice. Of *course* they weren't her initials. The very thought of it was absurd.

"She's . . . she's not well," he continued. "Got diagnosed with cancer a few months before I left to come here. It's my way of having her here with me."

His voice was calm and even. He didn't look at Corrie.

"Oh, I'm sorry, Ford. I shouldn't have . . ." She wanted to touch him. To put her arms around his shoulders and tell him it would be okay. Not that she knew whether it would be okay. But she wanted him to feel better, and she knew Ford well enough to know that as even-toned as he seemed, he was not okay.

"It's okay. It's hard being here sometimes, that's all," he said, glancing at her for a moment, then returning to the dishes.

"Only being able to speak to her on the satellite phone once a week. Not knowing the condition she'll be in once I get back."

"What about your dad? Is he handling it okay?"

Ford paused, gripping the side of the tub for a moment while staring straight ahead into the darkness of the jungle. "He died two years ago."

Corrie closed her eyes and silently winced. Jeez. Talk about a foot in the mouth. "Before you go apologizing again, don't. He's not worth it," Ford followed up, pulling his mouth into a tight line.

She remembered him talking about his parents that night in the library. The Sunday evening phone calls he never missed. The first time he'd watched *Raiders of the Lost Ark* with his dad. How much he was looking forward to his upcoming father-son trip that summer. Guess a lot had changed over those last several years. She had so many questions, but it was likely hard enough for Ford to reveal as much as he did to her, so she let it go. But why was he here if his mother was sick? Sure, this was his job, but it wasn't like finding Chimalli was Ford's passion like it was Corrie's. Ford probably couldn't care less about Chimalli, to be honest. He was always more interested in unearthing lost cities and structures, not necessarily the specific people who lived in them.

"Can we talk about something else?" he asked, breaking into her thoughts.

"Of course. What do you want to talk about?"

"What about that jaguar? Did you really outrun it?" He tipped his head at her and smiled. There it was again. And there were the flutters in her stomach.

Corrie laughed. "I swear, I don't know how that rumor got

started. No, it wasn't a jaguar. It was a jaguarundi. The size of a giant housecat. All people hear is 'jaguar' and now I'm a jag hunter. And I wouldn't say I outran it, but rather outsmarted it. Though, to your earlier point, no, it *wasn't* injured." She smiled back at him, and he chuckled.

Mm. She liked that sound. She *liked* making him laugh. Almost more than she liked getting under his skin.

Who knew?

"What about the whole necklace thing, then? The one where you allegedly stole *back* that jade necklace that had been stolen from the auction?"

"I mean, that one's *sort of* true. Though, in all fairness, you can't really steal what's already been stolen. And besides, I didn't take it, anyway. I still maintain that Bernard Sardoni gave it to me."

"Gave it to you? I thought I'd heard you got it from his bedroom?"

"Yes, that's right."

He cocked his head. "And? How did you even get in that situation in the first place?"

"Well, I'd gone to that auction with a friend of mine who'd been the one responsible for the necklace, and when the necklace went missing, they blamed him. So I did some digging, learned Sardoni was the likely culprit, snuck my way into a party he was having a few days later, and during the party he invited me to his room. And while we were in there . . . he put the necklace on me."

She nonchalantly glanced at Ford, who was hanging on to her every word. This was fun. And, admittedly, the time she fooled mob boss Bernard Sardoni *was* one of her favorite stories, even though, at the time, she had been terrified. But she couldn't let her friend take the heat for the necklace's disappearance.

"Wait . . . did you . . ." Although he didn't finish his question, it was obvious what he wanted to ask. The same question everyone asked: whether she'd had sex with Sardoni.

"Ew, of course not, Ford. I *do* have standards, thank you very much."

"But you *did* use your sex appeal to get in his bedroom," he said, more like a fact than a question.

Hmm . . . was Ford admitting that he found her sexy? She fought her smile back.

"Well, how else was I going to get up there? I mean, how the heck do you think I got into that party, anyway?"

Though, that *was* the reason Sardoni brought her to his room. Thankfully, she'd gone in with an exit plan.

"And that's it? He put the necklace on you and said, 'Here you go'?"

"No. About a minute later, his wife came bursting into the room, with the maid I'd paid a hundred bucks to snitch, and then I snuck out during the commotion. Seeing as he stole the necklace in the first place, it wasn't like he was going to report me to the police."

Ford covered his mouth to hide his shock. "No way. I can't believe you did that. That's so dangerous, Corrie. And ballsy. Maybe you *are* a badass."

She smiled and had to turn her head to keep him from being able to see her blush. For some reason, his acknowledgment felt like confirmation that all her outrageous antics had been worth it. They at least made for decent fodder at dig-side dinners.

"What about you? What's the wildest thing that's happened to you since you became Dr. Ford Matthews?"

"I don't do wild," he said, wiping the last of the droplets off the makeshift counter.

"Oh, come on. No Holy Grails? Or chasing Nazis through the desert?"

He snickered. "Nope."

"What about sword fights and snakes?" she jested.

"Certainly not."

"Don't you have any fun?" she asked, playfully tugging on his arm.

And accidentally brushing her breasts against his bicep. They both froze, each glancing at the place where their bodies connected, but neither making any effort to break apart. They hadn't been this close since . . . since that night in the library.

Dammit . . . it felt good being this close to him. Warmth rippled through her body, and her nipples hardened. Could he feel it? Did she *want* him to feel it? The pace of his breathing picked up, matching hers one to one.

A roar of thunder cracked through the sky, snapping them out of whatever daze they'd been in and forcing their bodies apart as if lightning had sliced between them. And with that one rolling boom came an onslaught of rain. The once-calm camp was now in an all-out flurry with people running for shelter and grabbing their things.

"The Jeep," Ford said.

"My things!" Corrie followed up. Within seconds, her bags, sitting on the backseat of the topless Jeep, would be soaked. Dammit.

"Come on," he said, grabbing her by the hand and running through the pouring rain.

By the time they reached the Jeep, Corrie's hair was plastered against her cheek. Her shirt clung to her skin. At least her shirt was black. Ford's white button-down, on the other hand, was practically see-through, highlighting every bump and divot of his perfect pecs and abs.

"Here, take this," he said, tearing her attention from his chest and handing her the smaller of her bags as he grabbed the other. "Now follow me."

They ran back through the camp, following the string lights as the rain came down so fast and hard that it couldn't even soak into the ground. Puddles started to form throughout camp, splashing up whenever Corrie and Ford ran through them. Finally, they reached one of the tents, and Ford pulled open the door to let her in. Once inside, a calmness settled over her, despite the loudness of the rain pounding on the roof.

"These are waterproof, right?" she asked as Ford came in and set her bag on the wooden platform floor.

"Yes. You'll be fine."

He ran his hand through his hair, shaking out some of the excess water while she took in her surroundings.

The space was large. Larger than any tent she'd ever slept in. There was a bed, a *real* full-size bed in one corner with a trunk at the foot. A desk covered with papers sat immediately across from it. A couple of comfortable-looking wooden chairs with a small table were in yet another corner. And by the entry was a bench with a pile of gear.

"This is nice," she said. A little fancy for her tastes, but, hey, it sure beat waking in a puddle in the middle of the night.

"You'll get one like this, too. If you stay, I mean," he said.

She couldn't help but feel *slightly* guilty that she hadn't made up her mind.

"Here," he said, handing her a towel and then taking off his glasses to dry them off.

She took it in her hand and pressed it against her hair and then her chest, trying to blot the water soaking through.

"Ugh, my stuff is probably all wet," she said, kneeling to open one of her bags to check.

"We can lay everything out to dry," Ford said, opening the other bag.

The *big* bag.

Oh no. Not that one.

"That's okay, I can do it," she said.

"It's not a problem. I don't mind," he continued, clearly not hearing the panic in her voice.

"No, really. I've got it." She started to get up, watching his arm disappear into her bag. "No, don't go in there!"

Ford pulled out his arm, and along with it a long purple contraption. "What is this?" he asked, eyeing the device suspiciously.

"It's . . . it's my vibrator."

He instantly dropped it, sending it to the floor with a loud *clunk*.

"My God, Ford, don't *break* it," she said, rushing to pick it up off the ground.

"Well, what is that doing in there?"

"What do you mean, 'What's it doing in there'? It's *my* bag. I told you not to go in there."

"Well, why didn't you warn me?"

"I *did* warn you. I said not to go in there."

"Yeah, but you could have said why."

"Oh, really? What was I supposed to say? 'Don't go in there, Ford. That's where I keep my *vibrator*'?"

"It certainly would have stopped me."

She turned it on to make sure the fall hadn't broken it. *Bzzzzzzzzzz.*

"Oh my God, what are you doing?" he asked, lifting his hands to cover his ears and turning away.

"Making sure you didn't break it."

"Now?"

"Yes, now. What, am I supposed to wait until I want to use it only to *then* realize that it's broken? If anyone should be embarrassed here, it's me, not you. Man up, Ford. It's just a sex toy. Lots of women use them. Men, too," she then added with a quick purse of her lips.

"It's time for me to go," he said, failing to look in her direction.

Interesting. Note to Corrie: Ford was uncomfortable with this. In fact, his discomfort made Corrie *more* comfortable with the fact that her purple monster, or Barney as she liked to call it, was on full display.

"Well, have a good night, Ford," she said, folding her arms with Barney still in her hand.

He glanced back at her one last time. "Good night. And don't use that thing in my bed."

A VIBRATOR. SHE'D ACTUALLY BROUGHT A *VIBRATOR* ON AN ARchaeological dig.

How was he supposed to focus on the dig—or, hell, how was he supposed to focus on sleep—when his mind kept wandering back to Corrie pleasuring herself in his bed? On his sheets that he would presumably return to the following night.

It was bad enough that Corrie's presence distracted him from the task at hand. He needed to get back his *eyes on the prize* mentality.

He needed this for his mom.

Fuck! He didn't want to think about his mom. Not now while his cock ached, picturing that long, smooth contraption whirring through Corrie's body. And worse yet? He couldn't do anything about it, not with three other guys sharing the same tent.

Guess he needed some new surroundings.

Under the darkness of the jungle, Ford crept out of bed in the middle of the night, confirming no others were out and about before making his way to the bathing area for a cold shower. Finally with some privacy, he stroked his cock under the cool spray, needing to relieve the tension so he could get some sleep. Once he returned to bed, however, he kept having dreams about Corrie, thinking about how it had felt when she'd pressed her breasts against his arm. The fact that she hadn't pulled away . . . well . . . Ford could only surmise what that meant. Based on the way her breath had hitched, he suspected she'd liked it as much as he had. Was that even possible?

When his alarm went off at six thirty, he could have sworn he'd just fallen asleep. Bringing Corrie here was proving to be a terrible error in judgment, even if just for the fact that her presence deprived him of much-needed sleep. He'd been erring a lot lately. He needed to get this morning over with. One way or another, it would solve his dilemma. Either she'd decide to leave—a real possibility after everything that had happened—or she'd hunker down and focus like the Corrie he'd known back in school. The one who wouldn't let anyone or anything stand in her way. The one who was determined and brilliant.

And the one who was supposed to have been given this job in the first place, not Ford. Had that been the case, she might have already found what they were looking for instead of spending the last three and a half months playing in the dirt.

That one. He needed that Corrie so he could get home to his mom.

With sixteen people in camp—well, technically seventeen now—and only four TTs and three showers, mornings tended to be chaotic. Ford tried to catch fifteen more minutes of sleep before getting up, but there was no use. So he tossed on a pair of dark camel cargo pants, his beat-up and well-worn hiking boots, and an orange-blue-and-white-plaid long-sleeved hiking shirt and set out for the day.

Everyone else was about wrapped up with breakfast by the time Corrie finally waltzed into the tent, looking fabulously well rested and chipper as all get out. Unlike every other person in this camp, Corrie appeared to have stepped straight out of a salon, with her hair flowing in long waves halfway down her torso. But the put-togetherness didn't end there. Her face was bright and cheery. If Ford didn't know better, he'd think she had makeup on. But she'd never needed it. She possessed a natural beauty that makeup would only hide. Her white button-down was knotted at the waist and with the buttons open at the top, revealing a skin-tight tank top barely containing her breasts underneath. That, coupled with a pair of charcoal fitted stretch hiking pants that highlighted her curves, drew Ford's—and likely everyone else's—attention away from their meals and directly at the vixen entering the mess tent.

Now she's fucking with me.

Except she wasn't. That was just the way Corrie was without trying.

Plain and simple: Corrie was all that and a bag of chips.

And Ford liked chips. A lot.

Like a sprite, she floated to Agnes, then grabbed a cup of coffee and a granola bar before eyeing the bowl of fruit.

Don't take the banana. Don't take the banana.

Apple.

Phew. Ford wasn't sure his dick could withstand watching Corrie put a banana in her mouth. Not after the night he'd had.

"How'd you sleep?" Ethan asked as she sat at the table.

"Wonderfully," she said, bringing up her shoulders and letting out an exaggerated sigh. "I know Ford didn't want me to enjoy his bed too much, but I couldn't help myself," she said, eyeing him over her mug.

His cock twitched as her gaze didn't waver.

Oh God. She did it. She used it in my bed.

Having Corrie around really wasn't good for his mental—or sexual—well-being.

"Ford, are you listening?" Ethan said.

"Huh?" Ford shook his head, trying to snap out of it. What had he missed?

"I said we should head out soon," Ethan repeated.

"Right. Yeah, sure. Let's get going."

He stood, gathering his tray, and was headed toward the bus tubs when Corrie ran up beside him.

"Hey, are you okay?" she asked, stopping him by the arm.

He glanced confusingly at her hand and then turned his gaze to her face. "Of course I'm okay. Why wouldn't I be?" he asked, unsure what she was referring to.

"Well, I didn't really . . ." she pulled in closer, "I didn't, *you know*, in your bed." She cast her eyes downward when she said it, as if it wasn't clear.

"Oh no? But I thought you slept 'wonderfully'?" he said with an uptick of his brow.

"I was teasing. Though I really did sleep well, so thank you for giving up your bed. And thanks for the coffee," she said, acknowledging that she knew the coffee was meant specially for her.

He hadn't intended the coffee to be a bribe. Frankly, Ford hadn't anticipated this turn of events or the potential that Corrie wouldn't immediately say yes. This dig was the culmination of her life's work. It was everything to her. He'd assumed that regardless of the fact that he was the lead, she would have jumped at the chance. The coffee had been intended as an added bonus.

But now, if she didn't stay, it was going to be an expensive mistake, replacing the entire camp's supply, seeing as it cost ten times as much as the crap they usually drank on digs. The investor might have been generous with certain expenses, but Ford still had a budget. Sure, he enjoyed it, too, and of course he'd much rather drink delicious Jamaican coffee over the acidic bean water they'd been choking down until a week ago, but it still cut into his bottom line. And his profits if things turned out the way he hoped.

Knowing Corrie Mejía, however, it was going to take more than a few coffee beans to keep her there. She might have been bright and chipper this morning, but Ford was well aware of the temporary nature of their getting along. Dammit. He'd done this for her and she was going to leave him here in the cold.

Or, rather, in the hot, sticky jungle.

"Let's get this over with so we have time to get back to the airport, okay?" he said, snapping back to the reality of a Mejía-Matthews partnership and shaking free from the hold she had on him.

She blinked twice, as if dumbfounded by his curtness, before he sighed and walked away. What was there to be surprised about? He knew how this would all end—with Corrie on an evening flight back to the States and Ford weighing whether he should press on or abandon the entire expedition. Honestly, he didn't know why they were even going through the motions by showing her the site, but moments later, ole Ethan was already hot on the trail, escorting Corrie through the thick brush of ferns and bromeliads.

Ford hung back as Ethan narrated the trek, telling Corrie about the land, warning her to mind her step, assisting her through the dense forest and the uneven terrain—as if she needed it. The woman ran through jungles and built rafts without tools. Pretty sure she could handle herself over a few rocks and fallen trees.

The two of them laughed and joked, catching up on their lives and reminiscing about old times. Ford tried blocking them out, but it was no use. Corrie's laugh was distinctive and intoxicating. He'd forgotten how much he'd enjoyed it. It started with a burst, and then turned into an uncontrollable rolling of laughter before ending with a couple of inhales to catch her breath. It was a real laugh, not one of those tiny, polite giggles. No, Corrie's laugh was anything but cute and was genuinely Corrie—an *I give zero fucks whether you like my laugh* kind of laugh. Ford had managed to trigger a few of them back in the day. Though the ones at the library were the most memorable, receiving several *shh*s and a threat that they'd get kicked out of the building if they weren't quiet.

It had taken lots of work, but he'd earned those laughs. Real laughs. And now Corrie was practically giving them away for free at everything Ethan said. Ethan was funny, but he wasn't *that* funny.

Why was it bothering him so much, though? Why was *everything* about Corrie's being here getting to him?

If only he didn't need her.

"And voilà! This is it," Ethan announced once they'd reached their destination.

The site really wasn't much to look at. From the top of the ravine, they stared into the work area: about a dozen square holes measuring six by six scattered about the cleared jungle floor, roped off in a grid for tracking purposes. Piles of sifted dirt sat along the outsides of the site, discarded after confirming the soil was free of any artifacts. Blue tarps covered the work site to shield from both the rain and the relentless sun. Even as deep in the jungle as they were, the sun still pounded on them every day. Great for a tan. Not great for working in ninety-degree heat.

Ford pulled up alongside Ethan and Corrie, then called out to the rest of the crew behind them, "All right, everyone. Go ahead and get started."

They watched and waited until the crew descended into the ravine, leaving Corrie, Ford, and Ethan standing alone at the top.

"So . . ." Ford started.

"So . . ."

"This is it."

"That I can see. What brought you here?" Corrie asked.

Wasn't that obvious? Wasn't she supposed to be the Chimalli expert, after all?

That was what he *wanted* to ask, but he knew better than to press his luck on Corrie's chipperness for the day.

"The Lacandon," he said, as if that were enough to explain. "And the distance from Tenochtitlán."

"And who found this particular spot?" she asked, crouching and putting her hands in the dirt.

Ford and Ethan glanced at each other. *What on literal earth is she doing?* So these were the stories he'd heard so much about. And not just the ones about her running down jags and schmoozing with mob bosses. No, the stories about her methods. How she felt the earth. Meditated during her lunch break. Lay in the dirt. Something about listening to the ancients speak to her or some woo-woo shit like that. They certainly didn't teach *this* in grad school.

Some people thought her methods were weird. Others thought she was spiritual, and that spirituality led her on the right path.

Ford was intrigued, though he also found lying around to meditate to be a giant waste of time. When he went on digs, he
wanted to find things. He didn't want to speak to dirt or ghosts.

"I did," he said, standing straighter and shifting his stance.
"And then Ethan came with me to scout it out about a month
before we broke ground."

She nodded slowly, as if taking what he said under advise-
ment. Ethan looked at Ford again and shrugged. The urge to
prod her for her thoughts nagged at Ford's senses, as did his
desire to beg her to tell him what they were doing wrong.

Because after the first couple of weeks of apparent success,
they'd hit a wall.

And not an ancient wall. That would have been a spectacular find. No . . . they hadn't found anything in more than two
months.

"What kind of artifacts have you found?" Corrie stood,
brushing her dirty hands against each other and descending
into the ravine without waiting for them.

Hot on her tail, Ford and Ethan followed.

"Um, a couple of flints. And a piece of obsidian," Ethan explained, trying to keep up.

"Where?"

"There," he pointed. "And also there and there."

She kept walking, past the crew, past the tents, past the holes
dug into the ground. She'd barely paused to look at what they
were doing.

"And let me guess, you haven't found anything in a while,
right?" she asked, finally coming to a stop at the far end of the
ravine and bending down again, giving Ford a view straight into
her cleavage.

"How did you know that?" he asked, trying not to stare.

She glanced up, and he quickly averted his eyes. "Because I wouldn't be here otherwise."

He looked back at her as she stared up at him, shielding her eyes from the sun shining through an open area in the tree canopy. "That's why I'm here, right? Because you thought you had the right spot, but now you're not finding anything?"

Admitting it to Ethan was one thing, but admitting it to Corrie was another. But she was right—she wouldn't have been there otherwise. If they'd been finding artifacts left and right, there wouldn't have been a need to call in reinforcements.

"All right. And? What do you think the problem is?"

"Well," she said, standing again and placing a lump of dirt in Ford's hand, "you're not in the right place."

No. No, that couldn't be right. Ford had scouted out spots for weeks. He'd read everything there was about Chimalli, including Corrie's hundred-page dissertation *three* times. Each account described the lush bowl-like oasis where Chimalli had settled, far from Tenochtitlán. Given the descriptions of the hot, muggy climate, heavy rainfalls, and abundant tropical rain forest trees, the location was most likely situated on the outskirts of the Lacandon Jungle. Old abandoned Mayan territory. A place beyond the reach of the Aztec Empire in the hope that Moctezuma II and his army wouldn't go looking there. This location checked all the boxes. Ford had trekked hundreds of acres in this jungle before settling on this location.

And Ethan had agreed. It made sense. It *had* to be the spot where Chimalli spent his final days.

Ford snickered at the absurdity of her proclamation. "I don't think so, Corrie. This is the spot, I'm certain of it."

"Oh, really? The accounts all place Chimalli's site in a bowl.

But only that side of the ravine is bowl-like," she said, pointing to the spot where they'd descended.

Ford glanced back at the high side of the ravine. With the ridgeline sloping to the flat area where they were standing, he couldn't deny that it didn't appear much like a bowl. But they were also in a rain forest where hundreds of years of rainfall tended to wash away soil. And when he and Ethan had first located the spot and they'd immediately found evidence of ancient Mexican peoples, well, it had all made sense. "It likely got washed out," he explained.

"Yeah, that's possible, but look at the soil." She pointed at the soil in his hand. The loose, crumbly almost-black dirt had a spongy texture as he pressed the substance between his fingers. "It's different than at the top. Up there it's more claylike. There would be some commonalities. And there's no evidence of any erosion. It's not the place."

This. This was the Corrie he remembered—the *I'm right, you're wrong* know-it-all. Ford rolled his eyes. She hadn't even looked at the artifacts they'd found or the dig pits. Like she could tell they were in the wrong place based solely on a handful of dirt. What a colossal waste of time. "Okay, Corrie. Well, thanks for this. Guess we should head back and get you to the airport."

He started to walk away. God, how could he have ever thought this was a good idea? Bringing her here? Ford could have put the tecpatl in her hand—*given* it to her, à la Bernard Sardoni—and she *still* would have said he was wrong. Because that was what Corrie did. She disputed everything he said. She was a contrarian, at least when it came to disputing whatever Ford believed. They would never see eye to eye because they'd never even started on the same page.

"I thought you wanted my help," she hollered after him. *Dammit.* He slowly turned, and there she was, sassy as all get out with her arms folded and hip cocked to the side.

"I *wanted* your expertise on where we should be looking. See if you knew something we didn't about how deep or in what spots to dig *here*," he called back.

"Well, I'm giving you my expertise, and you're in the wrong place."

God, she was irritating. And arrogant. Like she'd always been. *Expertise, pfft!*

"You can't possibly know that by standing here for five minutes and picking up some dirt."

"Then where's the river?"

"The river? What's the river got to do with this?"

"Mendoza claimed that Chimalli tended to his wounds as they sat beside the river with Yaretzi cooking their meal nearby."

He groaned. "Not again with Mendoza."

"And in the Spaniards' accounts they came upon a man suspected to be Chimalli by the river. Where is it? Where's the river?"

Fuck. He forgot about the Spaniards.

He pulled out the notebook he kept in his pocket at all times and unfolded the map tucked between the pages. Scanning the worn paper, he searched for the river. There. Not far from a few of the other locations he'd circled as possibilities for the site. Sites he'd never bothered to rule out once they'd found this location.

Great.

He'd been so desperate to start digging and find these damn artifacts that he'd convinced himself he was right. Desperation mixed with a tiny bit of pride—and a healthy dose of arrogance.

How could he have been so lazy and irresponsible? He didn't deserve to be called Doctor.

"I'm right, aren't I?" she said, smug as could be. It was smugness she'd earned, but the last thing he needed was a braggart.

"I didn't ask you to come here for a trip down memory lane, Corrie, so spare me the *I told you so*s, okay?"

She laughed, but not one of those intoxicating, genuine laughs that he liked. No, this was one of those *I despise you more than anything else in the whole wide world* laughs he'd had the unfortunate pleasure of being on the receiving end of one too many times.

He'd earned plenty of those, too.

She unfolded her arms and placed her hands on her hips as she took a few slow, swaggering steps toward him. "You can't say it, can you? Even now. Even when you tricked me into flying *thousands* of miles because you needed *me*, and you can't admit when you're wrong."

Ford matched her stance and narrowed his eyes at her, bracing himself for a fight.

"Okay, okay," Ethan started in, ready to play mediator yet again.

But Ford didn't want a referee. This wasn't about her flying to Mexico or some dirt. This was about *them* and the long overdue need to hash out this decade-long grudge.

He'd opened his mouth with vile words on the tip of his tongue when Sunny ran over waving the yellow satellite phone in her hand.

"Dr. Matthews! Dr. Matthews! You've got a call!" she called out from fifty feet away.

Sat phone rule number one: the phone was only to be used for calls from the investor and emergencies, and when it came to their investor, his calls were emergencies. At least in Mr. Vaut-our's eyes. Meaning chewing out Corrie would have to wait.

Sunny ran up, out of breath, and handed him the phone. Sat phone rule number two: don't delay. With the cost of the calls, running was a necessity. Otherwise, a single phone call could cost them a few hundred dollars. Again, cutting into their bottom line.

And Ford's profit.

He walked toward her, then took the phone and waited a few seconds for Sunny to hurry away. Rule number three: don't listen in. Once she, Ethan, and Corrie were out of earshot, he answered.

"Hello?"

"Dr. Matthews?"

"Yes?"

"This is Dr. Snyder over at Sacred Heart Hospital calling about your mother, Catherine Matthews."

Ford's heart sank. The doctors at Sacred Heart had never had to call before. His mother was still well enough that she could make her own phone calls, and they weren't scheduled to have another one until Friday. Something must have happened.

Oh God . . . no . . .

"Don't worry, your mother is fine," Dr. Snyder continued, and Ford let out the breath he didn't realize he'd been holding. "I know this number is only for emergencies, so I'll keep this short. A spot opened at Lakeview Rehab Center. Your mother can be moved as early as Thursday, although I recommend you wait until at least this Saturday, after she finishes the next round of treatment here."

Lakeview? Ford had been trying to get her into Lakeview since she'd first been diagnosed. Not only was it located closer to where he lived than Sacred Heart, meaning he could visit her multiple times a week rather than the every-other-week schedule they'd been on before he left, it also had the best care for cancer patients like her in world-class facilities.

Albeit at world-class prices.

He'd hoped that by the time a spot opened up, he would have the money to pay for it. The money from this dig. Although he was getting paid to be here, unless they actually found something worth discovering—like the tecpatl or Chimalli's bones— it wouldn't be enough to afford Lakeview. Only then would Ford get a nice fat million-dollar check. A check that meant his mother could live comfortably, and hopefully for much, much longer. It was unusual to get paid like this for work on a dig, but Dr. Crawley had assured Ford that Mr. Vautour had both the wherewithal and the obsession with Chimalli to pay for their success.

But how was Ford going to afford his mother's expenses in the meantime?

"That's great news," he managed to say. Because, yes, from one perspective, it was fantastic news, and with all the ups and downs with his parents over the last few years, he'd welcome any positive news. "What do I need to do?"

"They need a deposit, and on her move-in day, they need the first month paid in full. Her insurance will continue to cover the treatments she's currently on, but as I'm sure you are aware, the cost of Lakeview versus Sacred Heart is . . . significant."

Significant? Ford would have laughed if it wasn't so depressing.

"Do you know if they take credit cards?" Credit was all Ford had at the moment.

"I'm sure they do."

"Then I'll arrange for the payment today," he told Dr. Snyder. "Can you please tell them to hold the spot for her?"

"Of course. Look, I know this is a huge sacrifice, but your mother will be in excellent care over at Lakeview. Catherine is lucky to have a son like you."

Lucky to have a son thousands of miles away? A son who was gambling everything on an archaeological discovery that no one in hundreds of years had been able to find? Sure, Dr. Snyder. Sure. At least, had he stayed in New Haven, he would have been able to collect his comfortable salary. But his salary alone wouldn't have been enough, not in the long term. Having to settle all his father's debts and pay for his mother's apartment and living expenses since his father passed had eaten into Ford's savings.

So when the opportunity to lead this dig had come up with the potential to make out big, he'd taken it. Literally. Right out from under Corrie's nose, and she didn't even know it. If she ever found out—well, she'd probably murder him. This was her life's work. Corrie would probably go so far as to say it was her life.

But Ford's mother's life *actually* depended on this. So life's work or not, in his eyes, his needs trumped Corrie's. Besides, if she stayed, she could still get what she wanted while at the same time helping him get what *he* wanted.

"Thanks," he finally responded to Dr. Snyder. "I'd better get going. Tell my mother I'll talk to her on Friday."

The instant he got off the phone, he immediately dialed his assistant in Connecticut, asking her to handle the payment for Lakeview using his credit card. He wasn't supposed to use his assistant for personal matters like this, but being in a Mexican jungle left him little choice otherwise. Hopefully they'd make it back to the States before his assistant would have to start taking calls about his maxed-out credit cards.

He needed this dig to go right, and, until this point, the only thing he'd done was fuck it up.

He glanced at Corrie and Ethan, who were crouched over a small hole in the ground as Corrie lifted a trowel and traced it through the air along the ridgeline with Ethan nodding beside her. Great. She was right. The only way this dig had even a remote chance of being successful was if he trusted her.

Catherine Matthews was worth the hit to his ego. He'd do anything for her. He looked at the inside of his arm where his mother's initials had been tattooed on his skin, realizing that he was still gripping that clump of dirt Corrie had placed in his hand. Unfurling his fingers, he stared at the dark soil, listening to see if the ancient spirits could speak to him. Tell him what he was doing wrong. Tell him what he needed to do to make it right.

A quetzal cawed overhead, turning his attention to the sound and putting Corrie directly in his line of vision. Corrie. Maybe that dirt *could* speak. Maybe it was telling him that Corrie was the answer.

He shook his head and his hand, letting the dirt fall to the jungle floor and brushing the remnants on his pants. *Don't be ridiculous. Dirt can't talk.* But when he looked up again and stared at her, watching her animated discussion with Ethan, he couldn't let her go.

If he was going to help his mom, Ford would have to swallow his pride and admit—out loud, for the first time in a long time—that he was wrong. And to Corrie Mejía, no less.

Letting out a long exhale, Ford started toward Corrie and Ethan. They were so engrossed in their conversation that they didn't even notice him approaching until he was less than three feet away. And even then, it was a twig snapping underneath Ford's foot that managed to grab their attention rather than Ford himself.

"Everything okay?" Ethan asked as he and Corrie stood.

Ford nodded. He didn't want to get into the whole thing about his mother. He hadn't even told Ethan that she was sick. All that would have led to would be Ethan trying to convince him not to go on this expedition. In fact, he hadn't told anyone about his mother. Except Corrie.

"Yeah, just a call about an update," he responded. Which wasn't technically untrue, although he was sure Ethan and Corrie took that to mean a call from the investor looking for an update rather than someone else providing an update to Ford on his mom.

"So . . ." Ford said, looking at Corrie, "do you think you can do this? Help us, I mean?"

"Are you sure you actually *want* my help?" she asked in return. She didn't ask in a snarky way. It was an honest question.

"Yes," he simply responded.

Corrie glanced at Ethan, then at the dig site, as Ford waited breathlessly for her answer.

"Okay. I'll stay."

He stared at her for a solid beat, then nodded. "All right, then. Let's tell everyone to pack up. We're done here."

He'd turned and started walking toward the crew when Ethan and Corrie ran up beside him. "What do you mean, 'We're done here'?" Ethan asked, confusion written all over his face. "I thought you wanted Corrie's help? Didn't you hear her? She's going to stay."

Ford stopped and turned to face them. "I heard her. So, be-cause I was wrong," he said, exaggerating his words, "and this isn't the site, we need to pack up and shut it down. It's going to take a few days to return it to its natural state, so while everyone else is doing that, Corrie and I will go research some other loca-tions. I'll need you, Ethan, to stay here and direct the break-down. And if we're lucky, maybe we'll find the *right* site and can resume digging within the next couple of days. Now, we're al-ready way behind schedule because of this . . . error, so let's not stand around debating my decision, because I'm still in charge here, and I want to be confident about at least one decision I've made in the past three months, okay?"

Ethan and Corrie simply nodded. Speechless. Ford never thought he'd see the day the two of them were speechless. Too bad it had to come at his expense.

"Great. Glad you agree," Ford said, resuming his march to-ward the crew.

And, hopefully, this would finally be the start of good deci-sions he made on this disaster of a dig.

Five

CORRIE COULDN'T BELIEVE IT. SHE COULDN'T BELIEVE HE'D ACTU-ally said those three magical words: *I. Was. Wrong.*

Most women might look at a man like Ford Matthews and think the sweetest and best three little words they could ever hope to hear come from his mouth were more in the likes of *I love you.* But not Corrie. For Corrie, hearing *I was wrong* come from those sweet, delicious lips practically gave her an orgasm.

She could totally get used to this.

The only words that could possibly be sweeter were *I'm sorry.* Sorry for all the jokes and jabs. Sorry for snagging that fellowship out from under her. Sorry for somehow weaseling his way to get *this* gig—some connection through Dr. Crawley, no doubt.

And maybe even a sorry for that night in the library. For leading her on. There was no doubt in her mind that he'd wanted to kiss her. If they'd been given thirty more seconds, his lips would have been on hers. One hundred percent.

How they'd managed to be locked on Addison Crawley's

only a few days later was beyond her. And dammit . . . it had hurt.

Corrie was surprised by how much it had hurt, seeing as until that night she never would have considered having *any* interest in Ford Matthews. Well, okay, not, like, *serious* interest, at least. The man was damn fine, and she had a libido. Even despite how much she hated him now, she couldn't deny the way her body reacted to him. But that was sexual interest. Dating interest? *Relationship* interest? Not over her dead body.

But something had changed that night. That night she'd viewed Ford as more than her nemesis. And the next morning she'd pictured what it might have been like to have Ford waking up next to her and sitting at her kitchen counter while she made him breakfast. Or maybe *he* would have made *her* breakfast. And then perhaps he'd have pulled her into his arms, with her in his T-shirt that barely covered her ass, and he'd have kissed her. And the bacon would have burned because they'd been so engrossed in each other that they hadn't even noticed the smoke until the smoke detector went off.

Yeah . . . he needed to apologize for allowing her to picture those things—pretty things, when she didn't believe in pretty things—and then throwing it all in her face by replacing that vision with one of him doing all those same things with Addison Fucking Crawley.

"Corrie, you all right?"

The question snapped Corrie out of her rage, loosening her grip on the small, worn map Ford had handed her earlier. Wow. That memory changed her mood fast. Her gaze shot to Ethan, who stood in front of her with a worried look on his face.

Corrie allowed her body to relax before she spoke. "Yeah, I'm fine. Just worried I left the oven on," she said, forcing a joke.

She hadn't realized how much her past with Ford still affected her. She hadn't thought about Ford in *years*. Two days ago, he couldn't have been any farther from her mind. Honestly, it pissed her off that she was allowing him to get under her skin like this. Pissed her off that she had *any* feelings about him after all this time. Why couldn't she let it roll off her?

"Please. Like you ever use the oven," Ethan said, curling up his lip. "You're thinking about Ford, aren't you?"

Corrie blinked several times. Was it . . . Was it that obvious?

"What? God, no, Ethan. Don't be ridiculous," she said, trying her best to keep her voice calm and even.

"So you're not thinking something's up with him? Because I sure am."

Corrie cocked her head and squinted at Ethan. Hmm. This got interesting. "What do you mean?"

Ethan shrugged. "I don't know . . . something's . . . something's not right. I mean, we both know how he is, but lately . . . something's especially off. Ever since we started this dig. But that call just now? The way his demeanor shifted? Well, we both know he's not like that."

Since the dig started? That meant Ford's being *off* had begun before she arrived.

Meaning that she wasn't the cause. Or, wasn't the *only* cause.

Corrie scanned the site, spotting Ford talking to some of the crew members and demonstrating how to refill the holes throughout the site. Yeah, there was definitely a rigidity to him, more so than normal. It could have been the stress of the dig and not finding anything. And having to find and move to a new location certainly wasn't *un*-stressful. But yeah . . . there was something weird about that phone call. She might have been carrying on with Ethan, but she had been watching Ford out of the corner of her eye and noticed the way he rubbed his forehead. He'd looked relieved, yet worried. Maybe the investor was frustrated at the lack of progress. Maybe he was telling the investor that he'd brought someone else to help. Maybe the *investor*, and not Ford, had been the one who wanted her there and that person was telling Ford that he had to keep Corrie on.

Or maybe . . . maybe it had something to do with his mom.

Did Ethan know about her?

"When was the last time you saw Ford?" Corrie asked. "Before this dig, I mean."

"Jeez," he said, lifting his hand to his forehead as if needing to think back. "Maybe two years ago when we were in Peru? Right after his dad passed away. I really only get to see him when we go on digs together, but we haven't been on a dig since Peru. We were there when it happened."

Oh. Wow. There was a lot to unpack there.

"Has he ever talked to you about it?"

"No, never. I mean, we've hardly spoken these last few years, at least not anything more than a couple of texts here and there. He didn't want me to come to the funeral. And he passed on my numerous offers to visit. I even tried reaching out to Addison to see if he was okay, but she never responded to my messages."

A vomitous rumble swirled in Corrie's stomach.

"To be honest," Ethan continued, "I was a little shocked when he called me to join him on this dig. But when I arrived, he acted like we hadn't gone two years without talking. Like he was the same old Ford. Except . . . except now he's more reserved. He rarely talks about his personal life anymore. It's not like we're strangers, but what the hell has he been doing outside of all this?" he said, motioning his hands around their surroundings at the dig.

Interesting. Ethan *didn't* know about Ford's mother. Well, it wasn't her place to enlighten him.

Ethan finally let his shoulders relax, as if psychoanalyzing Ford was the most exhausting task of the day despite having to move thousands of pounds of dirt in the muggy ninety-plus-degree jungle. Which, frankly, wasn't all that surprising. Corrie, too, was exhausted trying to compartmentalize everything Ethan had said. Corrie had been trying to solve the Ford puzzle for a decade.

"You're asking me as if I would know?" Corrie asked some-what jokingly. "This may come as a shock to you, Ethan, but Ford and I haven't exactly kept in touch, either. Maybe you should ask someone who's been around him these last two years."

"Well, according to Sunny, as fascinating as he is in the classroom, out of the classroom he's about as interesting as a box of rocks. She said he doesn't even have photos in his office. Or mention any weekend plans. She's also pretty sure he hasn't had sex in forever. I tried to explain that maybe that's because he's got a girlfriend, but Sunny seems to think they're on the outs."

Corrie's brow quirked up at the mention of Ford's sex life. What the hell had happened with Addison?

Not that she could blame Ford for trying to maintain some boundaries. Sure, she wasn't *super* private when it came to her students. Unlike him, she had gobs of photos decorating the walls in her office. Photos from digs. Photos with her friends. Photos with her family. And she wasn't afraid to share details of her personal life. She didn't divulge TMI, but she'd talk about her weekend plans and her favorite shows. They knew when her niece celebrated her quinceañera and when her brother got remarried. And when she'd had to miss a month midquarter when her mother passed away, they'd known about that, too. A group of postgrads had even sent a beautiful flower arrangement for the funeral.

But her sex life? Absolutely not. That was private. They didn't need to know who—or how many people—she slept with. Not that she was ashamed of her healthy sex life. No, Corrie was comfortable with her sexuality and the casual hookups that comprised her dating life. But it was none of their business. Plain and simple.

Besides, Corrie didn't like airing out her dirty laundry. Or, better yet, airing out her rain-soaked vibrator.

"Don't you think it's a little inappropriate for Sunny to be talking to you about Ford's sex life?"

"Do you think Sunny cares about what's appropriate and what's not?" Ethan quipped with a head tilt and a smile.

"True, but I don't know. It's a little weird, that's all. I mean, do you think maybe she has a crush on him or something?"

"You think Ford and Sunny are romantically involved?" Ethan raised his brows and burst out laughing. "Trust me, that's not the case. Ford's not her type."

Not her type? Hmm. She *did* seem a little flirty with Corrie when they first met . . .

"Do you think maybe you could talk to him and make sure he's okay?" Ethan asked, catching Corrie off-guard.

"Me?" Corrie asked, pointing her finger at her chest.

"Well, yeah. I mean, he must trust you, otherwise you wouldn't be here."

Corrie took a moment to consider that. Despite their checkered past, it was true. There was no way he would have called for her if he didn't trust her. Not with something that had the potential of being this big. He also must have trusted her not to hold *too* much of a grudge.

But there were probably dozens of people who were better suited to talking to Ford about personal matters, and she wasn't even the best person at this dig site to do so. If anyone held that honor—if it could be considered one—that had to be Ethan.

"Ethan, I am one hundred percent certain you are the better person for that task. Besides, we don't really have that kind of relationship," Corrie said, though the word *relationship* gave her a funny flutter in her stomach when using it in reference to whatever she and Ford had together.

Ethan shook his head. "Well, like I said, we don't have that kind of relationship anymore, either. But I know something's up. For example, every Friday when we're done for the day at camp, he takes the sat phone and goes to his tent for, like, an hour, and I swear it looks like he's been crying when he comes back. And if you ask him about it, he brushes it off like it's allergies. I mean, come on. Allergies only on Fridays? It's weird."

Crying? *It has to be his mother . . .* It could be Addison as well. Maybe he missed her.

Another funny flutter roiled through her belly, though this one was of a fouler variety.

"Yeah, I guess that's a little odd. But you've been friends for a long time. If he won't talk to you about things, then I highly doubt he'll talk to me," Corrie explained.

"Maybe," Ethan said, looking disappointed. "But, then again, the most emotion I've witnessed from him lately comes from interactions with you."

Corrie laughed. "Perhaps it's not obvious, Ethan, but that's because we irritate the shit out of each other."

"Yeah, and what's the saying? 'We bug the shit out of those we love the most.'"

Corrie burst out laughing in an all-out bellow, garnering a few looks from the others who were a fair distance away. She wished her laugh wasn't so damn annoying. Lord knows she'd tried to work on it, at the behest of her older brother, Antonio, when they'd been kids. "You sound like a burrito," he would tease her, referring to what he called her "hee-haw donkey laugh," which had earned her the nickname "Corrito Burrito." *That* was not something she shared with her students. But it was safe to say that at this point in her life, she really couldn't help it. The laugh was there to stay, and people would just have to deal.

"I think the saying is 'We hurt those we love the most,' but either way, trust me, that's not it. There's no love lost between us."

Now, if the saying was *We bug the shit out of those we hate the most*, then Ethan might be onto something. Because in her entire life, *no one* could get under her skin with as much panache as Ford Matthews.

Ethan's face grew solemn, and the mood turned. "Do you think you could try?" he asked.

"Okay, this is getting weird. Why are you being so insistent? You know we hate each other. He's never going to open up to me."

"Hate? Please. I know you may still harbor some ill will for Ford and all, but we both know you harbor some other feelings for him, too."

Corrie's jaw dropped. In all their years, she'd never acknowledged to Ethan—or to anyone else, for that matter—her attraction to Ford. Partly because she suspected Ethan had had a thing for her at one point and she didn't want to hurt his feelings by expressing her love-hate for Ford. Or, rather, her lust-hate. But since nothing would *ever* happen between her and Ford, there'd never been a reason to reveal what that man could do to her panties.

"Look, Corrie. I'm not asking you to forgive him, but please do this for me. I'm worried about him. I know you think he's a dick and all, but he's actually a good person. And he's a great friend. I love the guy like he's my brother, and it's killing me that I don't know if he's okay."

Hmm. Corrie might not have trusted Ford, but she trusted and respected Ethan. If Ethan could care about Ford that much—if he could love him like a brother—then maybe Ford wasn't as bad as she thought. Maybe he *had* changed.

"Okay," Corrie said.

"Okay, you'll talk to him?"

"Okay, I'll try. I'm not making any promises, though. There's a real possibility that he won't open up to me. Also, if it's private, I'm not going to press him. And I'm not going to tell you what he says, other than to let you know if he's okay. All right?"

"Thank you," he said with relief. "You're the best."

Corrie shook her head and laughed. "I don't know if I'd go that far, but I'll see what I can do."

"Dr. Mejía!" Ford called out. "You ready to go?"

Ready as she'd ever be.

FORD FELT BAD LEAVING ETHAN WITH THE DIRTY WORK OF CLEAN-
ing up his mess. Well, *mostly* felt bad. After all, Ethan had
helped select that site and agreed to forgo any further searches
just as Ford had. They'd spent a week scouting before they'd
had supplies delivered and started digging. In an ideal world—
in a *fair* world—Ford would have been right beside the rest of
the crew, helping to pack up and return the site to its natural
state.

But Ford didn't have time for fairness. They needed to keep
moving and figure this out if he was going to get his mother's
finances straight. None of this would have been happening had
his dad not spent all their money secretly buying archaeological
artifacts.

"Artifacts" that they'd learned were fakes when it had come
time to sort out the estate after his death.

Even after everything Ford had accomplished as an archaeologist . . . there his dad had been, buying garbage off the internet.
Ford couldn't make sense of it. Why his dad had resorted to eBay

rather than certified auction houses and accredited antiquities dealers. Why he hadn't ever asked for Ford's opinion.

It hurt that Dad hadn't trusted Ford's expertise. And that was only the beginning of his string of disappointments.

He and Corrie walked to the camp in silence. Without Ethan there as his buffer, Ford worried about talking too much. No, they needed to get to the camp, pull out the topo maps, and make a plan. The less talking the better. The last thing he needed was to get in a fight with Corrie without a mediator.

The lack of talking did nothing to quiet his awareness of her, however. A cacophony in his head alerted him to her proximity whenever she drew near. Not that he needed a notification. His body was already more than cognizant of her closeness, reacting involuntarily to each movement she made. He tried not to stare at her ass when she was in front of him or at her long, beautiful neck when she lifted her water bottle for a drink. He had to keep reminding himself of the agenda: use Corrie's help to get out of this mess, not get into a *new* mess with *her*.

Back at the camp, a crew of men were erecting Corrie's tent, pounding and hammering to get the platform in place. Luckily, he'd radioed ahead for them to get started, so hopefully the tent would be ready before nightfall.

It would be good to get his space back. Agnes was right—sharing with the other men was gross. Ford liked his privacy. And the ability to take care of himself in case Corrie invaded his dreams again.

"Back so soon?" Agnes called out, in the middle of making lunches in the mess tent, with Lance going over paperwork beside her. Every day she packed a meal that got picked up and delivered to the crew at the work site. Some days a hot lunch. Some days cold. Today—a supply drop day—meant something with a fresh component: the food that wouldn't last through the whole week with their not-quite-sufficient refrigeration system. It did an adequate job, but they'd had two instances now where half a week's worth of food had gone bad.

"Uh, ran into a little hiccup," Ford said, walking into the tent and eyeing the spread of cold-cut sandwiches with lettuce, tomatoes, and the works.

"Hiccup?" Lance said, looking up from his papers.

"We're looking for a new site."

Agnes's eyebrow raised. "Sounds like more than a hiccup, if you ask me. But, hey, I'm not the archaeologist. You are," she said, pointing a butter knife at Ford and waving it around in a circle.

Usually Ford appreciated Agnes's jabs and taunts. They made it feel like she was a friend rather than a hired hand. Her tell-it-like-it-is attitude always made him laugh and set a light-hearted tone around camp. But not today. Today Ford didn't need anything or anyone else pointing out his failures. Especially not in front of Lance.

"Anything the investor should be worried about?" Lance asked.

Yes.

"Nah, I don't think so," Ford responded, earning a curious look from Corrie.

"Ford is thinking there might be *multiple* sites, that's all," she then chimed in.

Now Ford was the one tossing questioning glances.

"Yeah . . ." Ford let his words evaporate in the air. "Mind if we take a couple of these?" he asked, motioning toward the sandwiches. "We've got a lot of work to do."

"Of course. Need anything else?" Agnes asked as Ford loaded up a plate.

"Actually, think you could make some more of that coffee?" Corrie asked.

"You got it. Let me finish these and I'll bring it over. Where can I find you?"

"We'll be in my tent," Ford responded, noticing a slight curl in the corner of Agnes's mouth. "Working," he added.

He led the way to the tent, tying up the corners of the window flaps to let in some light. But when he entered, a blast of Corrie slapped him in the face. She was everywhere, or at least her things were: Gear set out to dry. Clothes dangling from every surface. Her things mingled with his own. Tangling her life into his.

"I see you settled in all right," he said.

"Oh jeez, I'm sorry," she said, rushing into the tent and swiping up her belongings.

"Looks like your bag vomited. Guess it's a good thing you aren't leaving right away."

"Yeah, well, everything got soaked last night. Sorry. I didn't think you'd see it like this. Give me a minute."

Corrie scurried around the room, snatching shirts and shorts and whatever else she'd had crammed in those bags. Seriously, the woman knew how to pack. It looked like she had an entire apartment's worth of stuff in there. Ford could have helped, but it didn't feel right to be touching her things.

Besides, he'd learned his lesson last night. Who knew what he'd find today?

"Thanks for not ratting me out to Lance, by the way," he said.

"Of course."

He paid her no mind as he made his way over to the desk, setting the plate of sandwiches and some cut-up fruit on the corner then sorting through the stacks of paper covering its surface. They'd need to take another look at the topographic maps to figure out where to search next. The maps had various areas marked. Places he'd already checked. Places he'd ruled out without visiting. But maybe Corrie would notice something he couldn't.

Upon finding the correct maps, he unfurled the giant rolls of paper across the desk, then pulled out a chair to sit.

And on the seat lay a black lace bra. The delicate fabric didn't look strong enough to tame Corrie's breasts. Even now he could tell she was wearing a bra with substantially more support than the thin, practically see-through lace contraption in his hands. It also didn't appear it would even fully cover her ample breasts. This wasn't a bra for digging up jungle dirt. He'd been on so many digs that he'd seen lots of things—including all sorts of people in various states of undress—and sports bras, or at least no-frills full-coverage bras, tended to be the standard. No, this was a bra for . . . *other* activities.

"Uh, here. Don't forget this," Ford said, walking over to Corrie shoving clothes in her bag.

She looked at the bra in his hands and surprisingly looked pretty nonchalant about it. Like Ford could have been handing her a pair of socks.

"Thanks," she said, taking the bra from his hands.

But for some reason, he didn't stop there.

"Does that even do anything?" he asked. *Why? Why had he asked that?* The moment the words were out of his mouth, he wished he could suck them back in.

She cocked her head. "Excuse me? Are you judging my intimates?"

"I'm sorry . . . It's none of my business."

"Then why did you ask?"

"Well, I mean, it doesn't seem practical for out here, that's all."

"And what would you know about it? Ever worn a bra, Ford?"

He furrowed his brow at her. Clearly it was a rhetorical question. She liked those.

"That's what I thought," she said. "You're right. It's *not* any of your business, but I didn't exactly know where I'd be going and whether there'd be any access to going-out places. And, frankly, sometimes I like to feel sexy, even if it's only for myself."

Ford swallowed. Hard.

"But don't worry," she continued. "I assure you, it has just enough support. Would you like me to show you?" she asked, holding the bra in front of her.

Oh. My. Fucking. God.

Show him? As in right here, right now? Corrie in . . . *that*? Blood rushed through his body like a fire sweeping over a dry plain.

"My God, Ford. Are you blushing?" she smirked.

Crap. Was he? He quickly reached for his ear, his telltale sign—it was hot, red hot—all while unable to take his eyes off Corrie.

"Working hard, I see," Agnes said as she walked into the tent with a thermos and a couple of empty mugs, forcing Ford to take a step back.

"Oh, just trying to explain to Dr. Matthews how bras work. He doesn't think this one has enough support for me," Corrie said, holding up the bra for Agnes.

Ford already knew he was never going to hear the end of it from either of them. Why he'd felt the need—or the right—to ask in the first place was completely beyond him.

"Mm," Agnes said, inspecting the bra from afar. "It's got plenty of support, depending on what you're using it for. I've got one just like it. Want to see?" she asked Ford.

Agnes and Corrie snickered, like the two of them had planned this.

"Ha ha ha," Ford exaggerated. "You two are hilarious."

"Your cheeks are a little red. Are you feeling all right?" Agnes said, walking toward him and reaching to touch his forehead.

But he swatted at her hand and backed away. "I'm fine."

Blushing, though? Seriously? Like he'd never seen a bra before.

"Here you go," Agnes said, handing the coffee and mugs to Corrie. "Made it extra strong. Now I'll let you get back to . . . work," she said, with a shimmy in her shoulders.

Ford walked to the desk, trying to ignore the suggestion in Agnes's voice. Why had he even opened his mouth? Since when did he start thinking it was okay to comment on a woman's—or anyone's—attire? Especially their intimate attire. His mother would be mortified.

Even more than he was.

"Sorry," Corrie said, setting the mugs and thermos on the desk next to the sandwiches.

"No, I'm the one who should be sorry. That was totally inappropriate of me."

"Yeah, but I wasn't exactly being appropriate in my response, either. I was trying to add a little levity to the situation. I mean, first my vibrator, now my bra? It's like a regular boudoir in here," she said with a slight chuckle.

Ford closed his eyes and cringed. He didn't want to think about Corrie's bra *or* her vibrator. Or boudoirs. Or anything else that might make him blush again. It was going to be hard enough working next to her every day, especially on days like this when they would be in close quarters. At least once they found another dig site, they'd be spread out and he wouldn't have to chance being close enough that he could smell whatever that coconut scent was that shrouded her entire being.

The scent that permeated his nostrils now that she was sitting across from him. Intoxicating him. Putting him in a daze.

"Sorry," Corrie apologized again. "Inappropriate."

"How about we get to work, okay?"

She nodded as she twisted off the lid of the thermos and poured the coffee, now filling the air with the aromas of Jamaican coffee *and* coconut. He sucked in a breath. Mm. It took him back to the night in the library.

He was in trouble.

"So here's where we are," he said, pointing out their location on the map and trying to focus. "The locations marked with an *X*? Those are the ones I've checked out personally and determined weren't right. The locations with a question mark? Well, it's obvious what that means."

Corrie stood and bent over the map while taking a sip of her coffee. Did she not realize what that did for her cleavage? Staring shouldn't have been an option, but Ford couldn't avert his gaze.

His eyes traveled upward along the crease between her breasts to the length of her neck, pausing momentarily on her wet, glistening lips before landing on her eyes. The ones staring right back at him.

Fuck. He quickly looked at the map and cleared his throat, waiting for another teasing browbeating from Corrie. When one didn't come, he glanced back at Corrie, who was deeply entrenched in the map.

"Do you have a copy of my dissertation?" she asked.

"Um . . . yeah. Let me find it."

The papers shuffled on the desk as he sorted through the stacks. Maybe he should have been embarrassed that he had been relying on someone else's work, even going so far as assigning her dissertation as required reading material for his students, but it was a great paper. He could admit it. Corrie was brilliant. It was one of the reasons he'd kept her close during grad school. Keep your enemies close, right? Not that he'd viewed Corrie as his enemy all those years ago. Back in the day, it had been more like friendly competition.

Though, since then, it had turned less . . . friendly. And when Ford had taken the Yale fellowship, well, he'd all but declared war.

"Here," he said, pulling out the well-worn copy of her dissertation. Dog-ears. Post-its. Handwritten notes in the margins.

He'd read it front to back a least a dozen times. A few passages he could even recite by memory. He remembered sitting there in the audience of her dissertation defense in awe— hidden in the back, of course, so as not to piss her off and screw her up. Had Dr. Crawley seen her defense, there was no way Ford would ever have gotten his job. In that moment, she'd earned that title of Dr. Socorro Mejía. She was the whole package—brains, beauty, fearlessness. A pang had shot through his chest. Regret possibly? And questioning whether he'd made a mistake.

Her eyebrows raised as she stared at his Frankenstein version of her paper. Okay, now he was embarrassed.

"Yeah . . . I might have read it a few times," he said, lowering his head and rubbing the back of his neck.

"I guess so."

Cringe again.

"Don't worry, I've read yours, too, and *also* took notes. I mean, my notes are more like holes in a giant bull's-eye, but the overall tattered effect is about the same. I'll let you see it sometime. You know, like if I ever ask *you* to join *me* on a dig in Peru."

Ford winced and thought back to his dissertation on the lives of the Incas in Machu Picchu. If he'd ever learned that Corrie had been hired for a dig there, and not him, it would have more than stung. "I deserve that."

"Yeah, you do. But I'm still grateful for the after-the-fact invitation. If I'd heard that you'd come here and found Chimalli without me, I would have murdered you." She smiled. God, why did Ford find it so sexy despite the fact that she was joking about killing him?

"Then I guess it's a good thing for me that I wasn't digging in the right spot." He smiled back, and a silence fell over the room as they stared at each other. Searching each other's faces.

What was happening here? Were they . . . getting along? Engaging in playful banter? Not wanting to murder each other?

The curled corners of Corrie's dissertation thrummed through her delicate, slender fingers. What was she thinking? He could see something was on her mind. Something she wanted to ask him. Her lips twitched and she pulled her bottom lip between her teeth. Ford fought to keep from looking at her mouth, but it was like a beacon begging for his attention.

"Ford," she said, finally breaking the silence, "is everything okay with you?"

This was *not* where he thought this would be going.

"What? Of course. I'm fine." He shifted in his seat.

"What did the investor want?"

He tilted his head. "What do you mean? I haven't talked to him in a few days."

"Then that *wasn't* who called you on the sat phone this morning?"

His mouth opened and then he shut it. He didn't want to lie, but he also didn't want to get into all that.

"That wasn't the investor. It was a call about my mom."

"Is she all right?" Corrie asked, sounding genuinely concerned.

"Yes, she's fine. She's being moved to another facility."

"Do you want to talk about it?"

"Not really."

"You sure? You seemed off after that call. Sometimes it helps to get things off your chest. I mean, maybe I'm not the best person for you to talk to and all, but maybe you can talk to someone else about it. Maybe call Addison or something?"

"Addison?" He pulled his face back. Addison was the *last* person he'd want to talk to about all this. "Why would I call her?"

Corrie blinked rapidly, clearly unaware what she walked into. "I . . . I guess I assumed you'd open up to your girlfriend about things like this. But I suppose every relationship is different."

Ford laughed, but not a fun, jovial laugh. No, this laugh—or, rather, this scoff—was accompanied by rolling eyes and disbelief.

"I see you haven't been keeping tabs on me. Addison and I broke up two years ago."

"Oh," was all she said. Three solid beats went by before she opened her mouth again. "Well, are you seeing someone else? Maybe you can talk to her?"

"No, Corrie, I'm not."

"What about Ethan?"

Jeez. Why won't she let it go? Can't she see I don't want to talk about this?

"I don't need to worry Ethan with my personal shit. We're here to work."

"It's not shit. And I think Ethan would welcome the discussion. He told me how he wished he could have been there for you after your dad passed away, and—"

"My dad? You were talking to Ethan about my dad?" Ford's body tensed.

"I'm just saying. Clearly something's bothering you. If not to Ethan, then it might help for you to get it out some other way."

"And how do you suppose I do that?" he asked, staring at her with a questioning gaze.

"Well, I mean, if you *want* to talk to me about it, I can listen." Her tone was gentle as she ran her index finger along the desk.

"After declaring that you're *not* the best person for me to talk to? Yeah, sure, Corrie. Sounds like a *great* idea."

"Hey, I'm trying to help."

"I get that, and thanks, but you wouldn't understand."

"Really? Wouldn't understand? Did you know my mom passed away after battling breast cancer four years ago now? I bought a house two blocks down from my parents so I could help my dad care for her that last year. I was there every day. And after she passed . . ." Corrie paused for a moment, clearing the croak in her throat. "I know that feeling, too. What it feels like when you lose a parent. You're crushed. Lost. And you can't stop wondering when and if that feeling is ever going to go away."

"I don't have any of that. The only thing I feel about my father is that he was a sack of shit." Anger started to roil under his skin, forcing Ford to pull his hands under the desk to hide his fists. He felt for her, but their situations were nothing alike.

"I don't believe that."

"Corrie, I'm telling you, you need to let this go," he said, his patience wearing thin.

But she didn't, continuing on as if she hadn't heard him. "I know how close you were to your parents—"

Ford couldn't take it any longer. "Yeah, until my dad died and left my mother with *nothing!*" he yelled out, jumping from his chair and leaning over the desk. "Nothing except a giant stinking pile of debt. So tell me, Corrie. Was that what it was like when your mom died? Because if so, I'd love to hear how you coped with *that* situation."

Corrie stood speechless across the desk. But what did she expect? That he was going to pour his heart out and cry in her arms? Screw her. When her mom had died, they'd probably celebrated her life. Had a party. She couldn't possibly understand what it was like when *his* father had died and he'd realized his hero was nothing but a selfish, spineless hack. Realized that the person he'd spent his whole life trying to emulate was now the only person he truly hated.

"So, what, Corrie?" he continued to drill, his knuckles now resting atop the topo maps. "Did you talk to your *boyfriend* about it? Did he decide that maybe it was a good time to tell you that your relationship wasn't working? Hm? Did you? Come on, Corrie. Tell me. I want to know if you truly *understand* what I've been going through. If you have experience dealing with *that*, too. Though what I *really* want to know is how talking about it with you is going to make me feel better, because right now I feel like shit."

Tears were on the verge of escaping, but he didn't even care anymore. Corrie already *thought* the worst of him. So what if she *saw* the worst of him, too?

It didn't stop him from turning his head away from her, though. "News flash, Corrie," he said, having calmed slightly from his outburst. "Maybe you have tons of people who care about you, who you can talk to, but the only person I have is two thousand miles away, and you know what? Unlike you, I *didn't* move closer to her so I could help. I left her alone while she's dying of cancer. So, again, no, I don't really want to talk about it," he finished, looking squarely at her.

He could sense the redness in his eyes as they burned, but there was no hiding them from her, not even behind his glasses. His pulse raced as he tried to slow his breathing. That calm, confident demeanor that he'd worked so hard to master over the years? That persona he'd tried so hard to maintain, to convince even himself that he wasn't a failure? Well, it broke into a thousand pieces.

Corrie let out a resigned sigh and cast a worried look at him as she ran her hand along the spine of the bound dissertation. She looked sorry. Not sorry for bringing it up. Sorry for *him*.

"You'd be surprised by how many people care about you. You might realize that if you ever let people in. From one stubborn wannabe loner to another, trust me, I know." She lifted the dissertation then continued, "I'm going to sit outside to read this over and think about things, but it's a standing offer. If you ever *do* want to talk about it, you know where you can find me. That goes for while we're here . . . and after."

With a shaky smile, Corrie walked out of the tent, leaving Ford sad. And confused. And, honestly, a little pissed. How dare she drudge up all his problems and then up and leave? What was with all that *I'm here for you* bullshit? Corrie didn't know him. Or at least not present-day Ford.

No one did.

Because Ford didn't talk to people anymore. Not *really*. Nowadays, Ford had surface-level conversations. Conversations that could easily be had with friends and strangers alike. Real conversations meant vulnerability, which Ford didn't have the courage to show anymore. Last time he let himself be vulnerable, it had ended with Addison packing her bags and moving out of his life, sticking him with the entire share of the mortgage payment. It might have technically been his place, but she'd been there throughout the sale, having always intended that someday it would be theirs. Maybe her reluctance to be on the title from the outset should have been a sign of her lack of commitment to their relationship.

And that was when he'd thought he had life figured out. How the hell was he supposed to let himself be vulnerable now?

He took off his glasses and rubbed his eyes. Not because he was crying. No. He wouldn't cry. Not over Addison. Or his dad. Neither of them deserved his tears. Not anymore.

But as he rubbed his eyes, another sensation washed over him. What was it? Like . . . a release.

Fuck. Corrie was right.

Everything that had been building inside. Everything that he'd been keeping to himself. He'd finally had a moment where

he let go. And, dammit, as much as it sucked balls, it felt surprisingly good.

Of course, he hadn't *really* gone into depth about what was
going on with him. But acknowledging to someone else—
acknowledging to *himself*, really—that he wasn't okay . . . well,
it felt *okay* that he wasn't okay.

Ford dropped into the chair and leaned back, directing his
gaze to the tent ceiling before closing his eyes and letting out a
huge sigh. Corrie deserved an apology. And a thank-you.

Seven

FORD WAS WORSE OFF THAN CORRIE HAD ORIGINALLY THOUGHT. She hadn't expected all . . . that. Or any of it, to be honest. When Ethan had asked her to talk to him, Corrie had thought maybe he would be sad about missing his mom. Or maybe he'd be stressed about the dig and the fact that they were practically starting over at square one.

But this whole thing about his dad? Yeah, Corrie didn't know what to make of that. Or Addison.

Was she a horrible person for feeling a slight sense of satisfaction that they were no longer together?

No. Don't be like that. High road. The man had just opened up to her, albeit in his own way. Now wasn't the time to gloat.

"Hey," Ford said, startling her out of her thoughts.

She looked up from where she sat on the covered platform outside Ford's tent to find him standing across from her, leaning against one of the posts holding up the tent with his arms folded. Good thing these tents were heavy-duty. They could not only withstand the heavy rains, they could also support a solid body like Ford's.

"Hey," she said back.

"Look, I'm sorry that I snapped. I get that you're trying to help. It's just . . . it's not easy for me to talk to people about this."

It wasn't quite the apology Corrie had waited eight years for, but she'd take it.

"I get it, Ford. Trust me, I get it more than you think I do. We may be different in many, *many* ways," she said with a friendly smirk, "but we're alike in many others. We don't like to appear weak. But talking about your feelings doesn't make you weak. In fact, I'd say the opposite is true."

He cocked his head and smiled. God, was it sexy. "You're very wise, Dr. Mejía."

"Thanks. I'd say I try, but it's natural," she said with a playful smile.

He snickered and bowed his head, giving it a slow shake. "Well, thank you. I mean it. You're the first person who's really tried to get me to talk, at least in a while. Even Ethan gave up trying a long time ago. Either I must be really good at hiding my emotions or everyone else is in denial that I might have actual feelings."

"Ford Matthews has feelings?" she said, scrunching her nose. "I'm kidding. But, in all seriousness, you're welcome. Perhaps it's weird, but I do actually like you in my own sick, twisted way."

"Well, as long as it's sick and twisted."

"Hey, I'd say this is an improvement, don't you think?"

He smiled again and it was doing weird things to Corrie's insides. "We haven't argued in at *least* fifteen minutes. *Huge* improvement."

Corrie laughed. "Huge. I suppose the fact that you were stewing inside for the last fourteen and a half of those minutes might have had something to do with it."

He stared at her, tenderly, like they were old friends rather than old rivals. She liked this. Liked this playful side of him.

"Could you have pictured this even a few days ago?" he asked. "The two of us in middle-of-nowhere Mexico, laughing and talking about our *feelings*?"

"Oh God, no," she said with a laugh. "I would have bet all my savings against it."

His smile fell a little. Was it her emphatic denial? Or something else? Great. She'd gone too far. *He's going to close up. He doesn't want to—*

"Does it get easier?" he asked with no context, his tone somber.

"Does what get it easier?"

"That lost feeling you had after your mom died?"

Did he . . . did he want to talk now?

Corrie didn't want to miss the opportunity to help him get it out. Who knew when he might open up again.

"Yes. It gets easier. Some days are better than others. I might go weeks without feeling sad. And then I'll be out, and something will suddenly remind me of her, and it's like the day she died again. But those days are less frequent now. How about you? Do you miss your dad?"

Ford looked up, clearly willing himself to maintain control. He'd looked like he might cry when they'd been in the tent, but those were angry tears he'd been holding back. These tears? These ones were sad.

"I try not to," he finally said. "I don't want to miss him. I'm so pissed at him and the mess he left for my mom. He's been gone for two years, though, and those feelings haven't sub-sided."

"Maybe anger is harder to let go of. Maybe if you let yourself miss him, miss those happy moments and the dad you loved, then eventually the other feelings might start to subside."

A quick scoff escaped his throat, and this time he looked down and scratched the corner of his eye behind his glasses. *Pretended* to scratch his eye, that was. He then wiped his hand across his mouth and opened wide, letting out a long exhale.

"I could use a drink. How about you?" he asked.

"What time is it?"

"Who cares?"

Hmm. He had a point. Besides, Corrie was never one to turn down a drink.

"Fine. But grab the sandwiches. We can't go getting wasted on empty stomachs at one in the afternoon, or whatever the hell time it is."

Ford popped into the tent, leaving Corrie while he rummaged for Lord knows what. She tossed the partially read dissertation on the platform beside her. Something told her they weren't going to get a lot of work done today. But it didn't seem like they were on any specific time frame, and Ford wasn't worried about it, so whatever. She could go with the flow.

Plus, she kind of enjoyed talking with Ford, just the two of them.

After a few minutes with the sound of glass clanking inside, he returned with a bottle of booze under his arm, a mug in one hand, and the plate of sandwiches in the other.

"What's this?" she said as he sat next to her, placing the food between them.

"Rye. My private stash," he said, twisting the cap off the

bottle of Rittenhouse and pouring it into the empty mug. "Sorry, I don't have any glasses."

"Can't we grab some from the mess tent?"

"And risk Agnes's judgy looks? It's only one in the afternoon, Dr. Mejía. We're working, remember?" His lip quirked up and Corrie had to laugh. First bras and now booze? They'd never hear the end of it. "Here," he said, handing the mug to her after taking a sip.

It reminded Corrie of that night in the library. Passing the coffee back and forth. Whispering in each other's ears.

She took the mug and downed the remaining contents.

"Easy, slugger. I thought you didn't want to get wasted?"

"Just warming the ole windpipes," she said.

Or, rather, she needed a little liquid encouragement.

She grabbed a sandwich and took a giant bite as he refilled the mug. "So," she said in between bites. "Tell me more about your dad."

He peered at her from the corner of his eye. "I see what you're trying to do here."

"Sorry. I thought that's what the booze was for. Come on, Ford. Let it out. Tell me about what he was like when you were growing up."

Much to her surprise, with a relaxing of his shoulders, Ford didn't fight it. As if she'd given him the permission he needed to talk about it. He talked about his father's love for archaeology, which had eventually turned into Ford's love for archaeology. About the first dig they'd gone on together as volunteers in the southwest United States and later digs in Central America and Peru. About their tradition of going to various natural history museums throughout the United States for Ford's birthday. Sometimes his mom had come along. Sometimes they'd go, just the two of them. But there'd always been somewhere new to see. Someplace new to explore.

But Corrie heard the doubt in his voice. Was Ford's love for archaeology ever truly his own? Would he have become an archaeologist were it not for his father?

It was hard for Corrie to imagine that anyone who spoke about their job with as much passion and excitement as Ford would ever second-guess their career path. The fact that Ford lacked any self-confidence came as a surprise, to be honest. What had happened to him these last few years?

With their lunch long gone, they passed the mug back and forth as they talked about their curricula and compared notes. Gave each other pointers. Debated hypotheses about various ancient civilizations. The longer they talked, the drunker they got. And the drunker they got, the louder they got. Corrito Burrito was out in full force, but Corrie didn't care. Ford's laugh had just as much . . . character, often leaving him out of breath and keeling over when he found something particularly hilarious.

Such as every one of her bad, ridiculous jokes. But Corrie couldn't help it that she was extra funny after splitting half a bottle of rye.

And as the booze improved Corrie's hilarity, it also softened Ford's features. He'd always been attractive. That much Corrie couldn't deny. But until that moment, it had always been more in Ford's hot and sexy sort of way. The *I want to fuck you so hard that we both forget our names* sort of way. Now, as she watched the corners of his eyes crease when he laughed and the perfect half-moon shape of his smile or the way he ran his fingers through his hair and looked up so his Adam's apple bobbed on full display . . . Well, now Corrie had a new revelation: Ford was possibly the handsomest man she'd ever met.

She liked this Ford. The loosened-up, talkative, friendly Ford. It was too bad he wasn't like this all the time. Perhaps they needed to start each morning with a shot of rye. A breakfast of champions.

"Okay, what about this?" Ford said. "Have you ever had a former student ask you out?"

She raised her brow. "You mean on a date?"

"Is there any other kind of asking out?"

Now he *had* to be drunk.

"You know," she said, "I don't know if I've ever had the pleasure." She leaned back, wrapping her hands around her knee, which was propped up on the other, as she took in this new, open Ford.

"What? Bullshit," he said, jutting forward then taking another sip of booze.

"No, it's true," she said, shaking her head.

"Well, that's because they're probably intimidated by you. I mean, you *are* pretty intimidating."

"That's because I'm so badass," Corrie said, puffing up her chest and pursing her lips.

"That . . . and for other reasons." Ford's gaze zeroed in on hers. Was he . . . was he flirting with her?

Warm fuzzies spread across her skin and radiated through her body.

"I take it *you've* been asked out?" she asked.

"Numerous times."

Of course he had.

"And what did you do about it? Have you ever . . . ?"

"God no," he said, leaning back. "I mean, I know they're adults and all, but it's pretty fucked up when teachers take advantage of that power dynamic over students."

"I thought you said they were former students?" Not that it made a difference to Corrie—even though they were teaching graduate-level courses, students were off-limits.

"They were, but it doesn't change the fact that I don't think about students that way, former or otherwise."

Corrie was relieved to hear she and Ford shared the same stance on student-teacher relationships.

"What I don't understand, however, is what they even want to get out of it after the fact," he continued.

Corrie laughed and rolled her eyes. "Oh, Ford, please don't tell me you're that naive."

"What do you mean?"

"The only thing they want out of it is to get *you* in the sack. They're hot for teacher."

He cocked his head and tossed her an unsure look. "Um, I don't think so."

"Oh, I think so. Don't act surprised."

"Well, now I'm confused."

"Confused?"

"I don't understand how is it that I've been asked out but you haven't."

"Perhaps my students aren't as shameless as yours," Corrie joked. "Or maybe you're one of those maniacal professors who waves their arms around like this," Corrie said, flapping her arms in the air, "and your sex pheromones go wafting through the air, drugging all your students."

Ford burst out laughing. "Yes, because, as you know, maniacal, frantic arm movements are my signature."

"Probably are. This cool, calm, collected routine is just an act."

"Oh yeah, totally. Because this is the real me," he said, wildly waving his arms in the air.

Corrito Burrito could barely keep it together. They were laughing so loudly they didn't even notice Ethan approaching, back from a long day working in the field.

"Nice to see you two hard at work while the rest of us were out in the scorching sun all day. Did you figure out where we should be digging?" Ethan asked, brushing away the dirt covering his khaki cargos and light blue hiking shirt.

"Um . . ." Ford and Corrie looked at each other, their eyes asking how they should respond. "Not yet?" Ford said, as a question and not a fact.

Corrie snickered and Ford had to cover his mouth.

"Glad to see you're getting along, at least," Ethan said, somewhat sarcastically, but the sentiment was sincere. Corrie cast him a knowing glance, though, hoping he would understand.

"Oh yeah, we're a couple of peas and a carrot," Ford said.

"Is that some sort of double entendre?" Ethan wrinkled his brow, and then his eyes darted toward the bottle of rye sitting between them. "Are you guys drunk?"

They looked at each other again. "Maybe?" Corrie responded.

"Are you kidding me? We've been out there all damn day and the two of you have been getting wasted?"

"Hey, we haven't been drinking the entire time," Ford protested, though drunk protests were never all that convincing.

And, as hilarious as the situation was, from Ethan's perspective, it probably wasn't quite so amusing. If only he could understand the breakthrough she'd had with Ford, though. *Don't worry, Ethan. It was still productive!*

"You two are unbelievable," Ethan continued. "One second you're about to bite each other's heads off, and now this? I mean, I love digging around in the jungle as much as the rest of you, but at *some* point, I would like to go home. And preferably go home having actually *made* a discovery, not just reburying mistakes."

Ouch.

Sure, Ethan might have wanted her to talk to Ford, but she had to remember that the rest of them had been there for much longer than she had. She'd been on many long digs, and they were great when you were finding things. Not so much when you came up empty-handed. And usually on the digs she went on, they knew where to look. This dig? Well, it was like a needle in a haystack, and they'd pricked their finger hard—only to realize they were looking in the wrong haystack altogether.

"I mean, jeez, Ford," Ethan continued, folding his arms. "We're going to run out of money eventually. And when the investor comes demanding answers about what we were doing the whole time, what are we going to do? Hide in a cave?"

A cave?

"Wait!" Corrie said, putting up her hand to stop Ethan from talking.

A cave.

"What is—" Ford started. But Corrie cut him off, placing her hand over his mouth, though not without noticing how soft his lips were.

"No. Shh." Her hands were outstretched as if needing to silence a room. *Cave. Cave.*

She grabbed her dissertation, still lying on the platform next to her, and started riffling through the pages. Searching for a passage from Mendoza's notes.

There. She found it. Ford had even circled it.

"Look," she said, scooting closer to Ford to show him the passage. Their thighs pressed against each other's and she paused for a moment, feeling the heat from his body. "Here," she said, turning back to the page and ignoring the hitch in her breath. "Mendoza talks about what Chimalli had told him about fleeing the city. They walked for more than three days and then hid in a cold, damp cave near the river for many days, the cave concealed by, quote, 'nature's curtain.' And once they thought they were safe, they settled in the bowl nearby, but whenever they heard noise, they'd run to the cave for safety."

"That's what we're looking for?" Ford asked.

"Yes."

"But what if Mendoza was wrong?" Ethan asked. "Like Ford said last night, his version has been widely disregarded."

"Yeah, Corrie. I mean, as much as it pains me to say it, I want you to be right, but I also don't want to be wandering around aimlessly for another who knows how many months," Ford said. "We've already wasted enough time."

He said it, not me.

"Okay . . . but what if Mendoza was right?" Corrie asked. "And we won't be wandering aimlessly. We have specific land-marks to look for: the river, a cave, and a depression in the shape of a bowl. Here . . ." she said, jumping up and running into the tent, toward the map unfurled on Ford's desk.

She smoothed her hand over the worn paper, circling around the desk to get her bearings. Her finger traced along the topo lines, searching for their location, as Ford and Ethan finally joined her inside, though not with nearly the same amount of energy that she displayed. But this felt right. Like she was onto something.

Her hair fell in her face, obstructing her view of the map, and she glanced at the guys walking toward her.

"Hey, Ford, can you reach inside that front zipper pocket on the purple bag over there and grab me a hair tie?" she asked.

"Uh-uh. I've learned my lesson when it comes to reaching in your bag," he said.

And Ethan raised his brow. "Is that another double entendre?"

"Gross, Ethan," Corrie said. "And how dare you compare my vagina to a bag," she said with a cocky tilt of her head.

Ford put his head in his hands. "Oh my God, if we were all actual coworkers, we'd be fired right now. I'm pretty sure this conversation violates at least half a dozen HR policies."

"Then good thing we're not. Now, can you please grab me a hair tie? Don't worry, the vibrator is in the other bag," Corrie said with a smirk.

Ethan burst out laughing. "I'm glad you haven't changed, Corrie."

Little did he know, Barney had already made an appearance. But finally Ford did as he was asked, peeking into the zippered pouch before diving in and emerging with one black rubber band. He handed the tie to Corrie with his arm outstretched, and when she took it, her finger lightly grazed his.

A flicker flashed in his eye. The graze hadn't been intentional, or at least she didn't *think* it was intentional. Was it? Well, she didn't have time to sort all that out at the moment. She twisted her hair into a messy bun, securing it in place with the rubber band. His gaze traveled from her hair, to her face, and along her now-bare neck before returning to hers. Something had changed between them over the last few hours.

"So what are you thinking?" Ethan asked, stealing her attention from Ford.

What was she thinking? She was thinking about Ford and what it would be like to kiss him.

But . . . Ethan didn't care about that.

So Corrie turned back to the map instead.

"Okay, we're here. And the river, it's here," she said, running her index finger along the curved line. "According to these topos, we've got a few potential options. Here, here, and . . . here," she said, pointing to each potential location on the map.

"What about over here?" Ethan asked, pointing to the eastern edge of the Lacandon Jungle.

She shook her head. "No, that's too far. Mendoza only made it just past San Lorenzo."

"Yeah, and we only have permission to dig within these boundaries," Ford said, tracing his finger along a heavy black line outlining their limits. Luckily, the sites Corrie selected were still within the borders. "This is the extent of the investor's land. Anything beyond this line will require new government and landowner approval."

Ethan and Ford both bent over to take a closer look. "Man . . . this one is really far," Ethan said, pointing at the location farthest north from them. "If that's the location, we're going to have to move the entire camp. There's no way we can hike to that every day."

"Well, this one isn't far. Maybe two miles? Depending on the terrain, it could take, what, forty-five minutes to an hour?" Ford said.

"Right . . . but we won't know until we check it out, so what are we going to do? Hike there, and then if it's not the right one, we hike to the next and then the next? You know how Murphy's Law works. You know it's going to be the last one. It will take at least a couple of days if we have to hike to all three of these and back," Ethan said.

"Well—and I don't mean to be a party pooper—but there's also a chance that none of these is the right spot. This might not even be the correct river. And as much as I trust this theory, Mendoza might not have come this way at all," Corrie said.

She hated admitting it, but it was true. And she wouldn't be doing her job if she didn't point out the potential that the whole trip could be a bust. Even though she wanted to believe in the Mendoza option, there was a real possibility that Mendoza *had* been a lying deserter.

She hoped that wasn't the case. If so, that meant her hypothesis and ancestral connection to Chimalli were false. But if she was going to try to prove her theory was correct, then she might as well do it on someone else's dime and on someone else's property. Thankfully, the investor's property encompassed the vast majority of the area that best fit the Mendoza account. If Chimalli's resting place lay beyond those borders, though, no amount of digging within them would make any difference.

Ethan and Ford glanced nervously at each other.

"Why don't we check the closest one and maybe we'll get lucky?" she said, not sure who exactly she was trying to reassure.

"It's been a long time since I got lucky," Ford said.

Corrie and Ethan both raised their eyebrows, dying to make the obvious joke.

Ford simply rolled his eyes and smiled. "Gutter brains."

"Hey, we've been out here a long time," Ethan joked.

"Yeah, then what's her excuse?" Ford said, motioning to Corrie.

"Oh, that's easy. I've got a dirty mind." She smirked, earning a muffled laugh from Ethan.

Oh, she had a dirty mind, all right. She was already thinking of all the ways she could help Ford get lucky. Was there any real truth to that statement, though? He'd already said he wasn't seeing anyone. Did *seeing anyone* only refer to dating? Because if that were the case, then Corrie wasn't seeing anyone, either.

That didn't mean she was unavailable for random dates and hookups, however. Not that they were a huge part of her life, but she had a solid rotation of guys she could call to . . . quench her thirst. A few of them wanted more. Every now and then one wanted . . . a relationship. Cringe. That was always her cue to cut things off. Corrie's lifestyle didn't really lend itself to long-term commitment. Not with moving around for jobs, or the weeks and months on end she spent out of town traveling the world.

But Ford was a tall drink of water and Corrie was getting *very* thirsty.

"If the two of you are done . . ." Ford said, using his *I'm the boss* voice, though a hint of the playfulness still rang through. Corrie and Ethan stood at full attention, pulling their mouths into tight lines. "Anyway . . . What about this? There's a road that goes all the way here," he said, dragging his finger across the map. "We have a raft. What if we drop into the river here and float our way down? Shouldn't take more than a day or two tops this way, rather than the three or four it would take to hike there and back. We check out each of these locations, and if one of them looks like the spot, great. If not, then we come back and reassess."

Corrie had to admit—it wasn't a *bad* idea, though it could potentially waste a lot of time. And there was always the chance that the river had rapids or other precarious obstacles. Then again, she was always up for an adventure.

Ford, on the other hand, was famously not. Ethan must have been thinking the same thing, because he hadn't responded, either.

"What?" he asked, noticing Corrie's and Ethan's blank stares. "You think it's a ridiculous idea, don't you?"

"No," Ethan said. "It's just . . . I'm a little surprised that you'd suggest something so . . . daring."

"Yeah, well, it must be the booze. I'm more open to risk-taking when I've been drinking," he said, tossing Corrie a quick glance with a half smile that sent her insides swirling again.

He really needed to stop looking at her like that or she would have to pull out that vibrator later. Though, who was she kidding? She'd be pulling it out regardless.

"Corrie, what do you think?" Ford asked.

"I mean, it would definitely save time *if* the closer spots aren't it. But we won't know that until we get out there."

Ethan sat on the edge of the desk. "How is this going to work logistically? We've still got at least two days left of cleanup at the old site. Even assuming one of these sites is the right one, we won't be able to get a solid crew together to scout until next week at the earliest."

Practical Ethan.

"Well, we only have one raft, anyway. It holds four to six people, max," Ford said. "I'll take a small team. Me, Corrie, and two of the other guys."

Ethan stood straight. *Uh-oh.* Corrie's eyes shifted between the two of them. Ethan didn't like this plan.

"I thought we were doing this together," Ethan said.

Is it warm in here?

"We are . . . we will. But I need you at the old site," Ford said.

"I can stay and close up the old site," Corrie said, taking a page from Ethan's referee book.

"No, I need you," Ford said. And there went those warm fuzzies again. "You're the only one who knows what we should be looking for. The only one who *truly* knows." He then turned to Ethan. "Look, man, you know I want you to be there with me, but if we wait, we're looking at next week, like you said. We can't afford to wait that long."

Ethan's face twisted, but he sat back down. "All right, fine. But if I hear you guys were battling cheetahs, I'm going to be pissed."

"Ethan, if we're battling cheetahs *in Mexico*, then we've got much bigger problems," Corrie said.

"Watch what you're saying." The corner of Ford's mouth ticked up. "If *anyone's* going to battle cheetahs in a Mexican jungle, it's Dr. Socorro Mejía, the living legend."

Corrie laughed and kicked her leg at Ford's hip as he shuffled to get away with that damn sexy grin on his face.

"Okay, do we have a plan?" Ford asked. The three of them looked around the desk at each other and then nodded. "Great. Then we've got a lot of work to do."

"You mean, *you two* have a lot of work to do," Ethan said, "seeing as you had a nice leisurely afternoon. *I'm* going to go take a shower."

"Actually, think we can take a break? I'd like to check on my tent," Corrie said.

"All right, how about this? Ethan, let me know who would

be the best two guys to join us. Not the students. We need professionals. Two people who aren't going to ask a bunch of questions or want to learn so we can get this done as quickly and efficiently as possible. A couple of guys who can deal with the physical demands of rafting and primitive camping for two days. Corrie, you check on your tent, and then maybe check in with Agnes about food. We should be able to do this in two days, but let's pack for three just in case. And while you're doing that, I'll figure out the rest. Okay?"

"Yessir!" Ethan said, standing at full attention.

Ford smiled and shook his head. "Jackass. We can go over notes during dinner."

"Sounds good, boss," Corrie said with a wink as she and Ethan got up to leave.

Ethan wasted no time jetting out to try to catch a shower before the line got too long. But as Corrie was about to exit the tent, Ford grabbed her hand and pulled her back.

The air seemingly *whooshed* out between them as they stood face-to-face. Close, but not close enough. One step forward and their bodies would connect as they had the night before in the mess tent.

"Thank you," he said, with her hand still in his.

"For what?"

"For today. For listening. And . . . for caring." His voice was soft and timid and his face sweet and sincere. Unlike the Ford who hours earlier had been yelling with frustration and on the verge of tears. Who was this man? Raw and vulnerable. Corrie almost wouldn't have recognized him as the Ford she used to know if it weren't for the way those emerald eyes warmed her body.

"Well, thank you, too. For trusting me and opening up. And

for trusting *in* me. Trusting my professional opinion, I mean. You have no idea how difficult it is trying to get taken seriously sometimes."

"You're welcome."

He stared at her for an impossibly long time. *Excruciatingly* long without his lips on hers. She searched his eyes as the pad of his thumb brushed over her knuckles before he finally let go.

"I'd better get to work on this," he said, clearing his throat and backing away.

"Right. I'll . . . I'll come for my things later."

A slight sense of disappointment settled over her. Disappointment that had no right being there in the first place. A few hours of playful banter shouldn't have been enough to make her overlook the years of contention. Oh, but it did. Especially when she saw him standing there with a look on his face that seemed to question the exact same thing.

"No snooping," she added, giving him a side-eye and finger wag.

"I make no promises," he retorted as she bounded down the stairs with a goofy grin on her face.

CHAPTER
Eight

CORRIE'S BAGS WERE BEGGING TO BE SNOOPED IN.

He was curious about what else she had in there. Like what kind of panties she wore. Her pants perfectly molded her curvy, round hips and ass. Did she cover them with plain, nondescript briefs? Or maybe *not* cover them with a thong? Or maybe they matched that bra of hers. Black. Lacy. Practically useless. Only there to make her feel sexy.

God. Stop it, will you? Who's got the gutter brain now?

But how could he stop thinking about her after the afternoon they'd had? It was the most fun he'd had in years, leaving him with a sense of contentment that he hadn't experienced since . . . since his father was alive. How did she do that? Yet another Corrie Mejía talent—the ability to release the contents of the bottle of emotions Ford had corked inside. And not only that. He *wanted* to tell her. He *wanted* to be free of his burdens. God, she really was . . . perfect.

Sharing that mug of rye had taken him right back to that

night in the library. Would he ever be able to drink rye and not think of her now?

Rye? Check.

Coconut? Check.

Jamaican coffee? Check.

Black lace bras and purple vibrators?

Stop, stop, stop! Ford didn't have time for this. If they were going to be heading out on a raft tomorrow, he needed to plan. Plot a route. Pack supplies. Strategize with the expedition team.

Bringing Corrie along wouldn't help with the hard-on that felt ready to unleash at any moment, but he'd meant it when he said he really couldn't scout new locations without her.

He stayed up late that night, plotting out their course and packing supplies. They'd take five people total in the pickup truck to the drop-in spot up the river. Jon, Guillermo, Corrie, and Ford to go on the actual trek. Lance would then drive the truck back to camp. He'd originally volunteered to go with them down the river, and as much as Ford would have enjoyed the friendly face, when someone had teased Lance for not being able to swim, Ford had told him he had to stay back. They couldn't have that kind of potential liability on their hands in case the boat tipped over or he fell out.

By the time they got to the drop-in location, they'd likely only have time to paddle to the first potential dig site. The one that was the farthest from camp. For many reasons, Ford hoped that would be the site. It would mean not only that they'd found it and could start digging but also that his rafting plan had been the right call.

At least he could have one adventure before having to call it a day and pack for home.

From there, depending on how much light they had left, they'd either keep going or set up camp. The next day, they'd paddle to the other two locations before pulling out of the river at the third spot. It would be a bitch hiking from the river back to camp with all their gear, so they packed light—the barest minimum of tools, four individual tents that weighed less than three pounds each, and one small dry bag of clothes and essentials per person. It wouldn't be comfortable, but comfort wasn't exactly the point.

"Okay, Dr. Matthews, this is it. You can still change your mind," Lance said as the rest of them unloaded the truck and pumped up the raft.

"We're good, Lance. If we're not back in three days, send someone to search for us."

"Will do."

They tossed any unnecessary items into the truck before Lance took off, and soon the four of them were all alone.

Ready for an adventure.

Ford had been rafting before, but he was hardly what would be considered a pro. And Guillermo and Jon had each been on a rafting trip, but never without a guide or an instructor. Unsurprisingly, Corrie knew a thing or two about rafting. Was there anything this woman couldn't do? She went over a few techniques. Gave some other instructions. And then they packed up their raft and set out on the river.

She looked cute over there, sitting across from him on the raft in her khaki shorts and life jacket. Her legs had a smooth sheen to them. Ford could only imagine how soft they were and how comfy it would be to nestle between them. It was the most he'd ever seen of her skin, and he had a hard time looking away.

Did she have this effect on all men? He'd never heard her talk about a significant other. In fact, he had no clue if she was seeing anyone. If he had to guess, he'd say no. There were a few times yesterday that had seemed like flirting, but he couldn't be sure. Ford was so out of practice ever since Addy left and all his focus had gone toward his mom's health that he didn't even remember *how* to flirt. He thought he'd felt something when he'd been holding her hand. A magnetism pulling them closer. If he'd had confirmation on her availability, he might have made a move. But if he'd been wrong . . . Well, knowing Corrie, it wouldn't have been pretty. So he let the moment pass.

Like the last time.

Besides, talking had been nice. And not just talking to anybody, because it had been a long time since he'd done that, too. But specifically talking with her. He couldn't remember the last time he'd laughed so much.

Or smiled when talking about his dad.

He had to admit, he'd woken up this morning without the seething anger typically present when he thought about his dad. Not that the anger wasn't still there. But it wasn't as intense as it had been these last few years. Maybe there was something to Corrie's theory: allowing himself to miss his dad might help ease the resentment.

Ford just hoped that wasn't the only theory of Corrie's that would work out on this trip.

"We're getting close to the first spot," Corrie said, glancing at the map, which was folded into a ziplock bag to keep it from getting wet. "Let's pull out there."

They paddled to a low bank on the river and dragged the raft onto the land. The area surrounding them looked much the same as it did near camp—wooded and untouched by humans. Hopefully not completely untouched, though. It would be nice if Chimalli had spent some time in these parts.

Ford went over the plan one more time while they situated themselves at the boat, ditching the life jackets and changing shoes.

"All right . . . let's split up. Dr. Mejía and I will take the ridge over there," Ford said pointing to a steep incline about a hundred yards away. "You two look for a cave somewhere nearby."

"What if it's on the other side of the river?" Jon asked.

"It won't be," Corrie chimed in. "Mendoza said that whenever they feared they were in danger, they would run to the cave, meaning it has to be accessible from the same side of the river as the bowl."

"How will we know if we find it?" Guillermo asked.

"You probably won't," she said, twisting her hair into one of those sexy messy buns that left random loose strands trickling down her neck. Strands that Ford desperately wanted to brush away from her beckoning skin. "It's likely going to be well hidden, so you might not even notice it right away. Keep your eyes out for any formation that looks like there might be a cave inside."

"Right. And if you find anything, mark it and we'll meet here in an hour," Ford said, grabbing a canteen and a small backpack of tools. "Use the walkies if there's a problem."

He tossed one of the walkie-talkies to Guillermo, and then the four of them split up.

Rough, jagged rocks littered the terrain from the river to the bowl. It was hard to imagine Chimalli and Yaretzi traversing this area every day for water. But Chimalli was a warrior, and warriors didn't shy away from treacherousness. So Ford held out hope that this was the right spot.

And that *he* was right.

Corrie flitted about on the rocks, hopping from boulder to boulder with ease and precision like a woodland fairy. No . . . like an elegant gazelle. No wonder she'd escaped that jaguarundi— which was still impressive even if it *was* only the size of a large housecat.

"Better be careful up there," he said from his position on a lower, much smaller set of rocks.

"I'll be fine. These giant things aren't going anywhere. It's those smaller rocks you need to watch out for. That's a broken ankle waiting to happen, and, no offense, Ford, but I can't carry you."

"Well, no offense, Corrie, but I don't *want* to carry you, either," he said, trying to be playful.

And botching it on one of the rocks.

"Shit!" he said as a rock rolled out from under him. He managed to catch himself in time to miss smacking his head against the hard stones, but not without also managing to scrape his forearm when breaking his fall.

"Are you okay?" she asked, rushing over.

But he put his hand up to stop her. He needed to spare some semblance of his dignity.

"Yeah." He picked up a small stone, as if that single rock was to blame, and threw it before picking himself up and violently brushing off his clothes. At least he didn't break anything. Just a couple of scrapes and a bruised ego.

"I told you, those little rocks—"

"Yeah, yeah. Got it. Size matters, ha ha ha." He rolled his eyes, then twisted his arm to assess the damage. The top layer of skin was curled back, exposing the raw flesh underneath. It stung, but he wasn't about to whine about it to Corrie. Give her more ammunition to tease him with.

"Come on. It's easier if you walk up here," she said, reaching her arm down for him.

God. How embarrassing.

But Ford didn't particularly care to fall on his ass again, so he took her hand, using his legs to push himself onto the rock with her. Not expecting their combination of strengths, however, they stumbled, almost causing Corrie to tumble backward off the rock. Ford wrapped his arms around her waist, pulling her toward him to stop the fall.

Which, except for the fact that the move had saved her, was a horrible idea. Because now, with her body pressed against his, he never wanted to let go. As he'd often suspected, her body was soft, molding into his as he held tight. Her breasts, which he'd fantasized about more times than he cared to admit, were wondrously full and pushed into his abdomen. But the most remarkable thing about her was her eyes, and the way they looked at him. The same look she'd given him all those years ago.

She gripped his shirt in her hands, twisting the fabric in tight fists, as her breathing kicked up a notch.

Should I? Dare I?

A crackle came over the walkie-talkie.

"Everything okay? We heard yelling. Over," Guillermo said.

She cleared her throat and loosened her grip as Ford released her and reached for the walkie-talkie.

"Yeah, we're fine."

"All right. Thought we'd check. Over and out."

Ford avoided eye contact as they resituated themselves.

"Well, that could have been bad," she said.

"See? I'm not built for adventures," he said, brushing off his pants again to give himself an opportunity to inspect whether the semi growing underneath them was noticeable. Thank God for all the chunky pockets and flaps on cargo pants.

"All archaeological digs are adventures. Some just have a little more action than others."

"Coming from someone who chases after thieves and swindles mob bosses, I'd say this is pretty weak sauce." He tilted his head at her and smiled.

"You're right. Hence your nickname shall be Dr. Ford Weak Sauce Matthews," she declared as if she were a royal at high court.

"Badass Mejía and Weak Sauce Matthews. We're quite the pair."

Corrie burst out laughing with that damn laugh Ford was coming to love. "Hey, I'd buy that book. *The Archaeological Adventures of Badass Mejía and Weak Sauce Matthews*. It's got a nice ring to it," she said.

"Don't go marketing it yet. I'd at least like to *try* to earn a better nickname."

Well, at least he wasn't as embarrassed about falling now. She was good at that—taking his thoughts from bad to good. Add it to the list of Corrie's talents.

From his higher perch atop the rocks, Ford got a better look at their surroundings. Eventually the rocks petered out, but he still couldn't imagine Chimalli spending his final days here. Perhaps that was the whole point, though. Live out your life in a place where no one would expect to find you.

"Does this look right to you?" he finally asked Corrie.

She winced. "I don't know. I mean, unless there is another water source up there, I don't see how they did this every day. Or, I guess, *why* they would do this every day."

Damn. She saw it, too.

"We're almost there, though," she said, looking at the base of the incline to the bowl. "Might as well check."

The steep slope also seemed an unlikely everyday trek, but who knew what it looked like from other angles. They started their ascent, digging into the hillside with their hands to pull themselves up. If this ended up being the spot—which was looking more and more doubtful—they'd need to build some temporary stairs because there was no way they could go up and down this hill every day.

"What do you think we'll find up here?" Ford huffed, trying not to sound too out of breath.

"Well . . . I'm hoping there's a small mound of dirt and over-grown vegetation, which could be evidence of the remnants of an adobe home. But who knows? If they lived in a stick-and-thatch hut, it might all be gone by now. Destroyed by the weather."

Soft grunts came from her as she continued to climb, and he had to force himself not to stare at her ass.

"Yeah, that's what we thought happened at the old place since it was pretty clear there wasn't going to be an adobe structure."

Which was true. Their first dig site didn't contain any remnants of a structure. But it wasn't until they'd been digging for a month that they'd made that determination.

Ford and Corrie finally reached the top, his heart pounding in anticipation of the *ah-ha* moment. The interior of the bowl, however, elicited more of a *whomp-whomp*. Downed trees and dirt that had eroded from the bowl's edge littered the inside. Besides the lack of any visible evidence of a structure, with the downed trees it would be nearly impossible to dig here without some serious—and expensive—equipment.

Ford might as well have kissed any profit goodbye. But whereas he saw the bowl as a financial disappointment, Corrie seemed to be brokenhearted.

"Dammit," she muttered.

"Not it?" Ford asked.

"Highly unlikely. I'm not sure it's even worth going down there to explore."

"Yeah . . . I don't want to get a splinter." He smiled, hoping his awful joke would at least earn him a smile in return.

She snickered and rolled her eyes. "You're such a dork."

Score.

"Let's check with Jon and Memo to see if they found anything," she then said.

"Jon and who-the-what-now?"

"Memo. It's Guillermo's nickname. Didn't you know that?"

He blinked. No, he didn't know that.

"Oh, I, uh . . . I forgot."

The wrinkle in her brow signaled that she knew he was full of it. But he didn't want to admit that in three months he hadn't actually gotten to know anyone, whereas she'd already managed to be on nickname basis with the crew.

"Well, here, give me the walkie." She held out her hand.

"No, I've got it. What do you want me to ask?" He pulled the walkie out of his backpack.

"Let me do it." Her voice was impatient.

But no. This was his job, after all. He was the one in charge.

"No."

She narrowed her eyes at him and lunged for the walkie as he twisted to keep it away from her. He raised the walkie above his head as she clawed for it. "Just give it to me!"

Flip.

Their wrestling knocked the walkie out of his hands. It flew into the air before arcing down the slope toward the rocks. "What is your problem?" she shouted at him.

"*My* problem? I'm still in charge here, you know."

He winced the minute he said the words. That wasn't him. Well, maybe the old him. The Ford who thought he was hot shit because everything magically worked out for him. All. The. Time.

Want this internship? Sure. How about admission to your dream graduate program? Don't mind if I do. And what about this Yale fellowship? Why, yes, please. And might as well throw a full-time teaching gig at Yale on top of it.

Easy-peasy.

It wasn't like he hadn't earned it. Ford was smart. And charming. And made the right connections. Because that was the way life worked. The more people you knew, the better your luck.

Until those connections dumped your ass and left you fighting tooth and nail to keep what you had left. Not to get ahead. Not to come out on top. Just to maintain.

It didn't matter that his classes were always the first to fill up during enrollment and that they always had at least a dozen people on the waitlist. Or that he'd been published well over thirty times in the last eight years. Or even that he'd helped secure hundreds of thousands of dollars in donations and grant funding because of his work. No, none of that mattered anymore. Not since Addison Crawley had decided she wanted nothing to do with him.

It was too bad that Dr. Richard Crawley now wanted nothing to do with him anymore, either.

Now he had to work. No, not work. Grind. These last few

years he'd worked harder than he'd ever worked before to ensure he kept his job, which only added to the stress of also having to care for his mom.

So what he was doing acting like Mr. Big Bad Boss to Corrie was beyond him. He really was a dick sometimes.

"Wow, Ford." Her eyes widened as she gave an exaggerated blink. "You know, I actually thought you'd changed for a hot minute. But I guess not. Guess you're the same old asshole that you've always been. I'll see you at the raft. Please don't slip and crack your head open on a rock."

Without waiting for a response, she barreled down the slope like a skier traversing gates on an alpine course as she swung her way around trees.

And there they were, back at square one.

CHAPTER
Nine

SHOULD LEAVE HIM HERE, STRANDED IN THE FUCKING JUNGLE. *We'll see if Dr. Charles in Charge can find Chimalli by himself.*

She glanced back at Ford, still navigating the rocks on his way to the raft like a tottering toddler taking their first steps, and shook her head. He looked fit. Had a body built for adventure. How the hell was he so uncoordinated? Maybe she *didn't* want to hate-fuck him. It probably wouldn't have been any good. He was probably one of those guys who comes and then forgets there's another person there. A *watches himself in the mirror* kind of guy. And then she'd only hate herself for letting him win. For letting him think he was in control of her. Because the one thing he *wasn't* was her boss.

And another thing he wasn't was in control. Ford would be lost without her, and not just physically lost in the jungle. No, he wouldn't have any clue where to look. If only she hadn't pointed out the other potential spots on the damn map. Then she could go claim one of them for herself.

Assuming one turned out to actually be the spot.

God, she hoped one of them was right, if for nothing else than to shove it in Ford's annoying, smarmy . . . gorgeous face that she was right, he was wrong, and he needed her. Maybe if someone like Dr. Ford Matthews needed her, other people might start taking her a little more seriously. Sure, it was flattering to be known as a badass to students, but the Lara Croft comparisons were starting to get old. She was tired of never getting an invite to speak at the International Institute of Archaeology's annual conference, the most prestigious gathering of the world's archaeologists. Aside from a few Women in Archaeology panels she'd done in the past, the only conferences she'd been invited to speak at were Comic-Cons. Fun, yes. But not exactly career-building opportunities.

No, she was the one who hadn't been able to land a good job after they'd graduated (thanks to Ford swiping her opportunity). The one who'd started teaching at some random third-tier school and only made her way to Berkeley after *Archaeological Digest* ran that ten-page story about one of her many digs that had gone awry but had a happy—and unexpected—ending. The story had included a couple of full-length color photos of her in a pair of short-shorts and a low-cut tank top. She'd become the talk of the town after that story, and whether it was because of her *badass* dig story or because of her *fine* ass, that story had led to her next teaching gig, which had then led to Berkeley. And even then, she suspected the reason Berkeley had hired her had more to do with trying to increase enrollment, given the buzz around her name (and picture), and less to do with her actual skills. She only hoped that someday people would stop thinking of her as *that one curvy, sexy Latina archaeologist* and maybe as *that archaeologist who helped discover Chimalli.*

Or, you know, maybe even *that archaeologist*.

One day she'd prove to all the stuffy old relics that she was a badass *and* a genius, and she'd prove it all on her own. In the meantime, maybe if they found Chimalli's remains on this dig, even if it was just an asterisk next to her name while Ford took most of the credit, maybe people would see beyond her tits, ass, and wild shenanigans.

Dammit. Guess she wouldn't leave him after all.

"Hey . . ." Ford said as he finally approached. "Look, what I said back there—"

Corrie cut him off by tossing the walkie at him. "Jon and Memo haven't found anything. They're on their way back right now."

"Can we talk for a minute?"

"Nah, I'm good." She stood and walked over to the raft, fidgeting with some of the bags to make sure they were secure.

Just because she wasn't going to leave him didn't mean she needed to be his BFF.

"Corrie, come on." He moved beside her, blocking her way.

"Yeah . . . you know, I'm all talked out from yesterday." She looked up from the raft and flashed him the brattiest smile she could muster.

"Oh, so when you want to talk and I don't want to, you keep pressing, but when it's the other way around then you're all talked out?"

"Oh, wow, Ford. Look at that. You finally get me." Standing tall, she batted her lashes and clasped her hands together over her heart. "Now move, please," she said, elbowing him out of her way and inspecting one of the oars.

"Okay. Got it. Glad we sorted this out, Cor. A real pleasure."

By the time Jon and Memo returned, the sun had started to dip. But *the Boss* wanted to keep going so they could make sure they made it back to camp before sundown tomorrow. Corrie thought about protesting. After all, they didn't know this river or any of its potential treacheries. But she wanted to get this over with as much as he did. They pressed on, agreeing to paddle until six o'clock so they could make sure they had enough time to pitch their tents and make dinner.

Jon and Memo carried on in the front of the raft, talking about not wanting to miss the World Series. Something about someone's brother's girlfriend's cousin's friend knowing an usher at Dodger Stadium and how they might be able to get seats during the playoffs. Corrie couldn't care less about baseball, but at least their excited discussion provided some entertainment and distraction. Because there certainly wasn't anything going on in the back of the boat, where she paddled with Ford.

She checked on him out of the corner of her eye—under the guise of boat guiding, of course. But he paid her no attention. Instead, he stared off to the side of the river, focused only on getting them to where they needed to go.

A few drops of water from Ford's oar splashed onto the inside of his arm. He wiped away the droplets, then stopped with his fingers brushing over his mother's initials tattooed on his skin, clearly deep in thought. Seconds later, he straightened up and resumed paddling, but not before Corrie noticed him rub the corner of his eye.

Okay, maybe she shouldn't have blown him off. It was pretty childish, after all.

But could he really blame her?

And it wasn't even that he was being a jerk. She was mostly

upset because she was disappointed. Disappointed that the guy she'd spent hours laughing with yesterday was still back at camp. Or maybe he didn't even exist.

And that sucked because she actually liked that guy. She'd almost *kissed* that guy. If only he hadn't let go of her hand and backed away last night, she would have made a move.

A rumbling in the distance snapped Corrie out of her thoughts. The others didn't notice. But no . . . something wasn't right.

She stood in the raft, finally catching Ford's attention.

"What are you doing?" he asked.

"Shh." She craned her neck to see in front of them. There. Rapids.

"We've got rapids." She rushed to sit. "Everyone, keep calm."

"Are they gonna flip us over?" Jon asked, all the color draining from his face.

"I don't know. I can't see how big they are." Shit. This was a bad idea. They had no idea what was on this river. For all they knew, they were about to head into class V rapids. And they were still far from any potential waterfalls.

Right?

Shit. Corrie reached for the ziplocked map and rechecked the topo lines. Phew. Didn't look like there were falls this far up the river. Hopefully that meant just a short section of rapids and then smooth sailing.

"What should we do?" Memo asked.

"Keep paddling. And try to keep the raft straight. But if you fall out, try to swim to the bank. And don't jump in after anyone. The last thing we need is to save *two* people instead of one." She glanced over at Ford. "Ford, you should take off your glasses."

"But I need them to see."

"Well, you're not going to see anything if they fall off in the river, so unless you have a spare pair, I'd ditch them now."

He stared at her for two solid beats before tearing off his glasses and diving toward the gear to tuck them into a pocket. His hands trembled as he fidgeted with a buckle, dropping the glasses into the raft before finally managing to find a secure place in his bag.

"Don't forget to secure that rope so the bags don't fall out," Corrie called over to him.

But he couldn't work fast enough. His hands malfunctioned as if he were a bumbling fool.

"Ford!"

"I'm trying!"

"Ford, grab your paddle! Just get back! Get back!"

Whoosh!

The first crash against the rapids hit with a spray, knocking Ford backward into the raft.

"Are you okay?" she called out to him.

"Yeah."

He climbed to his perch on the side of the raft and began paddling. Corrie called out commands to the group, though each bump and spin threw them off their rhythm. Under normal circumstances the cool spray would have been refreshing on a sweltering day like today. Under normal circumstances, though, they wouldn't have been in a boat in the middle of a Mexican jungle with limited supplies and no guide.

*Shit*s and *Oh fuck*s were mixed in with *Watch out*s and *Be careful*s. The first few seconds were a chaotic blur, with the raft spinning every which way, and never the way Corrie intended. She needed to get control.

"Guys! Stop. Listen to me. Memo, paddle hard. Ford, sink your paddle to help turn. Jon, get your paddle out of the water."

She commanded them back into a straight line, directing who should paddle and when. And they actually listened. Even Ford.

"Okay, looks like we're almost out of it," she said.

The rapids settled as they neared the clearing. Jon and Memo turned to celebrate, but they celebrated too soon. With a *thwack*, the front of the raft tipped up, lifting out of the water. Jon and Memo clung to the raft. But Corrie couldn't hang on. She fell backward into the water with a *smack*. Something hit her in the chest. Something from the boat. She tried to grab it, but her head went underwater, flooding her eyes so she couldn't see. Her body bobbed in the river as she caught breaths between submersions, though she still took a fair bit of water into her lungs.

For exactly three seconds the thought that she might drown crossed her mind. Until a firm, strong arm wrapped around her waist and pulled her to the boat. Having already felt that arm around her waist once today, she knew exactly who it was.

"What are you doing?" she managed to spit out. "I said don't jump in after anyone."

"Yeah, well, it's a good thing I don't listen to you," Ford said, reaching his free arm to the raft and slinging Corrie to the edge with the other as Jon and Memo reached to help her in. "You're welcome, by the way."

"I had it," she spat out, wiping her matted hair away from her face. Never mind that brief moment of panic. She had a life vest, after all. And they were right at the end of the whitewater.

Ford lifted himself into the boat without assistance from the guys. "Okay. Keep telling yourself that." Without looking at her, he crossed the boat, went over to his bag, and pulled out his glasses.

"Are you okay, Dr. Mejía?" Memo asked.

"Yeah, I'm fine." Aside from the fact that she looked like a wet rat, that was, and that she'd needed a man—and not just any man, but specifically Ford—to save her. "Maybe we should find a spot to camp for the night sooner rather than later." It wasn't much earlier than they'd planned to stop, anyway.

They paddled leisurely for another fifteen minutes until they finally came upon a location with an easy pull-out spot but that was also up away from the riverbank in case it rained. Once on dry land, Corrie tossed her life jacket to the ground and squeezed the water out of her hair. Every part of her was soaked. Including her ego.

"Jon, would you mind tossing me my bag?" she asked as Jon and Memo unpacked their things. She turned around to face the boat and then immediately froze, her mouth dropping at the sight of Ford on the other side, lifting his waterlogged shirt off his body.

And *oh . . . my . . . fucking . . . God*. Ford wasn't *built* for adventures. Ford *was* the adventure.

Corrie had been with lots of attractive guys. But they were always more of the *Oh, good, he looks like his profile pic* kind of guys. The ones who didn't disappoint when they walked into the bar or restaurant for the date. But she'd never been with a guy who'd caused her to stare. Or drool.

Which was exactly what Ford was doing to her right now.

She couldn't pull her eyes away. Instead, they shifted from his shoulders to his pecs, then to his biceps, followed by his abs.

Each area well defined. Smooth, with a little smattering of hair on his chest. Toned and muscular, but not too bulky. He clearly spent time in the gym, but not all his time.

Why? Why did she have to be attracted to him? Of all people.

"Um, Dr. Mejía?" Jon said, finally tearing her attention away from Ford's physique. "I don't . . . I don't see your bag. In fact, there are only three dry bags and the equipment and food bags."

"What?!"

She ran over to the raft and started sorting through the packs. *No, no, no!* Her bag was gone, and with it, the tent that had been strapped to it.

"It's got to be somewhere," Ford said, slinging the wet shirt over his shoulder with a *slap* as it made contact with his skin. Couldn't he put it back on? Did he have to torture her at this exact moment?

Corrie's eyes narrowed at Ford. This was his fault. "Well, it's not. I told you to secure the bags."

"You're going to blame *me* for this? I saved your life!"

Corrie scoffed. "Again, I didn't need your help."

Ford stared blankly at her. "You really can't accept it, can you? Accept that sometimes you need help from others?"

"Well, in case you haven't noticed, in this instance you have done the opposite of help me. Now I don't have any clothes *or* a tent for tonight."

"Like you think any of the three of us would actually let you sleep without a tent." He rolled his eyes. He then reached for his own bag, yanked off the tent strapped to the side, and tossed it at Corrie. "You can have mine. I'll sleep by the fire. At least that will give you one less thing to complain about."

Complain? She opened her mouth to protest, but he stormed

off, taking with him the rest of the equipment. Jon and Memo stood silent, clearly not knowing how to respond. But, frankly, as she looked at the tent in her hands, neither did Corrie.

Sure, she was pissed that her bag was gone, though luckily most of her belongings were still at the main camp. But . . . he *had* rescued her, whether she'd wanted him to or not. And he *did* hand over his tent. Why was she being so hard-nosed? Why was she letting him get to her?

They set up the camp, and Jon, Memo, and Corrie pitched their tents as Ford started a fire. The small individual tents didn't have much room, but at least they were easy to put together. Jon and Memo had resumed their pre-rapids conversation about the World Series.

"Here," Ford said, standing over her as she crouched next to her tent, tacking down the rainfly. In his hand was a wad of fabric.

"What's that?"

"A long-sleeved T-shirt and some boxers. I don't have much but thought you might want to change out of those clothes for the night."

She hesitated for a moment, with the urge to decline on the tip of her tongue. But, much to her surprise—and his—she took the clothes. "Thanks."

"You're welcome." He didn't wait any longer before heading back to the fire.

The evening was calm, much calmer than the day had been. Corrie and Ford let Jon and Memo do all the talking as they sat and ate their dinner in silence. Ford had been smart enough, at least, to bring a flask. They passed that around, allowing Corrie to take the edge off. After Jon and Memo went to sleep, Corrie and Ford sat by the fire in continued silence, their eyes never connecting. What was there to say, really? Practically every time they opened their mouths they got into an argument. That was the real problem. Corrie wasn't talked out. She was argued out.

Despite the lack of conversation and eye contact, however, Corrie's body was on high alert, reacting to every one of Ford's subtle movements. The flex of muscles in his forearms. The crack of his neck when he stretched. The pop of his lips when he took a nip from the flask. He handed over the flask without words, and she brought the small copper container to her mouth, soaking in the heavy rye scent. Would she ever be able to enjoy rye again without associating it with him?

She sighed to herself. Dammit. She loved rye now.

A rumbling sound came from behind them, likely from a paca or some other nocturnal animal, tearing their attention to the forest. *Well, this is going to make for a fun night.* Hopefully there weren't any actual jaguars in this part of the jungle. Sightings were rare in the Lacandon Jungle, but the giant ferns and wild elephant-ear plants surrounding them made the perfect habitat for them to stalk their camp overnight.

They both turned back to face the fire, catching each other's gazes for the briefest of moments. The flames were reflected in his glasses, but beyond them, a sadness hid behind his eyes. She opened her mouth to speak, to tell him this was silly, but he quickly tore his gaze away from her and resumed his fire entrancement. The croaks from the frogs, the babble from the river nearby, and the hoots and calls from the other forest creatures couldn't compete with the deafening silence between them. Yesterday was all but a distant memory at this point.

A drop of water hit Corrie's nose and she peered up at the sky. Was that . . . rain?

"Did you feel that?"

"Feel what?" he asked, as if being pulled out of deep thought.

"A raindrop."

He looked up, darkness shrouding the sky above through the thick cover of the trees. And *blink*.

"Shit," he said as he searched for cover.

Another drop. Then another. A shower was inevitable.

They both stood, hustling to put their gear away, before Corrie rushed over to the tent. Ford, on the other hand, grabbed a blanket and put it over his head.

"What are you doing?" she asked.

"Trying not to get wet."

For a brief moment, she debated her next words. But regardless of everything that had happened earlier in the day, she didn't really have any choice other than to speak them.

"Ford, just sleep in the tent with me."

"No, I'm fine." Stubborn, like she would have been.

"No, you're going to get drenched. Come on. Before I change my mind."

He stared at her for a second before hurrying over to the tent mere seconds before the rain came pouring down. The rain hit the tent in a thunderous clatter as they barely made it in without getting drenched. Again. But the small, one-person tent really didn't have enough room for the two of them, especially not when one of them had shoulders like Ford's. They twisted and turned, shifting their bodies to get situated. Bumping knees. Clocking their heads. But finally, after a minute of flurried movements, they found a comfortable-ish happy medium, with both of them on their sides facing away from each other.

The heat built between their bodies, though. Like that

two-inch space between them was a fiery inferno that they were both avoiding, for fear of getting burned. But it took all her might to keep her distance.

"God, it's loud," she said, more to herself than to Ford.

But he responded anyway. "You'll get used to it."

No shit. Not like it was her first time in a goddamn tent in the rain. But no need to rev the ole argument engine again.

"Camp in the rain often?"

"Used to. I mean, not like a 'Oh, hey, it's raining, let's go camping.' But more of a consequence of going camping often."

"Why'd you stop? Camping often, I mean?"

He paused and let out a quick breath. "Addison didn't like camping."

Oh.

The silence inside the tent was no match for the rain pelting against the rainfly. Or the questions swirling in her head.

"Why'd you and Addison break up?"

Another sigh.

"Do we really need to talk about this?"

"What else are we going to talk about?"

"We don't *have* to talk about anything. We could just go to sleep." She could hear the frustration in his voice.

"But it's too loud to sleep." Outside and in her head.

"I told you. You'll get used to it."

"Well, I'm not even tired." She should have been, given all the physical exertion from the day. But her mind was too wired with Ford close to her. "Are you?"

Nothing. No answer.

And then a simple, "No."

"Then let's talk about something." She turned over to her other side so she faced Ford's back.

"*Now* you want to talk?" He flipped onto his back, her breasts now barely a hair from brushing against his arm, and then he looked at her. "Again, you realize you want to talk now that it's on your terms, right? When *I* wanted to talk, you blew me off."

Why did he have to call her out like that?

"Fine. Then go ahead. What do *you* want to talk about?"

"What's the deal with you never accepting help? Why do you always have to be the doer?"

Hmm. Maybe she *didn't* want to talk. She bit her lip and stared at him, even though she could barely see him in the darkness of the storm.

"Mm-hmm," he mumbled, straightening his head and closing his eyes, "That's what I thought."

He folded his hands atop his stomach as if he weren't bothered one bit by the fact that they were sleeping together. Could he seriously close his eyes and doze off?

Ugh. He was winning. He might not have been trying to win, but it didn't matter. He was getting what he wanted—silence. Well, Corrie didn't want silence. She wanted to talk. And if that meant she needed to be the one doing the talking, then so be it.

"I don't want people to think I'm weak. Like I'm some featherbrained, helpless chick. I want people to respect me."

"I'm sure people respect you," he said with his eyes still closed.

"Not in the same way they respect you. I'm the real-life archaeologist with the tits."

His eyes opened and he tilted his head toward her, one brow raised. Now she'd gotten his attention. Tits usually did. And that was the problem.

"Oh, don't look at me like that. I'm sure you've heard it before."

"What, you mean because of that magazine article?" he asked.

Case in point.

"Like I said. I'm sure you've heard it before."

"I mean, not that exact phrase, but . . ."

"Then what have you heard? Let me guess. 'I know a bone she can search for.' 'I'd like to uncover her temples at Lake Titicaca.' 'Dr. Socorro Mejía, PH Double Ds.' I know what men say about me, Ford. I'm not oblivious."

"Hadn't heard the Lake Titicaca one. Gotta admit, that one's pretty clever."

"Oh my God, you're such an asshole," she said, shooting up and searching for her shoes.

He sat up, though, and pulled her back. "Hey, hey, I was kidding. You're always making sex jokes and I thought . . . I thought maybe that would take the edge off. But that was in poor taste. I'm sorry."

"I make sex jokes because I'm comfortable with my sexuality. Or, I don't know. Maybe I do it as a defense mechanism. And I talk like that with you and Ethan because we know each other. But I don't talk about sex or make jokes around other people. I'm not some sex-addled hornball. I *do* have a brain."

"I know you do."

"Really? Well, that's good to know, because sometimes I don't think other people do."

"Corrie, I didn't ask you to come here because of your tits. I wanted you here because you're the smartest person I know."

She paused, letting the atmosphere in the tent reset.

"Do you mean that?" she asked, quietly. She wasn't looking for feigned compliments. She truly wanted to know—did he . . . did he respect her?

"Of course I do. Honestly, Corrie, the only reason I did well in school is because I had you as my competition, always keeping me on my toes. I had to work a hell of a lot harder because of you. It was kind of annoying, to be honest," he said, finishing with humor in his tone.

"And yet you still came out on top," she said, looking away, "And no one recognizes that I was right behind you. People genuinely act surprised when I tell them I have a PhD. Do you know how insulting that is?"

It was one of the main reasons Corrie didn't like going on dates with new people. When she did, she often didn't tell them what she did for a living. The surprised looks and claims that *You don't look like a doctor* had gotten old long ago. Besides, they didn't need to know about her career if all they were going to do was grab a drink and bang.

"I'm sure plenty of people recognize how brilliant you are."

"Really? Then why wasn't I selected as lead for this dig? I mean, no offense, Ford, but this is my life's work. I've written articles and papers on it. Hell, it was the subject of my dissertation, the dissertation *you're* using as a guide."

Ford wrinkled his brow, as if uncomfortable with her comments. She hadn't intended to make him feel bad. But he'd asked why she didn't like receiving help, and this was the answer.

Because deep down, she knew she'd never earn the same respect as someone without a pair of double Ds. Not in this industry. And, unfortunately, not in many others, either.

"And so earlier today," she continued, "when you made those comments about being in charge, it hit me hard. I was actually starting to think that maybe you weren't the asshole I'd thought you were, but when you said that? Well, I changed my mind."

Ford winced and rubbed his face. "Corrie . . . I'm really sorry about that. It was a shitty thing to say and the minute I did, I regretted it. I was pissed about that not being the spot and pissed at myself for making the impulsive decision to come all the way here for nothing, wasting our time. Then you said we needed to tell Jon and Memo I was wrong. Between that and you pointing out that in the three months we've been here, I haven't taken the time to get to know anyone, well, it felt like you were egging me on again. Which, after I started thinking that maybe *you* weren't so bad, kind of hurt. So I pulled a dick move. But I'm sorry. I know I'm not better, smarter, or more qualified than you. I'm where I'm at right now, and you're not, simply because I dated the right woman at the right time. That's it."

Wow. Maybe she *was* wrong about Ford. Again.

"Thank you for saying that."

"Well, it's the truth. And you know how hard it is for me to admit when I'm wrong."

"So what you're saying is all I had to do was date Addison and *I'd* be a professor at Yale leading high-profile digs all over the world?" She waggled her brows and he laughed, lowering and shaking his head.

"Honestly, you would have been the better fit for her."

Corrie's curiosity piqued. "Oh yeah? Is she into ladies?"

"First of all, Corrie, you're no lady," he joked. "But no. She . . . I . . . I wasn't exciting enough for her."

Exciting enough? *Well, this just got a helluva lot more interesting.*

Their conversation had made its way full circle. Corrie stared at Ford as if saying, *Explain*, and he groaned, lying back on the ground. She lay next to him on her side, propping her head up in her hand. Waiting for more.

"Do tell, Dr. Matthews," Corrie said. "You can't lead with that and then leave me hanging."

"I can't believe I'm going to tell you this," he said, closing his eyes and rubbing his temples.

"What happened?"

He let out a long sigh, then finally started talking. "I honestly don't know when things started going the wrong direction with her. Things were good, or at least I *thought* they were. I mean, I was gone a lot, but as the daughter of Dr. Crawley, it wasn't anything new to her. But then my dad died when I was on a dig, so I ended up coming home early without telling her. I was so upset about my dad, I thought that if I could surprise Addison, her excitement to see me would make everything better. And she was surprised to see me all right—I walked in on her masturbating with a dildo."

Corrie fought to keep her face straight. *Well . . . this *was* unexpected.*

"What happened after that?"

"Well, first she screamed and threw the dildo at me because she thought I was an intruder. Gave me a black eye, in fact."

Corrie snickered.

"Don't laugh. It's not funny," he said, unable to keep himself from chuckling.

"I'm sorry, I'm sorry," she said, waving her hands in front of her face to stop herself. "I'm just picturing a dildo hitting you in the eye, and you have to admit—it's an interesting visual."

"I'll give you that."

"So then what?"

"We talked about it later and she apologized, but she also said that she was lonely because I was gone too much. I decided to stick around for a while, trying to rebuild our relationship, trying to satisfy her. I tried thinking of ways to reignite the spark so I thought, well, maybe we could experiment with toys *together*. We'd never tried that before, but I've always been open to exploring new things. Whenever we had sex, though, it was different. She . . . she was faking it."

Hmm. Maybe she was right about him not being any good in bed.

"Like, faking having an orgasm."

"Yes." He paused. "God, why am I telling you this?" he muttered as he shook his head, still looking up. "This is so embarrassing."

"Do you think she was always faking it?"

"I don't know. I don't think so. But at this point, who knows? Then we had sex less and less, and it was always she was tired or wasn't in the mood or was on her period or she'd just taken a shower and didn't want to get dirty again."

Mm, wasn't that half the fun?

"But I swear, Corrie, she'd say she was too tired and so she was going to go to bed and then I'd hear her later. Hear her muffling her moans. Do you have any idea how that messes with your head? Like, I don't know. Not like I'm God's gift or anything, but I always thought I was decent in the bedroom. Or, I don't know, thought our emotional connection was stronger than that. I suppose I was wrong."

This only stoked Corrie's interest.

"Did you ever talk about it?" she asked as she shifted over to her stomach and propped herself up on her forearms.

"Oh yeah," he said with a chortle. "Big mistake. That's when I learned I wasn't exciting enough for her. Our sex life was boring. And then she said our entire relationship was boring. What do I even do with that?"

In some ways, his admission didn't surprise Corrie. Not everyone could be Indiana Jones, even if they were technically named after him.

"Yikes."

"Yikes is right. Can you even imagine? Wait . . . no. You're the opposite of boring."

No, Corrie had never been described as boring in the bedroom. She'd also never been described as boring in a relationship. But, then again, she hadn't really been in a relationship since her early twenties.

"So you broke up?"

He turned over on his side, now facing her. His face weary and tired.

"Yeah. I mean, I guess. Honestly, we never even said the words. She literally said, 'Our sex life is boring. Our relationship is boring. And you're boring.' And after standing there dumbfounded, I responded, 'Well, okay then.' And we stared at each other for a few more minutes until she finally said she was going to go. And that was it. She took a bag that I thought was for the night, and she literally never came back."

"Ouch."

"Is it weird that it didn't hurt?"

"I mean, no. If the sex was as bad as it sounds toward the end, you were probably emotionally disconnected from her already."

"Yeah . . . maybe."

"How's it been since then?"

"What? Things with Addison? I haven't spoken to her even once since that day."

Interesting. But not what she meant.

"No, I mean how's sex been? Did the emperor get his groove back?" she joked with a shimmy, trying to bring a little levity to the situation.

But he didn't laugh. He blinked a few times. "I haven't had sex since then."

No. Fucking. Way.

Literally. No fucking way.

Corrie about choked.

"Why not?"

He shrugged. "With everything going on with my parents and some changes at work, I haven't had time for dating."

"There's always time for sex. Takes five minutes if you're efficient," she said matter-of-factly.

"I thought women didn't like men who couldn't last more than five minutes?"

"It serves its purpose. Sometimes all you need or want is a five-minute fuck."

"Wow. You really are comfortable with your sexuality, aren't you." He didn't say it like it was a question. It was definitely more of a statement. And a correct statement at that.

"Aren't you?"

"Not anymore."

"Maybe you need to try Tinder. It's great for boosting your confidence."

"You use Tinder?" His eyebrow raised.

She nodded. "Sometimes. What? Why are you looking at me like that?"

"I'm surprised, that's all."

"Why? Because it's slutty?" She hated that stereotype. Why couldn't women enjoy sex with random hookups as much as men did?

"No. Because I . . . I guess I thought you would be in a relationship."

Corrie laughed. "What? Me? Oh no no no. I don't think so," she said shaking her head.

"Like, never?"

"Not in a long time. As you've acknowledged, our lifestyle doesn't exactly lend itself to having stable relationships."

"I mean, it *can*. It just didn't work for me and Addison. Lots of archaeologists and professors are married or in relationships."

"Yeah, well, not this one. Think about it, Ford. Would I even be here right now if I were in a relationship? You gave me less than a week's notice to fly out. What would I say? 'Sorry, honey. Gotta go, but see you maybe in a few weeks or months'? And then, if you add kids to the mix, it only gets more complicated. I don't see how that's feasible. Not with all the things I want to do."

"Things like what?"

"Like find Chimalli."

"Okay, what if we find him here? What if, in a few weeks, we're packing up with a crate of his bones and all these years of research and study finally culminate with the biggest archaeological discovery of our time? Then what?"

Corrie had never thought about life after Chimalli. Maybe because she'd never thought she'd actually have the opportunity to find him. What *did* she want to do with herself after that, assuming there would *be* an after?

"Then . . . I don't know. But at least I have the freedom to explore the options."

"I have to say, Corrie. You never cease to amaze me."

"You're amazed because I don't want to be in a relationship and I use Tinder?" she asked, raising her brow and pursing her lips.

"No, I'm amazed because when I think I've started to figure you out, there's something new I learn about you."

Her insides tingled at the sound of him calling her *amazing* and at the look on his face. The genuine surprise. His sexy smile. She was amazed at herself, too—amazed at her incredible self-control in not reaching over and kissing those delicious-looking lips of his.

"Well, I guarantee I'm not as interesting as people think I am. I get home from work, watch TV, go to the grocery store, take walks, mow my lawn . . ." She tried to play it off.

"You mow your own lawn?"

"Yes, I mow my own lawn. Jeez, Ford. Don't you?"

"No . . . but I live in a condo." He stopped to laugh. "Seriously . . . could the two of us be more opposite?"

Corrie smiled. "Probably."

"Thanks for listening to me. I haven't actually told anyone what really happened with Addison, so it was nice to finally get it off my chest. Thanks for not making me feel like an ill-equipped doofus."

"Hey, I have no idea what kind of equipment you're packing under there and whether you know how to use it," she said motioning toward his crotch, "but anytime."

"And there's that Corrie Mejía humor again," he said with a chuckle.

"Would you rather I be more serious? Because I can do that, too."

"No, I'm good with this amount of seriousness."

"Well, then, I have to ask . . . how big was it? The dildo. I need to know what size I need. For self-defense purposes, that is."

Ford laughed and buried his face into his hands for a second. "Oh God. Corrie . . . it was big."

"Like how big, though? Like this big?" she said, putting her hands up.

Ford sat up and extended her hands. "Try more like this."

Corrie's eyes widened. "Seriously?"

"Mm-hmm. And like this big around . . ." He brought his hands together in a circle.

"No."

"Yes. So, you know, a total mold of the equipment I'm packing down here," he said with a slyness in his eye.

A Corrito Burrito laugh escaped, and she had to cover her mouth so as not to wake Jon and Memo. It was still raining, but the rain was no match for Corrito. "I'm sorry."

"You're really hurting my manhood here, Corrie," he said, jokingly.

"I know. I'm the worst."

"Yeah, pretty much." He smiled, and Corrie's heart swarmed with all sorts of feelings that a woman who didn't like relationships shouldn't have. Feelings that made her wonder what it would be like to fall asleep in bed next to Ford like this every night.

Dangerous feelings that made her question her decision to remain single.

She was grateful for the darkness so he couldn't see her blush, but she used every ounce of energy to keep from burying her face in the sleeping bag to hide her giddy smile.

"We should get some sleep. We've got a big day tomorrow," he said.

"Yeah." Though dammit if she didn't want to keep talking to him all night.

Or confirm what he was packing down there.

"Thanks for being the worst." He smiled again.

"Thanks for being the second-worst."

"Look at that. You beat me at something."

Corrie pushed her hand into his chest—his rather *firm* chest. "Yeah, and don't you forget it."

CHAPTER

Ten

FORD SAVED ALL HIS INDIANA JONES–ESQE ADVENTURES FOR HIS dreams. That was where he chased robbers over rooftops, swung from vines, and found lost treasure in ancient pyramids. He was always alone on solo adventures. And always came out on top.

But not this time. This time he was with Corrie. And this time, she was on top. Riding him with her gorgeous breasts swaying with the rock of her hips like the Ocean Motion ride at Cedar Point.

She leaned down to kiss him, her coconut-scented locks cascading around him like a fruity waterfall. The pressure increased in his cock. He was dreaming, but he didn't want the dream to end. It was too real. It was like he could smell the coconut . . .

His eyelids slowly creeped open, and in his face lay a mess of wavy brown coconut-scented curls.

And pressed against his cock were her full, fabulous hips. *Fuck.*

How long had they been sleeping like that? Spooning. It couldn't have been the whole night. Ford had made sure to keep his distance, as difficult as it had been in that tiny tent and with her magnetism trying to pull him in closer. Surely after telling her about his inadequacies in the bedroom, he'd lost any chance that he ever had with her. She was a sexual goddess. She could have sex whenever and with whoever she wanted. And chances were, she had no interest in having sex with a man whose last girlfriend had described their sex life as *boring*.

Ford really wished he hadn't told Corrie all that.

But too late for regrets. Now he needed to figure out how he was going to get his arm free from around her waist *and* his cock away from her before he had to explain his wet dream.

With the most minuscule of movements, Ford lifted his arm, inching from her grip. She stirred, wriggling her body against his, her ass grinding against his already firm cock. *Oh God. Please don't let me come right now.* Ford closed his eyes, trying to think of anything and everything that could tame his erection, but she wouldn't stop.

And then the moans started.

"Mm . . . Ford . . ."

Wait. What?

Did he hear that right? Did she moan his name while grinding in her sleep?

Her whimpers grew louder and faster. *Oh my God . . . she's about to orgasm.*

Should he wake her? What was worse? Letting her finish, not realizing that he was awake and next to her, or waking her and possibly risking another moment like the one he'd had with Addison when he'd caught her in the middle of the act? Why didn't they teach *this* in sex ed?

No . . . it wasn't right. This was a violation of her privacy, no matter how much he enjoyed it.

With a quick tug, he pulled back his arm and her body stilled. No . . . it tensed. She was awake. Her head moved, as if she was scanning her surroundings . . . assessing how much he'd noticed.

"Ford, are you awake?" she whispered.

"Yeah."

"Have you been up long?" Her voice was shaky. Maybe even a little nervous.

"No, not long." Which, sure, was the truth. But long enough.

She twisted and sat up as Ford quickly pulled the sleeping bag over to cover his erection. Her hair was a mess. She was wearing Ford's giant T-shirt. But she was still the most gorgeous being he'd ever seen. Like the way actors looked when they first woke up in the movies.

"What time is it?" She shifted her gaze around the tent, seemingly avoiding eye contact with him.

He reached into the pocket near the top of the tent where he'd tucked his glasses, then pulled his wrist to his face to check his watch. "It's six thirty."

"My God, I slept hard as a rock last night." Did she have to talk about things being hard? "How early do you think we'll head out?"

"Um, I guess we can eat something and then get going. No reason to stick around here much longer."

Well, Ford could think of a few things they could do. She *had* been calling his name a few minutes ago.

"Well, I'm going to find a place to go to the bathroom."

Ford didn't budge until she exited the tent, yanking on his boxers to adjust himself the minute she was gone. *What is wrong with you?* He could sleep platonically next to a woman. Jeez, it wasn't like he never spent time around the opposite sex. Half of his colleagues at Yale were female. And most of the nurses who'd been helping his mom. And he'd been around Sunny and Agnes every day for the last three months.

Though Agnes might as well have been his mom. And after knowing Sunny for a few years now, he was *pretty* sure she was more interested in Corrie than any of the other guys at camp. Not that he could blame her. Too bad Corrie wasn't interested in either of them.

It was weird, though—Corrie being unattached was both surprising and unsurprising at the same time. Surprising because Ford would have thought men would be lining up at her door, dying to make her theirs. But unsurprising because Corrie wasn't the type to belong to anyone. She was strong, independent, and could stand up to any man. It sucked that she didn't get the respect she deserved.

Then again . . . men like Ford were the reason she lacked faith in herself.

He'd ogled her more often than he liked to admit. Heard every single one of those "jokes" about her, even the Lake Titicaca one. Failed to speak up when another man sexualized her. Pictured her naked and *definitely* had inappropriate thoughts when he'd read that magazine article.

Who was he kidding? He hadn't read anything. *I get it for the articles* wasn't a line that applied only to *Playboy.*

But worse than that—he'd taken what should have been hers. Taken the fellowship with Dr. Crawley. Taken the Chimalli dig despite knowing with one hundred percent certainty that she was the better person for the job. And he'd gotten those things easily. Things that probably would have gone a long way toward earning that respect she so desperately wanted. And all it had taken for him to get those things was some light convincing and a smile.

Too bad it had cost him six years with a woman who couldn't have cared less for him and *any* chance he could ever have with Corrie. Sure, she already knew about the fellowship, though she didn't know the *full* story. If she knew the full story, maybe she would get over it. And, in all fairness, she might have thought she had that one in the bag, but it hadn't been a guarantee yet. She'd been close, but if all it had taken was for Addison Crawley to be interested in Ford, then Corrie probably hadn't been as strong a contender as she'd thought.

But she'd never forgive him if she knew about how he'd gotten the lead for this dig. He'd be lucky if she ever spoke to him again. The guilt that had seeped in when she'd mentioned the impetus of this dig last night still made him squirm. But it didn't weigh as heavily as the guilt he had for not coming clean when he'd had the chance. Now if she found out, there'd be hell to pay.

And that would be the end of *The Adventures of Badass Mejía and Weak Sauce Matthews.*

Had to admit, it had a nice ring to it, even if it meant highlighting Ford's faults. But he'd happily be Corrie's sidekick. He'd happily be her anything.

That meant she couldn't find out. No, now that he had her back in his life, he didn't want to lose her again, even if all they were was friends. Because friends were something Ford desperately lacked. Real friends, at least. People he could talk to. People who understood him and everything he'd sacrificed to get where he was. Sure, he had a cool job and he loved teaching, but he'd sacrificed real connections to get it. Corrie understood that, though. It sounded like she was in much the same place. But she seemed to genuinely prefer it that way.

Maybe Ford might prefer it, too, if he gave it a try.

God, why had he signed up for this expedition? Maybe he needed to scrap the whole thing and let Corrie take the glory as lead archaeologist on her dream dig. Maybe she *wouldn't* need to know about his whole scheme. It was actually a perfect solution to the predicament he was in.

Except for the fact that he couldn't fail. He needed the money too badly. His mother's life depended on it.

Which meant he needed to get his ass up and get that raft on the river.

He threw on his shoes and grabbed his jacket, then crawled out of the tent, finding Jon and Memo sitting directly across from him, stoking the fire with giant shit-eating grins on their faces. Great. They'd already seen Corrie come out. He could practically see the wheels turning in their heads.

"Good morning, Dr. Matthews," Memo said. "Sleep well?" The suggestion in his voice couldn't be missed.

"I slept fine." In actuality, he'd slept wonderfully. It had been the first night since he'd arrived in Mexico that he didn't lie awake thinking about his mother and worrying that they hadn't found Chimalli.

Jon and Memo shot each other a glance before turning to Ford.

"I know what you're thinking, and don't," Ford followed up. "It's not like that. It was dumping rain last night. Where else was I supposed to sleep?"

"Could have slept with one of us," Jon said.

"In those tiny-ass tents? Sorry, but I'll take my chances with Dr. Mejía any day in that situation."

"Take your chances with me how?" Corrie walked right beside Ford. How had he not heard her coming?

The guys pressed their lips together, afraid to comment. *Chickens.* But Corrie did that to people. Ford didn't believe that none of her students had crushes on her. They were just intimidated. And there was so much about her that was intimidating—her beauty, her accomplishments, but mostly her intelligence. But after everything they'd talked about last night, he didn't want to admit that they'd been talking about sleeping arrangements. Corrie wasn't oblivious. She'd know *exactly* where their minds were, feeding right into her complaints. Because if Corrie looked less like Corrie and more like any one of the other dozen men on the crew, there wouldn't have been any insinuation in Jon's and Memo's morning well-wishes.

God, men really were pigs.

"We were talking about the rest of this rafting trip," Ford offered.

Corrie scanned his face, then glanced at Jon and Memo. "Sure you were." She then walked up to Ford and put her hand on his shoulder. "You're a terrible liar," she whispered.

If that were the case, then she wouldn't even be there. Good thing he was only a selectively bad liar.

The light crested the trees, signaling that it was time for the day to begin. After eating a light breakfast and packing, they set out on the river. They'd finally gotten a feel for the raft, easily meandering through the swift waters. The lack of rapids—so far—made things easier. So long as they didn't have any more falling-out-of-the-boat incidents, they should be on track to hit both sites and make it to camp before dark. And, if they were lucky and site number two was *the* site, then they could skip site three altogether.

But they weren't lucky. Site two was a complete and total bust. Ford started to think this was one of life's sick jokes—luck had been on his side for the first thirty-eight years of his life, yet suddenly luck was nothing but a distant memory. The last two years had been nothing but *bad* luck. One crap event after the next. And this dig and rafting expedition were looking more and more like they might be adding to the string.

Even if the final site turned out to be the precious one—which Ford had no hope of any longer—all it meant was that they could have simply hiked to it from camp and saved themselves an entire day.

Add it to the list of bad decisions Ford had made.

They paddled leisurely on the river. The other three took in the sights and sounds of the jungle. Breathing in the air. Basking in the warmth of the sun. Brilliant red macaws sang from the branches, complementing the running trickle of the water. A mama tapir and her calf foraged for food near the riverbank, pausing and raising their proboscises, presumably to take in the unfamiliar human scents of their crew. Exactly the idyllic setting Ford had pictured before taking this job. Corrie leaned out to the side of the raft and let her fingers skate along the river. She was calm. Peaceful.

The opposite of Ford.

Corrie glanced over her shoulder, noticing Ford staring at her.

"What?" she asked with a friendly smile, warming his insides and quieting the anxiety in his stomach.

"Nothing. Just wondering how you're so relaxed right now."

She shrugged. "It is what it is, Ford. Why not enjoy being out here while we can?"

"'It is what it is'? Those don't sound like the words of someone who's been waiting their whole life for this moment."

"And what moment is that? Spending time with you?" she asked, pulling her hand out of the water and flicking the droplets at him with the most adorable, sexy smile Ford had ever seen.

How could he not smile back?

"Please. Don't act like I'm not growing on you." He smirked.

She shrugged again with a sultry batting of her long lashes. "Eh. You're not as bad as I remember."

"Thanks for the compliment. In fact, that might actually be the nicest thing you've ever said to me."

Though, in his humble opinion, the truly nicest thing she'd ever said to him had been his name when she'd been grinding her ass against him this morning.

Her smile started to fade. Uh-oh. Could she read his dirty thoughts?

She closed her eyes, not saying a word.

"Corrie?"

"Shh."

Jon and Memo turned around, but Ford shook his head, not knowing what was going on. Corrie sat still, turning her head as if listening to something in the wind. Listening to a rumble that hadn't existed before now. What was that? More rapids? A waterfall?

"This is it," she finally said, opening her eyes and speaking quickly. "We're here. Pull over to the side there. Quick!"

The guys immediately shot to attention, guiding the raft to the riverbank. They moved so fast Ford barely had time to contemplate what Corrie had said. *This is it.* How did she know? How could she tell?

Ford didn't have an opportunity to question her as she jumped out of the boat, planting her boots firmly in the dirt on the shore. She took several steps forward, then squatted to the ground, placing her hand on the dirt. Her back was to them, but Ford didn't need to see her face to know what it looked like. She was taking it in. Taking in the earth. The air. Everything around her.

She shot up from her crouched position and set out toward the trees.

"Where are you going?" Ford called out, still pulling gear from the raft.

"Come on!" she called without looking at him.

"Go. We got this," Memo said, situating the boat.

Ford grabbed his bag and a walkie, then ran through the trees to catch up with her. She jogged as if she knew exactly where she was going despite not having the map.

"Corrie, wait up."

But she didn't wait. She kept going. Going right until she reached it.

A slope in the jungle. The bowl.

With little pause, she started climbing. Ford trailed behind, cursing under his breath about her insistence. He clawed at the slope, pulling himself up by roots and trunks. This couldn't be it. There was no way Chimalli and Yaretzi had gone up and down this treacherous slope every day for water or food or whatever else was out there.

No way this was . . .

"Oh my God, this is it," Ford said, standing atop the rim of the crater.

Down below, a partially forest-covered adobe structure sat, undisturbed for centuries. Half of the structure was covered in dirt, moss, and vines, hidden from the world. Satellite imagery would have likely missed it. *Ford* would have likely missed it had it not been for Corrie.

No, if she weren't here, he would still be digging in that same wrong spot.

"Come on, let's go down there," she said, pulling him by the hand.

Now having found the place, they took their time descending into the bowl. Ford took in the surroundings, taking note of what Chimalli's life must have been like living here. To the right the earth had a gentler slope. Likely the way they'd gone in and out. Trees scattered throughout provided cover from the elements. And with its proximity to the water, this actually would have been a fine place to set down roots.

They tentatively walked up to the structure, careful not to disturb the area. Not without first taking photos and having their proper gear. It would never look like this again. Not once they were done with it. They took in the moment. Staring at the adobe hut for what felt like hours.

"Can you picture it? Chimalli . . . here?" Corrie said, her voice quiet and reserved.

Yes. Yes, he could. A perfect hiding place from the wrath of Moctezuma II and the army he'd abandoned. Far away from the dangers waiting for him—and Yaretzi, if she truly existed—in Tenochtitlán. And away from the sweeping conquest of the Spaniards. It was idyllic, really. Quiet. Secluded. Beautiful.

Safe.

Corrie took a few steps forward, kneeling next to the structure and placing her hand on the worn adobe. She closed her eyes, as if feeling Chimalli's spirit through the bricks, then opened her eyes and looked right at Ford.

"I'm so happy right now I could cry." She stared at him with her big, beautiful brown eyes glistening with the threat of tears. "Thank you, Ford. Thank you for bringing me here."

Ford's heart swelled—he'd done that. Ford Matthews had made Socorro Mejía so overjoyed that she'd almost cried. But he couldn't take all the credit.

"You brought yourself here. Thanks for bringing *me*."

She smiled at him, but something caught his attention out of the corner of his eye. Movement. Through the vines.

"Corrie, watch out!"

Ford barely had a second to react before a snake lunged out of the tangle of vines straight toward Corrie's hand resting on the brick. With speed he didn't even know he possessed, Ford lunged toward her, reaching one hand to grab the snake right behind its head, and the other to pull Corrie out of harm's way. She screamed as the impact caused them to tumble, with Corrie landing on her back and Ford kneeling over her, one hand on the ground next to her head and the other still holding the snake. Its mouth agape, fangs ready to sink into flesh as its tail end thrashed around, trying to get loose. But Ford kept squeezing behind its head, protecting them from its fury. Lifting himself as he straddled Corrie's hips, Ford gathered the snake and whipped it through the air as far as he could throw it.

Corrie breathed heavily beneath him, still clearly in shock, and he looked at her. Her chest heaved and her hair splayed out over the dirt, with sticks and other debris stuck between the strands.

Didn't matter—she still looked gorgeous.

He reached down, delicately plucking a twig from her hair. Much to his surprise, she didn't yell at him to get off her. Instead, her breathing slowed as her gaze softened, and she eyed him with purposeful intensity. His hand traveled to her face and brushed away a speck of dirt from her forehead, then another from her cheek, and another that allowed his thumb to linger dangerously close to her glisteningly enchanting lips.

"Did you literally grab a snake in midair to save me, Dr. Matthews?" Her voice was like thick warm honey. Sweet and viscous, coating Ford's insides with desire. She'd never said his name like that before. Said *Dr. Matthews* like a seductress. The only thing that had ever come close was when she'd moaned his name this morning in the tent.

"I believe I did, Dr. Mejía," he said to her with hooded eyes as he leaned in, placing his hands on either side of her head. His deep voice growled through his throat. "But are you acknowledging that I saved you? Because I *believe* that's the third time I've come to your rescue on this trip." His lip turned up with a quirk.

"Third?" She smirked.

Her hands reached to his waist, sending an inferno soaring through his body.

"Well, there was the time I saved you from falling off that boulder, then when I pulled you out of the river, and now here I am with my snake maneuvers."

He inched closer to her as she tightly tugged on his belt loops.

"Well, Indy's got nothing on you. He would have left me to die if a snake came at me."

"I guess it's a good thing I was named after Harrison, then, and not Indiana."

He leaned forward, their faces less than a foot apart. Her full lips begging to be kissed. Her entire body begging to be near his. Eight years. Eight years since he'd let this same moment pass them by in the library. He wouldn't be letting this moment pass again.

"Mayday! Mayday!" Jon's panicked voice yelled through the walkie. "Dr. Matthews! Dr. Mejía! Mayday!"

Fuck.

Corrie and Ford scrambled to get up, reaching for Ford's backpack containing the walkie-talkie. Worst-case scenarios ran through Ford's head. Broken leg? Puncture in the raft? More snakes? Cheetahs? Shit. While he and Corrie had been messing around, something bad had happened.

This time Corrie didn't fight Ford for the walkie. He pulled it out of the backpack and called back.

"Jon? What happened? Is everything okay?"

Crackle . . . crackle . . .

"Dr. Matthews! We need you. Come quick!"

"Where are you? And are you okay?"

Crackle . . . crackle . . .

"Oh . . . yeah. We're fine. But we think we found something. South of the raft."

Fine? They were *fine*? Did those two have *any* idea what they'd interrupted? After all their goading that morning, they deserved to be strangled.

"We should get going," Corrie said, standing and brushing the remaining dirt and debris from her clothes and hair. Ford's heart sank.

And like that . . . the moment faded. Again.

They hiked back to where Jon and Memo stood waiting beside a moss-covered boulder. Ford examined it, but there wasn't anything special about it. Another rock half-buried in the dirt. Nothing like what he and Corrie had found up top. They'd better have something good or Ford would never forgive them.

"So, what'd you find?" Corrie asked, striding up to them.

"Well, you told us to look for a cave. Something that might not be obvious. 'Hidden by nature's curtain,' I believe was what you said," Memo started.

Then Jon picked up the story. "And we saw this boulder and all the moss. And, honestly, we would have missed it if Memo hadn't tripped—"

"And I fell right through," Memo finished.

Corrie and Ford each scanned the boulder. There were no holes in the ground. No cracks in the stone. If this was what they brought them down here for . . .

"Fell through what?" Ford asked, his patience wearing thin.

Memo smiled. "Through this."

He reached his hand to the sheet of moss and pulled it back like a curtain. A cave. Hidden by nature.

"What the . . ." Corrie said, walking toward it.

"They're vines," Jon said. "Vines that have grown over the top of the boulder and are covered by moss."

"Yeah, when I fell and put out my arm to brace my fall against the rock, it gave underneath."

She stepped into the pitch-black crevice, placing her hand against the wet rock before resting her forehead against the back of her hand. Ford moved closer to get a peek inside, shining his flashlight into the dark abyss. The cool air from the seemingly never-ending cave hit him with a blast. Cold. Dark. Damp. He'd never truly believed Mendoza's account, but now . . . well, now it was looking to be the answer.

Nature's curtain.

CHAPTER

Eleven

SHE WAS THE LUCKIEST WOMAN IN THE WORLD. SOON THEY'D have to rename her Badass as Fuck Mejía. She'd done it. She'd found Chimalli's final resting place in less than three days.

Well, Ford, Jon, and Memo had helped. But they wouldn't have been there if it wasn't for her. Because they, like everyone else, had disregarded Mendoza's story. But Corrie knew. Mendoza had been right. And soon they'd *prove* he was right by finding actual artifacts. Finding evidence.

She hadn't wanted to leave. There was still so much to see and explore. But Ford was right. They'd be back in a few days with a crew and equipment. Then they could really dig down, no pun intended, into the mystery that had shrouded Chimalli's life—and death—for hundreds of years.

It was too bad that by the time they returned to the site, Corrie would no longer have the peace that she'd felt being there with Ford. No, when they returned there would be more than a dozen people with them. With noise. And crowding.

And protocols to follow. She wanted to be there alone, even if only for an hour. An hour with the adobe hut and the chilly cave. An hour to feel Chimalli in the earth and in the stone.

Though she'd be okay if Ford wanted to join her.

She hadn't been able to get him out of her head all night. He'd invaded her dreams. Commanded her thoughts. His ex might have said he was boring in bed, but he sure as hell wasn't boring in her dreams. No, the only thing *boring* was his cock pounding into her vagina. She'd almost come in her sleep. When she'd woken, she'd worried that she actually had. And with his demeanor that morning and the wet spot she'd had on his boxers she was wearing, she was only twenty-five percent sure she hadn't.

But even worse than that—or, honestly, better—was the way he'd surveyed her when she'd lain on the ground next to Chimalli's home. He'd saved her life. Yes, he'd saved her *again*. She could admit it. Corrie had spent enough time studying poisonous flora and fauna in the region, and Ford had had a coral snake in his hands without knowing it. That thing could have killed her with one bite, but Ford hadn't even flinched. They'd have to be careful when they got back and warn everyone about the snakes. But for now, Ford was her hero.

Three times over.

Damn Jon and Memo for interrupting their moment. She'd been so close . . . not even ten inches from finally tasting him. Finally sealing the deal on that kiss. The kiss that had eluded her for more than eight years. And boring sex or not, Corrie wanted to experience it for herself.

It was too bad they weren't forced to share that tiny-ass tent again. And now that they were back at camp, back with the other fifteen people on this expedition, their opportunities to be alone were dwindling.

A small part of her debated whether she should have told him so much about her sex life. It wasn't like she'd given him any specific details, but she'd definitely come off as being more . . . active than him. In the last eight years he'd been with only one person. The number of men in her sexual rotation this year alone more than quadrupled that number. He'd seemed surprised that she was on Tinder, and though he'd said it was because he thought she'd been in a committed relationship, maybe she should have clarified that she hadn't needed to use it for years due to said sexual rotation?

Or did that sound worse?

And this was one of the reasons Corrie didn't date. Monogamously, at least. Because having to explain her sexual prowess wasn't something she really cared to do. Not that she was ashamed of her sex life. Like she'd said, she was comfortable with her sexuality. And fuck those people who thought it was okay for men to sow their wild oats, but women who did were sluts.

For now, she wasn't looking for a boyfriend. She merely wanted to scratch the itch that had been nagging her for eight years. And Ford looked willing to scratch that itch despite her sexual past.

All she had to do was find another opportunity.

They got back to camp around four thirty. It had taken them longer to get back than they'd originally plotted, meaning each day they'd have to account for two and a half hours of travel time to and from the site, maybe a little less on the days they weren't carrying any gear. Moving the camp wasn't an option unless they built their own road through the jungle—which was not something the investor had given them permission to do on his land. Corrie didn't mind the hiking in and out from a physical standpoint, but in reality, it meant less time each day at the dig site.

"Well, well, well, look what the cat dragged in," Ethan called over to them as he and Sunny emerged from his tent. It looked like they and the others must have just returned from working for the day packing up the old site, most of them covered in dust and dirt, sitting around the campsite relaxing. "Tell me you have good news."

"That we do, my friend. Come join us in my quarters," Ford said, his voice bellowing with pride and excitement.

"Quarters? Well, this must be good if we've upgraded from tents to quarters," Ethan said, walking toward them.

They neared Ford's tent, and Jon and Memo started to walk away, but Ford stopped them. "Where are you going? We need a celebratory drink," he told them.

Jon and Memo perked up as if they were not only surprised . . . but . . . happy. Ford wasn't dismissing them like a couple of peon workers. They were one of the team. Adventurers. Explorers. Friends.

They all ditched their bags on the ground and took a load off on the platform outside Ford's tent while Ford went inside to grab the bottle. "Can someone grab some cups?" he called out.

Corrie ran to the mess tent and back, returning just in time to witness Ford emerging from his tent mid–shirt change. They were both filthy and hadn't showered, yet Corrie would still drag her tongue across his abs right now if she had the opportunity. Why was the Lord tempting her this way? Dangling Ford and all his forbidden fruits in front of her.

Now *that* was an adventure novel that Corrie was in for: *Ford and the Search for His Forbidden Fruits*. No, no. Better yet:

Badass AF Mejía and Her Search for Ford's Forbidden Fruits. Had a nice ring to it. As far as Choose Your Own Adventures went, Corrie knew exactly which direction she'd be taking. *Turn to page 42 if Dr. Mejía wants to research and look at boring, dusty maps. Or turn to page 69 if Dr. Mejía wants to explore Dr. Matthews.*

"Earth to Corrie," Ethan called out, snapping her out of her novel planning.

Her gaze shot to Ford's. He was watching her as he buttoned the final button of his shirt. Stealing his abs from her view. But the glint in his eye told her, *I saw you watching me.*

And Corrie didn't care. She wanted him to see. Wanted him to get the hint. Because she couldn't go on like this forever. Couldn't go on with this itch nagging at her.

She set the glasses down, and Ford poured a shot of rye into each glass before they all took one. "To all of us and the true first day in the quest for Chimalli," Ford said, raising his glass.

Their glasses clinked and they tossed back the brown liquid before Ford recapped the trip for Ethan. He went over all the important details, and the ones he missed, Jon, Memo, and Corrie were quick to fill in. Such as the rapids. And the snake. And Jon and Memo not so subtly brought up the sleeping situation, garnering an interested look from Ethan.

Ethan and the rest of the crew had finished at the old site, so they plotted their plan for the rest of the week: head out in the morning with all the equipment and set up, spend the remainder of the day taking photos and mapping the grid of the site, do some preliminary digging on Friday, rest over the weekend, then hit the ground running the following week by starting to uncover the structure in the bowl with one team while another team took to the cave. Ford's schedule was aggressive but doable. In order to spend more time at the dig site, he contemplated adding more tents to their supply drop the following week so they could camp at the site during the week rather than do the two-plus-hour hike each day. But it would have required a whole new plan as far as food and other supplies were concerned, only eating further into their budget.

Ford planned to make some announcements and unveil his plan to the entire group after dinner, which, judging by the delicious aroma wafting from the mess tent, looked to be in less than an hour. So he set everyone on their way to clean up and take much-needed showers before the evening's events.

The interns all clamored for information during dinner, but Ford kept telling them to be patient. Corrie could see his excitement to reveal the news. After dinner, he got up in front of the group and gave the update, which was met with cheers from the group and a celebratory hug from Lance. Once the excitement settled down, Ford went over the plan for the next few days. Ethan took the stage next, discussing specific techniques for uncovering the structure. When he mentioned watching for snakes, Ford glanced over at Corrie, heating her core. But the longer Ethan talked, the more Corrie realized she wouldn't ever be alone with Chimalli's home again. There would be more than a dozen of them swarmed over the structure by tomorrow morning. Picking at it. Touching it. Ruining it. She would no longer be the only person to have touched it in hundreds of years.

It would no longer be hers.

One more time. She needed to be there alone one more time, feeling Chimalli in her soul.

Drawing as little attention as she could, Corrie crept away from the mess tent, casually strolling over toward the bathrooms as if that were all she was doing. Eventually they'd disperse, and no one would even realize she'd been gone for a while. And by the time she got back, they'd all be asleep.

After a quick stop at her tent for a flashlight, she set out into the forest, careful not to shine the light until she could no longer hear or see the camp. Actions like this were typically forbidden. Going to a site alone could lead to injuries with no one to help or it could lead to damage to the site. Going alone was also a great cover for people with more nefarious intentions, such as theft.

Corrie marched through the forest with a knife drawn at her waist. Sure, walking an hour each way through a jungle in the pitch black with nothing but a flashlight and a knife was dangerous, but Corrie didn't shy away from danger.

And, frankly, she could die a happy woman now that she'd found Chimalli. Although she'd *much* prefer not to.

Snap!

Corrie froze and turned off her light. Someone . . . *something* was there.

Uh-oh . . . maybe this wasn't such a good idea after all. Ocelot? Puma? Please, not an actual jaguar. It was one thing to run from a jaguarundi during the day. Another entirely to run from a jaguar *at night.* She hid behind a tree, listening to the shuffling of leaves and branches coming her direction. Closer. Closer. She closed her eyes, trying to meditate and slow her breathing.

"Corrie?"

Ford?

Her eyes shot open and she moved out from behind the tree, right into the beam of Ford's flashlight. She shielded her face from the light and flashed her own at him.

"Corrie, what the hell are you doing out here?"

The truth wasn't an option. The truth could get her taken off this job.

"I . . . I needed some fresh air."

Believable. *Real* believable.

"Fresh air? Corrie, please tell me you weren't doing what I think you were doing?" When she didn't respond, he sighed. "You *can't* go out there. Not alone and *definitely* not in the middle of the night. Do you know how dangerous this is?"

She opened her mouth to deny his accusation, but what could she really say? She was obsessed with Chimalli. There really was only one possible explanation for her being out here.

"I wanted to see it once more before the site is crawling with people." Her voice pleaded. Ford could understand, right?

"I can't let you do that. You know the rules."

"I know, but just the one time. I promise, I won't mess with anything—"

"Just being there could potentially mess with things. Plus there are snakes and who knows what other creatures out there, which will only be harder to see and protect yourself from in the dark."

"I'll be fine. I know how to protect myself."

"Really? Because you didn't earlier today."

Corrie snapped her head back. "I don't need your protection, Ford. I would have been fine."

He scoffed. "Oh, we're doing *this* again, are we?"

"*This?*"

"Where you won't acknowledge needing other people's help. Because if I remember correctly, you seemed rather grateful for my help earlier today when I was on top of you."

She glared at him. "Oh, please. I was trying to boost your self-esteem."

Now he glared back. Sure, it was a low blow, but he was keeping her from going out there.

Crack-snap!

They froze and Ford grabbed Corrie, pulling her behind a tree. "You don't need to *save* me again—" Corrie started, but Ford covered her mouth.

"Shh. Someone's there," he whispered.

His large body blocked her in against the tree. Close. So close she could almost feel him and the warmth from his body.

"If it's a person then just tell them it's us," Corrie said.

"And then have to explain what we're doing out here? Or maybe they were up to the same thing as you," he pointed out.

They stood quietly and listened, hearing voices getting closer. And closer.

"Are you sure you saw them go this way?" one of the voices asked.

"I'm sure, boss. She got up from dinner and walked into the woods and then he followed a few minutes later. They must be trying to find it in the middle of the night," the other responded.

"Shit," Ford whispered, recognizing the voices. "It's Lance and Guiles. Fuck, fuck, fuck."

"So what?" Corrie asked.

"So what? They work for the investor. And sounds like Guiles thinks we're out here trying to rip him off."

"What should we do if we find them at the site? Are you going to fire them?" Guiles asked, getting closer and closer to their location.

"Fuck," Ford said. "Are you happy now? We're going to get fired."

No. No, they couldn't get fired like this. And, if anything, Corrie should be the one to get kicked off the job, not Ford.

This was her fault. Had she not snuck into the forest, Ford wouldn't have followed her. And Lance and Guiles wouldn't have followed him.

They needed another reason to be out there. Something plausible that wouldn't get them—or at least Ford—fired.

Quick.

Without further hesitation, Corrie put her hands around Ford's neck and pulled his face to hers.

"What are you doing?" he asked.

"Improvising."

He stared at her for a solid beat before crashing his lips on hers with a feverish fury. *This*. This was what she'd been waiting for. The kiss that had been eight years coming. The itch that needed scratching.

She tasted him. Tasted his tongue, which wrestled furiously with hers. Tasted his strong, supple lips against hers. But she wanted more. The itch still burned. Still needed satisfying. She let her hands glide down his firm, flexing chest, down his rippled abs, and to his waist, pulling his pelvis closer to hers. Pressing his core against her abdomen. Feeling him grow harder beneath those thick, rigid cargos. He let out a low moan into her mouth, and a smile broke across her lips. He sucked her lower lip before pulling his mouth away and moving to her ear lobe. Pulling. Sucking. Groaning into her ear.

With her backside pressed against the tree, Ford rolled his hips into her, massaging his erection between her legs. She tilted her hips for the perfect angle. The angle that satisfied her as much as him. A little harder. There. Right there.

A light cast into her eyes and she let out a scream.

Oh, right. Lance and Guiles. Corrie's mind had gone blank, momentarily forgetting the reason they'd started kissing in the first place. Ford released his mouth from her neck, but didn't back away, likely to conceal his hard-on.

"Can you turn off the light?" Ford growled with his hand shielding their faces from the beam.

"Sorry . . ." Guiles said, fumbling with the light.

"What are you doing out here?" Lance then asked.

"Isn't that obvious?" Ford responded.

Corrie's chest heaved, half from the apprehension of getting caught, but more from the fire caused by Ford.

"Well, I . . . I thought maybe you were . . ." Guiles stuttered, clearly flustered by finding them in the middle of whatever this was. Or whatever it looked like.

"You thought we were what?" Ford asked with confidence, as if they hadn't just been caught in a compromising position. His face was cool and assertive. Damn, it was sexy.

"Going to the site," Guiles responded.

"No, Guiles. We wanted some privacy. Privacy that's nonexistent in a camp without walls and doors."

"Guiles," Lance said, taking a few steps forward. "You can go back to camp. I'll handle it from here."

Guiles glanced at each of them, assessing the situation once more. But not moving.

"I said you can go now," Lance repeated pointedly.

"Yes, right. Right. Sorry. I . . . I'll leave you be."

They waited silently until Guiles scurried away. Once he was out of earshot, Ford spoke up.

"We'd appreciate it if you wouldn't tell the investor about this."

Lance waved his hand. "You don't need to worry about that. I wasn't brought here to snitch on you. And I'll talk to Guiles.

He's . . . perhaps a little overeager to impress the boss," he said with humor in his voice.

Corrie felt the tension in Ford's chest ease. "And we'd also appreciate it if you wouldn't tell the others about this at camp," she added. "We don't want people gossiping about it and not being focused on the dig."

"Of course. Trust me, I get it, and I appreciate you wanting to make sure the team is focused. Though maybe be a little more . . . discreet," he said with a friendly smile. Phew. "Not that there are any rules against fraternizing, but the investor has sunk a lot of money into this dig, and employees like Guiles may be looking for ways to prove their worth."

Good point. Corrie hadn't even considered that potential ass-kissing minions might be lurking around when she went tip-toeing out into the jungle.

"Absolutely. We thought coming out here would accomplish exactly that, but we'll be more mindful in the future," she followed up.

"Well, I'd better get back before Guiles starts blabbing. But don't worry, your secret's safe with me," he said with a final head nod.

"Thank you," Ford said with his arms still wrapped around Corrie's waist.

They watched Lance as he faded into the trees, once again leaving them in the dark jungle, before Corrie flicked on her flashlight and moved out from Ford's grasp. "Okay, let's go," she said, walking in the direction of the Chimalli site and *not* camp.

"Where do you think you're going?" Ford asked. "Camp's *that* way." He pointed in the direction that Lance had retreated.

"Right. And the site is this way."

Ford furrowed his brow and shook his head. "Do you not remember what happened literally a minute ago? We almost got caught, Corrie, doing the very thing that you're setting out to do again. We could have been *fired*."

"Right, and now Lance and kiss-ass Guiles think that we're making out, so they're off the trail and won't be coming to look for us anytime soon."

Ford looked incredulously at her. "I can't believe you. I swear, one of these days you're going to get yourself killed pulling dangerous stunts like this. Corrie, please don't make me kick you off this job."

Corrie's mouth dropped. "I saved your ass back there and now you're going to threaten me?"

"The only reason my ass needed saving was because *you* put it on the line by sneaking out here in the first place!"

"Yeah, and if you wouldn't have followed me, then your ass wouldn't have needed saving!"

"I'm not letting you do this, Corrie."

"I'm not asking for your permission."

"Well, I'm not asking, either. I'm ordering," he growled. His shoulders heaved as his eyes narrowed on her like lasers.

Corrie laughed. "Oh, we're doing *this* again, too. The ole *Charles in Charge* routine."

"Corrie, I *am* in charge. Like it or not. And if you take one more step in that direction, you're done. I really don't want to do that, and I know how important this is to you, so please don't test me," he said with his hands on his hips.

"And what if I don't agree? What if I take a step in this direction, you kick me off the dig, and I go anyway?" She squared up with him, crossing her arms.

"Then I'll drag you out of this jungle. I'm telling you. Don't do it."

"Drag me?" She leaned back and guffawed. "What, are you a caveman now? Ford, you won't be putting your hands anywhere on me."

"Really? Because it seemed like you enjoyed it a few minutes ago. Seriously, Corrie. Don't test me."

Don't test me? Who the hell did he think he was? Corrie didn't take orders from men, especially not men who lorded their positions of power over her. Her body tensed, fighting with the urge to disobey him. To show Ford he couldn't control her.

But then Ford would be the only name in the history books next to the discovery of Chimalli. And Corrie couldn't let that happen. Over her dead body.

She might have enjoyed his hands on her—no, not enjoyed, *savored* his hands on her—and her core might still be pulsing from the need for a release, but she wouldn't let him put his hands anywhere on her after that. *She* was the one in control on this front.

"Fine," she said, taking one step toward Ford.

"And you're going back to camp?"

"Mm-hmm." Another step.

"And you're going to *stay* at camp?"

"Mm-hmm."

"And I'm not going to have to worry that you're going to sneak out in the middle of the night?"

"Nope. I'll be too busy for that." Another step.

"Busy doing what?"

"Busy letting my vibrator go places I'll *never* allow you to explore." She smirked and brushed by him without waiting for his reaction, marching toward camp. Hearing his footsteps close behind her sent a satisfied grin spreading over her face.

With each step, the intensity in her core built up. If she couldn't—or, rather, *wouldn't*—hate-fuck Ford, she'd at least picture doing it while using her vibrator.

A few of the crew still lingered about in camp, but for the most part it looked like everyone had retired to their sleeping quarters for the evening. She marched right into her tent and tore off her clothes, changing into her sexy black lace bra-and-panty combo, the bra Ford had put his disgusting man hands over. Well, that would be the last time he'd get close to *her* intimates!

Fuck him and that obnoxious kiss.

Vibrator in hand, sexy lingerie on, and lying in bed, Corrie laid back and closed her eyes, picturing his annoying hard cock between her legs, and pressed the on switch.

Buzzzzzzssssssssss . . .

And like her hopes of visiting Chimalli's home once more by herself, her vibrator died.

CHAPTER

Twelve

SELFISH, LITTLE, TROUBLEMAKING . . .

Ford paced around his bed, half-tempted to march over to Corrie's tent to make sure she was actually there. Obeying his order. He should have sent her home. If it had been *anyone* else on this dig . . . *anyone*—Ethan, Sunny, *Agnes*—they would have already been on their way to the airport.

Why he was being soft when it came to Corrie was beyond him.

Well, no. No, that wasn't true. He was being soft on her because of those soft lips that he desperately wanted to taste again. The soft breasts pressing against his chest. And her soft thighs, forming the perfect nestling place for his pelvis. It was all those soft things—which he would never have the pleasure of experiencing again—that had turned *him* into a soft, spineless weenie.

He closed his eyes and got a whiff of coconut. Bringing his shirt to his nose, he breathed in deep, her scent soaked into the fabric. His cock started to swell thinking about her.

No. No, he couldn't let her invade his thoughts like this. He tore off his T-shirt and threw it on the bed as he readied himself for sleep. Stripping to his boxers, he climbed into bed and grabbed a book by the table next to him, trying to do anything to focus his thoughts away from her. But his cock throbbed, begging for a release.

He glanced over at the T-shirt at the foot of his bed.

Oh, fuck it.

He sat up, reaching for the T-shirt and bringing it to his nose. Breathing her in. His cock swelling. With the shirt in one hand, and his cock in the other, he lay back, slowly massaging his erection. Picturing his hand replaced with hers. Wondering what it would feel like with her lips trailing down his stomach and over the tip of his swollen head.

"Ford, do you have any—"

His eyes shot open to find Corrie entering his tent in only a purple robe, her eyes wide and shooting right toward his cock in his hand. Her mouth formed a smirk as she stared at him. With the fastest reflexes possible, he covered his crotch with the T-shirt and sat up.

"Get the hell out!"

"Well, well, well, Dr. Matthews. What do we have here?" She walked farther into his tent, arms crossed and sass in her step.

"I said get out." He pointed at the door with his free hand.

"I'll leave, I'll leave. And let you get back to your . . . business. But I need some batteries."

"I don't have any fucking batteries. Now can you please leave?" he growled.

"But my vibrator died. And I don't want to be the only one missing out on enjoying myself this evening. Don't you have anything I can take the batteries from?"

"Are you serious right now? No. No, I don't."

"Well, can you order some for me? Triple-As."

"Yes. Fine. I'll order some."

She stood there, watching him, the wheels clearly spinning in her head.

"Can I see it?" she asked.

He blinked several times, then shook his head. Was she asking . . . to see his penis? "See what?"

"Your cock."

His head jutted out and his eyes widened. "You want me to show you my dick?"

She nodded, lightly brushing her fingertips along the neckline of her robe.

Was she for real?

"I can't tell if you're actually being serious right now," he followed up.

"Dead serious. My vibrator won't work until I get new batteries, so I need something for . . . stimulation. Is it still hard?" she asked.

He blinked again. "What? Of course it is. You're standing there wearing *that* and talking about vibrators and cocks."

The room fell silent as they stared, each clearly waiting for the other to make the next move. Contemplating what was on the other's mind.

"Do you really want me to leave?" she asked, her tone shifting with the atmosphere. She was no longer goading him. She was feeling him out.

"Of course I don't. Not when you're wearing *that* and talking about vibrators and cocks," he said with a smile.

She laughed and, God, it was sexy. "Okay, then, let me see it. I'll show you my tits. I'm wearing that bra you liked, Dr. Matthews."

He gulped. That bra. That black, lacy, flimsy bra that he'd thought about numerous times over the past couple of days.

"You realize that coming over here in nothing but a flimsy little robe is the opposite of discreet, right?" he asked with playful humor. "Less than an hour ago you were biting my head off and now, what, you want us to show each other our naughty bits like we're a couple of kids hiding in a basement?"

She nodded and bit her lower lip, awakening his desires. His craving for her. Wanting her more than he'd ever wanted anything. And she hadn't come here for some batteries. She'd come for *him*. She could deny it all she wanted, but she desired him, too.

He needed her to admit it.

"Corrie, why are you here? In my room, I mean."

"I told you, I needed batteries."

No. Not good enough. He had to hear her say it. He reached his hand under the T-shirt and started stroking his cock through his boxers. She licked her lips, practically salivating. Yep . . . she wanted him.

"Right, but you could have asked anyone and instead you came here. To me. After everything that happened tonight."

He dragged long, slow strokes against his erection, building in intensity with her hungry stares.

"You were right. I enjoyed your hands on me. I enjoyed your mouth on me, too."

"You did?"

She nodded. "Of course I did. Ford, since you're oblivious to the fact that you've been propositioned by your former students because they want to fuck you, let me make it obvious—you're fucking hot, and it honestly makes me hate you even more than I already do. I think about kissing you all the time . . . about doing *many* things with you. So . . ." She took a step closer. "Did you like kissing me?"

There was a surprising nervousness in her voice at the question. Could she really not tell how much he enjoyed her lips?

"I think about kissing you all the time, too, often because I think it might get you to shut the hell up," he said with his lips upturned. Luckily, she smiled. "But most of the time, I want to kiss you because you're gorgeous, and brilliant, and you . . . and you comfort me. Sometimes those things make me forget that I'm *supposed* to hate you. So, yes, Corrie . . . yes, I liked kissing you."

"Show it to me," she commanded.

Maintaining his rhythm and pressure, he moved the shirt then reached into his boxers and pulled out his cock. He wrapped his hand around the shaft, then began stroking again as she watched and began to untie her robe. With slow movements, she opened the robe, revealing her fabulous body to him. Even better than he'd imagined. Full, round breasts barely concealed by that ridiculous bra. Her dark nipples beaming through. Wide, full hips. A soft tummy, toned but not too skinny. No, Corrie Mejía had curves, and her body was sexy as hell.

Her fingers danced over her flesh as she caressed her body. Two fingers swirled in circles along the outside of her bra, outlining her now-hard nipples, while her other hand trailed down into her panties and started massaging her clit.

Oh, fuck this.

Ford stood and pulled Corrie onto the bed so her back was flush with the mattress as he hovered over her. Her robe fell open, welcoming him to her body. "May I?" he asked, his hand hovering over her bra.

"Only if you kiss me first."

He pressed his lips against hers, savoring every movement of her mouth and tongue, before having the divine pleasure of cupping Corrie Mejía's breasts. No other breasts in his lifetime could—or would—compare. His mouth left hers, planting kisses down her neck and chest before stopping at that scandalous bra. He ran his tongue along the curve of her breasts before sucking on her nipple through the practically nonexistent fabric. She arched her back and moaned as the scratchy lace twisted around her nipple in his mouth.

He dragged the fabric down with his fingers, now fully taking her swollen bud between his lips. With quick flicks, he lapped against her nipple as his hands traveled all over her body, outlining every curve. Every inch of her. Every spot better than the last. Ford had never touched a woman so incredible. Someone he wanted to please as much as he wanted to please Corrie.

His hand grazed her stomach before diving beneath her panties and between her folds. Fuck. She was wet. So very. Very. Wet.

Ford's eyes practically rolled in the back of his head as his fingers glided along her slippery entrance. Was she always like this? Did *he* do this to her? Boring Ford Matthews?

He released her breast from his mouth and scooted down the bed toward her panty line. Kneeling in front of her, he took a good look. Her hair splayed out in a fan on his bed. Her half-naked body resting in her open robe. Her rich, dark eyes staring at him with a foreign intensity. Something was clearly on her mind.

"I want you to fuck me."

Not what he was expecting to come from her lips.

"Okay." Was there really any other answer?

"Do you have any condoms?"

Annnnnnd no. No, he didn't. And why would he? He hadn't had sex in years, and the only two women he'd *planned* on interacting with on this trip were Sunny and Agnes, neither of whom were options.

"No," he finally said.

"Dammit. Do you think Ethan has any?"

"I have no idea, but I'm not going to ask him."

"Then how are you going to fuck me?"

Good question. How *was* he going to fuck her? Because this could very well be a once-in-a-lifetime opportunity. Who knew how things would be between them by the morning with the way they ran so hot and cold? But he wasn't about to suggest they go without one. He had no idea how Corrie would take such a suggestion and he didn't want to upset her.

"I can order some."

Ford closed his eyes, wincing the moment the words came out of his mouth. Order some? Seriously? How unsexy could he be?

"You really know how to turn a lady on," she said. He could hear the smirk in her voice. Her body shifted as she pulled her legs out from under him.

Yep. He'd killed his chances. She was leaving.

But when he opened his eyes expecting to find her putting on her robe, he found the opposite. Instead, she kneeled in front of him, her robe now completely off.

"Why are you looking at me like that?" she asked.

"I thought you were going to leave."

"Leave? Ford, I want you to fuck me, but just because that's not going to happen tonight doesn't mean I'm going to leave. I'm horny. I'm wet. And the thought of having to postpone the inevitable boning is making me even more so."

Ford couldn't help but laugh. "Inevitable boning?"

She smiled and inched closer. "Yes. This is happening, Ford. Even if I left right now, you know what would happen." She placed her hand on Ford's pecs and trickled her fingers lightly along his chest and abs. "We'd both walk away from this sexually frustrated. We'd get into an argument about something ridiculous, because that's what we do. And then one of us would eventually kiss the other again. And we'd be right back here, ripping each other's clothes off, because we both know this is an eight-year-old itch that needs to be scratched."

Her hand reached into his boxers and wrapped around his cock, causing him to suck in a deep breath. Her delicate, slender fingers glided over his firm flesh. That, coupled with the look in her eye . . . heaven. Absolute heaven.

Ford brushed her hair behind her shoulders and wrapped his hand behind her neck. "Calling me an itch? You really know how to turn a man on."

She squeezed a tad tighter and pressed her lips to his. "Oh, I'm just getting started." With that, she backed up then bent over. Her ass high in the air. What Ford wouldn't do for a mirror. Although everything around him went blank the moment she took him in her mouth. The moan escaping his lips couldn't be helped. Not with the way her tongue rolled around his cock's head and the way her hand glided slowly along his shaft. And definitely not with the way her own hips rolled as she massaged him with her mouth, as if she was picturing his cock inside of her in a different way than at present.

He ran his hand along the arch of her back as she sucked on him. The last time he had a blow job was . . . damn. He couldn't even remember. Though maybe that was because none of them

were worth remembering. But this one? Oh, this was a blow job
he'd never forget.

Everything about this moment, he'd never forget. And he
didn't want Corrie forgetting it, either.

Well, that and he selfishly wanted to taste her, too.

He reached around and ran his hand around the curve of
her hip, then pulled her panties to the side, slipping his fingers
inside her. Feeling her wetness almost made him come, but no.
He couldn't come before giving her pleasure, too.

Their bodies broke apart and Ford climbed onto the bed
beside her. They both rested on their sides, heads opposite each
other, and he situated himself with his mouth in front of her
panties. With a slow glide, he slid her panties off then dove between her legs, alternating between lapping at her clit and dragging his tongue in long, wide strokes along her slit. Tasting her
like she was the best damn dessert he'd ever had.

"Oh God, Ford. There . . . right there . . ."

He gripped her ass, pulling her tightly against his face. He
had one mission and one mission only—to satisfy her. No, not
just satisfy. To worship her. But when she pulled him back into
her mouth doing the same, he wouldn't last much longer. Not
when hearing her moans, no, *feeling* her moans on his cock.
And not with the way she continued to roll her hips against his
face.

"Ford . . ." she said, pulling her mouth off him but continuing to pump his shaft, "I'm going to come."

"Me too," he said between licks.

She bobbed on his head a few more times before pulling
away and letting him come on her tits. Twelve years of tension
released. Twelve years since the moment he'd first laid eyes on

Corrie Mejía. A wave of ecstasy washed over his body as he buried his face and moaned into her as she convulsed against him, her satisfied cries sending another warm surge over him. He laid back, trying to catch his breath and placing a hand on his chest. The room was silent aside from their panting breaths.

"Don't forget to order those condoms."

CHAPTER

Thirteen

THERE WAS NOTHING BORING ABOUT FORD MATTHEWS. NOT THE way he kissed. Or the way he performed oral sex. And certainly not his body.

With Corrie's romantic life consisting primarily of casual sexual encounters—okay, *only* of casual sexual encounters—she'd grown pretty accustomed to men with nice bodies. She wasn't exactly swiping right because of their personalities, that was for sure. Sometimes that meant the guys she hooked up with were more into their *own* bodies than hers. Those were the ones who she'd pass on for a repeat.

Then there was Ford, focused on *her* pleasure and oblivious to his abs, chest, emerald eyes, and flawless cock.

How had this man not been banging women left and right? It was a shame, really, that he was keeping his body all to himself. He even smelled good, which, after being in the jungle for more than three months, was surprising. It was likely only his deodorant or body wash, but the juniper aroma was divine to Corrie's senses.

Which made it even harder to work beside him the following day without trying to find a place behind a tree or a boulder where he could go down on her again.

He acted normally, saying good morning to her and the others like it was any ordinary day. Said hello with the same face that had been buried between her legs less than eight hours earlier. Hmm . . . did his face still smell like her? He acted so casually, though, that she wondered if she was on his mind at all.

He ate his breakfast across the table from her, treating her no differently than he treated Ethan or Sunny. Frankly, it was pissing her off. She might not have been like those full-of-themselves guys she'd met on Tinder, but she had a rocking body. And she gave a *fantastic* blow job. So why wasn't he flashing her any suggestive looks? Or checking out her breasts, which she was not-so-subtly displaying in her low-cut tank? Hell, every other guy at the table—and Sunny—had checked them out at *least* once already. Ford hadn't even taken a peek.

Had Corrie let Ford play her again?

"Dr. Matthews," Sunny said, approaching the table, holding the sat phone, "They want to know if there are any more supplies to add to the drop on Monday."

Ford perked up and quickly glanced at Corrie before looking at Sunny.

"Um, yeah." He wiped his mouth and started to stand.

"Oh, I got it," Sunny said. "Let me know what it is, and I'll take care of it."

But Ford didn't back down, glancing at Corrie one more time. "No, I've got it," he said, reaching for the phone then walking away—far away—from the table.

Corrie couldn't help the smile on her face as she continued

eating her breakfast. Condoms. He was thinking about her after all.

"That was weird," Ethan said to Corrie. "Why wouldn't he
want us to know what supplies he's getting?"

Corrie shrugged, trying to play it off. "You know how he is."

"Well, I'm not sure if you've had any success getting him to
open up, but he still doesn't tell me anything."

"He's certainly private."

"Yeah . . . maybe he needs hemorrhoid cream."

Corrie snickered. "Nah. He's probably getting lube." Or
something like that. She smirked, knowing she wasn't too far off.

And Ethan's laugh signaled that he had no clue how spot-on
she'd been.

"What's so funny?" Ford asked, returning to the table.

"Oh, we were trying to guess what you needed to order in
private," Ethan said.

Another glance.

"Oh yeah? And?"

"Corrie over here guessed lube."

"Do the two of you seriously have nothing else on your
mind?" Ford asked in his typical bossy way.

A light tap hit Corrie's toe. She looked up from her plate to
see Ford's cautioning eyes.

"Hey, it was better than Ethan's guess," Corrie said, taking
another bite of toast.

"I don't even want to know," Ford said, hanging then shaking his head. "Come on . . . it's time to head out."

Everyone at the table gathered their trays and made their
way to the washtubs, but as Corrie passed Ford, he pulled her
back by the crook of her elbow and whispered in her ear. "I'm
pretty sure you have all the lubricant I need. Now quit looking

at me like that, because those condoms aren't coming for another four days, and I can't be walking around with a raging hard-on until then."

His warm breath tickled her ear, sending a chill down her spine and her nipples to full attention.

"As long as you're still thinking about me," she said, just to make sure, and turning her head to look at him.

"Corrie, I'm *always* thinking about you. And I'll be thinking about that pretty mouth of yours on my cock all day until we're in my tent tonight. But for now, we should focus on the dig."

"Well, if you want me to focus, then I need to stop by my room to change out of these wet panties because, Dr. Matthews, you've got a way with your words."

Corrie sashayed to her tent, not bothering to check Ford's reaction. She wanted him to be in as much agony as she was, waiting for the moment they could be alone together again.

With a fresh pair of panties, Corrie joined the rest of the group on their trek to the Chimalli site. It was as beautiful as she'd remembered.

The sun peeked through the mahogany tree canopy, casting a mystic atmosphere around the adobe building covered in vines and moss. Corrie pictured what it looked like in its prime—likely a single room with space only for sleeping and minimal furnishings aside from woven reed mats and a metatl table. A hearth outside the home. Maybe even a small garden for vegetables. Perhaps Chimalli returned over the ridge with a vessel of water to see Yaretzi sitting at the opening of the hut, weaving a basket and watching their child play in the dirt below her. Their quiet, idyllic life a far cry from that in Tenochtitlán.

After doing a group tour of both sites and laying the ground rules for the dig, they split into two teams and got to work setting up the site. Taking photos of each area. Marking various spots to dig. Erecting tents and other facilities, areas for eating, taking breaks, sifting, and going to the bathroom. Most of the day, Ford drifted back and forth between the bowl and the cave, answering questions and offering suggestions on techniques to carefully remove the vegetation that had consumed the structure. By the time they broke for a late lunch, they were halfway through setup. But at this rate, they wouldn't break ground until the next day at the earliest.

Digging was a painstakingly slow process. They couldn't simply jab their shovels in and go. No, every inch had to be carefully uncovered and any peculiarities marked. And then dirt needed to be sifted. And artifacts tagged then bagged. And then on to the next inch. Given the size of the adobe hut alone, they'd be there for at least another month.

Though, now that Corrie had someone to keep her company in the evenings, she didn't think she'd mind the added time.

"Dr. Mejía?" Ford said as everyone was sitting to eat their sack lunches, courtesy of Agnes. "Could you come look at something with me for a minute?"

Corrie paused midbite and set her sandwich on the wrapper. "Right now?"

"Yes. I want your opinion on another potential search spot."

She wrinkled her brow. Another spot? Maybe Chimalli had a storage area or Ford had found another cave.

"Do you need me to come, too?" Ethan asked, ready to hop up from his seat on the ground.

"No, just Dr. Mejía for now."

Ford led the way, far from the rest of the group and both dig sites. What on earth were they looking for over here? And how did Ford even find this spot? Perhaps there was something around the boulder ahead of them. But once they turned the corner, nothing.

"Ford, what are we—"

She couldn't finish her sentence before he pressed her back against the cold, hard stone and kissed her. Kissed her with the same passion and intensity from the night before. Reminding her of the things he could do with that fabulous mouth of his and that extremely talented tongue.

Who needed lunch when you could have a Ford snack?

Their tongues tousled in a frenzied flurry. Needing more. Wanting more. And not just wanting more from the kiss. Wanting more from each other in every possible way. Corrie wrapped her leg around Ford's waist, pulling his groin into hers. His hips rolled in long, deep strokes against her, pressing his thick, hard cock into her most sensitive area.

Maybe they didn't need a condom. He hadn't had sex in a few years after all . . .

No. Corrie put the thought out of her head. She had rules and couldn't break them simply because she was horny and Ford's cock was begging to be let in. It was a deal she'd made with herself when she'd decided to stick with casual sex. No condom, no sex, no exceptions. The last thing Corrie needed was an STI. Or a baby Mejía. A baby would no doubt set her plans back.

Slowly, he pulled his mouth from hers, planting a few final pecks on her lips, then stared at her face.

"How am I supposed to focus and get any work done when all I can think about is you?" he asked.

Sweet satisfaction washed over her.

"Were you really able to focus before this? Because I don't know about you, but I've been thinking about kissing you since the airport," she said. "Hate-kissing you, of course, but still kissing you."

"True, but it was easier to get work done when I was competing with you."

"Who said the competition is over? I still plan on being the first one to hold the knife." She smirked.

Besides, their friendly competition made the rest of it all sweeter.

"You're assuming I'm going to *let* that happen," Ford said, his eyes homing in on hers.

"Let it happen? Oh-ho-ho! Dr. Matthews, you're mistaken if you think I'm going to let you let *me* do anything."

"All right, then. How about a little wager?"

Wager. Hmm . . . Corrie was beginning to like the sound of this.

"Okay . . . I'm listening."

"Well, so we're not here for the next six months unable to focus, how about we add some skin to the game?"

Corrie waggled her brow. Oh, she was all for more of Ford's skin, especially the smooth, veiny skin of his cock.

"Dirty girl," he said. "Anyway, whoever finds the knife and holds it first gets to pick their prize."

"And what are the parameters for the prize?"

"Whatever you want . . . within reason of course."

"Do we have to want the same thing?"

He shook his head. "Like I said, whatever you want. I'll go first . . . if I win, I want that bra and panties you were wearing last night."

That was it? Hell, Corrie would have given him those even without the wager. Not that she'd let him know that. Particularly not with what it was she wanted out of this deal.

"Dirty boy." She hooked her fingers through his belt loops and pulled him closer. He needed buttering up for what Corrie was about to drop. She rubbed her hand on the outside of his pants and brought her mouth to his ear, sucking on the lobe. "If I win . . . I want my name listed first on every publication, museum plaque, history book, whatever it may be, as the person who discovered Chimalli."

He pulled his face back, the strain obvious. Wanting to call her out for being absurd but not wanting her to stop massaging him. "That's significantly more than what I asked for."

"I didn't make the rules, Ford. My proposal is reasonable. You can always ask for something else if you'd like. This," she said, motioning toward her hand around him, "doesn't constitute a handshake, so you still have time to change your mind."

"Fine. If I win . . . I want you to do an interview where you are quoted as thanking me for giving you the opportunity to come on this dig."

That. Little. Asshole.

She glared at him and took back her hand. "You realize that goes against everything that I believe in, right?"

"You realize it has nothing to do with the fact that you're a woman, and everything to do with us and this decade-long grudge, right?"

"Yes, it does. We wouldn't *be* in this competition if I weren't a woman."

"Okay, and you don't think that the reason you want your name first doesn't have anything to do with the fact that I'm a man? It goes both ways, Corrie. But again, it's the fact that you're *this* woman. *This* woman who drives me up the wall and makes me want to rip my hair out at the same time I want to rip her clothes off. Now, are you going to take my wager or what?"

Under any other circumstances, her principles would win out. But Corrie didn't have any intention of letting Ford win this competition. Meaning the risk of losing the bet was slim to none.

"Fine. But we need some ground rules. Rule number one, you can't pull that *I'm the boss* bullshit on me and assign me to some menial task so that I'm never in a position where winning could be possible."

"Okay. I can agree to that. Rule number two, no sneaking out alone. We come here together or we don't come at all."

"Is that an invitation, Dr. Matthews? Or perhaps another double entendre?" She waggled her brow.

"Hey, I've never been a fan of one-way orgasms."

No, he certainly wasn't. He'd proven that last night.

"Rule number three. When we're at the site, we focus."

"Okay. Then we need a revision to rule number one. I won't pull that bullshit *I'm the boss* routine, but you have to respect that out here, I *am* the boss," he said matter-of-factly. Which, fair. He technically was the boss. "I won't assign you pointless tasks or purposely do things so you lose, but you have to do what I say. No arguing. No challenging my direction—"

"But what if you're wrong? I mean, let's face it, Ford. You *were* wrong more than once already."

It was the truth. Had Corrie not challenged his decisions, they'd still be playing in the sandbox at the other site.

"I can acknowledge when I'm wrong, Corrie, and, yes, in those instances, I was wrong. But there's a difference between being wrong and merely disagreeing. We can both admit that our scuffles are often more a consequence of our differences of opinion rather than one of us being truly incorrect."

He had a point. Ford really was one of the smartest people

she'd ever met. A true and worthy rival as far as competition was concerned. He just didn't do most things the way Corrie would do them.

"Fine. Out here, you're the boss."

"And at camp."

"And at camp? That means you're the boss all the time."

"No, at camp only when we're with others. Rule number four, when we're alone, you can be the boss."

Corrie smirked. *Can* be? That was already a given.

She reached out her hand. "You've got yourself a deal, Dr. Matthews."

They shook hands, each of them smiling as if they'd already won. But there could only be one winner, and she'd come out on top.

CHAPTER

Fourteen

A LITTLE COMPETITION NEVER HURT ANYONE.

Unless you considered the fact that Corrie and Ford had been competing their entire careers, and, if he was really being honest with himself, Corrie had *definitely* come out on the losing end in the past—the Yale fellowship, Ford's ranking as the top student in their class, and even the cheers for him that had drowned out hers at graduation when he'd crossed the stage seconds before her. But this time was different. Sure, they were competing against each other, but they really wanted the same thing—to find Chimalli. And the odds of success were looking good. If he had to give up first billing on any publications, then fine.

It would be a small price to pay considering the *huge* price these artifacts were going to fetch. And now that they were back to focusing, and now that they had a wager going, things were going to move a lot faster on the dig. Which only made the time waiting for those damn condoms to arrive excruciatingly long.

The whole crew seemed to be ready to go home. They even

volunteered to work through the weekend. Though it might have been that everyone was eager once they uncovered an old grinding stone in the adobe house. It had been their first big find on the dig. It would definitely score Ford a few extra thousand in bonus money. Not the million-dollar reward he'd been promised for the tecpatl or the million-and-a-half-dollar reward if they found any skeletal remains, but with the luck they'd had, Ford would take whatever he could get.

But when they found a bowl and small hand-carved chest the next day, Ford's skepticism all but vanished. At the pace they were working, it would only be a matter of days before they'd uncover the rest of it.

Everyone had been so excited they'd celebrated that evening with a toast. And he and Corrie had enjoyed a private celebration later that night, complete with cunnilingus, blow jobs, and the best titty fuck he'd ever had.

Once Monday rolled around—supply drop day—he'd stopped fixating on the inevitable. Fixating on whether she'd be disappointed after the wait. Sure, every night for the last five days they'd met in his tent late at night. She kept coming back, which must mean *something*. Though Ford couldn't help but notice she never stayed. Sure, they'd agreed to keep what was going on between them a secret. The last thing they needed was for everyone to gossip about it, or for the investor to find out and question whether Ford was taking the dig seriously. And it was obvious that Corrie in particular was concerned about her reputation, which made sense given everything she'd told him about the rumors that had followed her over the years. But it would have been nice if she wasn't always in such a rush to get back to her own tent after they fooled around.

It would have been nice if every now and then she wanted to stay and talk. Or cuddle. Or sleep beside him.

But she was the boss. Her rules. Her orders. So whenever she got up to put her clothes on and leave, and that little ache of wanting her to stay stabbed Ford in the side, he didn't say anything. He let her go without so much as a second glance. Leaving him alone in his bed and alone with his thoughts.

Thoughts about what would happen after all this was over. What would happen with Corrie. What would happen with his mother. Whether any of this was really worth it.

He glanced over at Corrie as they all walked to the camp after a long day at the site. Her smile warmed his heart. The smile that she gave only to him. She smiled at others, but never like that. Never with that slight blush in her cheeks, or the nibble on her lower lip. It made him hopeful.

Yes. She was worth it. Was it terrible that he'd rather stay in the jungle with Corrie forever than go back to his life in New Haven? Did that make him a horrible son?

He shook the thought away, already suffering from enough guilt after missing his mom's call last Friday since they'd worked later than normal before a weekend.

Yep, he was a terrible son.

The sentiment was confirmed the moment they walked into camp and his cock started to stiffen upon seeing the supply crates. *You're going to hell, Ford.*

"Dr. Matthews," Agnes called out, waving him over once they returned, "Come here, please." The tone in her voice was firm and slightly perturbed.

Okay . . . weird . . .

Agnes stood with one of the delivery guys, Federico. Usually

Federico dropped off the supplies with Agnes when they were still in the field, and Agnes would start sorting things before they got back. They never needed to wait for Ford to sign off on anything.

He jogged over to the two of them, Federico clutching a clipboard as if his life depended on not handing it over to Agnes.

"What's the problem?" Ford asked.

"Oh, for some reason Federico here decided that you are the only one who can sign for the supplies this time. Even though I've signed for it the last *dozen* times," she said, glowering at Federico.

Federico leaned in and whispered, "I've got that special *thing* you asked for."

And with the worst timing possible, Corrie walked by. Federico's gaze traveled over in her direction, gave her a quick once-over, then turned back to Ford with a sly eye and a smirk. The reason behind asking for that *special thing* wasn't lost on him. At least Federico knew better than to say anything about it. But that didn't stop Ford from blushing, his ears radiating with heat.

"They're in this crate," Federico said pointing to a smaller wooden box next to him. Thankfully small enough for Ford to carry alone and take to his tent.

"Great. Thanks," Ford said, signing the order acceptance and handing the clipboard back to him.

"Have fun."

Oh, Ford planned to have fun. Lots of it. Hence why he'd ordered a box rather than just a packet of condoms.

Under Agnes's watchful eye, he took the crate to his tent as the others unpacked the rest of the supplies. Once in his room, he hid the box in the trunk at the foot of his bed, with a few individual condoms tucked in the drawer in the side table for easy access. Soon, once everyone else was asleep, Corrie would be in his tent, between his sheets, and, finally, he'd be inside her. All he had to do was get through dinner and the typical evening hangouts.

He showered. Made a quick call to the investor. Ate dinner. And followed the group to relax by the fire. Corrie was extra chill that evening. So chill that Ford wondered whether she even remembered the plan. That was, until she sat next to him by the fire and leaned over toward his ear, whispering, "I hope that package arrived, because I've got plans for you tonight, Dr. Matthews."

The hair on the back of his neck stood up straight. Something about the way she called him *Dr. Matthews* got him every time. He loved it. Loved the way she said his name. Loved that sexy, purring voice she used when they were alone. Even now that they weren't fighting every day like they used to, she still got his goat. But now, in a good way.

"In my tent, Dr. Mejía," he responded.

"Good," she said, leaning back and setting herself at ease. "Let's hope everyone remembers it's a Monday night and wants to go to bed early."

Ethan plunked down next to them, not giving them much hope for an early bedtime.

"This is still weird to me," he said, taking a drink.

"What's weird?" Ford asked.

"The two of you getting along. It's like I don't know who you are anymore."

"We're not getting along," Corrie responded. "We're tolerating each other to achieve a mutual goal. Huge difference."

"Yeah, besides . . . it's too exhausting fighting with her. She always wins," Ford said.

She smirked. "That's right, Dr. Matthews. I *always* win."

Oh, not this time, honey. He was winning this one.

"Dr. Matthews," Sunny said, walking over to them. "You have a call. From some hospital."

She reached out her arm holding the satellite phone and Ford's stomach sank. *Oh God, no. No . . . please don't tell me . . .*

He stopped himself from thinking the worst, but everything else around him faded to the back of his mind. Winning. The dig. Corrie. Nothing else mattered but his mom. He jumped up from the ground, snagged the phone, and took off for some privacy.

"Hello?" he asked once he'd reached the safety of his tent.

"This is Dr. Lee at Lakeview. Sorry for calling at such a late hour—"

"That's okay. Is everything all right? Is . . . is my mom okay?" He held his breath, waiting for Dr. Lee's response.

"Yes, she's . . . stable . . ." Stable? That didn't sound like a good thing. "But the transfer from the hospital to Lakeview didn't go as smoothly as we would have liked. I'd like to start her on the new treatment right away, tomorrow if possible."

"Okay . . ."

Where was the catch?

"But I wanted to talk to you about some . . . maybe . . . less expensive options we could try first."

The catch.

"Oh."

"Your mother explained that insurance has been covering most of her treatments thus far, and she was concerned about the cost of the treatment I'm recommending because it's . . .

well, the out-of-pocket expense will be significantly greater than what you've been covering, so she asked that I call you. There are several additional options for treatment, though they're not as aggressive as the one I originally recommended. But as her doctor, I would be comfortable with any of them at this point. She just wanted to make sure you are okay with the selection."

His mother wanted to make sure *he* was okay? As if his checking account mattered more than her health. It was official—he was a terrible son.

Although, in some respects, it didn't matter if he couldn't actually *pay* for the treatment.

"Tell me . . . if the other treatments don't work, does that mean you'll eventually recommend the more expensive treatment anyway?" he asked.

"Most likely."

"And if that happens, then it would end up costing even more money in the end?"

"Sure. It's a definite possibility."

"Then do whatever is most likely to make her better." Making sure she was better, or even simply comfortable, was the only thing he cared about.

"She knew you were going to say that."

"Well, she could have called me herself, and I would have told her that. I'm sorry to make you call to deliver the same answer she already knew."

"She said she'd tried to call but hadn't been able to get ahold of you . . ." A sickening gut punch hit Ford deep in the stomach.

"Can I talk to her now?" To assuage some of his guilt.

"I'm sorry, Dr. Matthews, but that won't be possible. Your mother is very weak, and the treatments take a lot out of her. I'm surprised she was even awake when she tried calling last

Friday, but she said it's the highlight of her week. The only thing she has to look forward to."

The phone dropped a half inch from his ear as he clutched it to keep from crying. The only thing she had to look forward to and he'd gone and forgotten after deciding instead to stay late at the dig site. He wasn't a terrible son. He was a *shitty* son.

"Well, can you tell her I love her?" he managed to choke out. Barely.

"Of course, Dr. Matthews. And she asked me to tell you the same. I'll follow up later this week with any updates. Take care, now."

The minute he hung up the phone, Ford crumpled onto his bed. What was he doing here? He didn't need to risk everything on this dig. There were other ways he could get the money. Pick up some additional lectures. Maybe that speaker series at the museum they'd been asking him to do. Sure, those things didn't pay much, but at least he'd be there with her and she wouldn't be alone. He could visit her in person, giving her something more than a thirty-minute phone call each week to look forward.

Hell, he could pick up gambling. Though, with the way his luck had been going the last couple of years, that perhaps wasn't the best option.

So why was he really here, given that there were other options? Was he here to get money, or was he here for his pride? Here because he wanted to be the archaeologist who'd discovered Chimalli? Here because even after eight years, and without even realizing it, he was still trying to compete with Corrie? Because he wanted to beat her. Pierre Vautour had wanted her. Yet Ford had waltzed right up to Vautour and boasted about his ability to succeed on this dig. So his being here, well, it was all his own damn idea, and now, as a result, he was missing valuable time with his mother. Time he'd never get back.

Add *shitty person* to the list of Ford's attributes.

He could tell himself all he wanted was the money—for his mom—but was that the truth or something he'd convinced himself of so he wouldn't look like such an asshole?

"Hey," a sweet, sexy voice called from the door of his tent.

Ford didn't need to look to know who it was. "Now's not a good time, Corrie," he said, turning away and removing his glasses to wipe the tears from his eyes.

"Hey, are you okay?" Not heeding his warning, she entered the tent and sat beside Ford. Typical Corrie, not listening to him.

"Please, Corrie . . . please go away, okay?"

"No, Ford, I'm not going to leave you like this. What happened? Is it your mom? Is everything okay?"

He couldn't even pretend not to be crying anymore. His body buckled under its own weight and he shifted on the bed to put distance between the two of them. But she wouldn't let him go far. She scooted closer to him, placing her hands on his back and pressing her head to his shoulder.

"Ford, please . . . please talk to me. You're worrying me."

"Why won't you just leave me?" he asked.

"Because I care about you, Ford."

"You wouldn't care about me if you really knew me."

"I do know you."

"No, you don't. You only know what I choose to tell you. And I'm telling you right now, I'm a horrible person," he said.

"You're not a horrible person," she said, rushing to the other side to face him. "And you haven't always been a shiny, picture-perfect person around me, and I *still* like you. You have flaws,

Ford. We all do. Now, please tell me what happened, because I'm sitting here imagining the worst."

She was thinking that his mother had died, but there was no way she was thinking the worst about him. That he'd betrayed her—again. And as much as he liked to think it had been an inadvertent betrayal, now he wasn't so sure.

"I missed her call last Friday," he finally said. "Missed it and honestly didn't even remember until well after the fact." He didn't care that his tears were on full display. There was no holding them back. She needed to see the person he was.

"I'm sure she'll understand." Corrie took his hands from his lap. "But she's okay?"

"She's alive, yes, but she's not okay. They need to start a new treatment, a treatment that isn't covered by insurance and that I can barely afford, and she was more concerned about me having to spend all my money than she was about getting better. Yet I couldn't even be bothered to take her call."

"Ford, it was an accident."

"No . . . I shouldn't be here. I should be there with her, help-ing her through this."

"Well, can you go for a few days to see her and then come back here?"

"But we're so close and . . ." he stopped himself. "And this is what I mean. I'm more concerned with this glorified treasure hunt than I am my mother. I told you. I'm a horrible person."

"That doesn't make you a horrible person, and just because you want to be here, too, doesn't mean you love her any less. You're being too hard on yourself."

She didn't even know the half of it.

"God, this is embarrassing. I can't believe I'm crying in front of you . . . again."

"It's nothing to be embarrassed about. You love and miss your mom. I'd be more turned off if you *weren't* upset by this situation."

Turned off? Did that mean she was turned on? Because despite all the waiting and the anticipation, sex was the last thing on Ford's mind.

"I didn't mean it like that," she answered for him, clearly reading his thoughts, "Not in a sexual way, I mean." The worry must have read all over his face. "I meant that I'd be turned off by you as a person if you didn't have a heart like that."

"I'm sorry . . . I know we'd sort of planned to . . . you know . . ." God, why couldn't he talk about sex like an adult? And *sort of planned*? Didn't he mean they'd counted down the days and the hours until the supply drop occurred so they could *inevitably* bone?

The warmth of her hand over his, however, calmed the nerves.

"Ford, I totally get it. It's not the right time."

"It doesn't feel right, you know? Not right now."

"I know. It's fine. Really." Her smile warmed his heart as she leaned over and kissed him on the cheek before standing to leave. But he grabbed her hand before she could go.

"You don't have to leave. You can still stay," he said, "and hang out for a bit."

All the self-loathing and sadness had evaporated ever since Corrie had stepped into his tent. Funny how someone who'd previously had the effect of irritating him now calmed his entire being. Though, if Ford was truly being honest with himself, it had never really been about being irritated by her. It had always been the tension of not being able to have her.

She smiled and said, "Of course."

They settled onto the bed, resting on their sides and talking. Talking about the dig. About his mom. Laughing about silly things that made him forget that hours earlier he'd been crying. But that was how things went with her. Hours passing in a blink. Easy conversation. Just like every time they'd ever been alone.

He couldn't help but admire her when she talked, and not just because she was breathtakingly gorgeous. Even aside from that, the woman had bravado and class. And she was fucking hilarious. Ford's sides hurt from all the laughing, his mouth from all the smiling. Not only that, but also her mannerisms. Like the way she tapped the tips of her fingers together in the air while she spoke. And the way she flipped over on the bed and leaned in whenever she got excited. He especially liked how animated she'd get when acting out a story.

He'd never met anyone like her. Seriously . . . anyone who'd ever spent a night talking and telling stories in bed with Corrie Mejía no doubt walked away from the experience completely head over heels for her, if they weren't obsessed with her already. Ford's insides tingled, warming his body as the evening wore on, when it finally hit him.

I'm wild about this woman.

Ford didn't do *wild*. He'd never been wild about anyone in his life. Although there'd been a flicker there once before.

And Corrie must have had the same thought.

"Why didn't you kiss me that night?" she asked.

The question came out of nowhere, but Ford knew exactly what she was referring to—the library. He'd asked himself that question—and dozens of variations—a thousand times. They'd been close. Only inches apart. Close enough he'd been able to smell that coconut of her hair with the coffee on her breath.

Was it bad that whenever Addy had gotten a coconut milk latte all he could think of was Corrie?

"The library was closing."

Oof. His response came out even worse than he'd planned. Worse than he'd rehearsed in his head all those years. And, sure, it was the truth. Had the librarian not barged in to tell them to leave, he *would* have kissed Corrie. But his response didn't tell the full story.

"Wow . . ." she said, propping her head in her hand. "Remind me never to go to the library with you again near closing time. Don't want you to break the rules."

"That's not what I meant," he said.

"Well, then, what did you mean, Dr. Matthews? Pray tell," she said, rolling onto her stomach and propping her head in her hands with her elbows on the bed like a teenager at a slumber party.

He leaned to his side facing her, lifting his head as he spoke. "I mean . . . yes, it was because the library was closing, but once we'd gotten outside I thought . . . I thought the moment had passed and that it would be awkward if I moved in for the kill. And, honestly, I wasn't sure you even liked me."

"Didn't like you? Do you not remember standing outside for fifteen minutes after closing? I was *waiting* for you to make a move."

"Yeah . . ." he drew out. "I realized that after I got home. Trust me . . . I kicked myself for that one."

She sighed and flipped onto her back, resting her head on the pillow. "And that was it. Our one opportunity for us to have gone down a different road, and neither of us even sought the other out after that."

"That's not true."

Her eyes perked up.

"What do you mean?" she asked.

"Corrie . . . the only reason I went to that gala was because you were going to be there."

She propped herself up again. "Funny, because I remember you sucking face with Addison Crawley that night." She pursed her lips and quirked her brow, but her tone was still playful.

But after all these years . . . all this time knowing she had the wrong idea, Ford needed to set things straight.

"*She* kissed *me*. I went looking for *you*."

The memory of Corrie finding them kissing in the alcove was firmly etched in his head. Her incredulous wide brown eyes. Her red dress hugging her gorgeous curves. Her matching red lips, trembling as if the sight of his lips on another woman genuinely crushed her soul. And not any woman, but Addison Crawley—the reason Corrie had gone to the gala in the first place. To schmooze Addison and hopefully boost her chances with Dr. Crawley at Yale.

Except Corrie never got that opportunity to schmooze. Not after Ford had unintentionally gotten to Addison first. He knew how it had probably looked from Corrie's perspective. She'd told him her plan to network with Addison at the gala when they'd whispered about their hopes and dreams in the library. At the time, Ford had no intention of going himself. Two days later, though, he'd gone in search of Corrie. But to Corrie, it looked like he'd gone to steal her plan. And given that his later relationship with Addison had sealed the deal for his job with Dr. Crawley, it was a plan that had appeared to work, cementing Corrie's hatred for him.

"You crushed me that night, Ford. I thought I'd been wrong about you. I *thought* I might actually like you. And then you did that . . ." This time her voice wasn't quite so jovial. The hurt was obvious.

"I know . . . I know how it looks," he said. "I'd actually tried avoiding her once I realized who she was, but she kept finding me at the party. I guess she thought I was playing hard to get. Thought I was a challenge that needed conquering. But, Corrie, honest to God, I did not go there for her. And we didn't start dating until four weeks later, after I had confirmation that there was no saving what you and I had in the library. I never intended what happened with her."

Her brows knitted together. "Wait . . . four weeks?" She stared off as if trying to piece it together, then looked straight at him. "Then how did you get the fellowship?"

Again, he knew how it looked to Corrie, especially when Dr. Crawley had originally planned to attend her dissertation defense during that four-week period but had been a no-show. Put together his making out with Addison and Dr. Crawley's no-show appearance and, yes, it had probably looked like Ford had something to do with it. But he hadn't.

"I don't know why Dr. Crawley didn't attend your dissertation, I swear. I didn't even see or speak to Addison again until the week after. But she took me to her parents' house to meet them for lunch shortly after we began dating, and he brought up the fellowship and how he'd been eyeing some people, but how he didn't have time for interviews, and then Addison asked him what about me, and suddenly we were in his study talking, and . . . and . . . honestly, Corrie, it all happened so fast," he rambled.

Eight years he'd been waiting to give her an explanation. Eight years and the best he could come up with was word vomit.

"I didn't go there with the intention of taking it from you," he continued, his mouth no longer a running faucet. "And I know I only got the position because of Addison. But I'm sorry. I'm sorry ~~because~~ I know how much it meant to you."

"You swear?"

"Yes, I swear. Corrie, I never meant to hurt you."

She sighed, her eyes cast downward. "Guess I didn't have it in the bag after all. Sounds like I wasn't even the only one in the running."

Ford didn't respond, but that was his understanding, too.

"God, I hated you so much for that. I feel foolish now. But I was so mad, thinking that you'd used me for that information."

"That wasn't it at all," he said, reaching across the bed and taking her hand. "Corrie . . . I liked you—a lot. I mean, you terrified me and frustrated the heck out of me sometimes—still do—but I'd been attracted to you from the moment you raised your hand in our first Archaeological Theory class. And not simply because I thought you were the most beautiful woman I'd ever seen. Though I'm sure you managed to inspire lots of crushes that day."

"Is that so?"

"Absolutely. Corrie, I know you think that when people look at you all they see is this," he said, swirling his hand in the air and waving it over her entire body, "but I see this . . ." He pressed his index and middle finger to her temple right above her eyebrow. "And this," he then said, touching his fingers to her lips.

"Hey, you try maintaining these brows and this lip in the jungle without access to hot wax," she said with a smirk.

He smiled. "No, smart-ass. I was referring to your brilliant mind and that sassy mouth that's not afraid of anyone or anything. Though, I'm not going to lie—I really do enjoy the rest of you, too."

"I really enjoy most of you as well."

"Oh, really? Only most of me?" he said, pulling her toward him so their bodies were flush on the bed.

She nodded. "Mm-hmm. I like this," she said, pointing to his eyes. "And this," touching her hand to his head, then running her fingers lightly through the tips of his hair. "And *all* this," she said, waving her hand over his taut physique. "And most of the time, this," she finished, placing the tips of her fingers on his lips.

"Most of the time?"

"I mean, I don't like when they're telling me no for various reasons, but I like it when they're smiling. And kissing me. And saying I'm sorry."

Without hesitation, he pressed his lips to hers. The feeling was mutual. He'd never enjoyed kissing anyone as much as he enjoyed kissing her. That feisty mouth of hers teased him in more ways than one. From her smart-alecky taunts to her sultry pouts and unrivaled intelligence, he yearned for that mouth every hour of the day. And for the talents she'd perfected with it.

His hand reached up the back of her shirt, caressing her soft skin, as she glided her hands along his chest under his shirt, her elegant fingers trailing each ridge of his muscles, causing his body to shudder with goose bumps. He anticipated her every move yet was always surprised.

"Ford?" she asked as his lips moved to her neck.

"Mm-hmm?"

His mouth traveled along her sweet skin, tasting her like she was the most delicious thing ever to hit his taste buds.

"I know we said not tonight, but . . ." Her panting breath trailed off.

"Mm-hmm?"

A soft purr tore from her throat. "But . . . Ford . . . I want you so badly. I've always wanted you."

He removed his lips from her and hovered over her body, one arm on either side of her. Those lustful eyes were staring at him, begging him to take her. Begging him to end the torture that had consumed them for the last decade.

"I want you, too."

"Where are they?" she asked.

He stepped off the bed and walked over to the table, pulling a condom out of the drawer. Then, standing there, staring at beautiful Corrie, he slowly took off his clothes. Tossing his shirt on the floor, kicking his boots to the side, he removed his pants and boxers and everything else until he stood stark naked in front of her.

Her eyes roamed over him, taking in every inch of his body, before she kneeled on the bed and removed her own clothes. Perfection. All the buildup. All the holding out . . . It had been worth it to be with her in this moment.

She inched toward the edge of the bed, then stepped off, moving closer to him and taking the condom from his hands. With delicate movements, she tore open the wrapper and un-furled the condom onto his aching cock, then backed up onto the bed, opening her legs wide for him. A sight that would be forever imprinted in his mind.

Like a sculptor studying his next subject, he stared at her, taking her in. Memorizing each curve of her body and every wisp of her hair. His own body consumed by the pleasure of gazing upon her.

"Waiting for something?" she purred, her fingertips trailing along her breasts down her impossibly soft skin and toward her opening.

"I'm trying to take my time to make sure I remember this."

She smiled and propped her body up on one elbow as her other hand traced her sex, her fingers glistening with her own wetness. He had to pull on his cock to relieve the pressure.

"Don't worry. I won't let you forget."

He moved toward her, took her hand, and sucked her wetness off her fingers. Then, without any more hesitation, he thrust into her body, both of them simultaneously releasing moans that had clearly agonized them for the last several years. Warm fuzzies swathed his entire being. Not just from the physical pleasure of being inside her or the fact that he hadn't had sex in a few years. But from the desire seeping from her pores. She wanted him. It warranted repeating: she—Dr. Socorro Mejía—wanted *him*. And by the sound of her moans and the arch of her back, he satisfied her hunger. Being able to sate a woman like Corrie almost sent Ford over the edge.

"Why does this feel so good?" she asked, writhing underneath him.

He could have asked the same thing. Sure, it had been a while, but God . . . he'd never had sex like this. Sex where every thrust, every brush of friction, released a euphoric surge throughout his body. He smiled at her, then turned his blushing face away.

"What?" she asked through her own smiles.

"I feel like a silly teenager smiling at you. But my God, Corrie, you feel incredible."

She flashed him a sultry smile before reaching up and pulling his face toward hers for a kiss. Their mouths locked, tongues rolling over each other, and she wrapped her legs around his waist. The heat from her body was no match for the fire soaring through his veins, however. Every ounce of him was full with her spirit. Her presence. Every ounce of him wanted nothing more than to prolong this moment.

They twisted and turned until Ford's back lay flush with the mattress with Corrie perched atop his hips. With long, slow strokes, she rolled her hips against him, her hands steadying herself on his thighs. Like a goddess riding through the sky, her breasts swayed with her movements. He couldn't help but watch her, admiring her from his position below, taking in every movement. Every wisp of her hair. Every whimper in her throat. Did she have this effect on all men or only Ford?

She leaned over, placing one hand on the side of his head and the other on his chest. Her long locks fell all around them, shrouding his face in her coconut scent, intoxicating him more than he'd already been. She took his hand and placed it on her chest, and he massaged her soft breast, brushing her nipple between the pads of his thumb and index finger. Her delectable moans were pushing him to the limit.

"Ford . . ." she hummed. "Ford, you're going to make me come."

As if he needed any further encouragement. With one hand on her taut bud and the other guiding her hips, Ford drove into her until they both cried out in pure ecstasy. And Ford sank into complete and total infatuation.

Corrie Mejía could do anything she wanted with him. Chew him up. Spit him out. Fuck him hard then dispose of him in a dumpster. And he wouldn't care one bit. Because being with her, even for a moment, was worth any and all devastation that might follow.

CHAPTER

Fifteen

JUST FIVE MORE. FIVE MORE MINUTES AND THEN I'LL GO TO MY *tent.*

Five more minutes in the warmth of his bed and with the hum of his deep sleepy breath. Five more minutes to linger in his juniper scent.

At least, Corrie only *intended* to rest her eyes for five minutes and bask in the after-sex glow. And bask she did. Sex with Ford was better than she'd ever imagined. He knew her body better than any man. Knew what she wanted. Knew how to please her. Perhaps the last several days of penetration-less foreplay had helped him learn his way around her body, but she'd never had such a relaxed, seamless, and pleasurable first time.

Or second time.

Or third.

But so much for her intentions. The early-morning stillness settled over the camp, leaving no doubt, once she flicked open her eyelids, that she'd stayed well past the five intended minutes.

The view was nice, though.

She admired Ford, still asleep next to her, and his flawless body. He was a sexy sleeper, if there was such a thing. Maybe other men were sexy sleepers, too, not that Corrie would know. No, she never let sex turn into sleepovers. Sleepovers led to morning coffee. Which led to breakfast. And eventually to reading the morning paper together with your feet propped up on the coffee table, a dog on the rug underfoot, and children screaming in the background. No, Corrie's no-strings-attached lifestyle didn't lend itself to forming real relationships.

This thing with Ford? It was absolutely *not* a sleepover. And it was absolutely *not* a relationship. Things were just different in the jungle. The same rules didn't apply. Like in Vegas. Besides, like she and Ford could *ever* be in a relationship. Badass Mejía and Weak Sauce Matthews, the two most unlikely candidates for Couple of the Year. Corrie rolled her eyes and laughed at herself for the idea.

That didn't mean she couldn't enjoy the view for another minute or so . . .

No! You need to get back to your tent!

With subtle movements, Corrie rolled out of bed and searched for her clothes among the sea of discarded articles scattered about the floor. It had seemed so calm in the moment, so why did his tent look messy? Each movement had been fluid at the time—so . . . right. It was funny to see the aftermath this morning; their mess was a metaphor for their chaotic relationship.

No. Not a *relationship*. She needed to quit using that word. A relationship between the two of them was an impossibility. With their personality conflicts and Corrie's aversion to feelings, not to mention the fact that they literally lived on opposite sides of the country, at best they could be sexy stopovers when traveling. Nothing more.

Why didn't that sit right with her?

She picked up his T-shirt as she looked for her own, then brought the shirt to her nose, closing her eyes to inhale. The prior evening flooded back to her. The two of them in bed. Talking. Sharing. Comforting. Her heart swelled, recalling those feelings. The feelings of someone actually wanting to know her. Of seeing her for something more than a sex symbol or a bossy bitch.

Oh God.

Corrie had . . . *feelings* for Ford. And not just the kind that made her panties wet.

She tore the shirt away from her face and tossed it several feet away like it contained an infectious disease.

"Do I really smell that bad?"

Corrie jumped at Ford's low timbre, shooting her gaze over to where he was watching her from the bed with his head propped up by his hand. His mischievous smile sent a warm wave over her body, pulling at her to climb back into that toasty bed and snuggle against his red-hot body.

"How long have you been awake?" she asked.

"Long enough to catch you judging my stinky clothes . . ." Far from it. Ford never smelled—not bad, at least. Even after long days working in the sweltering jungle, he still smelled delightful. "And long enough to catch you sneaking off."

"I'm not sneaking." She scrunched her face when she said that, since she had clearly been sneaking. "It's just . . . it's already getting light out and I should get to my tent before people start getting up."

"What time is it?" he asked, motioning toward his watch on the table beside the bed.

"It's a little after five."

"That's it?" he said, smiling and rolling out from under the covers, revealing his naked body in all its glory. There went Corrie's feelings again . . . though this time the ones that got her hot. "No one gets up this early except Agnes."

He reached over to the table for his glasses, sitting with legs spread on the side of the bed, his cock starting to stiffen. Why? Why did the gods tempt her like this?

"I see you looking," he said with a smirk.

Corrie grabbed her shirt from the floor, then stood in front of him. "Well, Ford, it's kind of hard not to when you're sitting stark naked in front of me and it's doing *that*," she said, pointing at his growing erection.

"Well, *Corrie*, it's kind of hard for it *not* to be doing that when you're crawling around on the floor in nothing but your bra and underwear. Come here," he said, pulling her toward him by the waist. She stood between his legs and looked at him, running her fingers through his hair and letting her shirt fall onto the bed as he massaged his hands over her body.

"Last night was nice," he said.

"Nice? Wow, what a compliment," she replied with a smile.

"I mean, the *sex* was incredible . . ." He flashed that sexy smile. "But I was referring to everything else. Thank you for making me feel better . . . for not leaving me to stew in my mind by myself."

"Anytime."

"Really? *Any*time?"

Uh-oh. That simple one-word question held a lot of meaning. Ford wasn't simply asking her if he could give her a call whenever he was down. No, his inflection signaled he was asking if there was something more to their situation. Something more than what was happening in the jungle.

As if he was curious about what might happen once they left. Shit. Ford was developing feelings, too.

"Yep!" she said, leaning to kiss his forehead and shimmying out of his grasp. "Except for right now because I should get going before it gets too late."

Like a Tasmanian devil, Corrie tore through the tent, Ford sitting on the bed all the while, silently laughing to himself as he also got ready, though with much less chaos. With a flick of her wrists, she twisted her hair into a high, messy bun, then squatted to lace her boots.

"You know you can admit it," Ford said, zipping his pants next to her.

"Admit what?" she asked, cocking her head to the side as she looked at him.

"Admit that you like me. You don't need to run off like that."

"I told you . . . I don't want anyone to see me—"

As she stood from her crouched position, Ford pulled her into his arms and planted a kiss on her lips. And in an instant, Corrie's body turned into goo. She let him take her. Take all of her. Giving in to his kiss.

She melted into his arms, completely lacking any ability to pull away. She didn't need to say the words—her actions told him everything he needed to know. She liked him. A lot. If each passing minute didn't increase the odds that they'd get caught, she would have pushed him back on that bed and torn off the clothes she'd spent so much time searching for.

Their lips pulled apart, and he stared at her with a smarmy grin.

"I hate you," she said, her lips pursed into a smile.

"I know you do." He planted another quick kiss on her lips and sat back on the edge of the bed to put on his shoes. "You'd better get going before someone sees you," he said, giving her a light tap on the ass.

Corrie couldn't help but smile. But as she turned to leave, a rapping came from the outside of the tent.

"Ford? Ford, are you awake?"

Ford and Corrie froze at the sound of Ethan's voice. They glanced at each other, assessing the situation. Both had on clothes. And it wasn't *super* obvious what Corrie was doing there. So she shrugged, giving him unspoken approval to answer.

"Yeah, come on in, Ethan," Ford called out.

Corrie braced herself for the inevitable confusion on Ethan's face. Three, two, one . . .

"Hey . . ." he said, wrinkling his brow at the sight of the two of them together so early in the morning and halting in place. "What's going on?"

Ford finished tying his boot and popped up from the bed. "Corrie came by to discuss today's plan."

"Never took you for much of a morning person," Ethan said to her. The skepticism in Ethan's voice couldn't be missed.

"I'd like to finish this dig before Christmas, that's all," Corrie retorted. If there was one thing that couldn't be questioned, it was Corrie's sass.

"What is it, Ethan?" Ford cut in, clearly trying to draw attention from Corrie's presence in his tent in the wee morning hour.

Ethan's eyes lingered on Corrie for another second, clearly not buying their act, but a moment later he turned his attention back toward Ford. "We've got a problem."

"What sort of problem?"

"You might want to come with me." He didn't wait before exiting the tent, leaving Corrie and Ford to exchange glances. Even though he'd only come for Ford, they both followed.

What on earth could be so important this early in the morning?

The camp had only started to stir for the day, and those who were awake were paying little attention to Ford, Corrie, and Ethan trudging through the camp. Past the tents. Past the bathrooms. And straight for the storage facilities.

They stopped in front of the structure on the outskirts of the camp, not a problem to be seen. Perhaps this was all a ruse. Perhaps Ethan had known she was in Ford's tent and was simply wanting to confront them.

Though that made no sense. Sure, they had a history and probably *shouldn't* be sleeping together for many reasons. But sex on digs wasn't an anomaly. Given Corrie's attitude toward sex and relationships, frankly, she was surprised that last night was the first time she'd ever done it on a job.

"Okay, Ethan, what's the problem?" Ford asked.

"See anything unusual?"

Corrie scanned the structure—everything seemed to be in order. No holes in the siding. Lock secure. Roof attached.

"Everything looks normal to me," Ford responded.

"Yeah, that's what I thought, too. But look here . . ." Ethan said, pointing at the lock, "Someone's been tampering with this."

Corrie and Ford moved in closer, peering at the metal latch for the lock. The screws were stripped and there were gouges in the siding around it, as if someone had tried to remove the entire hinge rather than cut off the lock. What the . . . ?

"Sunny and I got up early today to catalog some of the smaller items we found yesterday," Ethan continued as they inspected the structure. "I didn't notice it at first, but the hinge had a distinct jiggle when I opened it. A jiggle that's never been there before."

"Was anything taken from inside?" Ford asked.

Ethan shook his head. "Not that I could see. I went through the entire list. But someone was clearly trying to get in."

"Robbers, you think?"

"Who can say? Someone might have found out what we were doing here. Followed the supply truck, perhaps."

"We might have to put someone on security watch."

"Guys," Corrie chimed in, "what if it was someone on the inside? Someone already here in camp?"

"What? No way!" Ford protested. "I personally vetted most of these people, and the others are employees of our investor. He wouldn't select someone who might be a thief."

"We don't know that. People do strange things when money is involved," Corrie said, and noticed a slight awkward shift in Ford's stance. "It could be anyone in this camp."

"Yeah, but except for the three of us, since we have our own tents, you'd think someone might notice if one of their tentmates took off in the middle of the night," Ethan said.

Ford's hand brushed against Corrie's, signaling how Ethan had no clue what had been going on in Ford's tent last night. But now wasn't the time for flirting.

"People get up in the middle of the night to go to the bathroom. Clearly, whoever did this didn't succeed. They might have realized they were taking too long and went back to their bunk. For now," Corrie pointed out.

"Okay. Then what are you saying? Since we can't trust

anyone except maybe the three of us, we send everyone else home and start fresh with a new crew?" Ethan asked.

Ford quickly snatched his hand away as he straightened up. "What? No! That would take months. We don't have months."

Corrie eyed Ford curiously. Sure, no one wanted to be out here longer than necessary, but starting over with a new crew really would be the only way they could guarantee that the source of the attempted theft didn't come from within, and something about the way Ford protested seemed off.

Like he had a different timeline than everyone else.

"Okay, then, what do you think we should do?" Corrie asked.

Ford glanced between the three of them and the structure, then paced while stroking his chin. "We keep this to ourselves for now. Just the three of us. We don't let anyone else know there might be a thief among us. But we keep watch. Note anything fishy. And if we discover the knife or any remains, we figure out a plan to keep them guarded at all times. If that means one of us sleeps with that damn knife under our bed, then so be it."

"If that's the plan, then we shouldn't be loitering around here anymore. Someone might notice and get suspicious," Corrie said.

"You're right. Let's head back. And remember, trust no one," Ford said.

"We can trust each other, though, right?" Ethan asked. "I mean, I think I trust the two of you, but I'm sure we all have our own motivations for being here . . ."

Fair question. Though she could trust Ford. Whenever they weren't in the field, they were in his bed. She would have noticed by now. Not that she wanted Ethan to know that.

And Ethan was as honest as the day was long. Like that time he'd admitted to their professor that he hadn't done the assigned reading instead of bullshitting his way through the answer like the rest of them.

"What are you trying to say, Ethan?" Ford asked, his voice growing impatient. "I know where I was last night. Do you?"

"I'm just trying to say . . . it seems like something's been bothering you lately. You've been even more irritable than usual. Is there something else going on that we should know about?"

Ford's nostrils flared and his eyes widened. Oh no.

"Perhaps I'm irritable because of accusations like this. Or maybe I'd just like to get out of this goddamn jungle sometime before the end of this year."

"I'm not accusing you of anything, I just—"

"Save your feigned concern. We've got work to do."

Ford stormed off to the camp, leaving Corrie and a stunned Ethan in his wake. Irritable was only the half of it. Just a week and a half in and she'd seen all sorts of reactions from Ford. But none like this. Ethan had questioned his integrity, and that clearly didn't sit well with him.

"I didn't mean it to come off that way," Ethan said to her once Ford was out of earshot.

"Well, what way *did* you mean it to come off? Because to me it sounded like you were accusing Ford of being the thief."

"He's still acting weird. And not in his normal Ford way. Like last night . . . again, with the calls . . ." he said, his voice trailing off.

Corrie debated revealing Ford's confidences for a moment. On one hand, it wasn't any of Ethan's business. But on the other, she had to clear Ford's name.

"It's his mom. She's really sick, Ethan. And he's worried he might not make it back before she passes away. He'll never forgive himself if that happens."

"Oh no . . . God, I'm an asshole. Why didn't he say anything?"

"Because you know how he is."

"I know, but I thought he and I were friends. I mean, I know I asked you to talk to him, but I can't believe he'd tell you all this but not me. It hurts, you know?"

She shrugged. "Maybe he feels like I already pass enough judgment on him, so what's the difference if he reveals his insecurities to me, too."

"Well, do you think those insecurities might cause him to do something extreme?"

"You mean break into the storage structure to steal the artifacts he's been hired to find?" Corrie lifted her brow. "No, Ethan, I don't."

"But how do we know that?"

There was no way around it. Ethan needed an answer, and Corrie couldn't lie to him.

"Because I was with him."

"Wait . . . what?"

Corrie sighed. "Last night. I stayed the night with him. When you found us this morning, I was getting ready to leave. That's how I know. He never left the tent. I was with him the entire night and would have noticed if he'd left."

Now Ethan was the one with wide eyes.

"Are you going to stand there staring at me without saying a word? Go ahead. Let's have it," she said, palms face up and waving as if to say, *Bring on the teasing comments.*

"I . . . I have no words. Just, wow. How long has this been going on?"

She sighed again. "Oh, I don't know, Ethan. I mean, there's always been something lurking between us, I suppose. But as far as this dig is concerned, a couple of days."

"I can't say that I'm surprised. I always knew he had a thing for you. I mean, it was obvious that your beef with each other was fueled by your sexual tension. I've never seen two people who needed to fuck more than you." He smiled, causing Corrie to laugh and easing her nerves. "And I have to admit, when I asked you to talk to him, I sort of hoped you two would finally bury that beef. I love you both, and I know you two never wanted to see it, but you're pretty perfect for each other."

Corrie smiled. Yeah, she could see it now, too.

"I hope you can understand why we didn't say anything about it earlier."

"Of course, Corrie. Your sex life is no one's business but your own."

"I know, but people talk. And I don't need anything to give actual cause to the reputation that I have."

"Still with that magazine spread?"

She rolled her eyes. "Always. Seriously, you'd think I'd posed for *Playboy*."

"I hope you don't take this the wrong way, but for any archaeologist or aspiring archaeologist over the age of fourteen, it was better than *Playboy*." He tried to make light of the situation. "Seriously, a living, breathing, gorgeous woman interested in digging up bones and playing in the dirt? You're young Indiana Jones's wet dream. The Latina Elsa from *The Last Crusade*. Or, better yet, a real-life Lara Croft."

"Did you just compare me to a Nazi?"

"You know what I mean. Come on, Corrie. I'm trying to lighten the mood."

"I know you are. But look . . . I don't want anyone to know about this, okay? It's bad enough that Ford got picked for this job instead of me in the first place. The last thing I need is for word to get out that we slept together, giving people another reason not to take me seriously."

"Your secret's safe with me. Now, come on. Let's go look for some bones. Unless you've had your fill of bone hunting for the day," he said with a sly look in his eye.

Corrie laughed and rolled her eyes. "I've always got time for a bone hunt or two."

Sixteen

WHEN WERE THEY GOING TO FIND SOME GODDAMNED BONES on this dig? Or that tecpatl? Something? Anything aside from boring household items that could have belonged to anyone? Maybe on any other dig, Ford would have been ecstatic upon finding a wooden bowl, but not now. Not when the stakes were this high.

Everything Corrie had predicted was right. An adobe structure hidden in a bowl-shaped landscape. The cave. The river. But after seven days straight of digging at the new site without a single day off, they still hadn't hit the jackpot. And the cave hadn't resulted in jack shit.

Unless the thief had gotten to it first.

Ford had been on edge ever since they'd discovered the storage hut had been tampered with. He didn't want to believe that someone on their team could have been the culprit—they'd been a family these last three months. Even Vautour's guys. He enjoyed talking with Lance as much as he enjoyed his time with Ethan. And you didn't steal from family.

Well, maybe some people did. But so far, no one from their team had vanished, and no one seemed off, so even if the thief *was* someone among their ranks, they probably hadn't found anything, either. Otherwise, what were they still doing there?

Ford's mind raced in bed that morning, running through each member of their team and analyzing the likelihood that they were the bad guys, all while stroking his fingertips over Corrie's bare shoulder next to him. Corrie was the only thing making this dig bearable. Even on the roughest of days, the ones when they found nothing and news of his mother only worsened, once he found himself beside Corrie at night, all his worries faded to the background. Some days he imagined this was their home. That they could stay here forever.

But that was an impossibility. Someday, and likely soon, they'd all have to go back to their normal lives.

What would that mean for Ford and Corrie? Would that be the end of their tryst? Would they go their separate ways, living on opposite ends of the country?

One thing was certain—he had to come clean to her about the circumstances that had brought them here if he had any hope that there would be something more between them. But the moment never seemed right. And if ever the moment felt right, Corrie would do something sweet and caring that would make him question whether he wanted to mess up such a perfect moment by revealing how big an asshole he really was.

Perhaps things would be better if they simply said their goodbyes at the end of all this and she never knew the truth. Corrie didn't deserve to be hurt—again. She deserved so much more than she'd been given credit for. Who knew that behind all that sass and beauty was the smartest, kindest, most badass chick ever?

He didn't deserve her.

"What are you thinking about?" her sweet voice asked, startling him out of his thoughts.

Was this it? Was this the *right* moment? His opportunity to tell her the truth?

"I was thinking about the attempted break-in."

Chicken. Corrie sat up, her tits perky as ever and barely concealed in that flimsy white tank top she liked to sleep in—and that he liked her sleeping in, too. Like he could change the subject now. Not when she was looking at him like that.

"Babe, you're going to send yourself to an early grave if you keep festering about that," she said, running her long, smooth fingers across his chest.

Babe?

"Did you call me 'babe'?" he asked. No woman had ever called him *babe*, and certainly not a mere week into their relationship.

Wait. Relationship? Was that what was happening between them?

Her eyes went wide, and she opened her mouth to answer, but a light rap on the door pulled their attention away. "Shit," he muttered as he climbed out of bed and pulled on some clothes. Corrie didn't bother hiding, but Ford knew better than to reveal her whereabouts as he squeezed out the door to find Sunny standing there with a worried look upon her face.

"Sunny, what is it?"

"Are you sick?" she asked.

Ford shook his head as he wrinkled his brow. Sick? Sick with what?

"We think it's food poisoning. From the dessert," Sunny continued. "Half the camp is lined up at the TTs."

Ford peered around the corner of his tent, and sure enough, several of the crew stood hunched over and holding their stomachs, waiting to use the bathroom. Ford and Corrie had been so quick to get to his tent the night before that they'd passed on dessert. Guess it had been a wise move.

"Are you serious?"

"Dead serious. Agnes is beside herself, claiming she'll never cook again."

"Where's Ethan?"

"Puking his brains out."

"What about you?"

Sunny shrugged her shoulders. "I don't eat sugar."

Wait . . . all that energy was . . . natural? Ford internally shook away the thought with a laugh.

"What are we going to do?" Sunny asked.

Good question. What *were* they going to do? They couldn't exactly go out in the middle of the jungle with half the crew keeled over with food poisoning.

"I don't know. I need some time to think. Let me finish getting dressed and I'll find you in a bit," he said, returning inside and leaving Sunny on the porch.

He walked over to the bed and collapsed on his back next to Corrie, then ran his hands over his face.

"What's wrong?" she asked.

"They've all got food poisoning," he said, muffled by his hands.

"Then that settles it. We're taking a day off," she said.

With a swift movement, he tore his hands from his face. "We can't take a day off." They needed to push on if he was going to get the money for his mom's treatment.

"Ford, it's food poisoning. We can't expect people to work

out there with diapers and barf bags. Thank God that's all it is, though. In a day or two, everyone will be back to normal. Besides, you need a day to clear your head."

"I'm not going to be able to take my mind off the dig." Or his mom.

"Really? Because I can think of some ways to take your mind off things," she said, reaching her hand under the waistband of his boxers and stroking his cock. He closed his eyes, taking in the delicate touch of her fingertips along his skin.

"Well, that's certainly working," he said, pulling his lower lip between his teeth.

"I can do this all day. Or we can do other things," she said, shifting her body to straddle him, their underwear providing little by way of a barrier between their insatiable bodies.

"People are definitely going to talk if we're in here all day with the window flaps closed." Not that he cared what other people said if that meant she was going to keep rolling her hips against him the way she was doing right now.

"Then we go somewhere else. We can go explore. Go for a swim."

"In the river? It's way too fast in this area."

"No, Weak Sauce," she said, nudging him in the side. "Down below. There's a huge pool below the waterfall. And we can bring a blanket to fuck on when we're done."

"I like that idea," he said with a waggle in his brow.

"I knew you would. Now, I'm going to head to my tent, get some things, snag some snacks, while you make your way around camp, letting everyone know they've got the day off," she said, hopping off the bed and leaving Ford hanging.

Well, maybe the opposite of hanging. His erection stood at full attention.

"Do you have to leave right this second? Maybe stay a few more minutes?" Between his hard-on and the desperation in his voice, there was no hiding the obviousness of his request. He had to pull at the fabric of his boxers to relieve the pressure.

But judging by her smirk and her lack of hesitation as she put on her clothes, it was clear Corrie had other plans. "We'll get to that," she said with a smile that would be sweet if Ford didn't know the meaning behind it. "But first we need to clear our schedules. I want the whole day with you, Ford. Not only another five minutes before I need to sneak away again. I want you all to myself with no time constraints. No duties. No thinking about Aztecs or archaeology. Just the two of us fucking in the jungle without a care in the world for one day."

How could it be that Corrie's little speech about fucking in the jungle was the most romantic thing he'd ever heard?

"Can't wait."

Today. He'd tell her the truth today.

· · · · · · · · ·

"WHEN DID YOU DECIDE YOU WANTED TO BE AN ARCHAEOLOGIST?" Ford asked as they treaded water in the crystal-blue pool below the waterfall.

"Uh-uh. No archaeology, remember?" she responded, playfully flicking water in his direction with her foot.

"I'm not asking about archaeology. I'm asking about you. I want to know what brought you to this point in your life. I want to know how Dr. Socorro Mejía came to be."

"Why in God's name would you want to know that?" she asked, making a silly face.

"Oh, it's part of my next term's curriculum—how to end up swimming naked at the base of a spectacular waterfall in the middle of the Mexican jungle with Dr. Ford Matthews. It's a working title."

She laughed with the full-throated laugh he loved. Excellent. Now she was nice and relaxed. The perfect opportunity to ease into the Conversation. Get her talking about the start of her career. Learn more about her interest in Chimalli and the importance of her being on this dig in an effort to focus on the positives and not his deception.

You know . . . deceive her into thinking it was no big deal that he'd snatched this job out from under her without her even knowing.

"Seriously, though. Was it Indiana like everyone else? Or because of your ancestry?"

She pursed her lips. "Let's talk about something else instead. Or, better yet, we can skip the talking and do *other* things with our mouths," she said before she disappeared beneath the surface of the water. Typical Corrie. Avoiding any topic that focused on her. Even when he tried to lighten things up with a joke, she never took the bait. And despite how perfect everything seemed between them—*seemed* was the operative word.

Because . . . the day itself *was* perfect. The team was grateful for the break. The hike down to the waterfall had been unhurried and stress-free. The crisp blue water was both refreshing and calming, with the sounds of the waterfall resonating through the air. And Corrie . . . Corrie was carefree and comforting.

She was perfect.

But Ford needed to come clean, and for once he could be assured they wouldn't have any interruptions. Today was the day, even if his attempts to ease into a tough conversation were going to hell. He couldn't afford to put it off any longer. And maybe . . . just maybe, Corrie's carefree attitude meant she might actually take the news okay.

Maybe kick some more water at his face, then play-dunk him under the water before taking him—again—on the picnic blanket.

God . . . he really was a piece of shit.

No. He had to do this now.

She swam toward him through the clear water like a mermaid. Something else to add to the growing list of Corrie's talents. Slowly, she emerged from below mere inches in front of him, droplets clinging to the delicate features of her face as she smiled with that sexy-as-hell smile intended to make him forget about the conversation they needed to have.

"Corrie . . . we need to talk," he said.

"Do we, though?" She nuzzled closer, tangling her legs around his own, almost crushing his will to resist. It couldn't prevent his lower half from involuntarily reacting, though. Hot, naked woman pressed against his body? Yeah . . . his dick couldn't fight back the blood pumping through his veins.

"Please don't do that," he managed to eke out as she planted soft kisses along his neck and jawline. "I'm trying to have a serious conversation here."

"My origin story doesn't qualify as a serious conversation," she teased, nipping at his skin. "Besides, we have serious conversations all the time. Come on, I don't want to talk about work. Let's let loose and relax while we have some peace and quiet. Enjoy each other without distractions and having to hide."

"I don't want to talk about work, either. I want to talk about you . . . and me . . . and what we're doing here."

She froze and inched away with her eyes wide as a doe in the headlights. Shit. That didn't come out right.

"No, not like that," he tried to explain. "I'm not talking about our relationship—"

"Relationship?" A nervous laugh escaped her lips. "Ford, you know how I feel about—"

Hmm. He didn't really like the way she laughed at that. But, no . . . that wasn't where he was trying to go with this conversation, though that was a conversation for another day. If she didn't kill him before then.

"No, that's not what I mean—"

"Then what *do* you mean?"

"Well, if you'd give me a minute, I can explain—"

"Shh!" She lunged forward and placed her hand over his mouth. But when he went to pry it away, she shushed him again. "Listen," she whispered. "Do you hear that?"

He lifted his head and listened to the sounds around him. "I don't hear anything. If this is your way of trying to change the subject—"

"No. Wait . . ."

They stilled, trying to hear over the crashing waterfall, when . . . there. There it was.

"Ford?" a faint voice called out.

"Dr. Matthews? Dr. Mejía?" called another.

"Corrie? Ford?"

Their names were being called in the distance.

"That sounds like Ethan," Ford said.

"And Sunny. And they're getting closer."

The possibility of getting caught was always there. Heck, Ethan had almost caught them the day before. But not like this. Not when completely naked with a hard-on that refused to go away. And not with one of Ford's students there to see. And who knew? Maybe there were more of them searching for Corrie and Ford. Maybe the whole team would pop out of the jungle at any moment, catching Corrie in the exact kind of scandal that she'd so desperately fought to avoid.

Luckily, their things were well hidden under a tree where they'd enjoyed a shady respite from the sun. Unluckily, they couldn't chance running toward it in time to get dressed. Ford and Corrie twirled through the water, each looking for an escape route. But with the voices getting closer, they had no time.

"I think I see something," Corrie said, pulling on Ford's arm and swimming *toward* the waterfall.

"What are you doing?" he asked.

"Look," she said, staring into the cascade. "We can hide on the other side."

Ford cocked back his head. "The other side? Corrie, have you lost all sense?"

"No. Check it out," she said, before disappearing beneath the surface. He tried to reach for her hand, but he was too late.

Ford's heart rate increased. With the churning falls, he couldn't see below the surface. Not that the falls were massive by any stretch, but they still pounded the surface of the water with a steady thrum. Where was she? Where did she go?

Ford could swim, but he couldn't swim *that* well. And he didn't know CPR. Panic settled over him. How long had it been? Thirty seconds? A minute?

He lifted his hands to scream out her name, not worrying anymore about Ethan, Sunny, or anyone else who might be looking for them, when, suddenly, there she was, waving at him from the other side of the sheet of water. What the . . . ?

She signaled for him to follow her. This was a *horrible* idea.

Sure, Corrie had made it under. But Corrie was a badass who could do pretty much anything.

Well, here goes nothing.

Ford took off his glasses, clutched them in his hand, took a deep breath, then prayed for his survival as he plunged beneath the falls. With the churning water, it was hard to see where he was going. Even harder without the aid of his glasses. He swam with his arms outstretched in front of him to avoid butting his head into a rock as the crashing falls beat against his skin. But the beating faded along with the deafening noise. Once he determined he was out of harm's way, Ford slowly rose to the surface and found Corrie staring at him with a huge smile on her face.

"That was incredibly dangerous," he said, putting his glasses back on, as if he could see any better with water-covered spectacles. "What if something had happened to one of us?"

She rolled her eyes. "Ford, you really need to live a little. We're fine. It wasn't even that bad. Now, come on . . . How awesome is this?" she asked, lifting her head and gazing at the cavernous space.

Ford closed his eyes and let out a huge sigh. *Live a little.* Tipping back his head with his face toward the ceiling of the cave, he opened his eyes and took in his surroundings. Jagged, wet rock defined the space. Cold, damp. Yet beautiful.

"Wow . . ."

"Wow is right," Corrie said, sidling up beside him as they stared into the dark space.

"How did we not notice this hours ago?" he asked, unable to stop his eyes roving over their backdrop.

"That waterfall. It's like a curtain."

The instant she said the word, Ford and Corrie snapped their gazes to each other. "'Nature's curtain,'" Ford said. "The real one."

"Oh my God, Ford. This is it. *This* is Chimalli's hiding place!"

It would make some sense, seeing as the cave they'd previously found hadn't amounted to anything.

"Do you think it's possible? I mean, to come through the water every time?"

"I don't know . . . maybe. What's up there?" she said, pointing to a crack in the rock.

"It's too dark to see," Ford said. Corrie started climbing onto the rock. "Corrie, wait. You won't be able to see a thing up there. I know you want me to live a little, but I want you to live, too, and that's a recipe for disaster."

She sighed. "Fine. You're right. I'll be right back," she said, swimming toward the waterfall.

"Where are you going?"

"I've got a waterproof flashlight in my bag. I'm going to get it. Wait here."

And she disappeared again.

The cave felt colder and darker without her. *As if that wasn't the most appropriate metaphor.* He shook his head. Way to come clean. But could she blame him? This clearly wasn't any old cave. And it ticked all the boxes—nature's curtain, close to the bowl, damp and hidden. And the other cave hadn't led to a single artifact. They'd assumed it was simply because Chimalli must not have left anything in it. Which could still be the case. But with Corrie hot on the trail with this new potential discovery, Ford would be hard-pressed to resume their prior conversation anytime soon.

Moments later, Corrie popped up from the water wearing a black tank top. "Here," she said, tossing Ford a pair of sopping-wet boxers.

"Seriously?"

"Hey, I'm not about to embark on what might be the biggest Aztec discovery in a hundred years while naked and staring at each other's genitals."

Fair point.

"Did you see anyone out there?" he asked as he pulled on the boxers underneath the water.

She shook her head and flicked on the flashlight. "No, they must have moved on." She shined the light around the cave, taking in every inch of the damp space. "Come on."

They carefully made their way up the slippery rocks, a task made even more treacherous without shoes. If this *was* the place, it was going to be a bitch to work in. But they took their time, inching along the stone toward the narrow slit in the surface. Corrie reached her arm in to shine the light inside and sucked in a breath.

"What? What is it?" Ford asked, unable to see around her.

Corrie turned back toward Ford, her face full of relief and something else . . . What was it?

Disappointment? Loss?

Sorrow?

"We found him," she said, tears filling her eyes. "Ford . . . we found him. All of them."

"All of them?"

She nodded. "There are three bodies in there . . . two adults and a child."

A . . . child? Wait . . .

"It has to be them. Chimalli, Yaretzi, and their child. I mean, what are the chances that they could be anyone else?"

"Let me see," he said, inching closer and taking the flashlight.

With his outstretched arm, he leaned into the crevice, illuminating the tight space. And there . . . on the ground were the remains of three bodies, clearly two adults and a child, like Corrie had described.

But if this was Chimalli and his family, that meant they hadn't made their way to a local village to live out their days like Corrie had predicted.

Meaning Corrie wasn't a descendant of Chimalli after all.

Seventeen

S HE'D DREAMED OF THIS MOMENT HUNDREDS OF TIMES SINCE she'd read her first Hannah Hollis book. Finding Chimalli. Confirming her ancestry. Being someone. Hannah Hollis and her archaeological adventures had given Corrie something to aspire to. And once her grandfather had told her that they were descendants of an Aztec warrior, she'd become obsessed. Obsessed with being the person to find this fabled warrior who no man had been able to find. Her discovery would prove to all those girls from junior high school that she'd amounted to more than a bimbo. Prove to everyone who'd underestimated her that she was a triple threat—beauty, brawn, *and* brains.

In terms of archaeological digs, their discovery was the equivalent of hitting the jackpot. Three bodies. Drawings on the cave walls that told the story of who they were and how they'd come to rest in that cave. And even what appeared to be the hilt of a knife, adorned with turquoise and a shell mosaic, poking out from beneath the dirt. It was Chimalli, no doubt about it.

There was so much to take in that their hour or so in the cave only scratched the surface, and half that time was spent merely working out the logistics. They'd know more once they returned with better lighting and tools—and definitely some clothes and shoes—but waterproof gear was a must. And the space wasn't big enough for more than a few people, so they'd have to plan accordingly. But they had found everything they'd hoped to find and then some. Corrie was right—it was the greatest Aztec discovery in a hundred years.

So why, now that they'd found Chimalli, didn't she feel like she'd accomplished her goal? Why did it feel like a failure?

At least she wasn't naked when it had happened.

At least Corrie garnered some relief finally having found Chimalli. At least now she could get on with her life, once this dig wrapped up, without it hanging over her head anymore. What that life looked like, however, was anyone's guess.

The walk to camp was relatively quiet. The day had started out so perfectly, but then Ford had to go mess it up with his prodding questions and talking about their *relationship*.

Sigh. She couldn't be mad at him for wanting to talk about where they were going with this whole thing. It's not like she could avoid the topic and hope that on the last day they could go their separate ways without ever having to mention the future.

Or admitting to the fact that she'd grown feelings for him and didn't *want* them to go their separate ways.

No, Ford hadn't ruined the day. Chimalli had. Or, rather, based on what she'd gathered from the drawings on the cave wall, whatever affliction had overcome Yaretzi and their child had ruined the day. Hopefully she'd learn more with better lighting. So many people had told her that there was no way she was a descendant of an Aztec warrior. As it turned out, despite all her protests, they'd been right. Leaving her a gullible fool.

With her grandfather gone, she'd never get a chance to confront him. Thankfully, her father wasn't one for *I told you so*s. He'd never believed her grandpa, anyway. And though she'd surely get a ribbing or two from her brother, eventually everyone would forget about her obsession with finding her *ancestor*.

Hopefully.

But her disappointment couldn't be masked. She'd almost cried when she'd first seen the bones, and not from happiness. Ford must have sensed it, too—as excited as he should have been for their discovery, his subdued reaction told her that he understood her disappointment. They went from smiling, laughing, and making love to analytical, emotionless diagnostics.

God, why couldn't they have just spent the day having sex without thinking about anything, like she'd planned? Today should have been a day to put all their troubles out of their minds for a bit. And now she was sulking around and avoiding having any more *real* conversations with Ford, which probably only added to his stress.

She was a self-centered piece of garbage. Here they were, having made a *huge* discovery, and she was having a private pity party in her head.

"Hannah Hollis," she said, breaking the silence and looking straight ahead as they walked to camp.

"Huh?"

"You asked when I knew I wanted to be an archaeologist. It was after I read *Hannah Hollis and the Search for the Jade Dragon*."

"Hannah Hollis," he repeated, as if trying to place the name. "That was that series by Denise Phillips, right?"

"Mm-hmm. Ten books in total, and I devoured every single

one, starting in seventh grade. One after another . . . Hannah Hollis was my escape."

"Escape from what?"

Corrie looked at her muddy boots as they trekked through the jungle. This was the part she'd wanted to avoid when he'd asked her at the waterfall earlier.

She chewed on the inside of her mouth before finally answering. "Escape from the other girls in my school. They weren't . . . they weren't fond of me. It was a new school and, well, let's just say that I drew a lot of unwanted attention from the boys because I was a little more . . . developed than the other girls that age."

"Did they bully you?"

She laugh-cried. "Tormented me is more like it. When the boys weren't snapping my bra, the girls were calling me 'whore,' and spreading rumors about me letting a whole slew of boys feel me up. I never even kissed a boy until the summer before my senior year of high school, yet by midyear in seventh grade, I'd earned the reputation as school slut."

Ford stopped her, grabbing her by the shoulders to face him. "Corrie, that's horrible. I'm sorry I even brought it up."

"It's okay. You didn't know."

"That doesn't make it okay."

"No, it's fine, Ford. I mean, I push you all the time to talk about things you don't want to talk about. I suppose it's only fair that you do the same to me."

"When you push me, it's because you're trying to help me. This? This is me being nosy."

"Well, maybe that's what I need. Maybe it will be good to get it off my chest. No pun intended," she said with a slight smile.

"Why do you do that? How do you make light of your body when it's been a source of constant trouble for you?"

"I wasn't always like this. I used to be insecure about my body. That twelve-year-old girl? She hated the attention it got. But the school librarian told me about Hannah Hollis, who led this double life, one as an outcast and the other as an adventurer. By the end of the series, Hannah had proved to everyone who'd ever doubted her that she was a force to be reckoned with. So, once I realized that those girls were likely jealous and insecure themselves, I determined that I was going to show them, show everyone, that *Socorro Mejía* was a force to be reckoned with. And that meant, among other things, taking control of my body. I can't help the instant judgment it garners me. We all make snap judgments about people based on the way they look. Judgments about me just happen to be focused on my sexuality and often a presumed lack of intelligence. That'll never go away. But I don't hate my body anymore.

"I suppose it's probably a defense mechanism, though. The jokes, I mean. If I make the jokes first, then others don't have the opportunity to do so. It's part of being in control of my own body. The same reason I didn't want to talk about this earlier, because it wasn't something *I* brought up."

"You could have told me about Hannah Hollis without mentioning the rest of it."

"But that wouldn't be the whole story. I got into archaeology because I wanted an escape from my insecurities by desiring to emulate a badass female archaeologist."

"Well, you've succeeded," he said, smiling at her. But Corrie's shoulders deflated and she looked away. "Corrie . . . I know you're disappointed. I know you were convinced of your ancestry." He tucked a loose, wavy hair behind her ear.

"I feel like such a fool. My grandfather told me we were descendants of Chimalli. I mean, why would he do that?"

"Maybe because you were in pain and were into those Hannah Hollis books, he told you a story to boost your self-esteem." He wrapped his hands around her waist.

"By lying to me? And even worse, he made a liar out of me! I've been spouting off this story for the last two decades, and it was all nonsense. I should have listened to my parents. They tried to tell me not to believe my grandpa and that he was fond of tall tales. But, Ford, he even had fake documentation."

"Then maybe he was convinced, himself. And you didn't *know* it wasn't true, so you couldn't have been lying. That was your truth."

Corrie rolled her eyes. "Sounds like something my grandfather would say to defend his actions. But the truth always comes out. And the only thing that's worse than a liar is one who tries to convince you the lie was for your own good."

Ford paused, his hands falling to his sides. Something clearly on his mind.

"Corrie, there's something—"

But movement behind him caught her eye. "Wait," she said, crouching.

Ford groaned. "Not this again."

"No, seriously. Look. Over there," she said, pointing through the trees. "Is that . . . is that Sunny sneaking around?"

"What?"

Ford crouched next to Corrie as they inched toward the tree line. Sunny circled the artifact shed, her gaze shifting around like she was up to no good, checking to make sure no one was watching her before she slipped inside.

"That little . . ." Ford mumbled as he straightened up.

"You don't think she's the thief, do you? I mean, Sunny? Really?"

Memories from her interactions with Sunny over the last couple of weeks swirled through her head. Her bubbly personality. The fangirling. It didn't make any sense. Not Sunny. Though maybe that was her cover. Play the sweet, awkward intern. Get people to love her so she'd be the last person suspected.

Yeah, this sneaking around the shed business didn't look good.

"Sure looks that way. I thought it was a little strange that she was one of the only ones who didn't get food poisoning."

"You think *she* poisoned everyone?" Sneaking around was one thing, but poisoning?

"Hold on . . ." Ford then said, putting his hand on Corrie's forearm. "Is that . . . is that Ethan?"

Sure was. Ethan, snooping around the shed, looking right as rain and not at all like he'd spent the morning *puking his brains out*. Were he and Sunny *both* in on it? No. No way. If Corrie felt she could trust anyone on this dig, Ford, Ethan, and Sunny—and possibly Agnes—were the ones.

Ethan checked his surroundings, then entered the same shed Sunny had entered.

"I . . . I don't believe it," Corrie said. A wave of nausea swept over her.

"I don't know what the hell to believe anymore." Ford sat on the ground, clearly upset by this revelation. As Ethan had said—they were like brothers. If Corrie was crushed by seeing Ethan sneaking around, Ford must have been devastated.

"What do you think we should do?" she asked.

He hopped up, as if her question had snapped him out of his

thoughts. "I don't know, but I'm not going to put up with this," he said, marching toward the shed.

Uh-oh.

Corrie ran to catch him as they made a beeline straight for the shed. Standing outside the door, they listened for a moment as clanking and groaning sounds carried through the walls. What the hell was she doing in there? Trying to steal heavy equipment?

Not wasting any more time, Ford flung open the door . . .

And there was Ethan, on his knees, with his face buried between Sunny's legs. Corrie's eyebrows raised. *Well, this got interesting.*

"Dr. Matthews!" Sunny screamed, hopping off the workbench and pulling up her pants as Ethan scrambled to his feet. "We've been looking for you everywhere."

"Certainly looks that way," Ford responded, and Corrie couldn't help but snicker.

Or feel somewhat of a sense of relief. No, they weren't stealing. They were fucking. All those moments seeing them together and Ethan's comments about what were some extremely personal conversations with Sunny suddenly made sense.

"I mean, not as in right this minute," Sunny continued, "but earlier, you know, before we came in here to . . . uh . . . to keep an eye on the shed. I mean, it's not what you think. Or, I mean, *that's* probably what you think," she said, motioning between her and Ethan.

Ethan put his hand on her wrist to stop her from talking. "Ford, this is all on me," he said, his voice solemn and apologetic.

"Ethan, I don't give a shit about that, though I suppose I *am* a little surprised. But you're both adults and she's not your student."

"Surprised about what?" Ethan asked.

"I thought she was into Corrie."

So did I.

"Oh, I am," Sunny chimed in.

Annnnd now I'm confused.

"Wait . . . I thought you said she wasn't into men," Corrie then said to Ethan.

"No, I said *Ford* wasn't her type," Ethan said with a smirk.

"Oh, yeah, totally. I'm into men, women, whatever. Blonds really aren't my thing, though. Nor is that whole professor-student thing. I mean, how cliché. No offense, Dr. Matthews."

"Why is it that every time you say 'no offense' I feel like I should be offended?" Ford said, playfully, and Corrie let out a full-throated Corrito Burrito laugh.

"Well, now that we got *that* out of the way, I thought you were sick with food poisoning?" Ford asked Ethan.

Ethan's face twisted as if wincing inside. "Yeah . . . so, that may not have been true."

"What the hell, man?" Ford said, now his tone agitated.

"What the hell, *me*? Where the hell have *you two* been all day? We were looking for you hours ago," Ethan spat back.

"We . . . we were . . . exploring."

Nice save, Ford. Real believable.

"Well, while *you* were out *exploring*," Ethan said with a pointed look to Corrie, "*we* were here investigating our situation and keeping an eye on the artifact shed. I faked being sick with the rest of them so I had a reason to hang around camp, in case someone else was faking sick so *they* had an excuse to be alone in camp. The thief. It appears he's back."

Oh no. It seemed Ford had been right to be worried this morning. Corrie and Ford looked at each other, then back at Ethan.

"Come on. Follow me," Ethan said, leading the charge out of the shed and around to the back, still within sight of everyone and everything but far enough that no one would be able to hear them. Aside from a few glances from the others, no one paid them any mind.

"Okay," Ethan said once they were situated, "see the panel at the back here?"

Corrie and Ethan looked over, but, again, nothing seemed unusual or out of place. "Yeah, what's the problem?" Ford asked.

"The whole thing has been removed. See?" Ethan said, easily lifting the wood panel from the frame.

"Did they take anything this time?"

"They did. Do you remember that wooden bowl? Well, it's gone."

A sickening sensation washed over Corrie's stomach. That bowl had been a huge find. It was almost intact and even had a small amount of grain in the bottom.

"Well, then, that settles it," Corrie said. "Ford, you've got to send everyone home."

"Are you serious right now? We found—" Ford started but stopped himself when Corrie's eyes widened and she started shaking her head.

"Found what?" Ethan asked, his brow furrowed.

"Maybe it's better if we talk about this later," Ford said, glancing briefly at Sunny then back toward Ethan.

"Maybe we all need to start trusting each other," Ethan said, crossing his arms.

Ford opened his mouth as if to protest, but then quickly shut it. Good. If there was one person Corrie trusted on this dig as much as she trusted Ford, it was Ethan.

"Okay," Ford said. "But trust goes both ways, man."

"Fine. Sunny and I have been . . . keeping each other company for a while. I didn't tell you because, well, because she's your student. And, honestly, things haven't really been the same between the two of us since your dad died."

Corrie winced internally, ready for Ford to blow a gasket. But instead, he sighed.

"I know. I'm sorry. I've been having a hard time these last few years. My mom . . . she's sick," he said, sinking his shoulders.

"I know," Ethan said, placing his hand on Ford's shoulder. "But I'm here for you. Always. We all are," he said, motioning around the group.

Ford smiled at them, and it warmed Corrie's heart. "I know."

"So, what is it? What did you find?" Ethan asked, clearly satisfied with that small acknowledgment.

Ford glanced at Corrie again, as if looking for permission. She nodded.

"We found Chimalli."

"What! Where?" Ethan said.

"*Behind* the waterfall."

"Behind the waterfall?"

"Nature's curtain," Sunny said.

Corrie smiled, proud that Mendoza's recounting of Chimalli's life was right.

"But that's not all," Ford continued. "We didn't just find Chimalli. There were drawings on the wall. Two other bodies. And it looks like the tecpatl is buried beneath one of the bodies."

"*Three* bodies?" Ethan started, but Corrie finally chimed in.

"It's Chimalli and his family. According to the drawings, Yaretzi and their child became ill, and it appears Chimalli may have taken his own life."

"But I thought—"

"So did I. Turns out I was wrong."

"So you're not a descendant of Chimalli?" Sunny asked.

Corrie shook her head. "Appears not."

"Well, I know that would have been pretty awesome, but you two still made one of the greatest archaeological discoveries of our time! You're going to be famous!" Ethan said.

"It was all Corrie," Ford said.

She shot a look at him. "No, we both found it."

"We wouldn't have even been here if it wasn't for you. And you know I *never* would have swum under that waterfall without your goading."

"Oh, please, you just didn't want anyone to see your naked ass," she teased, momentarily forgetting they were in the company of others.

Now Ford was the one staring wide-eyed.

"Naked ass? Sounds like your afternoon has been . . . surprising as well," Ethan said with a smirk.

"We were . . . uh . . . we didn't have swimsuits and we didn't want to get our clothes wet," Ford rambled.

It was actually kind of sweet hearing him try to protect her honor. But, man, he was a terrible liar. She had to put him out of his misery. "Relax, Ford. Ethan already knows."

"Ethan knows?"

"Oh, Ethan knows," Ethan said. "And now Sunny does, too."

All three of them looked at Sunny. "Yeah . . . I figured it out this morning when I came by your tent. You looked freshly fucked, and, jeez, it's about time."

Corrie snickered. Sunny wasn't into that whole teacher-student thing in more ways than one, as evidenced by her complete and utter honesty when talking to him.

"How long has Ethan known?" Ford asked Corrie.

"A couple of days."

"She told me to clear your name after I accused you of being the thief," Ethan clarified.

"Well, this is fun and all," Corrie said, "but back to the big picture. What are we going to do? Until we know who the thief is, we can't tell anyone else. This discovery is too big."

"Then we do what you suggested. We send everyone home," Ethan said.

"We can't do that. Now that we've made the discovery, we need to get it out of here before someone else figures it out, too," Ford said.

"Then we need to confront everyone. Give the thief a chance to come clean, and if they don't, we search their things."

"We can't search their things." Ford said, he and Ethan going back and forth.

"We can if they give their permission. And they'll give their permission unless they're guilty."

"So we figure out who it is by process of elimination?"

"Exactly. Anyone with anything to hide will turn themselves in before we figure out the truth on our own," Ethan said.

"Yeah, because the truth always comes out. Like I said earlier," Corrie chimed in.

The truth always won in the end.

CHAPTER

Eighteen

T HE TRUTH ALWAYS CAME OUT. APPARENTLY, HEARING IT ONCE wasn't enough. It was like the universe trying to hammer the point home. Trying to warn him that he was walking a dangerous line, as if he wasn't already aware of his predicament. Warning him of Corrie's anticipated reaction.

But what was he supposed to do? He'd tried telling her twice now and both times he'd been interrupted. Was he supposed to blurt it out? Interrupt the biggest archaeological discovery of his career with a *Hold that thought, Chimalli, I need to tell Corrie something*?

Yet with each passing minute, anxiousness built in the pit of his stomach. A dread of what was to come. Add a thief in the camp on top of that, and Ford was sure he was about to have a heart attack from all the stress.

One by one, Ford and Ethan questioned the team members. Asked them if they had anything they wanted to confess to. Prodded for a voluntary confession. And when a confession didn't come, Ethan would reveal the situation and ask if they would be willing to submit to a search of their bunk and bags.

"The truth always comes out," Ethan said each time. *Thanks for the reminder.*

So far, everyone had agreed, with each protesting that they had nothing to hide. Like Corrie had suspected. And after each questioning and search, they were sent off to a separate area of the camp monitored by Corrie and Sunny so they couldn't warn those who had yet to be questioned. It was slow, but it was necessary at this point in the dig. They simply couldn't chance that the thief had learned of their discovery.

Five down and eight more to go.

Agnes plopped into the seat across from Ethan and Ford.

"Is this really necessary?" Ford asked Ethan. Seriously. The *last* person he suspected was Agnes.

"Better safe than sorry," he replied.

"What's this about?" Agnes asked, crossing her arms and leaning back in her seat. "Are you firing me for this alleged food poisoning incident? Because I don't serve rotten food."

Hmm. Maybe the thief had done that, too.

"No, Agnes. That's not what this is about. You're a fabulous cook, and I'm pretty sure I can't live without you on another dig."

Agnes flashed Ford a sultry smile, clearly proud of herself. "All right. Well, I see you going through everyone's bunks. Coming to check out my knickers?"

Ford couldn't help but snicker. "Yes, Agnes, that's it. We're the knicker police," Ford said. "But in all seriousness, we've got a problem in camp."

"Well, if you wanted in my knickers, you could have come to

my bunk after everyone else was asleep. Though you've been . . . preoccupied every night already," she said, waggling her brow.

Ford straightened in his seat. "How did you . . ." His voice trailed off.

With a devilish quirk of the lips, Agnes cocked her head and said, "It's easy for people to forget I'm here. Ignore the cook. But I see everything that happens in this camp, even when people *think* no one is looking."

Ethan and Ford glanced at each other as if thinking the exact same thing. A human security camera.

"Agnes," Ethan started, "we've got a situation. It appears there might be someone in camp who has . . . ulterior motives for being here."

"If you're asking whether I've seen someone sneaking around the storage bunker, then the answer is yes. You don't need to beat around the bush and play coy with me," she said, and then turned toward Ford and raised her brow. "Unless you're trying to get in my knickers, that is."

"I'm sorry . . . did you say you saw someone sneaking around the storage bunker?" Ford asked, ignoring her inuendo.

"Sure did. Didn't see who it was, though, unfortunately. Caught my attention because I thought it was odd seeing someone wearing a black hooded sweatshirt. It's a little hot for a sweatshirt. But then he was walking around the storage bunker. Like he was eyeing it real close. Like trying to find a way in. Didn't see whether he did, though. Kind of hard to see from this angle."

"Was there anything else about him, like, physically, that you can remember?"

"No, like I said. He had on a hood. Sort of hard to tell from afar. Though I suppose he seemed on the smaller end of the spectrum, as far as the men here go."

"Small? How small?"

"Small like I could crush him. Maybe yea tall," she said, putting her hand up no higher than her own head. "And definitely didn't have shoulders like yours." Another flirty smile.

Ford mentally ran through the men in camp. Only a few could possibly fit the bill, though Agnes's vague recollection was anything but definitive. "Do you remember seeing any black hoodies in the bags we've searched so far?" he asked Ethan.

"No. Though if we're narrowing it down to guys on the shorter side, we've really only got Guiles left."

Guiles. That brownnosing little kiss-ass. Hmm.

"Have you noticed anything else strange around here lately?" Ford asked.

"Couple of weird things on the supply list. And I'm not talking about your special delivery," she said, wiggling her brow at Ford again.

God dammit, Agnes. Ethan raised his brows. "Condoms," Ford begrudgingly admitted. Good thing Ethan already knew about him and Corrie, otherwise he would have had a lot more explaining to do. "Can you please focus now, Agnes? What kind of weird things?"

"Well, I don't know a whole lot about what you all do out there and all the tools you use, but the bolt cutters and a screwdriver on the list threw me for a loop. Not the most efficient digging tools."

The culprit must have used them to break into the shed.

"Why are you telling us all this now?" Ethan asked.

"I'm paid to cook, not babysit and play detective," she responded, sassy as all get out.

Ford opened his mouth to ask another question when Sunny came rushing over carrying the sat phone. "Dr. Matthews," she said out of breath, "it's the investor."

Now? Great. What was he supposed to tell him? That they had a thief among their ranks? Taking the phone and stepping away from Ethan, Agnes, and Sunny, Ford braced himself for a lot of explanation.

"This is Dr. Matthews."

"Do I need to ask what is going on at my camp?" Vautour barked. He'd never taken this tone before, but there was no mistaking his voice—he was not pleased. "What's all this about you questioning employees and searching through their belongings?"

He'd already heard? How could that be?

Ford glanced at the others, waiting patiently for him to get off the phone. Surely Sunny hadn't called him.

"Sir, we've had some trouble over the last few days. Someone's broken into the shed where we keep the artifacts."

"And do you know who it is?"

"No. That's what we're trying to figure out, though I'm afraid it might be one of your employees. We might have to shut down the dig for a short time while we—"

Vautour cut him off. "Absolutely not. In fact, you need to stop these interrogations right now and get to work."

Ford cocked his head even though Vautour couldn't see. "Sir, you don't understand what we're dealing with. We can't continue without finding out who the thief is."

"You can and you will. I'm not paying you to take days off questioning *my* employees . . . or frolicking in the jungle with your sexy little assistant."

A lump caught in Ford's throat. How did he know about

that? He couldn't have Vautour thinking all he was doing there was fucking around. Sure, there was *some* of that going on, but both Ford and Corrie took their jobs seriously. Besides, what they did in their private time really wasn't anyone's business. Not even Vautour's.

"Sir, I don't know what you've heard, but—"

"You can stop right there. I don't need your excuses or your lies. That's what you were going to do, after all, isn't that right? Tell me I have it all wrong? That you weren't found sneaking off in the middle of the night groping that woman under the cover of the jungle?"

Guiles.

Ford should have known, what with Guiles's watchful eye and tattletale mouth. Vautour's spy. Guess Lance wasn't able to convince him to keep quiet after all.

"You're lucky I don't fire you on the spot. But maybe we'll leave that up to Yale and whether they want to fire you for fraternizing with a student intern. If you don't start producing, then I might have to let them know."

Wait. Vautour thought Ford was messing around with Sunny? And—hold on a minute—was he blackmailing Ford?

"Sir . . . are you threatening me?"

"Call it whatever you'd like. I'm paying you to do a job, Dr. Matthews, and I expect that it's going to get done. I want that goddamn knife and I want it now. Not a month from now. Not a year. The longer you're out there, the more suspicion it raises. If that means I have to apply a little more pressure on you, then so be it."

The hell with that. Ford wasn't going to play this game. "Then I quit."

He'd find some other way to earn the money to pay for his

mother's treatments. Extra courses. Teaching gigs at other schools. Hell, he'd even take up the library's offer to do a ten-week speaking series that paid only seventy-five dollars a pop if it meant maintaining his integrity. Vautour could take his threats and shove them right up his pompous asshole.

So why was Vautour laughing?

"I don't think so," Vautour said, his voice unwavering. "This is not only your reputation we're dealing with here, Dr. Matthews. If you quit, then I'll make sure each and every person on your team never sets foot on an archaeological dig again. And that tasty treat you've got? Well, I hear she's quite the looker. I can't wait to see the photos my man got of the two of you by the waterfall this afternoon. I'm sure others will be interested in them, too."

Fire surged through Ford's veins as his grip tightened around the phone. It was one thing to threaten him. Ruin his reputation, fine. There wasn't much left of it after he'd pissed off Dr. Crawley, anyway. But it was another thing entirely to threaten his team.

And Vautour would be damned if he thought he could soil Corrie's reputation and violate her privacy by capturing nude photographs of her.

"Listen, motherfucker—" Ford growled.

But Vautour cut him off again. "No! You listen, you insignificant pillock!" The spittle practically seeped through the phone. "I don't give a shit about your self-righteous ideals. The minute you accepted my offer, you stepped into a whole new ball game, Dr. Matthews, and this one doesn't have rules. Now, you're going to get me that *fucking* knife. But don't test me or I *will* destroy you and everyone and everything you care about. You have one week."

Click.

What the hell just happened? Ford stood motionless, stunned by Vautour's reaction. Vautour hadn't ever given Ford warm fuzzies but up until that moment, he'd also never given off criminal vibes. He never should have taken this job.

Never in his life had Ford felt so powerless. He stared at the phone. It felt heavy and dangerous. As if he was holding the weight of everyone's lives in his hands. A burden for him to carry. Alone.

A sinking nausea settled over him. There would be no getting out of this unscathed. No scenario could guarantee a positive outcome. Because no matter how Ford proceeded—standing up for his morals or standing up for the others—he'd be destroyed regardless.

If he was truly being honest with himself, he could admit that he'd compromised his morals the minute he took the job. Took the job right out from under Corrie.

Was this who he was? Was he any better than Vautour?

He glanced around the camp—at Ethan, at Sunny, at Agnes, at the other interns and workers—and guilt washed over him. Guilt that all of them were there because of him. Unknowingly putting their livelihoods in his hands.

He could never let them take the fall for his mistakes.

Then Corrie walked into his line of sight. An ache swelled in his heart. Not an ache over the fear that he was going to lose her after this. That much he was certain of. An aching at the thought of her getting hurt. He couldn't let that happen. Wouldn't let that happen.

Because that ache . . . it was love.

CHAPTER

Nineteen

WE'RE DONE," SUNNY SAID, FINALLY RETURNING TO THE HOLD-ing group.

"We're done?" Corrie asked. "What do you mean, 'we're done'? We haven't even talked to half of the camp yet," she said.

Sunny shrugged. "Dr. Matthews said we're done." She then turned to the group that had already been searched and questioned. "Everyone can go back to your tents. Or to whatever it is you want to do. Dinner's still at the same time tonight."

The group grumbled as they dispersed. Not that Corrie could blame them. They'd been in lockup for the last two hours, and for what? To go on their merry way without any explanation?

Better yet, where was *Corrie's* explanation?

"Did Ford say why he's called it off? Did he figure out who it was?"

Yes! That had to be it. Though the last person he and Ethan had questioned was Agnes. And no way could Agnes be the bad guy. Right?

"I have no idea. The investor called, and then Ford came back, told us to shut it down, and walked away."

What?

Corrie scanned the camp, Ford nowhere in sight. Something wasn't right. No, Ford had his weird ways and all, but leaving a crook running around camp didn't make any sense. And they couldn't chance it. Not now that they'd actually found what they came for.

She had to talk to him.

"I'll be back," Corrie said to Sunny, before marching through camp searching for Ford.

Not in the mess tent. Or his tent. Or the bathroom. Yes, she checked. So where was he?

Ethan had no idea. Agnes had no clue. He hadn't gone back to the waterfall, had he?

No. Ford wouldn't do that. Sneak off to continue digging by himself. Not after he'd chastised Corrie for trying to sneak off alone to the site over a week ago. They had rules. But that was also before they'd hit the jackpot.

She considered that thought for a moment, but quickly batted it away. She trusted Ford. So she waited.

The rest of the camp carried on as if the day hadn't been disrupted by scandal. Sure, a few murmurs carried throughout the camp, but no one acted upset by what had happened. Upset that they'd essentially been accused of being thieves. By dinnertime, though, everyone had moved on from the whole ordeal. Everyone except Corrie, who couldn't focus on anything except Ford's whereabouts.

Corrie's mind wandered as Ethan told the interns a story about an expedition he'd gone on in Belize. The engrossing story and laughter kept everyone else's attention on Ethan, so they were paying no mind to Corrie, who was focused on the outskirts of camp. Watching. Waiting for Ford.

What's that?

A flicker of light came from beyond the trees. The unmistakable zigzag of a flashlight. And then nothing.

She squinted, zeroing in on the tree line.

There. There he was, emerging from the jungle. Dirty and wet. *What the . . .*

Fire burned in Corrie's belly. That sneaky sack of turds. He'd gone back. Back to the waterfall. Without her, or anyone else.

Corrie had started to rise from her seat when Ethan caught her attention. "Right, Corrie?" he asked.

She shot her gaze to Ethan, then glanced around the table, all eyes on her. "Um . . . sorry. I missed what you were saying," she said, settling back onto the bench so as not to draw too much attention to the situation.

"I was telling them about that time you tricked the museum director with that fake gold necklace, convincing him it was a five-hundred-year-old relic, when in actuality you bought it from, what, a mall kiosk?"

"Claire's boutique," she clarified matter-of-factly, though her focus remained on Ford at the outskirts of the camp in the corner of her eye.

Ethan and the others laughed, even though she wasn't trying to be funny. "Oh my God, yes. You should have seen his face when she admitted it was a fake," Ethan explained to the group.

Call it a knack, but Corrie could smell a gullible person from a hundred yards away. And sorry, but that director should never have been hired if he couldn't tell the difference between Claire's costume jewelry and the real deal.

That little act hadn't earned her any fans with the "serious" experts in her field, though. She probably should have thought about that before pulling such a stunt on the husband of the International Institute of Archaeology's conference director. All right, fine. Maybe she was partially to blame for her less-than-stellar reputation.

With the conversation focused on her, however, she couldn't exactly leave to go confront Ford. She bided her time, planning in her head what she was going to say to him when she finally had her chance. And the instant dinner wrapped up, Corrie hightailed it straight to Ford's tent.

"Care to explain where you were today and what the hell is going on?" she demanded, blasting into his tent without even the barest attempt at a knock.

Though her commanding presence immediately softened upon finding Ford standing in the middle of his room wearing nothing but a towel wrapped around his trim waist. Water droplets dripped from the tips of his blond tresses onto his chest. His clean, fresh juniper scent wafted in her direction, intoxicating her senses. She rubbed her fingertips against her thigh, picturing them grazing his hard abs. Pulled her lower lip into her mouth, ready to feast upon his skin. Damn. She should have joined him in that shower while everyone else was distracted by dinner.

"Jesus, Corrie," Ford said, startling at her presence. "You scared the shit out of me. Think you can give me a minute? I'm trying to change," he said, clutching the towel around his waist to keep it from falling.

Trying to change?

"Ford, we literally spent half the day naked together. It's nothing I haven't seen."

"Yeah, well, things are different now."

She cocked back her head.

"Different now? What the actual fuck, Ford? Are you going to tell me what's up with you? Or, I don't know, tell me why your clothes are lying in a pile over there soaked and completely covered in mud?" She nodded her head in the direction of his clothes.

"We're done here. I got the knife. We can pack up and leave now."

Corrie's jaw went slack. Not that she didn't already suspect he'd gone there alone to investigate, but this? Excavating the tecpatl on his own in a mere matter of hours? The odds were highly unlikely that he followed the proper protocols.

"Why the hell would you do that? What were you *thinking*?" she demanded.

"I was thinking it's time for us to go. Get back to our lives. Put an end to all this . . . this thievery nonsense. Now that I've got the knife, we can all finally go home."

"But what about Chimalli and Yaretzi? And their child? We still need to excavate—"

"No, we don't. The investor wants the knife, that's it. He doesn't care about the rest of it, so neither should we."

"You're joking, right?" Corrie examined Ford like he'd come down with an illness. "Ford, this is one of the greatest Aztec discoveries in decades. We can't forget about it and leave."

"Well, this is what the investor wants, and seeing as it's his money and his land, sorry, but you don't have a choice."

"So that's it?" she asked, watching him nonchalantly get dressed as if it were any old day, though he took care not to flash his ass to her as he pulled on his boxer briefs under the towel. As if she hadn't already seen his goods dozens of times. But Ford was right . . . things were different now. Like everything they'd shared was of no consequence anymore.

"That's it."

"And what happens after we leave here?"

"I guess the investor will either sell the piece to a museum or keep it for his own private collection."

"That's not what I'm talking about." She paused, trying to settle her heart, which was about ready to pop out of her chest from pounding so hard. "I mean . . . what about us?"

Us. A word Corrie had never used when discussing relationship status with any of her partners.

Though *relationship status* was also a foreign term in Corrie's vocabulary.

Ford stopped what he was doing and turned to her. Searching her face. Clearly scouring his own thoughts. Why wasn't he saying anything? She couldn't have been wrong about the connection they'd made. Sure, the sex was great. Fantastic, in fact. But there was so much more beneath the surface. And pain at the idea that she'd never see him again after this.

"Ford . . ." she said taking a few steps toward him, her voice soft and timid, "what happens to us once we leave here?"

He stared at her, unflinching.

"You go back to Berkeley and I go back to New Haven. That's for the best, don't you think?"

"No. No, I don't think that's for the best. Please tell me you aren't being serious. You know there's something more between us. I don't know why we didn't see it before."

"We'd never work, Corrie. You know that. We'd end up arguing all the time," he said as if exhausted, then resumed getting dressed.

"So what? Maybe that's exactly why we *would* work. They say opposites attract."

"But we're not opposites. We argue because we're both stubborn, egotistical know-it-alls—"

"Who happen to understand each other better than anyone has ever before," she said, inching closer still and tracing her hands along his chest and collarbone. She gazed at his face, twirling her fingers along the nape of his neck and into the wet tips of his hair. Warmth spread over her body as he wrapped his hands around her waist and succumbed to their magnetic energy. Yes . . . he wanted it, too.

"What if I took a sabbatical? Moved to New England for a few months." The words came out of her mouth without any forethought, but it felt right hearing them aloud.

A life with Ford no longer seemed an impossibility.

It seemed a necessity.

"Corrie, what are you saying? Are you saying you want to move . . . move for me? Because I thought you didn't do relationships."

"I don't. Or at least I didn't. But at least over these last twelve years, maybe that's because deep down I always wanted you. You're the only person who can occupy my mind, no matter how much I've tried to keep you out. The only person I've ever truly wanted to know. And the only person I've ever wanted to know me."

He brought his hand to her cheek, brushing his fingertips across her warm skin, flushed from her reveal. She hadn't intended to tell him all that. But something told her she needed him to know.

"I . . ." he started, staring into her eyes. "I want those things too . . ."

Corrie's heart warmed, soaring with elation. She'd finally opened her heart to someone else and they'd reciprocated.

"But," he continued, sending a sinking knot into her stomach, "we can't be together. I'm not the man you think I am. You deserve better."

He pulled away from her, leaving an emptiness in her arms.

"That's not true," she said. "Ford, I know you. The real you."

"I wish that were true."

"Then tell me."

"Corrie, please don't make this any harder than it already is," he said, his voice exasperated.

"Harder? Ford, you're literally breaking my heart right now," she said, her voice shaking. "Why are you doing this? Why are you pushing me away when a few hours ago you were pulling me closer? What happened between then and now?"

"I'll tell you everything tomorrow. At the airport on our way back to the US."

"The airport?" She cocked back her head and stared at him incredulously. "Ford, no. Whatever it is, I want to know now. There's no reason this has to wait."

"Yes, there is. Because once I tell you, you're never going to want to speak to me or see me again."

"So instead you're going to leave me to fret about it all night? How can that be better?"

"It just is."

"But how?"

"Corrie, let it go."

"No, Ford, I can't let it go. I have to know now because . . . because . . . because I'm in love with you!" she blurted out.

Silence fell over the tent as they both froze. He then hung his head and spoke. "Please don't say that."

A lump formed in Corrie's throat. Thirty-five years of her life, and the first time she tells someone other than a family member that she loves them, the response is *please don't say that*? So that was what it felt like when men told her they loved her and she didn't reciprocate.

Except Corrie *hadn't* loved them and she was pretty sure Ford *did* love her.

"Ford . . . please. I—" she said, taking a step toward him. She needed to hold him. Hold him so he could feel her love.

But he cut her off and stepped away, turning his body to the side. Closing himself off to her. "I'm not even supposed to be here," he said, stopping her in her tracks.

"What are you talking about?"

"Here, leading this dig." He closed his eyes for a moment, then looked her straight in the face. "I learned about this dig through Dr. Crawley and that the investor was planning to hire you, so I called him and convinced him to choose me instead. Told him that I knew as much about Chimalli as you did."

Corrie blinked several times before fire rose through her belly as his words sank in. "You . . . you took this from me?" She was unable to contain the confused anger rising through her voice.

"Yes."

"Why? Why would you do that? You know how much this dig meant to me."

"Because he was going to pay me a lot of money if I succeeded."

"You did this . . . for *money*?" She scoffed and shook her head. "How much? How much is he paying you?"

He slumped his shoulders. "A million dollars. One-point-five million with any skeletal remains, but all he really wants is the knife."

A torrent of fury whirled through every inch of her. Money? He wanted fucking money?!

"What world are you living in? That's ludicrous, Ford, for someone to pay an archaeologist that much to find an artifact. No one does that. And that's not why *we* do what we do. We do it to preserve history. And for the adventure. We don't do it to line our pockets with gold."

"Well, I needed the money!" he shot back. "For my mom's treatments."

"So you compromised an archaeologist's moral code and your integrity to get it?"

"My integrity? I did this for *her*. I'm broke, Corrie. Completely and utterly broke. My father wasted everything they had on phony artifacts and left my mother with nothing. And I've been support-ing her ever since, even after I got a pay reduction due to budget cuts that conveniently happened to coincide with my breakup with the boss's daughter. So, yeah, I did this for her. I did it so I can pay for treatments that might save her life," he argued.

"Ford, there are other ways to get money. Once word gets out about this dig, our reputations will be that of money-hungry gravediggers. No one in the professional archaeology world will respect us after this."

"What do you care about those people? They don't respect you anyway."

Thwack!

Corrie's open hand flew out and smacked Ford's face as tears rolled down her own. Cheap. He'd made her feel cheap. Con-firming all the whispers and crass jokes made about her all these years. Except she wanted to believe Ford was different. That he saw her for more than that.

Clearly, she was wrong.

"Corrie, I'm sor—" He moved toward her, but she snatched herself away.

"Fuck you, Ford. It's because of people like you that I've acquired this reputation. People who've treated me like a joke—a caricature," she said, her voice shaking.

"That wasn't what I meant. You're better than those people. Who gives a damn what they think about you?"

"I do!"

"Well, maybe you shouldn't."

Corrie laughed, numb and filled with disbelief. "That's rich coming from someone who's gotten where they are by keeping others down. I trusted you, Ford. I trusted you with everything. Gave you parts of me I haven't shared with anyone. And here you are, throwing it all back in my face like none of it ever mattered."

"I tried to tell you. Two times today—" he pleaded.

"After you slept with me."

He paused, clearly having no retort.

"You lied to me," she continued, pointing her finger at him. "From the moment I got here—no, before even—you've been lying and manipulating me so you could get what you wanted. Was this your plan all along? Get me to fuck you—to *fall* for you—so you could finally win?"

"What? No. Absolutely not," he said, standing straighter. "I would never do that."

"Really? How do you expect me to believe you?"

He sighed. "I don't. And I'm sure you never will. But those moments we had? They were real. And if you can believe anything, then believe that."

Real? They could never have been real. Not when all of it had started with a lie and deception.

"Okay . . . if those moments were real, why this? Why this now?"

"Because it's fine to accept that this needs to end." He bowed his head.

"I don't buy that. Something happened. Something between our meeting with Ethan and Sunny and your decision to get the knife by yourself. So what was it? Was it the investor?"

"Let it go. This isn't going to do anyone any good."

Thanks for the confirmation.

"So it *was* him. What did he say to you?"

"Corrie . . ." he said, sounding tired and dejected.

"You owe it to me. After everything that's happened, I deserve to know the truth."

"Fine, you want to know?" he said, his voice raised. "He threatened you, Corrie. He threatened you, me, and everyone else in this camp. He knew about everything. Told me to halt our inquiries into the thief and told me that if we didn't deliver the knife to him within a week, he'd go after every single person here."

"And you believed that? What on earth could he possibly do to us? Not offer us jobs in the future? Well, fine by me. I don't need to work for blackmailing asshats."

"He has photos, Corrie. Photos of us by the waterfall today."

A pit formed in the bottom of her stomach and she swallowed. Hard.

"Of us . . . naked?" She could hardly get the words out.

Ford's features softened and he rested on the edge of the bed. "Yes," he said, his voice low and gentle. "On the plus side, he doesn't know who you are. But on the minus side, he thinks you're my intern and he plans to release the photos to Yale if I don't do what he says. It won't be hard for people to put two and two together and figure out it's you."

Corrie wrapped her arms around her body, shrinking into an unknown abyss. After all these years trying to preserve her reputation. All her efforts to combat the impact of that goddamn *Archaeological Digest* spread. And now someone had photos of her and planned to use them against her. Photos of *her* body.

It belonged to her. Her and no one else.

Ford was right—it wouldn't take much for her identity to be figured out. Certainly no one would mistake her for the auburn-haired, fair-skinned Sunny. But, worse yet, Corrie knew how these things worked. Once the photos were out, there would be no way to control who got their hands on them. No way to protect her body.

"This is all your fault, Ford. You let this happen," she said, her anger rumbling through her voice. But it was time for Corrie to take matters into her own hands. Fuck this *Ford's the boss* bullshit. Corrie was in control now.

He hung his head. "I know. Which is why I want to give him what he wants so we can all get out of here."

"Well, I'm not leaving."

"What?" He shot a look to her. "No, Corrie. Please don't start this again. We're all packing tomorrow and heading out. It's nonnegotiable."

"Who said I'm negotiating? I'm staying, Ford. I'm not going to let some rich asshole dictate my decisions. If he releases those photos, then fine. But it's going to be because *I* made the decision to stay and not because he scared me off. I came here to do a job, and I'm not leaving until we pack up those goddamn bones. And the way I see it, we still have seven days."

"Corrie, we shouldn't mess with him. He's got multiple people in camp watching and reporting our every move."

"So what? What are they going to say? That we're doing our jobs?"

"Look, I went there tonight so we could get out of here. So I could hopefully avoid the investor coming after you."

She threw up her hand to stop him. "Save your chivalry for some other damsel. You did this to protect your own ass—and your investment."

"Nothing about me being here is for me."

She scoffed.

"Tell me something," she said, ticking her head to the side and crossing her arms. "What if this dig had been destined for someone else? One of your male colleagues, perhaps. Would you have handled it the same way? Taken it from them? Or did you only do it because it was me? Because you knew you could?"

"How can you possibly expect me to answer that? I'm here because of my mom. But no matter what I say, either you're not going to believe me or you're going to hate me more than you already do."

"Well, you sure are right about that. We're staying, Ford. And in one week, after we're done with this dig, you'll never see me again."

Twenty

GETTING YOUR ASS HANDED TO YOU SURE SUCKED.

Not that Ford expected anything different from Corrie Mejía. The woman had fire—and self-respect. A few hours into the dig the following morning and her position was loud and clear: Ford better back the fuck up and stay away.

He gave her space those next few days. Took his meals alone in his tent. Helped at the bowl dig site while Corrie, Sunny, and Ethan focused on the cave. Sunny and Ethan didn't ask questions, at least not of Ford. Who knew what Corrie had told them. But if she'd told them the entire truth, that was fine with him. They deserved to know. Everyone deserved to know what a terrible person he'd been. Because Corrie was right—as much as he wanted to convince himself that he'd done this for his mom, there were other ways he could have helped her without compromising his integrity.

Or breaking Corrie's heart.

His own heart ached whenever he looked at her. Thought about what they could have had together. Remembered what it was like to touch the warmth of her skin. Remembered what it was like to feel love—real love. Love from his equal.

Except he wasn't Corrie's equal. She wasn't a snake like him. A liar.

They kept what they were doing at the cave under wraps, trekking to the site in circuitous ways and never together. Despite everything, they still had a thief lurking about, and Ford had his sights set on Guiles. Maybe Vautour wasn't concerned about it, but Ford sure was. They had what he wanted, and then some. The last thing they needed was for someone to skedaddle with the knife four days before they went home.

He considered talking to Lance about it to see if he could reason with Vautour. But reasoning with a blackmailer seemed like a waste of time. After all, to Vautour, Ford was nothing more than an *insignificant pillock*. What did he care if he destroyed Ford's life?

Answer: he didn't.

Ford and the rest of the bowl crew returned to the camp long before the cave crew. While the others went about their afternoons, Ford sat outside his tent, watching them carrying on without a care in the world. What he wouldn't give to be in their shoes. To focus on the dig without the backdrop of a sick mother or a blackmailing boss. Would he ever go back to being someone like that? To smiling? To being happy?

To finding love?

He shook away the thought. How could he expect anyone to love him when this was the kind of person he'd become?

"Hey, Ford," Ethan called out as he, Sunny, and Corrie emerged from the jungle. Dirty. Wet. And laughing and smiling.

Well, at least Corrie *had been* smiling. Her mouth quickly turned down at the sight of Ford.

"Hey, guys," he responded, straightening up on the porch as they approached. "How are things going out there?"

No matter how hard he tried, his gaze kept wandering to Corrie's, though she never made eye contact. A shell of Corrie stood in front of him. Empty and mentally absent.

"Good, good," Ethan said. "We're making great time. We'll definitely be able to hit your goal, maybe even a day or two early."

Ford tilted his head. "My goal?"

"Yeah, Corrie told us how you wanted to surprise everyone and wrap up by the end of the week so we could all finally get home. Everyone's going to be stoked when you tell them. Thanks, Ford," Ethan said, completely oblivious to reality.

Ford shot a glance at Corrie, catching her eye for an instant before she looked away. She'd lied. Lied to protect them. Protect them like he'd tried to do. At least she'd been successful. Ford had failed miserably at protecting anyone.

"That's great," Ford said, forcing his voice to keep up the facade.

"You should see it, Dr. Matthews. The bones are in excellent condition because they were protected by the cave. And we found some clothing fragments," Sunny said, hardly able to contain her excitement.

It *did* sound exciting. Despite what Corrie had accused him of, he did actually care about archaeology and not just the money. But there was no way he could work in such close proximity to Corrie. Meaning there was no way *she'd* allow it.

"Awesome," Ford responded, trying his best to feign his composure.

"It also appears that Mendoza may have been the one who got Yaretzi and their child sick," Ethan added.

Ford cocked his head. "Mendoza? But didn't Mendoza write about them settling in another village?"

"Well, according to the wall drawings, they caught something from Mendoza. Look," Ethan said, pulling a camera out of his bag and handing it to Ford to scroll through the digital photos. Close-ups of the murals. The paintings unmistakably depicted a sick man—a Spaniard. Chimalli's family nursing the man back to health. And becoming sick themselves. "He must have lied about it to cover his guilt. I mean, clearly they didn't live out their days in another village."

"Yeah, like his later accountings were his atonement. Let them live forever through his words," Sunny chimed in.

Atonement. What would Ford's atonement be? A lifetime of unhappiness without someone to share it with as punishment for the devastation he'd caused others?

"I know you probably want to be down there, too," Sunny continued, pulling Ford out of his thoughts. "But I really appreciate you encouraging Dr. Mejía to bring me for the learning experience."

Another lie. And another glance from Corrie. Lies, lies everywhere. Mendoza. Ford. Corrie. At least Mendoza's and Corrie's lies had been used for good.

"Of course," Ford said, handing the camera back to Ethan.

"Oh, hey, before I forget," Sunny said, pulling the sat phone out of her backpack. "You got a call today from Lakeview Rehab Center. They said something about a credit card getting declined."

This time Corrie didn't simply glance. She looked straight at Ford with worry in her eyes.

"Oh . . ." was all Ford could muster.

"Yeah, they said they'd sent several notices and need

payment by tomorrow, but I didn't catch the rest. The connection in the cave wasn't good. I'm sorry. I didn't mean to take the phone."

"It's okay."

It wasn't okay. How the hell was he supposed to find the money by tomorrow? All his money was riding on this dig, and he wouldn't get paid until he delivered.

And he still wouldn't be able to deliver for a few more days.

"Is everything all right, Ford?" Ethan asked.

"Yeah, totally," he said, his voice straining to choke out the words. Did he actually think that sounded convincing?

"Ford, how much?" Corrie asked, all eyes shooting to her.

He stared at her. They were the first words she'd spoken to him since leaving his tent the other night. Under normal circumstances he'd be pissed at someone bringing up his finances in front of others. But Ford had no pride left. And if he was being perfectly honest with himself, a tiny sense of hope formed in his heart at the fact that she was speaking to him at all.

"Thirty thousand."

"Thirty thousand *dollars*?" Ethan asked. "For what?"

"For my mom's treatments."

"Do you have it?" Corrie asked.

He searched her face again before responding. "No."

"Can you get an advance on the dig?" Ethan asked.

An advance? Ha. He wanted to laugh out loud. Seeing as he was being blackmailed, Ford wasn't exactly in the position to be asking for advances.

"Don't worry about me. I'll figure it out. Anyway," he said, clapping his hands and trying to change the subject, "you guys should get cleaned up. Agnes has been slaving away on some red beans and rice, and it smells amazing."

"You should eat with us," Sunny said.

"Nah, I'm good," he said, waving it off. "Trying to get paperwork done since we're wrapping up in a few days."

Corrie cocked her head at him. Of course it was a bogus excuse. Ford was meticulous about staying current on paperwork. The only thing he had to do to wrap things up was pack his bags.

"Aw, come on. I haven't talked to you in days," Ethan said. "And we're all going home soon. It'll be months before we're all together again."

Ford looked at Corrie. No, they'd never all be together again. As she'd already acknowledged, he'd never see her after they left the jungle.

But where he expected to see daggers in her eyes, or at least a warning to stay away, there were the sweet brown eyes he'd fallen in love with so many times.

"I've gotta go shower. See you at dinner, Ford," she said before finally walking away.

. . . .

FORD'S MOUTH HURT FROM SMILING. THE STORIES ABOUT WHAT everyone planned to do once they got home ranged from the practical—planning to take a nice long, hot shower and sleep for a solid day in a real bed—to the downright hysterical—booking a trip to the ice hotel in Sweden to recover from the sweltering Mexican heat. Around the table, they told their stories. Laughing. Teasing. Joking about returning to real life. It was definitely better than eating alone in his tent and wallowing in his own pity.

"Your turn, Ethan," one of the interns said.

Ethan tipped back his head, looking toward the tent ceiling

as he twisted his face in thought. "Hmm . . . well . . . I'll go to the movies. Pig out on popcorn. Recline in a plush chair. Bask in the air-conditioning. Who knows, I might even watch the movie."

Imagine that. So much of them returning home had more to do with the mundane than anything else.

"What about you, Dr. Mejía?" Sunny asked.

The pace of Ford's heart picked up. A glimpse into Corrie. A glimpse into her thoughts over the last few days.

"Me? Oh, I don't know," she said, pushing her food around on her plate with her fork.

So much for that glimpse.

"Oh, come on, you have to have *something* in mind," Ethan said.

"Well, I was sort of thinking of taking a sabbatical," she said, briefly glancing at Ford. "I don't know, though. I need a break."

"Corrie Mejía knows how to take breaks?" Ethan said with a smile.

"I don't," she said with a laugh. "But maybe it's time I try something new."

Something new. Ford wanted to smack himself for everything he'd caused, because if it weren't for his dickhead moves, a relationship with *him* could be her something new.

But now Corrie would find some*one* new.

The thought of her with someone else sent a wave of nausea over him. Picturing her laughing with that hee-haw boom in another man's arms. Twisting her delicate fingers through another man's tresses. Carrying on in her badassery but returning home and giving her warmth to someone else.

He had no right to be jealous. And no right to be hurt. But damn . . . what he wouldn't give to take it all back.

"How about you, Dr. Matthews?" Sunny asked. The question snapped Ford out of his daydreaming. "What's the first thing you're going to do when you get back?"

That was easy.

"Visit my mom."

He'd tell her everything. Everything about how he'd gotten the money. About Corrie. And then he'd ask for her forgiveness. All these years he'd been so angry at his father and promised his mother that he'd never become him. Spent countless hours furious that his father could do that to his mother—leave her penniless, all for his own selfish reasons. Yet there Ford was, falling right into his father's footsteps and swindling the woman he loved to get what he wanted.

"My mom *wishes* I'd put visiting her on my list," one of the guys said.

"Please. Dr. Matthews is probably trying to impress the ladies, right Dr. Matthews?" Mateo joked.

A sarcastic laugh resounded in Ford's head. "Me highlighting the fact that I'm a mama's boy isn't all that impressive," he responded. Nothing like reminding Corrie of how he'd screwed her over for his mother's sake.

"Well, it's sweet," Sunny said with a smile.

"What about you, Dr. Mejía?" Gabriel asked. "Do women eat that up when a man openly expresses how much he loves his mom? I need to know if I should be taking notes."

Why? Why did they have to poke the beast? The proverbial elephant in the room. The guys were only joking, having gotten comfortable with such banter at camp. They were all more like family than students, teachers, and coworkers. The only sign that they recognized boundaries at all was the fact that still, after four months, they called him Dr. Matthews.

"Well . . ." she started, seizing Ford's attention, "there's no shame in admitting that, no matter who you are. If my mother were still alive, I'd want to see her, too." A hint of sadness twinkled in her eye.

"Though I don't think Dr. Matthews said that to impress anyone," she continued. "He loves his mom and would do anything for her. At least he stands by *something*. Now, if you'll excuse me, I still need to log some items from today's dig before I forget."

She stood from the table, leaving a gut punch in Ford's stomach. *At least he stands by something.* Ouch. The others likely had no clue what was going on. Not even Sunny or Ethan. But her choice of words had been no accident. Despite the glances and the unspoken permission to join them for dinner, Corrie Mejía was *not* over what had happened the other day.

And chances were, she'd never be.

WAS IT CORRIE OR WAS THIS THE HOTTEST, MUGGIEST, LON-gest night of this entire goddamn expedition?

She reached over to the table beside her bed to check the time—again—only one twenty-two a.m.? How was that even possible? She flipped over, kicking the extra blanket and sheet to the foot of the bed. That was all it was—the heat. Yes, the heat kept her up. It had nothing to do with Ford. Or that fact that his mother might not be able to get the treatment she needed to live. Or the fact that even after he admitted all the things he'd done, she still had feelings for him. *Strong* feelings. *Warm* feelings. Sexy *hand down my shorts I can't stop thinking about him* feelings.

Okay, so her insomnia had *everything* to do with Ford.

But how was she supposed to sleep when he was less than a hundred feet away? Especially when her insides twisted when-ever she thought about what she'd said at dinner. *At least he stands by something.* She'd regretted the words the instant she'd walked away. Why had she said that? Why had she stooped to such a level?

She needed a walk. Tire out her legs, and then she could finally fall asleep. Because after three nights of barely sleeping, she desperately needed it.

Corrie didn't bother putting on more than the tank top and shorts combo she'd been (trying to) sleep in. Sure, the tank top barely contained her breasts, and her ass cheeks were a thread away from peeking out the bottom of her shorts, but no one else would be out and about. Not at this hour, at least.

The hum of the jungle filled the air, but the tents otherwise remained silent. As suspected, the camp was vacant. And judging by the silence, Corrie seemed to be the only person suffering from another sleepless night. Though . . . a soft glow came from Ford's tent. A light, perhaps?

She wandered closer to his quarters, straining her ears to hear, but nothing. Not even the rustling of sheets or the soft purrs of his sleepy whimpers she'd come to know all too well. The tent canvas was extremely thick, though, so the chances she'd hear anything were slim anyway. After all, no one seemed to have heard them having sex, and Corrie wasn't exactly what most would refer to as quiet, even though she had practiced lots of restraint these last few weeks.

Shh. Someone might hear, Ford would whisper in her ear. She could hear his deep timbre, the warmth of his breath and moisture from his lips sending a shockwave to her core as he rocked into her body.

A smile slowly crept over her, before she tamped it down. *No. Stop thinking about him.*

Moving away from his tent, she wandered through the camp.

But her gaze never strayed far from the glow. Wondering if he was awake. Wondering if he had come up with a plan for his mom. Wondering if he was thinking about her.

Fuck it.

Corrie meandered back toward Ford's tent, creeping up the porch and pressing her ear against the door, which creaked at her touch. Listening for any indication that he was awake.

"Is someone there?" Ford quietly called out.

That was indication enough.

Corrie pulled the door open and entered his tent. He was lying in bed with one arm lifted above his head, wearing nothing but a pair of black boxer briefs, sweat glistening against his skin.

"I couldn't sleep," she said, crossing her arms to cover her now hard nipples. Maybe this wasn't such a good idea after all.

"Neither can I," he responded, sitting up and rubbing his hands over his face.

"Is it me or did the jungle decide to turn it up a few thousand degrees tonight?" she asked with a smile.

A half chuckle escaped his lips. She missed that laugh. She missed everything about him. Well . . . almost everything.

"It's hot as balls," he said.

Balls. Why couldn't he have used a different word? Corrie couldn't help but glance at his crotch when he said it. She chastised herself for being unable to get her mind out of the gutter. Despite the missiles firing in all sorts of directions inside her upon seeing him in all his half-naked glory, her sexual attraction to him accounted for only a small fraction of her thoughts.

Okay, a large fraction. But those weren't the *real* reasons she couldn't get him out of her head.

"I'm sorry for what I said earlier. About standing up for your mom," she said.

"Corrie, please," he said, hanging his head. "You have nothing to be apologizing for. You're only going to make me feel worse if you think you ever need to apologize to me. Not after what I've done."

"I know, but . . . I know how much your mom means to you. It was a low blow."

"I deserve worse."

"Not when it comes to her. You don't deserve to worry about her."

His face softened as he looked up at her, as if finally accepting her words.

"Have you figured out what you're going to do yet?" she asked. "About the payment, I mean."

He shook his head. "I called the bank today to see if I could get a line of credit, but they said it would take a few weeks for the paperwork."

"Could you get an advance on the . . ." Her voice cracked. "On the money from this dig?"

"Based on my last conversation with the investor, I'm not in a position to be asking for favors. I haven't even told him about the knife yet."

She cocked her head. "Why not? Isn't that what he wanted?"

"Yes, but that's *all* he wanted."

Oh. Corrie didn't need Ford to spell it out to her—the minute he told the investor about the tecpatl, they'd be pulled out. And even though it meant Ford would have the money he needed for his mom's treatments, it would also mean Corrie couldn't finish what she'd set out to do.

She couldn't let his mom suffer because of whatever this was that was happening between them.

"Where's the sat phone?" she asked.

"It's on the desk. Why?"

Corrie walked over to the desk, grabbed the phone, then brought it over to Ford, having to ignore the rise in temperature at being so close to him. "Call the treatment center."

He looked at the phone like it was a foreign object. "What? Why? I already told you, I don't have the money."

"Call them," she demanded, thrusting the phone in front of him.

He stared at her for a moment, then did what she said. But the moment the phone rang on the other end, she took it from him.

"Lakeview Rehab Center. How can I help you?"

"Quick, what's your mom's name?" she whispered to Ford.

"Catherine. Catherine Matthews," he said, clearly clueless as to what she was planning to do.

Corrie nodded once, then brought the mouthpiece to her lips. "Hi, I'm calling about the payment for Catherine Matthews."

"What are you doing?" Ford whispered.

"Our accounts and billing department won't be open until eight a.m., but I'd be happy to see if I can help you," the voice on the other end said.

"Well, I'm in a remote location overseas and might not be able to call when they are open. Is there any chance you can accept a payment now over the phone?" Corrie responded.

"What?! Corrie, no. You can't—" Ford said, trying to take the phone from her. But Corrie swatted him, and his hard sweaty body, away.

"Sure thing. I've got Mrs. Matthews's account right here," the receptionist said.

"Great!" Corrie said, moving away from Ford so he couldn't grab the phone. "I'm ready with the credit card number whenever you are."

"Ready."

"Okay, it's—"

Ford snatched the phone from her grasp. "I can't let you do that."

"Give me the phone." She reached around him, their bodies grazing against each other, sending a satisfying zap to her senses.

"No. It's thirty thousand dollars, Corrie."

"And you can pay me back as soon as you get paid. Now hand me the phone, Ford. I'm doing this whether you want me to or not."

She held out her hand as he searched her face, debating his options. As if he really had any. His shoulders finally relaxed with a resigned sigh. But after reluctantly letting go, Corrie proceeded to give her credit card info to the receptionist then wrapped up the call before finally handing the phone to Ford.

"Thank you," he said.

"You're welcome."

They stood silently for a moment, Ford running his thumb back and forth over the phone.

"Why are you being so kind to me? You shouldn't even want to speak to me right now."

She sighed. Wasn't that the truth? But she couldn't deny that pain in her heart.

"Ford . . . I hate what you did. Like *close my eyes and picture your face on a dartboard* hate it. But . . ." She paused. "But I can't say I wouldn't have done the same if I'd been in your position."

"I don't believe that."

"You don't? Even taking out the mom component, you don't think I would have taken the chance to get back at you for stealing my opportunity with Addison? You don't think I would have thrown you under the bus to take this from you?"

"No, I don't."

Corrie had to admit, she was a little insulted at his disbelief in her ruthlessness.

"That's because," he continued, "under all this fire and attitude, I know you have too much pride not to earn your spot based on your merit. That's why you care so much about what people think of you. You'd never throw someone else under the bus to get what you wanted. Not even me. It's not your style. You have too much class for that."

He was probably right. Sure, she'd fantasized many times about the ways she could get back at him, then and now. But revenge would only highlight her own weaknesses, and her satisfaction would be short-lived. Because how could she feel good about getting ahead if the only reason it happened was because of someone else's failure instead of her own success?

Besides, she'd been wrong about the whole Addison thing anyway.

"Fine," she said, letting her arms fall to her side, palms facing forward. "I did it because, after everything, I still care about you. I hate how much I wish you'd never told me about it. How I wish you'd kept this from me so that I could love you with blissful ignorance. How messed up is that, Ford? That I'm madder at myself for wishing you'd never told me than the fact that you screwed me over in the first place?"

He didn't answer, but his pained eyes said he understood.

"We're still going our separate ways after this and never have to see each other again," she continued. "But that doesn't make the other feelings go away. And I feel like a fool for even saying that. Like I'm some silly girl with a crush on a guy who doesn't care about her at all but would still do anything for him. But I can't watch you worry about her, and I can't let her suffer just because I feel foolish."

"Corrie." He said her name breathlessly. "I never said that I didn't care about you. I care about you so, so much. So much it makes me feel like I'm choosing between the only two people in this entire world that I truly care about, except that the damage occurred before there was any other option.

"You say you hate what I did, but I guarantee I hate it even more. Hate it because I hurt you. Hate it because it will hurt my mother, knowing how I got the money. Hate it because I became the one thing I promised myself I'd never be—my father. But I hate that it's planted this seed of self-doubt in you. Socorro Mejía, you are anything but a fool. I'm the fool for letting you slip through my fingers."

His face strained, as if it pained him to speak those words. She chewed on her bottom lip, trying to force herself not to cry. Hopeless love. That was what this was.

"Will you hold me?" she asked.

His eyes were full of pain and uncertainty. "I'm completely sticky and gross."

"I don't care. Even you sticky and gross is better than the emptiness that I'm feeling at the thought of saying goodbye to you in a few days." Her voice quivered. Tough chicas didn't cry.

Maybe she wasn't so tough after all.

He pulled her in toward his body and, yep, she was right.

Even with the humidity and the sweat, it still felt better to be in his arms than not.

"I'm sorry," he whispered into her hair. "If I could take it all back, rewind all the way to that night in the library, I would. I'd go back and kiss you and maybe . . . maybe we would have had a chance."

She squeezed her eyes tight and buried her face in his chest, as if she could will the tears away. If only time worked that way.

She lifted her head and stared at him looking at her. Like that first night in the library—well, aside from the whole half-naked thing—but the look. That questioning in his eyes.

Should I kiss her? they asked.

She lifted herself on her toes and answered him by placing her lips on his. He took her in, holding her tighter in his arms as their tongues glided together. Much like their wet bodies. She needed his kiss, needed it once more before she never saw him again. Needed to implant the memory of his touch in her head so she could judge future relationships against this feeling. Because if she didn't feel this, it wasn't worth it.

But he pulled away and let go of her body, and the feeling of emptiness returned.

"Stop, stop. We can't," he said, backing up toward the bed. "We're making it harder for ourselves."

They'd never see each other after this. She couldn't let that be their last kiss.

"Then kiss me one more time. One more time before we say goodbye."

He took two slow steps toward her, his chest heaving and matching her breaths, one to one. Her heart pounded, fearful of this final kiss. Afraid that it wouldn't be enough to remember him. Reaching one hand to her face and tucking a loose strand behind her ear, he pulled her into his body with the other hand once more and planted his lips softly upon hers. A kiss that said everything that his words couldn't.

I love you.

I'm sorry.

And goodbye.

Twenty-Two

HOW ON EARTH WAS IT POSSIBLE TO WAKE UP WITH A HANGOVER despite not having a single drop to drink in several days?

Ford sat in bed, his mind still processing the evening before. Corrie's presence both eased and complicated things. Eased his immediate worries about how he would cover his mom's treatments. But just about everything else made his life much more complicated. Complicated because he was one hundred percent certain that he was in love with Corrie and ninety-nine-point-nine-nine percent certain he'd never love another woman like this. Complicated in that he was ninety-eight percent certain she loved him, but one hundred percent certain she *would* love another man someday. A man who deserved her and had earned her love.

But mostly complicated because, without a doubt, had he not stopped them, things would have ended with them in bed. He'd have been tormenting himself. Selfishly savoring her. Momentarily fooling himself into believing they still had a chance. A glimmer of hope that wouldn't be fair to either of them.

The sooner they got out of Mexico, the better. If they stayed any longer, he couldn't guarantee they wouldn't have a repeat of last night. Worse yet, he couldn't guarantee he'd have the willpower to stop. All he wanted at this point was to get himself as far away from her as possible so she wouldn't get hurt. Not by him. Not by Vautour. Not by anyone.

The entire camp dragged ass that morning, zapped of their energy from the unrelenting heat. Even though a light breeze had eventually kicked up in the middle of the night, finally providing some relief, the early-morning sun already warned of another scorcher. Too bad he'd promised himself he'd stay away from Corrie, otherwise he'd join them at the waterfall cave to cool down. But at least she'd be comfortable. He deserved the sun's punishment. Preparation for his eternity in the underworld.

Okay, perhaps he was being a bit dramatic. But, then again, a life without Corrie would be hell.

The line at the shower was longer than normal for a workday morning. Ford's skin had a thin coating of last night's sweat. Others must have had the same.

"Sleep all right?" Ethan asked, patting Ford on the back as he got in line for the showers.

"No. Slept like garbage. You?"

"Lucky you slept at all. I spent half the night on the porch butt-ass naked."

Ford laughed. Glad someone could find humor during all this. "Good thing no one was up to see you."

"Oh, I'm not sure about that. Not about anyone seeing me, but about no one else being up."

Ethan quirked his brow at Ford. Corrie. He'd seen Corrie.

"What is it, Ethan? Just come out with it. I'm too hot and exhausted to play coy."

"Why was she crying? She barely made it to her tent before collapsing on the porch. What did you do, Ford?"

Ford's insides ached. Sure, last night had been tough on both of them, but when she'd left his tent, she'd seemed okay, or as okay as she could be, all things considered. After that perfect yet torturous kiss, she'd smiled and told him good night like she'd done almost every night for the past few weeks.

And why did Ethan automatically assume it was Ford's fault? Oh right.

"We ended things," he responded without further elaboration.

"What? Why? You two are perfect for each other."

"It'll never work. Not beyond the confines of this camp. And she's the one who's perfect, not me."

"So you're going to let her go?" Ethan asked, his voice full of disbelief.

"I'm not letting her go. Look, it's complicated."

"Yeah, complicated because you're being a dumbass," he argued back.

Ford narrowed his eyes at Ethan. "Okay, Ethan. Maybe you should stop acting like you know anything about this situation and drop it. Besides, it's none of your business."

"Well, you made it my business by making her cry. I'm not going to let you hurt one of my best friends—"

"It's too late for that, Ethan!" Ford yelled, spinning around to face Ethan head-on. A few of the other campers turned, then Ford quieted his voice. "I fucked things up, okay? I fucked it up and there's no taking it back. No fixing things. So I don't need you standing here telling me what I should do, because none of it will make a lick of a difference."

Ethan gave Ford a sad smile, then said, "Come on, let's take a walk," patting Ford on the shoulder and heading away from the showers.

Ford growled to himself. Why wouldn't Ethan let it go?

A shower opened, and for a moment Ford debated letting Ethan go off on a solo sojourn so he could get ready and wash away the evening. Wash away the vision of Corrie crying alone in the darkness. But with a heavy sigh, he gave in, following Ethan away from the rest of the camp. They walked over to the fire pit area, deserted and empty, where Ethan took a seat on the ground, resting his back against a log. Tension filled the air. Ethan was waiting—waiting for Ford to spill it. Explain what *he'd* done so then Ethan could chew him out. What was the point in trying to hide it any longer though?

Ford plopped onto the ground beside Ethan and stared at the sky for a moment before unloading everything—his dad's debt, his mother's treatments, the payout from the dig, the blackmailing, and his deception. He didn't leave anything out. Not his failed relationship with Addy. Or his unsuccessful attempt at tenure. Not even Corrie's late-night loan. And with every bit of information, every flaw, he sank deeper into his shame. Did he have *any* good qualities?

"That it?" Ethan asked, almost jokingly, when Ford finally finished.

"Yep." Ford mangled a stick in his hands, twisting it around and around until a piece snapped off. "Though I'm sure I've done some other terrible things that I'm forgetting. Or, more likely, that I've blocked out. Like I said . . . I fucked it up. I'm a selfish piece of shit. I honestly don't even know how you can stand being next to me right now."

"Eh, you're not so bad. And you may have made some bad decisions—I mean *really* bad," he said, causing Ford to wince.

"But you're anything but selfish. Selfish would mean you took this job to get rich. Or you let that dickwad ruin the rest of us. Or you didn't tell Corrie the truth. You could have easily gotten away with her not knowing. And *that* would have been the ultimate douchebag move. But you didn't do those things. And the fact that you're letting her go . . . that's the least selfish thing you could do. Because she's amazing and you'll never find another woman like her."

Ford sighed, resting his head back on the downed tree trunk behind them and staring at the green-and-blue-speckled canopy above. "Please tell me something I don't already know."

"All right. Did you know I've only ever seen Corrie cry two times in the twelve years I've known her and both times were because of you?"

He lifted his head and raised his brow. Two times? "Is this supposed to make me feel better?"

"No, it's supposed to make you realize that despite everything, she probably still wants to be with you."

"When was the first time?"

"Back in school. After the whole Addison thing."

"Wait . . . she told you about that?" Ethan nodded. "Why didn't you ever say anything to me about it?"

"Honestly? Because I had a crush on her. I mean, can you blame me?"

Ethan had had a crush on Corrie? Ford's mind swirled in a thousand different directions.

"It was always obvious that the two of you had some little thing going on, but then the whole Addison situation happened. She cried about it, tried to act like it was about the fellowship, but I knew deep down it was because of *you*, and for a brief moment I thought maybe I had a chance. Maybe I could show her that *I* was a great guy. But the way she looked at you? She'd never looked at me that way. I'm her buddy. Her compadre.

"Don't worry . . . I'm over her now," he continued, waving his hands like it was no big deal. "But the minute Corrie saw you at the airport, there was that flicker in her eye. That heartbreak still lingering even after all these years. She's even got it right now," Ethan said, motioning his head toward the rest of camp.

Ford looked over, finding Corrie watching them from a distance, then quickly averting her gaze.

"I don't deserve her," Ford said, throwing the broken stick into the empty stone fire circle as he forced the ache in his heart to forget that look Corrie had been giving him.

"Oh, screw that. Ford, people make mistakes. Sometimes big ones. But it's what you do after that that matters. Nothing is unforgivable."

"Yeah, but—"

The roar of several Jeeps rolling into camp cut him off. They didn't bother parking by the other vehicles. No, these guys torpedoed straight toward the mess tent, kicking up a cloud of dust behind them.

"What the . . ." Ford said, lifting himself off the ground.

A few men jumped out of the Jeep and started questioning those in the camp, but Ford and Ethan were too far away to understand what they were saying among all the commotion. Ford didn't recognize any of the people. But the vehicles had a seal on the sides of the door: DEPARTAMENTO DE ARQUEOLOGÍA.

The regulatory agency for any archaeological digs taking place in Mexico. Something wasn't right.

Ford and Ethan rushed over to the others, pushing through the crowd.

"Who's in charge here?" one of the men asked.

"I am," Ford said, finally making his way to the crowd.

"And your name?"

"Dr. Ford Matthews," he said, reaching his hand out. But the man didn't take it.

"Well, Dr. Matthews, you're undertaking an illegal archaeological dig on these lands. We're shutting you down."

The crowd erupted with questions and concerns. *Illegal?* There was nothing illegal about what they were doing.

"Excuse me, and who are you?" Ford asked.

"My name is Jaime Castillo, director of the National Department of Archaeology."

"Well, Mr. Castillo, I can assure you that we've got the permits to dig here."

"Ford," Corrie said, squeezing through the crowd. "What's going on?" Her voice was worried.

"Don't worry, I'll take care of this," Ford said. Although the pit in his stomach said otherwise.

"Let me see your permit," Castillo said.

"I'll be right back."

Ford marched over to his tent, his mind racing a million miles a minute. This needed to be set straight. Once he showed them the permit, everything would be fine. Grab the permit, go back, and then—

"What the hell?" Ford muttered to himself as he walked into his tent. Papers tossed. Bedding on the floor. Drawers open. Had those assholes already made it to his quarters to search? And what the hell were they even looking for?

Ford went straight for the desk, retrieving the permit from the remaining papers in the top drawer and hurried back to Castillo to set things straight.

"Here," Ford growled, whipping the permit at Castillo. "And maybe next time stay out of my things."

Castillo raised his brow at Ford before taking and examining the document. "How did you get this permit?"

"The property owner applied and gave it to us before we got here. See?" Ford said, pointing to a signature on the form. "His name is right there."

"I have never seen this man a day in my life," another man called out while climbing down from one of the Jeeps.

"Who the hell are you?" Ford asked. This situation was getting old.

"I'm Juan Carlos Moreno. The property owner. And I can assure you, Dr. Matthews, that I have not given you permission whatsoever to be on my land."

No. This couldn't be right.

"No, Pierre Vautour is the owner—"

"Vautour?!" Corrie called out. "Ford, Pierre Vautour is a smuggler."

Ford blinked several times. What was happening?

"What? No . . . no, you must be thinking of someone else. He's a friend of Dr. Crawley's," Ford said, trying to convince Corrie. Trying to convince himself.

"Oh, I'm sure. There's only one Pierre Vautour. Please don't tell me he's who hired you for this job."

Ford stared at her, his nonanswer all the answer she needed.

"Well, this permit is a fake," Castillo chimed in, handing the bogus document back to Ford. "And perhaps this Mr. Vautour thought you would go unnoticed on hundreds of acres in the middle of the jungle, but trying to sell artifacts on the black market raises eyebrows."

The thief.

Everything was starting to make sense. Vautour's blackmailing. His insistence that they quickly wrap up before suspicions were raised. The large sum of money. Money that probably didn't even exist. Ford was a gullible fool.

"I'm sorry . . . I need a minute to process all this," Ford said, putting his hand to his forehead. "This . . . this doesn't make any sense."

They were in trouble. No . . . deep shit. If they were digging for artifacts without permission and without a permit, they could all be arrested. Thrown in Mexican jail. Who knows how long they'd be stuck there, drowning in red tape and paperwork? And what about his mother?

"Clearly we are as shocked as all of you," Corrie chimed in, touching Ford's arm. "Can we have a minute to make a few calls and try to sort this out?"

"Go ahead, but we're not leaving . . . and you're not going out to dig," Castillo said.

Ford stood in a daze, pulled away from the crowd by Ethan and Corrie yanking on his arms. Between his mom, the legal trouble, the potential media frenzy, and their fraternization with criminals, they'd stepped into a full-on shitstorm.

"You have to call Vautour," Corrie said, snapping him out of the haze.

"And say what? 'Hey, Pierre, I know you've been blackmailing me, but by any chance, were you mistaken when you said you owned the land we've been digging on?' I'm sure that will go over well."

"Put him on speakerphone. Get him to admit that this was all part of his little scheme so they can hear. Otherwise, we're going to get arrested, Ford. For all they know, Vautour doesn't exist. All they see is a group of people trespassing and digging up Moreno's property."

"We're all screwed," Ford said, pacing between them.

"How did this even happen? I thought you said Dr. Crawley told you about this dig," Ethan said.

"He did"

"Crawley had to have known about Vautour," Corrie said.

"There's no way. Dr. Crawley is highly respected in our field. He encouraged me to fight for this spot," Ford said.

Corrie blinked. "You mean, *he* told you to convince Vautour not to hire me?"

Ford nodded. "He said Vautour wanted you, but he was pretty sure that you would decline. Then he told me about the money because I needed it."

"Ford, there is no way Dr. Crawley didn't know exactly who Vautour is. He set you up."

Ford cocked back his head. "What? No. He wouldn't do that."

"Why not? He's clearly been looking for a way to get rid of you. This was his opportunity. Send you off on a bogus dig, and when it falls apart, he's got a reason to fire you. He knew you were desperate."

God, how could he have been such a fool? Of course this dig had been too good to be true. And it had fallen into his lap right at the time he needed it most . . . right after he'd gotten his pay cut and explained to Dr. Crawley how much he needed the money.

"How do you know all this? About Vautour, I mean?" he asked Corrie.

"I met Vautour at Bernard Sardoni's party. The encounter

was brief, but a few days later I ran into him again. He knew I was the one who'd taken the necklace and that I'd beat him to it. He said we were two peas in a pod, but I assured him that I wasn't there to steal anything. I was there to return what had already been stolen. But he said one day he'd call me to work for him, and I said it would never happen. Guess I was wrong about that."

"Well, this is all fascinating, guys, but what the hell are we going to do?" Ethan asked.

"Maybe we need to give them everything we've found? Cut out Vautour. Moreno gets the goods. And we get out of here, hopefully with a slap on the wrist. I mean, it's still a fantastic discovery. Let's take them to the site and show them everything, and, Ford, you can give them the tecpatl and then . . . Ford?" Corrie asked as Ford stared blankly at her. "Ford, what is it?"

"My tent . . . it was ransacked."

"What do you mean it was ransacked? When?"

"I don't know. When I went to get the permit, it . . . it was trashed. I thought maybe Castillo's men trashed it, but now . . . well, there's no way. The timing, I mean."

"It had to have been one of Vautour's men," Corrie pointed out.

"Guiles," Ford said, finally coming to the realization. "Vautour knew about that night . . . when Guiles found us in the jungle. It has to be him." How had he not realized it before? Not only was he one of the only guys on the smaller side, per Agnes's observation of the person sneaking around the storage shed, but he was gunning for a gold star from the boss.

They all turned back toward the group, scanning for Guiles. There, nonchalantly approaching from the TTs . . . in a black hoodie.

"Son of a—" Ford grumbled under his breath, making a

beeline toward Guiles. "You!" he said, grabbing a wide-eyed Guiles by the shoulders of that fucking black hoodie.

Ethan rushed over, trying to loosen Ford's grasp as Guiles trembled. "Ford, Ford, ease up, man!" Ethan said.

"No! This asshole is a snitch. And a thief!" Ford's voice thundered, rumbling from his throat all the way through his fingertips wrapped around the black cotton, as the veins in his neck throbbed.

"Thief? I'm not a thief. I swear . . . I . . . I haven't taken anything!" Guiles protested. The color drained from his face as he stuttered.

"Bullshit! It's been you all along. Spying on us in the jungle. Sneaking around the storage sheds in this hoodie. And snitching on us to Vautour! Where are they, Guiles? Where are the fucking pictures?"

"Pictures? What pictures?"

"Don't play innocent with me. You know what goddamn pictures I'm talking about."

"I swear," he said, putting his trembling palms up to his chest. "I don't know what you're talking about. And . . . and . . . I don't know Mr. Vautour. I've never spoken to him in my life. I was hired by Mr. Soldat."

Ford scrunched his face. *"Who?"*

"Mr. . . . Mr. Lancelin. Mr. Lancelin Soldat."

Corrie narrowed her eyes. "Lance."

What? Ford loosened his grip. No. It couldn't be. Lance was his friend. Guiles was the one who was sneaking around. Lance had made sure to protect them. Unless . . . unless it was all a lie.

Was there no one on this damn dig who was honest?

"He told me to keep an eye on things. Patrol the camp. But that's it, I swear! I haven't taken anything."

A sick, gut-wrenching churning roiled through Ford's body. It was Lance all along. Pretending to be on their side. *Now* he felt like a gullible fool.

Ford turned toward the group, scanning for Lance, but of course he wasn't there. He put his hands to his mouth and called out, "Has anyone seen Lance?"

Memo raised his hand. "He headed toward the site with his pack when the Jeeps pulled in."

"That son of a . . ." Corrie didn't wait to finish her sentence before sprinting toward the jungle.

"Corrie! Wait!" Ford called out. But there was no stopping her. Nor going after her. Not with Ethan and Ford still in their pre-shower flip-flops. "Shit," he said, rushing toward his tent.

"What are you doing?" Ethan called, hurrying behind him.

"I need shoes."

And to check on one more thing—his hiding spot for the knife.

Twenty-Three

THAT MOTHERFUCKER.

They needed Lance's confession if they were going to make it out of this predicament unscathed. Or at least partially unscathed. But there was no way she was letting that rat Lance get away with this. Not after he'd gotten those photos, too.

She charged through the forest. Weaving in and out of the trees. Leaping over rocks and fallen timber. After three weeks out here, Corrie knew every obstacle. Every landmark. So long as she kept her pace, she'd find Lance in no time.

Or, rather, Lancelin Soldat.

Her heart pounded as she ran. Pounded faster than her feet, with a mixture of nerves and exertion. She hadn't run this quickly since the jaguarundi incident. But her drive had kicked in. This was what she was made for.

The roar of the waterfall grew louder, and she slowed her pace upon noticing a black backpack on the ground near the river. But Lance was nowhere to be found. Dipshit probably needed a piss break. She crept over to the bag, inching with caution and stealth. *Quick. Search the bag.*

She slowly unzipped the front pocket, trying not to make noise, and rummaged through the contents when a sharp prick nicked her neck.

"Looking for this?" Lance said from behind her, pressing a blade into her flesh. "Stand slowly with your hands in the air." His accent faded, now revealing his true French voice.

Corrie did as he said. Okay . . . maybe she *wasn't* made for this.

"Turn around."

There, staring back at her, was a white flint blade. "Not so smart after all, are you?" he said, with a smirk.

"Cut the crap, Lance. You're never going to get away with this."

"Oh no? I believe I already have. I got what we came for."

"You think Vautour is going to give you a dime from whatever profit he makes off that thing?"

"Oh, pretty lady, I've got much more than this. I warned you to be discreet. Lucky for me, you didn't heed my advice. I already have a buyer for those lovely photos of you. Vautour considers it my bonus. Besides, Vautour knows better than to screw me over."

How had she missed it? His accent? His smarmy face? His beady eyes? The man could have been picked straight out of a lineup in a *Dick Tracy* comic.

"You're kidding, right? That's what he does. That's what people like *you* do. Screw each other over the minute you get the chance," she spat back.

"Oh, you mean like your boyfriend did to you?" He tapped

the blade lightly against his temple. "I figured it out. Or, well, I was eavesdropping. That's how I learned about this beauty," he said, tracing his finger along the knife. "It's too bad he turned out to be an asshole. You two really . . . enjoyed each other. Thank you for providing me with the entertainment. Gets lonely out here," he said, his hooded eyes raking over her body.

The sudden urge to vomit overcame her. "Fuck you."

A flash came out of the corner of her eye. *Ford*. She tried not to reveal her relief, but Lance must have noticed the recognition in her eye. With a swift yank, he pulled Corrie in front of him and held the knife against her throat.

"Don't come any closer!" he yelled to Ford, his warm, reeking breath hot against her ear.

"Whoa, whoa," Ford said, putting his hands in the air. "Lance, calm down. Just let her go."

"And lose my safety net? I don't think so."

Corrie squirmed to get away, but Lance held firm, pressing the knife harder against her skin, causing her to squeal.

"Please!" Ford called out. "Please don't hurt her," he pleaded.

"Hurt her? What kind of animal do you think I am?" he asked.

"What do you want? Whatever it is, it's yours," Ford said.

But Lance laughed. A hoarse, sickening laugh that sent a cold shiver down Corrie's spine. "But you don't have anything that I want, Dr. Matthews. Except . . ." He paused. And something about the way he paused sent a wave of nausea over Corrie's skin. "Except maybe I need her to come with me to ensure my safety."

"You asshole—" Ford started, taking a step toward them. But Lance only grabbed tighter.

"Ford, please," Corrie cried out, tears streaming down her face. Her prior escapades seemed like child's play now. In all her years, all her adventures, she'd never been more terrified.

"Back up!" Lance commanded, his words blasting in her ear. "Back up or I'll slit her throat. It would be a shame, but don't test me. You're not going to stop me from leaving with this knife."

"Well, that's not the knife," Ford said, "so if you want to leave with *Chimalli's* blade, then you're going to have to let her go."

Now was not the time for games. And based on Lance's laugh, he clearly agreed.

"Nice try, Dr. Matthews, but I found it in your super-secret hiding place under your mattress."

"You found *a* knife under the mattress. You didn't find *the* knife. I made a fake. A decoy. I knew someone had been lurking around. The real knife has been with me the whole time."

"Prove it."

What was he doing? Ford reached around his back and pulled out a handkerchief with something rolled up inside. Slowly, he unraveled the fabric, revealing a sheathed blade with a mosaic hilt glinting in the light.

"The knife for her."

"You're not in a position to be making demands," Lance responded.

"Take the knife and let her go, and you'll never see us again. We won't come after you. We won't even tell them which direction you went. Or . . . I throw this in the river," he said, raising the knife in the air. "It's one or the other, but something tells me Vautour would rather have this over those damn photos. You choose."

"Ford, don't," she called out. "Don't give it to him."

"I know what I'm doing," he said, focusing only on her.

His emerald eyes stared at her holding so much hope. Holding on to the chance that her trust was still a possibility. She wanted to give it to him, but there *was* a knife grazing her neck. This wasn't just him tricking her into coming on this dig. This could get her killed.

But the thought of getting out of this situation with his arms wrapped around her provided her comfort.

She nodded her head slightly, telling him okay. She trusted him. His worried eyes relaxed a fraction, and then he turned his attention back to Lance.

"Do we have a deal?"

"Fine. Bring it to me and I'll let her go."

Ford took a few steps closer, rewrapping the knife in the handkerchief. "Toss the knife over there," Ford said, pointing to a spot several feet away, "let her go, and then I'll give this to you."

Lance waved the blade away then tossed it to the ground before pushing Corrie toward Ford. She resisted the urge to grab the knife from Ford's hands and run to camp. *Trust me*, his eyes spoke as she walked behind him, shielding herself with his body.

"Here," Ford said, outstretching his arm with the handkerchief. "Take it and go."

Lance greedily snatched the knife from his hands. "Nice doing business with you."

"Come on," Ford said to Corrie, pulling her into his side.

They took a few tentative steps forward to head to camp, then Ford reached down, grabbing the knife that Lance had discarded. What was he doing?

"On the count of three, run," he then whispered.

Run?

"One . . . two . . ."

"What the hell is this? What do you think you're trying to pull?" Lance growled.

"Run!"

Ford pushed Corrie out of the way as Lance lunged with the knife, but not fast enough to avoid the rusty blade slicing his forearm. He winced, grabbing his cut arm as Corrie screamed his name.

"Go! Run!" he screamed at her.

And leave him there alone?

"Give it to me!" Lance yelled.

Lance waved the knife at Ford, slashing it through the air, Ford narrowly missing the blade each time. They danced around in a circle, lunging and swiping at each other, while Corrie stood motionless off to the side. Their bodies finally connected, wrestling each other next to the rushing river.

She'd run from bandits, tricked mob bosses, outrun wild animals, and rafted down rivers. But for the first time in all her archaeological adventures, Corrie felt utterly helpless.

No. Corrie was anything but helpless. She couldn't let this animal hurt Ford. She was a motherfucking badass.

"Let him go!" she screamed, searching for something to use to fight back. A stick. A rock. Anything.

"Corrie, go! Get help!" Ford called out before throwing back his head with a loud cry as Lance fell into his body. His grunting continued as Lance stumbled, tripping over his backpack on the ground and sending both of them hurling into the river with a loud *splash*.

"Ford! No!"

Corrie rushed to the river's edge, where Ford hung on to a root protruding from the riverbank, Lance clinging to his back, the waterfall rushing less than a hundred yards away. A hundred yards toward certain death.

"Help! Help!" Lance screamed, his face terrified as he pushed Ford's head under the water trying to climb out.

She dove to the ground, pulling on Ford's arms to help him out. But Lance used Ford's body as a ladder, clawing to escape the rolling rapids. The pounding waterfall sent a deafening thunder through her ears, adding to the chaos and franticness.

"No! Get off him!" Corrie yelled, using her legs to kick Lance. Ford twisted beneath him, fighting to hold on to the riverbank while elbowing Lance out of the way and gasping for breath. Finally, Ford broke free from his grasp, sending Lance bobbing in the depths of the river and over the edge with a blood-curdling scream.

Ford rested his head against the muddy riverbank, panting and exhausted from the struggle.

"Do you think he made it?" Corrie asked, still holding on to his arms.

"Honestly . . . I don't fucking care."

"Come on. Let me help you out."

She used her legs to pull him out of the river, tugging under his armpits as he crawled up the bank. Once on dry land, they both collapsed. Out of breath. Out of harm's way. Corrie stared at the blue sky poking out through the tree canopy, panting at how close they'd both come to death. All because of . . .

"Ford! The knife!" she said, shooting up to a seated position.

"Don't worry . . . I've got it right here," he said, pulling a knife from his pocket. The one Lance had pointed at her neck.

"Wait . . . I thought this was a fake."

"No. The other was the fake. A little trick I learned from you. Besides, I needed something to do in the evenings," he said, turning his head toward her and flashing a smirk.

She couldn't help but smile. "Oh my God, Ford. Do you know how dangerous that was? We could have both been killed."

"Well, I knew you'd never forgive me if I let him get away with that knife. And I'd never forgive myself if you got hurt. What else was I supposed to do?"

Her heart pounded. He'd saved her. Saved her *again*. Badass Mejía had needed saving by Weak Sauce Matthews, and in his mind, he'd had no other options.

"Ford . . . I—"

"We should get back," he cut her off. "They're going to be looking for us soon and we don't want them to think we took off."

He started to sit up, then cried out in pain and collapsed on the ground.

"What's wrong? What is it?" she said, scooting closer to examine him, his arm wrapped around his waist. "Is it your arm?" she asked, seeing the blood everywhere.

But he lifted his shirt and it was so much worse. Blood pooled out of a wound in his side. "Oh my God, Ford! He stabbed you!"

As if that wasn't obvious.

"It's fine," he said, sucking in a breath and closing his eyes. His lips pulled into a tight line as he tried settling his breaths. "I just need to get to camp."

"No, Ford, it's not fine. You're losing a lot of blood. Here," she said as she pulled off her shirt and bundled it into a wad to press against the wound. But Corrie was no medic. Sure, she'd found herself in enough scuffles to know her way around a first aid kit, but she'd never encountered a wound like this. Never something life-threatening.

He cried out once more when she pressed the shirt against his body. "Okay, maybe it's not fine," he said.

"Then come on. We need to get you back," she said, trying to wrap his arm around her neck. But his body was like dead weight, impossible for her to lift. And he winced again.

"I can't," he said. "I don't think I can move."

"Then we'll wait. Like you said, they'll be looking for us soon."

"You should go get help."

"No, I can't go."

"I don't . . . I don't think I'm going to make it if you don't get someone."

"No, Ford! Don't say that. You'll make it," she said, tears streaming down her face. "I'm not leaving you alone out here!"

Her body trembled as she pressed firmly against his wound, willing the blood to stop. *Let him live. Please, God, let him live.*

"Corrie?" His voice was calm. Serene. She studied his face as he brought his hand to hers. "Corrie, I love you."

What was this? Was he . . . was he saying goodbye?

"Ford, please just relax. Conserve your energy."

"I want you to know," he continued, completely ignoring her pleas, "these last few weeks have been the best weeks of my life. You brought adventure to my life. Passion. A reason to live. I'd say I'm sorry for everything I've done, and in many ways I am, but . . . I'm not sorry for any of those moments I had with you. And I'm not sorry that I fell in love with you."

"Shh," she hushed, touching his lips and chest and hands. "Quit talking like that. Quit talking like this is the end."

"Isn't it, though? I can't feel the pain anymore. Not in my stomach. The only pain I have is in my heart for having to say goodbye to you."

"No! No, Ford. You're not leaving me!" She shot her hands on both sides of his face, forcing him to hold her gaze. "Stay with me!"

"I'll always be with you. Part of the legend of Badass Mejía. When Weak Sauce Matthews saved her life half a dozen times," he said with a slight chuckle, followed by a wince.

She laughed through her cries. How, even after everything, could he still make her smile? Still make her heart sing? Even in the worst of times.

"Hey . . . I saved *you* this time," she said through her sniffles.

"Corrie . . . you've saved me in more ways than one." He took her hand and squeezed. "Promise me something."

"Anything."

"Promise me you won't change for anyone. Embrace who you are, because you're the most amazing woman I've ever met."

She brushed her tears away and smiled. "I promise. I love you, Dr. Matthews. I always have and I always will."

"Same, Dr. Mejía. You won, Corrie. You won my heart and no one will ever be able to take it away from you," he said, smiling, with a tear running from the crease of his eye.

She leaned down and pressed her lips to his, tasting his mouth for what she was sure would be the last time, then lay beside him. And as he wrapped his arm around her, she was comforted. The comfort that only he could give. He loved her for who she was—wild adventures, ridiculous antics, and all. It didn't matter that she wasn't the ancestor of a great Aztec warrior, or that she'd probably never get that speaker invite to the international conference. Yet she'd made him proud.

She'd made herself proud.

The only thing she'd ever wanted.

CHAPTER

Twenty-Four

One Year Later

THE RED CARPET BECKONED CORRIE TOWARD THE ENTRANCE OF Chicago's Field Museum of Natural History. Banners hung near the top of the building: FROM TENOCHTITLÁN TO NOWHERE: THE LIFE OF AZTEC WARRIOR CHIMALLI. The signs, illuminated by the spotlights below, featured a rendering of Chimalli standing on top of the waterfall, with Yaretzi and their child standing beside him. Ethan had outdone himself with this one.

"Come on, let's head in," Miri said, taking Corrie by the arm.

Dozens of limos lined the front of the museum, with at least a hundred guests climbing the stairs to enter—men in tuxedos and women in evening gowns. But none as bold as Corrie's—a deep red mermaid-style dress with a sweetheart neckline, accentuated by her French twist updo. Finally, an opportunity to get out of dirty khakis and hiking boots. It was her night, after all. Had it not been for her research and belief in Mendoza's recounting of Chimalli's life, his bones and the tecpatl would likely still be in that damp cave. And the truth would never have been known.

It had also taken some finagling with the Mexican Department of Archaeology and Juan Carlos to get them to agree to loan the artifacts they'd uncovered for a six-month exhibition in Chicago. The deal entailed that she volunteer to assist the department with another dig in Mexico, free of charge. But with her sabbatical in effect, she had plenty of time. And with all the press from the Chimalli dig—magazine and newspaper articles, talk show appearances, and book deals—she could volunteer her time without financial worry. The International Institute of Archaeology had even offered her a paid keynote opportunity at next year's conference.

But that one she'd turned down.

Corrie and Miri entered the gallery, immediately greeted by a waiter holding a tray of champagne flutes. After two hours of travel by Jeep on a dirt road, followed by five hours of planes and airports, yes, champagne. Corrie took the glass and took a sip, but no. This wasn't her.

She reached her hand to the waiter's arm before he walked away. "Actually," she said once she had his attention, "would it be possible to get a pour of rye? Neat?"

"Absolutely. I'll be right back, miss."

She smiled to herself as he walked away, reminiscing over her newfound love of rye whiskey.

"Dr. Mejía!"

Corrie turned to find Sunny, in a bright yellow floor-length gown, running toward her and flinging her arms around Corrie's shoulders.

"Sunny. So good to see you," she said, pulling back and bringing a smile to her face. "This is my good friend and colleague Dr. Miriam Jacobs."

"So great to meet you!" Sunny said, pulling Miri into a hearty embrace. Miri's eyes went wide, and Corrie had to duck her head to keep from laughing. "Are you a kick-ass archaeologist, too?"

"Um . . . y-yes," Miri said, pushing her glasses back up the bridge of her nose. "I mean, not like Corrie, but—"

Corrie waved her off. "Give it time and you'll see. She'll be swinging from vines in no time."

Miri blushed and bit back a smile. She might not have been as outgoing as Sunny or as adventurous as Corrie, but Miri had potential.

"Weren't you literally at the dig this morning? You look *uh*-mazing. This dress is killer," Sunny said, motioning toward Corrie's dress.

"I was going for badass," Corrie joked.

"Oh, your ass certainly looks bad. You're getting plenty of naughty glances, I can tell you that," Sunny said with a smirk, and nodding her head toward the other guests.

Corrie didn't bother checking whether Sunny was right. This dress was designed to catch plenty of glances. None, however, compared to the way that Ford looked at her. Looked at her not just like she was a pretty face or had a killer body, but like he *saw* her. Truly saw who she was.

She missed his glances. She missed everything about him.

"Have you gone through the exhibition yet?" Sunny asked, cutting off Corrie's thoughts.

"No, not yet. Did you help Ethan and Gabriel with all this? Because what I've seen so far looks incredible."

Sunny smiled and stood straighter. "Thank you. We designed it together."

Sunny had stayed with Ethan and hadn't gone back to Yale, not after everything that had happened. Not with Ford no longer there. And certainly not with Dr. Crawley still lurking around, denying all culpability for the Vautour scandal. His tenure might have kept him at the university, but at least his reputation had been ruined. Corrie hoped he enjoyed his new position sitting in a crusty, dusty old office, shielded from the outside world.

"I haven't seen Ethan yet. Where is he?"

"Over here, my dear," Ethan said, taking a bow.

Corrie burst out laughing, good ole Corrito Burrito back in action. God, it had been a long time since she'd laughed like that.

"You are stunning, Dr. Mejía. Not that there was ever any doubt," he said, taking her hand and kissing it before saying hello to Miri, then wrapping his arm around Sunny and kissing her on the lips.

Corrie laughed and rolled her eyes. "Quit being ridiculous."

"I shall not!" he said, puffing up his chest like a knight in shining armor. "I do, however, have a surprise for you." He relaxed his shoulders and offered his arm. "Come with me, milady."

"I'll be back," she said to Miri and Sunny. She took Ethan's arm and he escorted her to the exhibition entrance, still blocked off with a red velvet rope.

"After you. Before we open it to the masses," he said, unclipping the rope to let her through.

"Are you sure?" she asked.

He nodded. "This one's for you, Corrie. Have it all to yourself and soak it in."

She reached over the velvet rope and grabbed his face, kissing him on the cheek. "Thank you."

Then she left the bustling entrance hall, went through the velvet curtain, and entered the Aztec Empire. Room by room, the exhibition detailed stages of the Aztec Empire and Chimalli's life. Her heels echoed on the floor tiles as she slowly weaved through each room. She stopped at the glass case holding the tecpatl and sucked in a breath. Now that it was cleaned up, you could finally see it in all its glory. A far cry from the last time she'd seen it lying next to Ford's bloody body.

The image of him lying beside the river flashed through her head, and she quickly shook it away. *No. Don't go back there.* That day frequently invaded her thoughts, but the vision of Ford's bloody body wasn't something she ever wanted to relive.

She moved on to the next room to a new display titled, "Love Begets Love." *Hmm.* Corrie made her way to the wall, to a photo of her and Ford at the dig site. She'd never seen this photo before, of the two of them kneeling beside the foundation of Chimalli's adobe home, smiling at each other as if no one was watching. Underneath the photo read a caption: LEAD ARCHAEOLOGIST DR. SOCORRO MEJÍA AND ASSISTANT ARCHAEOLOGIST DR. FORD MATTHEWS.

Lead?

Corrie turned as if to ask the question, but no one was there.

She moved on to the next photo in the display, this one of her and Ford laughing in the mess tent. Seeing his smile made her hurt. Who'd taken this photo? Where had they gotten it? Moving on, there were dozens of other photos of the two of them. Candid shots of them being real. Shots when they hadn't thought anyone was watching. A plaque beside the collection of photos read:

An extraordinary warrior and an ordinary villager. An un-likely pair brought together by their own ideals of what life should be. Out of the search for these two lost souls came another unlikely pair—this one an ordinary professor and an extraordinary adventurer. Also lost souls, albeit in a differ-ent way, these archaeologists found in each other what Chimalli and Yaretzi had found in the same jungle hundreds of years earlier: true love.

They say a picture speaks a thousand words. These photos were taken without their knowledge—every reaction is 100 percent real. The photographer had planned to use these photos against them (see the "Sex, Smuggling, and Black-mail" display in the next room). The only thing he caught, however, was proof that even the most unlikely of pairs can fall in love.

Corrie wiped a tear from her eye as she looked at the photos, placing her hand on one at the waterfall. A *clothed* one, thank God, though the nude ones had already been well circulated by now. She'd expected more slut shaming, but, surprisingly, the community had rallied behind her. This time, however, rather than shy away from the attention, Corrie embraced it. What did she have to hide, anyway? That she'd had sex with a man she loved and that some Peeping Tom had tried to exploit her? Sure, she'd prefer that her colleagues—or anyone else who'd not shared her bed—*not* know what she looked like naked, but she figured their prying eyes said more about their character than her own.

She couldn't believe that rat Lance had actually survived his dive over the waterfall and that he'd had the forethought to create digital backups of the photos. But at least he was behind bars for multiple counts including voyeurism, kidnapping, and attempted murder.

"Dr. Mejía."

A smile formed on her face at the sound of that luscious timbre. It might have only been a few hours since they'd spoken on the phone, but hearing that voice in person and knowing this time she'd be able to touch him—well, she couldn't help the butterflies swirling in her stomach.

Slowly, she turned, leaning against the wall. There he was, sexy as hell in his tuxedo. Hands in his pockets. Leaning against the doorway on the other side of the room. Far too distant for her liking.

"Dr. Matthews," she responded with hooded eyes, the desire dripping from her lips.

"I hope you don't mind," he said.

"Mind what?"

"This," he said, motioning his head to the wall behind her. "Lance had been watching us from the moment you arrived."

"Well, aside from the fact that he was the source, I love it. I hate to admit it, but he had a knack for photography. Caught the exact moment that I fell for you."

"Oh really? Show me."

He pushed off the doorframe and strode across the room toward her, sending a jolt of heat between her legs. She hadn't seen him in person in three months, not since she'd joined another dig in the Yucatán. Even after a year together, he still made her heart sing whenever he was around, whether in person, on the phone, or only in her thoughts. It had been hard being apart, especially after she'd almost lost him from the stabbing. Things had been touch-and-go for a few weeks in the hospital, between the loss of blood and a later infection, but he'd eventually pulled through. They'd spent as much time together as possible since then, which, between Corrie's sabbatical and Ford's resignation, had made things a lot easier—up until she'd left for Mexico again, that was.

The instant he was beside her, she wanted to pounce on him, and it took all her strength not to. They were in a public setting, after all. But he took her hand and stood beside her, staring at the collection of photos on the wall.

"This one," she said, pointing to the photo of them doing dishes her first night in camp.

He craned his head and looked at her. "Really?"

"Mm-hmm. It was when you were talking about your mom and I realized you were actually a good guy. Speaking of?"

"She's out with Ethan. Sorry again I couldn't pick you up from the airport. Her doctor's appointment went late today, but she's looking and feeling great."

"That's okay. I'm just glad you're here. That you both are."

He wrapped his arms around her waist. "I've missed you."

"I've missed you, too."

He planted his lips on hers, sending a fire roaring through her body. Not even three months and thousands of miles apart could tame the blaze from his kiss.

"When did you know?" she asked.

"Know what?"

"That you were in love with me?"

"In the library. When you were drinking that coffee. I knew it the minute I wanted to *be* that coffee."

"You wanted to be coffee?" she asked with a smirk.

"Absolutely. I wanted to touch your lips and be consumed by you. There might not be a picture of it hanging on this wall, but it's here," he said, placing his fingertips at his temple, "and here," he said, taking both their hands and holding them over his heart. "That picture will forever be etched in my soul. And no one can take it away from me."

Just like no one could take his heart away from her.

A low rumble of words and whispers came from the other room. The exhibition must have opened to the public. After one more quick kiss, they separated their bodies and mingled with the guests. Answering questions. Telling stories. Catching each other's longing gazes throughout the evening.

The exhibition was a hit. Experts and archaeology enthusiasts had come from all over the world—though Dr. Crawley had conveniently been left off the guest list. In this field, reputation meant everything, and Crawley's had sunk to the bottom rung with the likes of Pierre Vautour and Bernard Sardoni. But for the first time in her life, Corrie was recognized for more than her antics and appearance. The old boys' club asked for *her* opinion. For *her* assistance on their own archaeological mysteries. Ford hung back and watched, allowing her to shine in the spotlight all on her own. Whenever a question was directed at him about the Chimalli dig, he deferred to Corrie, "as she was the lead," he'd explain. Never once taking credit for her accomplishments. And he was even quick to point out the mistakes he'd made early on.

As the evening wound down, Ford and Corrie made a final pass through the room to say their goodbyes. Sunny and Ethan offered to take Miri back to the hotel, though they all made plans to meet for brunch in the morning along with the rest of the gang. The whole crew had come—Mateo, Gabriel, Jon, Memo, and even Agnes.

"I'm glad to see the two of you still together. Though, Dr.

Matthews, if you ever want to settle down, you know where to find me," Agnes said with a wink.

"What makes you think I haven't settled down?" Ford asked.

"There's no settling down with this one. Something tells me life will always be an adventure so long as you're together." She pulled them in for a three-way hug. "Call me the next time you need a chef for another dig. Most excitement I've had in years."

Agnes walked off, leaving them alone beside the knife case. "So, do you think what Agnes said is true? That you'll never settle down?" Corrie asked.

Ford pulled her into his arms and smiled at her. "I don't know. My life has definitely been more . . . entertaining since you've been in it. But there's no one else I'd rather spend it with. And nowhere else I'd rather be." He then homed in on her eyes. "Except maybe somewhere with this amazing dress in a pile on the floor and me between your legs."

"About time you said something."

"I've been spending the last few hours trying to talk myself off the proverbial ledge. I mean, clearly it's no secret that I'm deeply, madly, and truly in love with you—as evidenced by not one, but *two* displays in this exhibition focused on our relationship—but I don't need to be making any more headlines by pitching tent at the opening gala."

Corrito Burrito unleashed a laugh, echoing in the exhibition hall, so loud she had to bury her head in his chest.

"I love your laugh."

"I love you."

He pulled her in for a kiss again, savoring every last ounce of her. Every now and then Corrie regretted all the years they'd spent loathing each other, but whenever he kissed her, those regrets went away. No, they'd come together at the perfect time and in the perfect way, tying a neat little bow on her life's work on Chimalli. It might not have ended the way she'd anticipated— or even the way she'd hoped it would when Calvin had first appeared in her office offering her the job. But she wouldn't change a thing.

"Ahem, excuse me. Doctors?"

Ford and Corrie separated their lips, but not their bodies, as they turned toward the voice. A short, round man in a tuxedo stood beside them.

"Hello, I'm Eugene Larity. I was hoping I could chat with you about a proposition."

Corrie and Ford glanced at each other, then back at Mr. Larity. "I'm sorry, but we're on sabbatical," Corrie said. "We can refer you to someone else, however."

"No, I'm afraid no one else will do."

"Well, unfortunately we can't help you," Ford said. "Thank you, and have a nice evening."

"You don't understand. You'll find a lot of . . . *value* in my proposition."

Oh, they understood all right. "We don't do jobs for payouts," Ford said. At least, not anymore. Though, seeing as Ford had never been paid a dime by Vautour, technically they'd never done any job for a payout. He took Corrie's hand and they started to walk away.

"I'm not talking about money. I'm talking about revenge. I believe we have a mutual enemy, Doctors. A Mr. Pierre Vautour?"

Corrie and Ford halted in their tracks.

"Excuse me, did you say Vautour?" she asked.

"I did. He stole something from me. Research on the location of the Lost City of the Moon."

"The City of the Moon isn't real," Ford said.

"I assure you, Dr. Matthews, it is. And I need you to find it before Vautour does."

The Lost City of the Moon. A mythological city in the Amazon full of riches beyond the imagination, swathed in shimmering precious stones and metals visible only in the moonlight. Hundreds of explorers had searched for the fabled lost civilization for many centuries to no avail. They might as well have been searching for Atlantis. What made this Mr. Larity think he'd found it?

But Corrie's interest had been piqued.

"How do we know we can trust you?" she asked.

"What? Corrie, no. You can't be serious," Ford whispered, pulling her away from the man.

"You said it yourself, Ford. We'll never settle down."

"But we have no idea who this man even is."

"Here are my credentials," Larity interrupted, handing a folder to them. "You can contact the authorities if you would like. I have nothing to hide."

"Who *are* you, exactly?" Ford asked.

"I'm an explorer like yourselves. Though, unfortunately, only a hobby explorer. I'm not built for expeditions and knife fights. I need professionals. I need the two of you, for not only your physical strength, but also your knowledge. And hopefully your taste for vindication."

Revenge. How sweet it would be to see Vautour behind bars right next to Lance. Corrie relished the thought.

"What say you?" she asked, turning toward Ford. "Are you ready for another adventure, Weak Sauce?"

He hung his head, shook it, then smiled. "With you, Badass? Absolutely."

Author's Note

I T STARTED WITH A TWEET: *WHAT KIND OF JOBS DO YOU WISH YOU saw more of in #romcom books for both the hero and the heroine?*

I—a lover of archaeology and fun, sexy rom-coms— responded: *Archaeologists. Plenty of "bones" to examine.*

I grew up watching movies like *Romancing the Stone*, *The Goonies*, *Indiana Jones and the Raiders of the Lost Ark*, and the rest of the Indiana Jones franchise. Later came franchises like Lara Croft, *The Mummy*, *National Treasure*, and *The Librarian*. I loved these stories about lost civilizations, treasure hunts, and ancient mysteries, and they were even better when they threw in a little romance. I dreamed of being an archaeologist and even participated in a Mayan dig in a Belizean jungle—one of the coolest experiences of my life. Ultimately, my career led me in a different direction, but that didn't bring an end to my fascination with archaeology and love of adventure movies.

So back to that tweet. It had been intended as a joke, but days later, I couldn't stop thinking about it. I thought, what if a badass adventurer, à la Lara Croft, teamed up with a *This belongs in a museum*-type stickler, à la Indiana Jones (yes, I know Indy is *also* a badass, but bear with me)? Picture it—Harrison Ford, I mean, Indy with those wire-rimmed glasses flashing that sexy, almost bashful smile at the heroine? Sign me up! And what if this Lara Croft–type character was Latina and she was searching for remains of her Aztec ancestor? My Mexican heritage is extremely important to me, so I wanted to include Latinx/e representation—especially since in the list of movies above, not a single one has any (at least not with any of the leads). Once I settled on the premise, I immediately decided to name the heroine Socorro after my great aunt Corrie, who was a badass in her own right. Also, the name Socorro means "help," which is so fitting of Dr. Mejía's character. And so, *Raiders of the Lost Heart* was born.

While I spent hours researching the lives of the Aztecs, I took certain liberties with this book for the sake of storytelling. Tenochtitlán, Moctezuma II, and the downfall of the Aztecs following the arrival of the Spanish are all real. The Aztec warrior Chimalli and the Spaniard Mendoza mentioned in this book are not. I tried to be sensitive to Aztec culture by acknowledging their way of life and by not condemning practices, such as human sacrifice and castration, that might seem ruthless in modern times. These were religious rituals that we might not understand today but were very important and meaningful to the Aztecs to ensure their gods were satisfied and their lands were fertile. I have included details of Aztec life in this book with the utmost respect and hope that it comes through in my writing.

I've traveled to Mexico and parts of Central America on multiple occasions, but I have not visited the Lacandon Jungle, the primary location where most of the events in *Raiders of the Lost*

Heart take place. The landmarks described in this book are generally fictional to allow Corrie and Ford flexibility on their adventures. In addition, while the Aztec Empire did not extend into the Lacandon, it was a perfect location for the type of flora, fauna, terrain, and climate I was seeking, while also not being too far outside the geographical range that Chimalli could realistically flee.

Finally, as much as I wish I were, I am not an archaeologist. I know being an archaeologist is not as easy as hiking through the jungle and stumbling upon a half-buried archaeological site. As Indy pointed out in *The Last Crusade*, X never marks the spot (though he thought otherwise later in the movie). The actual process of locating a site requires lots of education and tons of research, and it's extremely methodical. But I didn't think you would enjoy reading about hours upon hours of researching in a library or months of scouting in the jungle, so this book requires you to suspend disbelief and accept that Corrie is simply *that* good of an archaeologist.

In the end, *Raiders of the Lost Heart* is intended to capture all of the thrills and swoons of the aforementioned adventure movies, albeit with a little imagination along the way to allow Corrie and Ford to shine. Besides, what's an archaeological adventure without a little fortune and glory anyway? Hope you enjoyed!

With love,
Jo

Acknowledgments

Publishing a book has been my dream since the first grade. While my first book, *The Dog and the Dog in the Pet Shop*, required no assistance from others since the story, pictures (I couldn't spell "illustrations"), and glued binding were all done by myself, *Raiders of the Lost Heart* wouldn't have been possible without the support and hard work of so many people—and in particular, so many badass women.

First, thank you to my agent, Eva Scalzo, and the team at Speilburg Literary Agency. When we spoke on the phone a few days after you'd liked my PitMad tweet and you were already halfway through reading this book, I had that warm, fuzzy feeling. Only fate can explain the fact that we sold this book on the anniversary of my one-year commitment to pursuing this whole writing thing in earnest.

To my editor, Sarah Blumenstock: Thank you for allowing *Raiders* to interrupt your vacation (sorry, not sorry). I loved writing this book, but I truly cannot believe how much I love it even more after having worked with you and incorporating all your amazing feedback. Thank you to assistant editor Liz Sellers, production editor Alaina Christensen, and managing editor Christine Legon—your fine-tuning has really made this book sing! Also, I promise someday I'll get lay/lie/laid/lain right. Hopefully. To the rest of the Berkley Romance team: Kristin Cipolla, Jessica Plummer, Hillary Tacuri, and the copyeditor, Abby Graves, you all rock! And, finally, to artist Camila Gray for the stunning cover—you really brought Corrie and Ford to life. Extra thanks for the bird.

I can't imagine having made it this far without my writing group, the Ponies! I've laughed so much (and so hard) with this group of badass chicks. Special thanks to Jen Comfort, my agent-sister and critique-partner extraordinaire! Your feedback was invaluable (and hilarious), as are you. I'll be your writing dom/sub any day. To Melora François—you've pretty much been (stuck) with me since Day One when we sat at the same table during our first ECWC pitchfest. Thank you for always being up for a brainstorming session and for reading all my nonsense. I will never eat (an entire bag of) honey mustard pretzels and not think of you. And to the rest of the Ponies who've been with me since the start of my journey: Elle Beauregard, Lin Lustig, Jasmine Silvera, Kelly Blake, Alexis De Girolami, and Kate Wallis. You are seriously not only amazingly talented writers, but you are also amazingly wonderful friends.

Thank you to all the Berkletes (of which there are too many to name) for the advice, industry info, feedback, commiseration, publishing guidance, and NSFW laughs. In particular, thank you to the Latinas de Berkley (Alana Quintana Albertson, Isabel Cañas, and Liana De la Rosa) for welcoming me with open arms.

I've also had the support of so many other authors along the way. Seriously, so many awesome people. But since I can't name every single one, there are a few that need a shout-out. Thank you to my dear friend Kathy Swoyer for teaching me what "querying" is and attending my first ever writing conference with me. It was scary! But you taught me so much. Thank you to Sierra Hill for reaching out and introducing me to so many fabulous authors. And thank you to Danica Winters for (politely) calling me out at ECWC and forcing me to join social media. See? I finally did it!

To all my non-writing friends who've supported and encouraged me along the way: Thank you, LB, for taking the time to read this book and for always being there for me, even when I'm being weird. Thank you, Natalia, for pushing me to write that very first manuscript and actually putting up with reading the whole thing in all its terrible, cringeworthy glory! I would not be here without you. Thank you, Meredith, for all the book talk, being my biggest cheerleader, and promising to buy a hundred copies of this book. And to those who've read my many other manuscripts and gave feedback that ultimately helped me to become a better writer: Anna, Candace, Charli, Cindy, Elaina, Geneva, Jen, and Mary. I'm so grateful for all of you.

To my family, Mom, Dad, Elaina, and Phil: My dream of publishing a book, and in particular, *this* book, would not have come true without the arts (performing, visual, and literary)— and movies like Indy—being such a huge part of our lives. Mom always says, "Life is a musical," and that has certainly rung true. What would life be, after all, without music, dancing, art, and books? "Thank you" doesn't do justice to express the gratitude I have for all of you, so how about this instead? *You . . . are . . . good, you are good, you are good, you are good!*

Jo Segura

READERS GUIDE

Discussion Questions

1. As evidenced by her many outrageous escapades, Corrie is an adventure seeker. Do you seek out adventure? What's the most adventurous thing you've ever done? Does taking risks scare you or does it energize you?

2. If you could participate on an archaeological dig, would you? If so, where would you like to go?

3. After Ford comes clean to Corrie regarding his hiring for the dig, she asks whether he would have handled things the same way if the Chimalli expert had been someone other than her—and specifically, a man. Do you think Ford would have acted differently if he was dealing with a male counterpart? What role do you think sex and gender factored into Ford and Corrie's animosity?

4. Corrie's sexuality is front and center in her relationships and her career. Despite the impact it has had on her reputation,

Corrie embraces her sexuality. Do you think Corrie's sexuality is a hindrance or an asset? Do you think Corrie's appearance and sexuality are the primary factors that have influenced her reputation? How do you think people would perceive Corrie if she were not a woman?

5. They say "a little friendly competition never hurt anyone." Do you agree? If not, are there ever times that competition between colleagues can be a positive thing?

6. Ultimately, Corrie gives Ford a second chance (though some might say, a third chance). Do you think people deserve second chances? Why or why not? Under what circumstances would you give someone a second chance in a relationship?

7. Although still rooted in deception, Ford's reasons for tricking Corrie into coming on the dig could be seen as admirable. Do you think Ford's reasons excuse his behavior? Is there a different or better way he could have handled the situation? Do you think he redeemed himself by the end of the book? Are there ever times when deceiving someone might be justified?

8. Corrie and Ford joke about their lives as a *Choose Your Own Adventure* book. If you had to give your life a *Choose Your Own Adventure* title, what would you call it? Describe a situation in your life where you had to choose between two drastically different options. Which did you choose and why? If you could go back, would you make a different choice? How do you think that would have changed your life (if at all)?

9. Archaeology sometimes receives criticism for the harmful effects of its past colonial practices: removing artifacts from their native lands and displaying them in other countries, disturbing ancient and often spiritual sites that have ritual and historic significance to local communities, and even creating harmful—and often racist—narratives related to perceived inferiority of colonized groups. Do you think Corrie, who believes she is the descendant of Chimalli, has more of a right to search for his remains than people who do not share that culture or heritage? Do you think artifacts should be left undisturbed or do you think archaeology still provides value in today's world? What do you think archaeologists should do to ensure their practices are respectful of the cultures and countries in which they work?

10. Indiana Jones, Lara Croft, Rick O'Connell, Benjamin Franklin Gates—these popular action/adventure movie characters seem to have the same mind-set: find the artifact at any cost. However, despite all the explosions, destruction, and lack of any scientific technique, they are always portrayed as the heroes at the end of the movie. Makes for an exciting movie, but what do you think about these characters? Should they be applauded for their tactics? Do you think Corrie falls into the same category as these characters?

11. The author of *Raiders of the Lost Heart* loves a good internet quiz. Silly, trivia, food-related, you name it. If you were to craft a quiz to determine what character you are from the book, what would the title of your quiz be? What types of questions would you ask?

Author photo copyright © Sean Hoyt

JO SEGURA lives in the Pacific Northwest with her husband and two doggos, Gus and Henrik, who vie for her attention with their sweet puppy dog eyes whenever she's trying to write (her dogs, that is . . . though sometimes her husband, too). Her stories feature strong, passionate heroines and draw upon aspects of her life, such as her love of good food, her Mexican heritage, and her fascination with archaeology. When she's not writing you can find her practicing law, shaking up a mean cocktail, or sitting out on the patio doing Buzzfeed quizzes (though she doesn't care what the chicken nugget quiz said—her favorite fruit is *not* banana).

VISIT JO SEGURA ONLINE

JoSegura.com
🐦 JoSeguraBooks
📷 JoSeguraBooks

Ready to find
your next great read?

Let us help.

Visit prh.com/nextread

Penguin
Random
House